MW01134862

TURN LEFT
AT THE
CORNER

TURN LEFT
AT THE
CORNER

Nancy Donnell

Cover photography by Nancy Donnell
Cover edits by Randy Allen and Walt Wilson

ISBN-13:978-1547223336
ISBN-10:1547223332
Library of Congress number: 2017909858
Printed in the United States of America
Books may be purchased on Amazon.com.

To my family, past and present. I love you all.

ACKNOWLEDGMENTS

I offer my gratitude to the many people who stood by me on my journey. What a wild ride this has been. Our yesterdays are gone, and our tomorrows are never guaranteed, so thank you all for being here for me today!

I thank all of my wonderful friends and family for listening, being my sounding board, and supporting me, especially Marie, John, Chris, Beth, Kim, and Debbie.

Justin, you inspired me to reach for my dreams. You motivated me in difficult times when I needed words of encouragement. I appreciate you more than I can ever say.

James, your constant encouragement and support got me through many tough days. Thank you for believing in me. I'm blessed to have you in my life.

Thanks to Nancy Nagel for offering her time and comments and to Sharon, Pam, Uma, Robin, and Danielle.

Words can't express my gratitude to my editor and now dear friend, Pamela McManus, for her professional advice and tireless assistance in polishing this novel.

Thank you, Patti Lee, for helping me with the nuances of word processing.

My thanks to Walt Wilson for generously offering his time and helpful advice on the cover.

Thank you, Peggy Nehmen, for your invaluable assistance on the interior page layout and guidance in the publishing process.

My profound appreciation to Randy Allen for his friendship, talent, and the finishing touches on the book's design.

Lastly, I thank *you* for taking a chance on a book about friendship, fortuitous encounters, and the ripple effect relationships have on our lives.

TURN LEFT
AT THE
CORNER

CHAPTER 1

Rosie Perón blamed herself for choosing to stay. She'd made a sacred vow in the presence of God. For better or worse. Until death they did part. Rosie watched her husband clutch last night's chicken wings, lick his thumb, and dig his teeth under his nails. The pungent sauce burned her eyes from across the room. Rosie rinsed her cereal bowl and dabbed the dishcloth inside her favorite china cup.

Carlos drew a breath and exhaled hard and fast. "Don't just stand there. Get me some water. Hurry up!"

"I'm not your servant." The words tumbled off her lips, and Rosie knew she'd invited trouble. Life was easier if she kept silent.

The carcass dropped into the Styrofoam box. Carlos wiped a greasy hand on his shirt and charged across the kitchen, an angry bull. His nose almost touched hers. Rosie turned away and focused on a stain on the floor. Carlos snatched the Limoges cup from the counter and without hesitation released his grip.

Rosie reached and spread her fingers to catch it, but Carlos had her pinned against the counter. The delicate antique crashed against the floor, shattering into irreparable pieces. Her lip quivered. "That was from my grandmother. How could you?"

"Don't be such a drama queen. Maybe next time you'll think before you open your mouth." Carlos stomped away, leaving splintered porcelain across the linoleum and gnawed chicken bones on the table.

Rosie swept the pieces, dropped them in the trash, and escaped to the bedroom. She shut the door to block the blare of the television and lay across the bed. She'd provoked him with her remark. Would it have been so tough to get him the water? They'd been fighting for months, but this was a first. A small action done with intention and cruelty to teach her a lesson.

Rosie rolled on her side and caught a glimpse of her wedding dress in the corner of the closet. The satin gown had once glowed under the bridal shop's hot lights. Now it hung shrouded in yellow plastic, a symbol of everything wrong in her life. Two years ago, nothing could have canceled her dreams to walk down the aisle with Carlos *and* get out of her parents' house. Fed up with the pressure and the overwhelming responsibility of being the oldest child, Rosie had seen Carlos as the perfect solution. She reached for their wedding portrait on the nightstand. She examined the beaded gown and Carlos, wearing a camel-colored suit, his bronze face darker than the jacket, his short, black hair combed back. God, he was good-looking then.

Rosie held her breath, thinking back. She'd been too eager the day they met in the grocery store, immediately accepting his dinner invitation to Applebee's. Understated signals should have warned her. "Oh, you wore pants? I like my women in skirts," he'd said. "Are you sure you want the steak?" She'd blushed and changed her order.

Rosie pushed the picture aside. After four dates, Carlos had asked her on a picnic at Forest Park. She'd brought a liter of Coke. He had passed her the pizza box. On the inside cardboard flap, *Will You Marry Me* had been written in black magic marker. A silver engagement ring topped with a diamond she could barely see sat in the center of the pie's mozzarella topping. She had wiped off the sauce and examined the ring. "Yes," she had said.

Twenty days later, she had walked down the aisle in St. Joseph's Catholic Church. Carlos was undeniably handsome and had a strong personality—and she was willing to be rescued. Two years later, he had proved himself manipulative, aggressive, and controlling.

Rosie flipped her rings around in a circle, riding them up and down her knuckle. Wishing life were different never changed a thing. She tossed the plastic frame on the dresser, squeezed the pillow against her chest, and gazed at the neat row of black skirts lining her side of the closet, certain they hid defects or at least disguised them. Shoe boxes stacked in tiny towers held pairs of three-inch heels, elevating her to five-foot-seven. Height was powerful, but she knew the heels were an illusion, a trick. She fantasized how a stiletto might be used with sadistic glamour.

Carlos called from the family room, "Hey, big butt, get me a beer." Rosie ignored his remark. She had tried to tell him how his words hurt her, but he'd insisted his insults were jokes and informed her she was too sensitive. Or he would give her the silent treatment to punish her. As if silence wasn't the best option. She wrapped her arms around her waist like thread around a spool, closed her eyes to banish the thoughts, and drifted in and out of restless sleep.

Her cell phone vibrated in her pocket, waking her.

"Hello, Mamá."

"Rosie, I haven't heard from you."

"I worked full time this week. You think it's easier because I work from home? I'm tired, Mamá."

"Why do you need to work? Carlos said he would take care of you. You're never available to help me. I hoped you could watch your brothers today."

Rosie stopped herself from saying something she'd regret, but anger rose in her chest. After the wedding, the first argument she'd had with Carlos had been about her seeking employment. He'd insisted he wanted her home. Carlos reluctantly had conceded after she found a job allowing her to work from their house.

"I can't come running every time you call. Ask one of my siblings," Rosie said. "They're old enough. When I got married, I said you had to stop depending on me."

"But you're the most responsible. The little ones love you best."

"Mamá, I can't." She paused. "Carlos and I had another argument."

Her mother breathed into the phone. "You promised to stand beside this man in good times and bad. Life is full of disappointments and difficulties. If times are bad, try harder, Rosie."

"He broke one of Lita's cups. On purpose."

"I am sure it was an accident."

"I'm hiding the others. I'm scared, Mamá. Carlos drinks all the time. Last week he threw an empty beer can at the television."

"You are a newlywed. All marriages have difficulties. The Church says—"

"We've been married two years. I'm not happy."

"Give him time, Rosie. God did not stutter when he said he hated divorce. You're twenty-two years old. Take responsibility. Perhaps you should speak with the priest."

Carlos bellowed from the kitchen. "Where are you? Where's my lunch?"

Rosie tossed Carlos's pillow off the bed. "No, and say nothing to him. I have to go, Mamá." Rosie clicked off. Overhead, the ceiling fan's wooden blades spun like bicycle spokes going nowhere. The last few months, Carlos had been moodier. An angry undercurrent brewed beneath his critical words.

"All right!" she said. In the kitchen, she lifted a loaf of bread from the cabinet. She stacked three pieces of ham, spread a generous amount of mustard between each slice, and set the plate in front of him. Carlos took a bite and shoved the plate at her.

"Are you so stupid you can't even make a sandwich? Where's the cheese? You forgot the damn cheese."

Rosie searched the refrigerator for the cheddar, pushing aside the leftover half-cup of chai tea she'd bought yesterday at the Jumpin' Jive Café. The barista at the espresso bar always wrote comments on people's cups. What was her name? Hanna.

Rosie had been in a hurry and hadn't bothered to check. She tilted the container to read the inscription: *Be careful.*

CHAPTER 2

Saige never dreamed she'd win the People's Choice contest. Coworkers clapped as Saige went to the podium to accept her prize. Mr. Seers, her manager, fixed his tie and posed for the photographer. Familiar warmth flooded her cheeks. The red would betray her. Always did.

"Saige Santoro, we're proud to announce that our patrons have voted you Employee of the Year." He removed comment stubs from the voting box and read, "'Always cheerful.' 'Greets me with a smile.'" He presented her a gift bag overflowing with tissue paper. "Congratulations."

A teller called to her, "What'd you get?"

Saige held up a device no bigger than a couple of double-A batteries. Someone at the front table said, "Wow—an iPod shuffle!" More clapping. "Thank you," Saige said. Mr. Seers shook her hand, and she hoped he didn't mind her sweaty palm. She hurried to her seat.

Marcy, the new hire from the loan office, leaned close, and Saige tried not to look at Marcy's exposed cleavage bubbling out the top of her scoop-neck top. "You know that gizmo has two gigs of storage? I've always wanted one."

"I've seen customers with them," Saige said. "It's for music, right?"

"Yeah, you put in your favorite songs."

"Do you know how?"

"Through your computer," Marcy said in a tone that made Saige feel like a small child. The clock on the wall reminded them that the doors opened in twenty minutes. "I'll explain later. It's a nice gift."

After the ceremony, Saige caught up with her boss. "Mr. Seers, could I have a word with you?"

"Yes, Saige?"

"I'm grateful for the gift, but I wondered if I might be up for a promotion? I've been here a long—"

Mr. Seers cleared his throat. "Now, Saige, I'd advise you to hang in there. We don't have any openings right now."

"But two months ago—"

He patted her shoulder. "Stick with what you know. I believe they're about to start serving. You best get in there. You're this year's recipient. Be proud."

"Yes, sir."

Chocolate cake and coffee were served. Saige finished her slice and tossed the empty plate in the trash.

"So," Marcy said, "do you feel like a big shot?"

"No. Never have." Saige dabbed her mouth. "I was hired to work Saturdays, but I stayed on full time. I wonder what it would be like to work somewhere else."

"What did you study in college?"

Saige shook her head. "I didn't go. For almost five years, this is what I have done every day." She gestured around the lobby. "I greet the customers and send them to the appropriate station."

"You were voted the People's Choice."

"It's easy to smile, say hello, and point."

"You don't give yourself enough credit."

"I expected to be a teller by now."

Maybe Mr. Seers had never intended to promote her. Saige glanced at the gift bag: a token, a substitute for a career headed nowhere.

"You should celebrate," Marcy said. "Take a friend and check out this place." She jotted an address. "It's a coffeehouse. The Jumpin' Jive Café." Marcy winked. "Have fun in life or what's the point, right?"

Throughout the day, customers saw the award photo and offered congratulations. After work, Saige hurried home, eager to show her father her prize. "Dad, guess what?" She hung up her coat and entered the kitchen. Her father sat at the table playing solitaire. "I was voted Employee of the Year."

"Wonderful! Did you get a raise?"

"No, but I got this." Saige held the iPod shuffle like a trophy and offered him the package.

"What is it? What does it do?"

"It plays music, but you have to have a computer to transfer the songs."

"No raise? Instead they give you this little piece of junk?" He shook his head and put the device on the counter. "The things they try to get away with these days."

"Maybe we could talk about a computer?"

"How many times do we have to have this conversation? Buy a computer, and you'll waste your life. It's a thousand times worse than a television. I won't have one in the house." He swept the iPod into the trash can. "Technology didn't help your mother, did it?" He stormed out of the room.

Saige called after him, "Why won't you talk about her?" She picked her gift from the rubbish and used a dishcloth to wipe the package clean. Even if he didn't mean to, her father had a way of turning her heart to ashes. Saige opened the junk drawer beside the dishwasher, a catchall for knickknacks and worthless objects they didn't use but refused to throw away. Saige stashed the iPod under a bag of rubber bands.

CHAPTER 3

Adam McGuire collapsed to the ground, hard. He pushed away from the rough concrete, dazed and embarrassed. He touched his cheek. No blood, the best he could tell without a mirror. He brushed away pieces of loose dirt stuck to his forehead. The few gawkers who had slowed after he hit the ground were gone. Cars whizzed past. The paved path behind him was empty. There were no stones, loose gravel, or uneven section of sidewalk that could have caused his leg to give way.

Adam adjusted his book bag and made his way toward the brick building ahead. Footsteps pounded the pavement. He turned, and Brad Reynolds loped behind him. Brad, an energetic sophomore and basketball enthusiast, often rounded up the guys for a game.

"Hey, McGuire. If you're up for playing Wednesday night, we can have a four-on-four."

"I don't know—"

"Come on, we need you. We're a man short."

Adam hesitated. "All right, count me in." He brushed a dried leaf from his jacket. "One of the guys said you're transferring to Truman State after the semester ends."

"Yeah, I feel lost in the crowd here. I think SLU has about thirteen thousand students to Truman's five thousand. Figured I'd try a smaller school," Brad said. "A more rural setting suits me just fine. It's only three hours from here, but I'll feel like I got out of my hometown."

"I know what you mean. St. Louis is great, but I'm anxious to experience another city. Everything here is too safe, too familiar," Adam said.

"You aren't far from graduation. You're pre-law?"

"I've applied for admission to Harvard. I've always wanted a career in law."

As a kid, Adam had been fascinated by the way one courageous act could change history—Rosa Parks refusing to surrender her seat to a white passenger, or the unarmed rebel in China who stood defiantly in front of army tanks in Tiananmen Square.

Adam had never done anything significant with his life, but if Harvard accepted him, he'd find an apartment in Boston, obtain his law degree, and fight narrow-mindedness and discrimination. He daydreamed of uncharted territory to explore, fresh seafood, new friends, and people whose accents were unlike his Midwestern style of speech. *Bah-stin.* He practiced saying it while imagining weekend trips to Rhode Island, New York, and Maine, places he'd never seen.

"Wow, you're a planner." Brad laughed. "Or a dreamer. Jeez, I can't even decide on a major."

"You'll figure it out. Hey, I'll see you Wednesday, our usual time. Right now, I need to ace this test in business law."

Brad's eyebrow cocked. "I thought your business law class met on Tuesday."

"Yeah," Adam said.

"This is Monday, dude." He clapped Adam's shoulder. "You have another whole day to study."

• • •

On Wednesday night, Adam ran out on the court, fist-bumping a couple of his buddies on the way.

Tennis shoes screeched across the gym's wooden floor. Adam

dodged the opposing guard and waved, signaling he was open. A teammate passed the ball, and Adam drove for the basket. Another player cut him off. Adam turned and dribbled toward the line to take a shot. His leg stiffened. He fell sideways onto the floor.

Brad yelled from across the court, "Hey, you okay?"

Adam sat up, aware that the game had stopped. "I'm fine."

Brad picked up the ball rolling across the floor. "You sure?"

Adam struggled to his feet. "Positive."

CHAPTER 4

She would be thirty this year, still single and too busy for a boy-friend. Alana Hudson's motto had always been "Complete one more project." She spread the last three months' magazine issues across her coffee table and considered the extensive work that had gone into assuring that each issue of *Slick* was a success. She knew she should hire more employees or cut the magazine's monthly output to six times a year. Or consider the offer from Borg Larson.

Success in this trade was a gamble; the speed at which things changed left the industry unstable. Clients here today could be gone tomorrow. There were repeat patrons, but businesses every-where were going down faster than a martini at happy hour.

Alana opened the window and filled the feeder with sunflower seeds. Wrens, cardinals, and finches took turns on the perch, cracking the shells with their beaks. She envied their simple lives.

She crossed the room and stopped at the hall table, which displayed photos of family and friends—memories of yesterdays. Alana's thumb brushed a picture of her younger sister, Natalie. She called every Saturday at nine.

Her cell rang. "Hi, Natalie," Alana said, without looking at the ID screen.

"You busy?"

"Yes. I have to review files, and promised myself an hour of yoga this morning."

"I thought we could hang out later," Natalie said.

"I can't today. How about next weekend?"

"Okay."

Natalie's disappointment stabbed her. Soon Natalie would have her own life with a boyfriend, and a big sister wouldn't be in the picture.

"Are you still investigating the man who contacted you about your publication?"

"I am," Alana said.

"I found his magazine, *New Heights*, online. The guy's a real tech geek. I wish I could play with toys like that. You need to fix your website. There's no way to download your magazine."

Alana sighed. "Yeah, I know we need to update."

"I love my Kindle," said Natalie.

"People still enjoy magazines. I happen to love the smell of paper and ink, pages that crinkle. You can't cuddle with a Kindle."

"Very funny," Natalie said. "I found a picture of the publisher, Borg Larson. What kind of name is Borg? Is he Swedish? Whatever, he's hot."

"That's not a reason for blending the magazine."

"Have you discussed it with Daniel? He's such a great lawyer."

"Not yet. I'm still researching. Sorry, Natalie, I have to go. Call you later, okay?"

Alana settled in front of her laptop and clicked on a folder titled "New Heights." The previous week, the California publisher had contacted her, expressing interest in a deal he said would send her circulation skyrocketing. Borg Larson had asked her to consider something she had sworn she'd never do: share her magazine.

CHAPTER 5

Adam hadn't seen Dr. Martin since his mandatory physical required by the university. In the waiting room, the woman beside him coughed and blew her nose. Adam moved to another chair. A moment later, a nurse with a badge identifying herself as Courtney called his name. Adam followed her into an exam room. The young woman couldn't have been much older than he was. She wore green scrub pants, a flowery top, and a cute smile.

"What's the reason for your visit?" she asked, and draped a blood pressure cuff around his arm.

"I'm having balance issues and trouble focusing on my homework. It's never been like me to have memory problems, but lately, I redline my calendar to keep track of what day it is."

The cuff tightened around his arm. "Are you experiencing dizziness?"

"No, it's more weakness in my legs. I fell twice this week."

She pecked the keyboard as Adam described his symptoms. "The doctor will be right in." She placed the chart in a slot outside the door and disappeared.

Adam had almost memorized the posters on the wall by the time Dr. Martin greeted him and took a seat. "I understand you're experiencing balance problems?"

"Yes, it happens without warning. Bam, I'm on the ground. It's pretty embarrassing. Lately, I can't concentrate, and I'm forgetting things. I'm worried because I have to keep my GPA up to get into law school."

Dr. Martin put a cold stethoscope against Adam's chest and told him to take deep breaths. He examined him and typed more notes. The doctor swiveled his chair to face Adam. "You're not describing vertigo. I'd like to refer you to a neurologist." He took out a pen and wrote on his pad. "Here's someone I'd recommend. Make an appointment as soon as you can."

• • •

Adam's razor scraped away the last bit of stubble. He rinsed his face and patted it with a crumpled towel. His fair skin and dark hair framed the circles under his bloodshot eyes. He'd studied for his logic test past midnight and then spent several hours thrashing the bed, anxious about the MRI scan.

The previous day, Dr. Harper, the young neurologist, had questioned Adam about his family history. Adam had informed the doctor that his relatives were in good health.

"Adam, do you know what an MRI is?"

"Magnetic imaging?"

"Yes. It can provide us with a lot of information. I'd like you to schedule a test this week if possible."

"All right."

"Would you like a prescription for a sedative? Many people feel nervous inside the machine. It's very enclosed, so if you're prone to claustrophobia, a Valium would relax you."

"No. No drugs. If you don't mind, I'd like to bring in a picture or something I could tape to the ceiling of the machine."

"I haven't heard of that, but as long as it doesn't damage the equipment or contain metal, there shouldn't be a problem," Dr. Harper had said.

Adam tore off a picture from an old calendar of two wood ducks paddling in a lake and tucked the page into his book bag. Something about the water always calmed him. The microwave clock warned that he should leave. On the drive to the hospital, he thought about the papers he had due. These tests and medical appointments took away from his study time.

Adam signed in, and a technician escorted him to a tubelike piece of equipment. A giant magnet. Adam wondered if the decision not to take a Valium had been foolish.

"This won't hurt, but you need to hold very still in the machine."

"Okay."

The tech instructed him to lie on the table, placed two small cushions around his head, hooked a Velcro strap over his forehead, and gave him an aviator-style headset for communication. Adam's palms began to sweat. Inside the scanner, a fan moved the air through the machine, but the restraints left him agitated—a prisoner.

The headphones reduced the noise, but the banging and snapping as the MRI took pictures of his brain sounded like machine gun fire, and Adam startled each time it stopped and started again. *Rat-tat-tat-tat.*

The tech's voice came through the headphones. "Are you all right?"

Adam's back muscles tensed from lying still, and his mind tired from controlling his instinct to panic. His answer, more like a plea: "How much longer?" He hoped he hadn't whimpered.

"About another fifteen minutes."

Adam focused on the picture, the ducks in the water.

Twenty minutes later, he hurried to the changing area to get dressed.

"Your doctor will call you after he reviews the images," the technician said.

Late Friday afternoon, Adam called the office. "This is Adam McGuire inquiring about the results from my MRI."

"I'm sorry, sir, but we can't give information on the phone. The doctor needs to see you. I can work you in Monday at 11:00 a.m. We recommend bringing someone with you."

Adam hung up and reassured himself that Dr. Harper was being thorough. Adam considered calling his family but didn't want them to worry. It was going to be a long weekend, and none of his classes in critical thinking, persuasion, or logic would help.

CHAPTER 6

Rosie dragged the trash bin to the street. Pickup was between nine and nine thirty, and she hated if Carlos forgot. The garage would stink if they had to wait until the following week, and the smell of rot would seep into the house.

A moving van squealed to a stop and parked in front of the house next door. An older couple trailed behind, parking ten feet from Rosie's driveway. The woman, whom Rosie guessed to be in her mid-seventies, retrieved a cardboard box from the backseat. Her pink and white checkered pants and aqua sneakers stood out in the drab day. The woman's voice carried in the crisp air. "I've got them," she said to the man exiting the driver's side.

"I told you I'd carry the box." He frowned, came around to her side of the car, and took the container from her. "Don't lift anything heavy. You'll injure your back again."

"Fine." She relinquished her hold. "And you let the movers take care of the rest. Lord knows we're paying them enough." The woman waved at Rosie and headed toward her, retying the belt on her double-breasted coat.

Rosie was curious. The house had been empty since the previous summer, the For Sale sign being put up and taken down, never once advertised as sold.

The woman appeared to be slim, though it was hard to tell. Her coat covered her from neck to mid-thigh. Her cheeks were flushed from the cold.

"Hi. I'm your new neighbor, Penny Albright."

"Rosie Perón."

"John, this is one of our neighbors, Rosie."

A portly man with a thin white mustache turned around and nodded. "Nice to meet you," he said and disappeared through the garage.

"Your husband is in charge of the breakables, I'm guessing."

"Yes. The box contains the wine, the vodka, the whiskey . . . the valuables." Penny laughed. "We'll need it tonight. I'm exhausted. A few years ago, we bought a condo in Florida and decided to downsize our St. Louis home." She tugged the collar closer to her neck. "The hardest part of the move is purging your possessions. I suppose it's all the memories associated with the stuff, not the items themselves, don't you think?"

"We haven't acquired much," Rosie said.

"Married long?"

"Two years. Feels like forever."

"It goes by fast," Penny said.

Rosie changed the subject. "I didn't know the house sold."

"We've been inside once and taken the virtual tour online several times. I think it will suit our needs."

Something small and white sniffed Rosie's ankle. "Aww . . . hello, little guy." Rosie squatted and offered her hand.

"This is Jo-Jo, my baby girl. The movers must have left the door open. Good thing she's afraid of the street."

"She's cute. Can I pet her?"

"Sure. She loves people."

Rosie scratched behind the dog's ears and stroked her neck.

"Rosie!" Carlos hollered out the window.

Penny jerked. "Oh, he startled me."

"I'm calling you. You hear me?"

The garbage truck pulled up in front of the women. A man jumped out, placed the can into the rear loader, waited, returned the can, and went on his way.

Rosie grasped the bin's handle. "Good luck with your move."

"Come by for coffee sometime." Penny glanced back at the window, picked up Jo-Jo, and waved good-bye.

CHAPTER 7

The neurologist's office had advised Adam to bring a family member to the consultation, but he'd declined, and now he held his breath while Dr. Harper explained his prognosis. "I know this is a lot of information to deal with." Dr. Harper's mouth was set in a hard, grim line. "Huntington's disease doesn't usually occur until people are in their thirties, forties, or fifties. Because of the early onset, you have Juvenile Huntington's, which progresses more rapidly."

Adam tried to think of the right questions to ask the doctor, but his thoughts turned cloudy, and it was difficult to register the foreign language of medical terminology. His mind wrapped itself in a cocoon of disbelief. But he understood Dr. Harper's statement: "I'm sorry. There is no cure."

Dr. Harper continued, "I think it would be helpful for you to discuss this with a therapist and others with the same diagnosis." He offered Adam the name of a Huntington's support group.

• • •

A week later, Adam found the small meeting room on the fourth floor of the hospital. Including himself, five of those present had been diagnosed with HD, and another four attendees were there as support: a friend, two wives, and a husband. The nine of them plus the group leader sat in a circle of folding chairs. Adam was the youngest in the group.

The group leader welcomed everyone, introduced Adam, and started the meeting.

A slender woman in her forties spoke. "The doctors say I have about two years until my life is unbearable." She talked about the things she had given up: career, driving, even her marriage, because her husband "couldn't hack it." An unshaven, overweight man slapped his chair. "If I go out in public, they call me a drunk because I stagger," he said. The other man, stricken with dementia, informed the group several times he could no longer go fishing. A thin woman using a wheelchair warned the group not to eat popcorn, Doritos, or anything hard to chew for fear of choking.

"I decided to stop attending my college classes." Adam hunched low in his seat. "I can't keep up with the workload."

"Too bad," the woman in the wheelchair said.

"Arm yourself with information now, so you won't be blindsided as your symptoms worsen," her husband said, and added, "I suffer from sleep apnea."

Adam bit the inside of his cheek. "Sleep apnea?"

"Yes. I have to wear one of those masks at night. It's just awful. You can't imagine."

All day, Adam's head had pounded. Now the anger he'd suppressed crackled through his arms to his fingertips. Adam the pacifist dissolved. His eyes closed. He stood up and punched the guy—hammered him until blood splattered the little alligator on his designer shirt.

Adam opened his eyes, the daydream over. The man was still blathering something about the apnea mask. Adam's fists perched on his thigh, his knuckles white. He wasn't sure if the support group was for the patient or for the family members, but he'd seen enough. These people represented what was waiting for him. A visual timeline peppered with a hefty dose of reality. Now, he needed an anger-management group.

The woman in the wheelchair said, "By the time I die, I won't know who I am."

Adam excused himself and decided to go back to his apartment. But first he stopped at the store and bought a big bag of Doritos.

• • •

A few days after the meeting, Adam drove to campus. He'd timed it hoping to run into the guys. To throw the ball instead of a lamp. Tonight, however, the gym was quiet. No feet trampled down the court, no voices hollered, "I'm open. Shoot. Go!" The only person roaming the hall was the janitor.

Adam left the gymnasium, yanked his woolen cap over his ears, and tucked his scarf inside his coat.

"Hey, McGuire!"

Adam turned. "Brad. Hey. No game tonight?"

"Naw, two of the guys have exams tomorrow. I haven't seen you in a while."

"Have time to get some coffee and catch up? My car's across the street."

"Sure."

• • •

For a Wednesday night, the Jive was unusually quiet. Over a cup of decaf, Adam told Brad about his diagnosis and about his support group experience.

"I don't know what to say," Brad said. His voice wavered; he was shaken by the news.

"There's no right or wrong reaction."

"What did your family say?"

"I haven't worked up the nerve to tell them," Adam said. "I feel like I'm disappearing. I'm not Adam anymore. I'm my disease. Jeez, no matter what I say, I sound maudlin."

"You are your disease," Brad said, as if to let it sink in. "Maybe, but for now, you have minimal symptoms. You aren't those people in the group. Huntington's hasn't beaten you. Not yet. Can't you focus on that?"

"Some days I can."

"Can I offer some suggestions?"

"I guess."

"You said you'd decline at a faster rate, but right now, your mind's sharp. You're dwelling on what will be, not what is. What about talking to a professional?"

"They'll offer me pills and a couch. Not interested. I keep asking, why me?"

"You're going to need help. There's no way to win this one."

"Interesting," Adam said.

"What do you mean? About help?"

"No, about winning. I can't beat this, but maybe I can call some of the shots."

"I'm missing something," Brad said.

Adam searched his cup for the words, the wisdom he'd come to expect from the barista. But Hanna wasn't working tonight.

"Let's change the subject. Tell me about Truman State. Have you found an apartment?"

CHAPTER 8

The doorbell rang. Rosie peered through the half-closed curtain. The new neighbor stood on the stoop holding a pie; slits in the crust revealed cherry filling. The pie was still warm, as evidenced by steam venting from its top. Jo-Jo was at Penny's heels, sniffing the welcome mat.

Rosie hesitated. Carlos had gone to shower and shave. Surely he wouldn't object to Penny's visit.

"Hello, neighbor." Penny held out the hot pastry dish.

"I've been meaning to stop by," Rosie said. "I feel terrible. I should have brought something to welcome *you*."

"I baked two, and it'll take all week for us to eat one. I enjoy cooking. It's therapeutic."

"I buy cookie dough from the refrigerator section. Never attempted a pie," Rosie said. "Looks delicious. Thank you."

Jo-Jo skirted past Rosie and beelined into the living room.

Penny passed the dessert to Rosie and bent down and clapped. "Come back here, baby." Penny shook her head. "We're still training her."

Rosie turned to see where the dog had gone, and Penny stepped through the entryway. Jo-Jo jumped on the couch, her short legs barely making the leap. She curled alongside the armrest, her head snuggled against the throw pillow.

"No, come!" Penny said, and moved toward the divan. "Sorry. We let her on our furniture."

Carlos moved into the room like a tank. "What the hell? Get that dog out of here." Jo-Jo leapt up and barked.

"Go on, get out of here."

Penny's eyes widened. She and Carlos stepped toward the dog at the same time. Penny continued to move in the direction of the couch, seized Jo-Jo, and backed toward the door.

"I'm sorry," Rosie said.

"So am I." Penny gave her a look, not of anger, but pity. She stuffed Jo-Jo inside her coat and rushed out the front entry.

"Keep the mutt away from here!" Carlos hollered after her. "You know I don't like dogs," he said to Rosie.

"Penny's our new neighbor. She brought this." Rosie lifted the pie. "The dog wandered in by accident."

"Tell her to keep it in her own yard."

Rosie wanted to scream at him. Or just scream.

CHAPTER 9

The cursor blinked. Waiting. Alana clicked, and a folder spilled files about Borg Larson across the monitor. She examined a photo of him cutting a ribbon to kick off the opening of an overseas plant. His short hair glowed light as wheat in the summer sun. He was tanned, trim, and well-tailored, but Alana wasn't convinced Larson was the answer to her conundrum.

Times were tough for the magazine industry. Many had folded or been bought out. Alana's keen sense of responsibility to her employees was always foremost on her mind every time she took on a new project. She wouldn't let her team down.

She studied each article. Borg Larson had everything most people dreamed about: charm, money, and power. Another document noted that Larson had graduated from the Wharton School of Business at the top of his class. The article stated that his intuitive business sense sent him into the world with a Midas touch, enabling him to build his empire. He had traveled to Europe after college, making and breaking international business deals, and, Alana guessed, a string of hearts with women he encountered along the way.

Her phone lit. A California area code flashed across the screen.

"Alana Hudson," she said.

"Good morning. I'm Borg Larson, owner of *New Heights Magazine*. Hope I'm not interrupting."

"Not at all. I'm reviewing information regarding your company and the paperwork your manager faxed me."

"Very good. I believe we need to press on with a decision."

"Mr. Larson, we write articles on current events, cuisine, and art. We run book reviews, and we promote events related to St. Louis entertainment, such as our symphony, botanical gardens, and the art museum. *Why* are you interested in my magazine?"

"Your magazine is appealing and informative, but you're missing two key components," Borg said. "Technology and fashion—two strengths we can offer."

"But *New Heights*'s emphasis is on tech gadgets, health, and fitness. I saw nothing related to fashion."

"We've recently become involved with a company in Paris. La Chic Boutique is a new haute couture house interested in expanding. I'd like to represent the company and showcase their ads in *Slick*. We sent them a copy of your magazine, and it was well received," Borg said. "The boutique has young, eager designers and an owner willing take risks to get American buyers."

"The idea of sharing my magazine isn't something I take lightly." Alana moved into the kitchen and paced around the counter. She twisted a grape from its stem, rolling it between her fingers.

"I'd like to suggest you come to my L.A. office for further discussion. My assistant can set up a flight. Today. First class. I'm eager to sign the boutique as a client and have an exclusivity clause in the contract."

"Let me review the information and get back to you," Alana said. She hung up and thumbed through the illustrations faxed by Andrew Stinson, Borg's department manager. La Chic Boutique's clothing appeared high-end and the pricing affordable. A tingle ran down Alana's spine. To survive, she needed to take risks. But one mistake could cost her the magazine. This decision could be a deal-breaker.

Alana had started the magazine after college, and *Slick* had soon hit the shelves monthly. She currently juggled the demands with a staff of six. Alana was editor-in-chief. She had an assistant and layout designer, Michelle; a supervisor of marketing and sales, Sean; a photographer, E.B.; and two contributing writers, Taylor and Murphy. Alana valued their loyalty. The six were family, and their combined talents produced *Slick*. She enjoyed the relationship with her employees, the weekly lunch meetings, the summer picnics and Christmas parties.

When newsstands had quickly run out of *Slick*'s first issues, Alana had given everyone a bonus to show her appreciation. Paid subscriptions had begun to roll in, and Alana had employed additional freelancers to keep up with the workload. Sales had been excellent until two years ago, when the economy had tanked. Retail sales had gone down, up, and then down again by several percentage points. The first thing people cut back were frivolities like magazine subscriptions. Forced to prune extra personnel, Alana had worried about her publication's future and her devoted staff, who were logging extended hours. She picked up her phone and debated. Alana didn't doubt her lawyer, Daniel, and his legal ability, but *Slick* was her baby. Alana popped a grape in her mouth and squished the soft flesh between her teeth. She wouldn't call Daniel. Not yet.

She tied her hair in a French braid, found her yoga mat, and took a downward dog position. Breathe in, breathe out. No distractions.

After her workout, Alana decided a double espresso from the Jumpin' Jive Café might provide a needed edge. She wrapped herself in a warm coat, and halfway to the Jive, she realized she had forgotten her phone. Two hours later, she saw Michelle's text: CALL IMMEDIATELY.

CHAPTER 10

Adam's reluctance to tell his family the news was burning a hole in his gut. He paced around his apartment and decided to phone Brad. "Hey, game on tonight?"

"You forgot. This is finals week before spring break, remember? The gym is locked. Have you checked outside? The Alberta Clipper unloaded at least four inches of snow, and it's still falling."

"So?" Adam didn't care if four feet pounded the city. He scratched a line of frost from the edge of the window pane. "March in St. Louis is so twisted. I need to get out of my apartment. Do you own a sled?"

"Are you serious? It's a blizzard out there." Brad laughed. "God, I haven't done that since I was twelve."

"Been to Art Hill?" Adam asked.

"Do I live in St. Louis?" Brad chuckled. "All right, let's do this. I'll borrow my brother's Sprint Racer. Should we meet there?"

"Why don't I pick you up?"

• • •

Adam packed a thermos of coffee and tossed a couple of paper cups in a bag. He found his old ski mask and tried it on. His aunt had given it to him years ago for Christmas. He never wore the thing, certain he'd be mistaken for a bank robber or a terrorist. Tonight he didn't care. Adam stuffed it in his pocket and tucked his jeans in his boots.

He drove to his parents' home and quietly removed his old wooden Flyer from the backyard shed. As he drove to Brad's house, the weather app on Adam's phone predicted more snowfall and high accumulations before morning; a freak storm had hit the entire Midwest. The city already was enveloped in a downy-white blanket, and the highway was now a whiteout, a ghostly, magical place. Fresh snow was cradled in the curves of branches and sloped rooftops. Tire marks from an occasional car quickly disappeared. Adam revved the engine. In preparation for Boston's harsh winters, the previous summer he'd gotten a blowout deal on a used Subaru Outback. His foot pressed the accelerator, testing. His heart thumped when the steering wheel slipped in his hand. He straightened the wheel and slowed with a gentle press on the brake.

For the rest of the ride, the silence was a melodic reprieve. The wiper blades swooshing across the windshield relaxed him. Street lamps lined the road like candles on a frosted cake, their lights emitting a warm glow. Another two inches had fallen since he'd phoned Brad. Soon, the salt trucks would begin scraping the roads, and more four-wheel drives would venture out. In thirty minutes, the virgin landscape would be gone.

Adam arrived at Brad's, pulled into the driveway, and beeped the horn. Brad threw his not-to-be-missed neon yellow sled in the back and jumped in the front with Adam. The rail-thin sophomore stood over six feet tall, but tonight his slender build appeared massive with all his layers. Not a shred of his sandy hair showed around the edges of his bright orange woolen beanie topped with a green pom.

Adam backed out of the driveway. "Dude, you're more padded than the Michelin tire man."

"Mind if I crack the window?" Brad asked.

"Maybe we're too suited up," Adam said and turned off the heat.

"You'll regret those words when we're climbing the hill. It's windy and twenty-five degrees."

The highway appeared deserted, but by the time they reached Art Hill, the parking lot was packed with people.

"This brings back memories," Adam said. "My dad used to drive my sister and me here every winter."

They lined up their sleds, jumped belly first, and raced down the hill. Adam won the first round; the next two were ties. The slope became crowded, the snow deeper, and the trudge up the hill more tiring. The fourth time down, Adam began to feel like a bowling ball, trying not to smack into the pins of people plodding against the tide, making their way to the top. Adam veered to the right to avoid a man and a boy about five years old, but lost control.

The sled rocketed down the slope. The man shouted, "Turn!" He picked up the child, but his movements were as sluggish as someone running in a swimming pool.

Adam rolled off the board, sliding on his back headfirst down the hill. He rolled again so he was on his stomach and dug in his toes to slow his descent. Brad soared behind him and coasted to a stop. He leapt off and bent over Adam.

"Jeez. Are you all right?"

Adam stood and faced Brad. It could have happened to anyone. Adam spotted the father halfway up the knoll, clasping the boy's mitten and tugging the rope attached to a saucer-shaped sled.

"I'm fine." He ducked in time to avoid the large snowball Brad hurled at him. But Adam's forced grin melted like the slush under his boots, certain the scenario was some kind of warning.

CHAPTER 11

Time wasn't on Adam McGuire's side. Neither was hope. Doctors couldn't give a definite answer. They never could.

Adam lumbered past barren trees lining the campus quad, and he shifted his backpack to keep the straps from digging into his shoulders. He passed through the student union, ignoring the cafeteria as it exhaled the aroma of his favorite pizza. Adam shuffled to the bookstore's return counter and emptied his backpack on at the register. Textbooks thudded in a pile.

A girl about his age, seated on a stool, asked, "Can I help you?"

"I want to sell these books back."

She scanned the hardbacks. "Sorry, man." Pink gum snapped in her back teeth. "We can't buy any of these books back due to edition changes."

"Fine, whatever." He turned away.

"Wait. You forgot your books."

"I don't need them anymore." He thrust the empty backpack under his arm and dug his phone out of his back pocket. He couldn't put off the call any longer.

"Marigold, it's me. Can you meet this morning at the Jive? I need to talk to you. It's important."

CHAPTER 12

Saige checked the directions on the paper taped to her dashboard. The rest of the world relied on GPS. The yellow-lined paper served as *another* reminder that she was out of step with everyone—all because her father didn't like the way technology changed things he could count on. Marcy's note read: *Turn left at the corner—at Manchester and Braden.*

Beyond the traffic signal, a neon sign flashed Jumpin' Jive Café, its lettering a beacon in the dull, tarnished sky. Saige waited for the light to change, her little Toyota wobbling in the hostile March wind. As soon as she accelerated, a zippy candy-apple-red convertible traveling through the intersection cut her off. Saige slammed on the brakes. The blonde in the convertible, oblivious, drove into the Jive's lot.

Saige parked and got out of her car. She placed a thin glove across her nose and mouth and cursed the lifeless St. Louis weather. The sky spit bits of moisture on her cheeks, cursing back.

For years, she'd dreamed of beaches, ocean waves, and accidental sunburns. If she saved her money, she could go somewhere warm. Wiggle her toes in the soft sand and let the tide lap at her legs. Maybe dance naked under the tropical sun?

No, she'd never really wanted to do *that*. Only to feel normal. For the past to stop haunting her. For the memories to fade, like an old newspaper in the summer sun. She'd probably pack her sorrows in the suitcase and take them with her. As if she could forget her mom's cries for help, the fear as she struggled to breathe, and her father's blunt "Buck up" meant to console Saige in their darkest hour. The doors to the bistro swung open. She stepped inside.

The Jumpin' Jive Café's wide room reverberated with the crowd's energy. Conversations blended as a single sound, rising and falling like breathing. Saige waited behind a crush of people to give her order. After a short wait, her name was called, and she picked up her tea. Words trailed beneath the cup's rim: *This is your lucky day.* A young woman she guessed to be about her age moved quickly, filling drinks and writing on cups. The barista's short hair, dyed black and copper against patches of platinum, mimicked a leopard's pelt. She nodded an acknowledgment to Saige and turned back to filling orders.

Marcy was wrong; it hadn't helped to get out. Saige cradled the warm drink, but there was no hope in her cup. She scoured the room to find a seat. Tables were spread through a large main section, with another wing on the building's back side. Every plush, oversized chair and high table was occupied. A sign above the room at the rear said, "Available for speed dating. Inquire at counter." A peek inside told her the area was packed.

At the far end of the main room, opposite the entrance, was an empty chair. Saige wove through the crowd, ready to claim a spot at the table. She stopped. The woman who'd cut her off at the intersection sat next to the vacant seat.

"You're welcome to sit here." The woman smiled through perfect teeth and polished lips. "The place is elbow-to-elbow today." The blonde scooted her chair to accommodate Saige. "I'm Alana," she said.

Saige noted that the woman carried herself with the easy elegance of a ballet dancer: upright posture, graceful, confident.

Saige introduced herself and scratched at a scar in the wooden table. Her hair tumbled forward in thin strands. The blonde removed a laptop from its case. Riveted on the screen coming to life, Saige didn't think she'd ever own a sleek, dark machine with glowing buttons.

Her father, Raphael Santoro, had no use for frivolous gadgets and had never allowed a computer in their home. Saige considered him a bit of a neo-Luddite, opposing specific kinds of technology.

After her car and insurance payments, gas, and other incidentals, there wasn't much money left from a paycheck that paid little more than minimum wage. Living with her father helped, allowing her occasional books, new clothes, or a little spare cash to store in her checking account, but a computer purchase and cell phone bills weren't in her budget. The equipment in front of her was alien. "Nice laptop," Saige said.

"Thanks." Alana leaned closer to the screen. "I'm trying to figure out features from the recent update." Alana plied the keyboard with ease and speed. Saige's fingers were competent on the family's typewriter and piano but were foreign to a computer keyboard.

"Your coupe's a real beauty," Saige said.

"How do you know what I drive?"

Saige's cheeks warmed. She wrapped a strand of hair around her finger and hoped to sound nonchalant. "It caught my attention while I waited at the light."

Alana beamed. "I love my car, but it doesn't drive well in the snow. I should have brought the other one. I think they're predicting more bad weather."

Saige nodded. Alana wasn't wearing a wedding band. How could a person so young own *two* cars?

"Did the barista write on your cup?"

"Pardon me?"

"There's a message on my cup."

"I'm guessing it's your first time here."

"Yes."

"That's Hanna's writing; it's her trademark." Alana turned her drink. *Choose wisely.*

"Is it meant to be advice?"

Alana sipped her coffee and eased back against the chair. "I'm not sure. You'll find Hanna a surprising individual. I have a decision regarding my company. I didn't mention anything. I have no idea how she comes up with these suggestions."

"You own your own business?"

"For now, anyway." Keys tapped in quick succession. Alana shifted her gaze to the clock overhead. "I have to go." She gulped her last bit of coffee, snapped the laptop shut, and zipped her coat. They exchanged nice to meet you and good-byes.

Moments later, Saige watched out the window as the convertible gave up its spot to another vehicle. Its male driver entered the Jive, his steps heavy, as though his loafers were lined with lead. He leaned against the wall, arms folded against his chest, waiting.

A teenage girl sprinted through the door, brushing a few wet flakes off her bulky sweater. "Hey, Adam!" She waved.

He moved toward her. "Where's your coat?" He hugged her, adding, "I figured you'd get here first, Marigold."

"Mom held me up. Wow," she said, "the Jive is packed today." Two women vacated a table, and Marigold threw her sweater on one of the seats. "I'll get the drinks. You sit." She hurried to get a place in line.

· · ·

Marigold waited for the Jive's favorite barista. Hanna had an uncanny ability to observe people. Her comments or advice on customers' cups surprised the Jive's patrons. It developed Hanna's loyal following there.

"One caramel latte and one coffee, black," she said. "The names are Adam and Marigold." She paid and moved to the next counter. "So, Hanna. How's business?"

Hanna shrugged. "Crazy busy today. What's the matter with your brother?"

"Nothing, he's fine."

Hanna capped her black marker, tucked it behind her ear and drizzled caramel on top Marigold's drink. Marigold's cup read: *Be ready. Today will bring something unexpected.* "What's this mean?"

"I don't know. I can't explain it. I talk to a person and everything slows down. Feelings wash over me. I used to think it was intuition, but sometimes I get images."

"Like what?"

"Well, last week I saw a customer at a table holding a Maltese with a blue collar. I went to tell her we had a no-pet rule. I got closer, and there was no dog."

Hanna started smoothies for the next couple. The next guy in line yelled over the blender crushing ice. "So what happened?"

"I wiped down the table next to her and asked the woman if she had a dog. She showed me a photo of a Maltese with his name embroidered on his blue collar. Said she was in town for a meeting and missed him."

Marigold sipped her drink. "You have a gift. Don't stop the comments."

"I won't. . . . I can't," Hanna said. "Take care of yourself. And Adam."

Marigold passed Adam his coffee and got comfortable in the seat across from him.

• • •

Saige crushed her empty cup and pushed back from the table. The heavy wooden chair scraped the floor, making more noise than she had intended. The sad-faced young man didn't look up, and the bubbly teenager across from him continued chatting away. It occurred to Saige they could have been twins, but he was older and a head taller. They both had the same slender build and pale, blue-gray eyes. Saige picked up a magazine from the table and flipped the pages. Three feet away, their conversation drifted to her table.

• • •

"I need you to listen," Adam said.

"You sound so serious."

"It *is* serious. I didn't want to tell you on the phone or at home, and maybe the Jive wasn't the best choice." His voice trailed off. "We have to talk. I'm having health issues, and the doctor got my test results back. The doctor's opinion is . . ." Adam forced out the words: "I'm dying."

Coffee sloshed over Marigold's cup. Her head shook back and forth in disbelief. "That's impossible. You're only twenty years old."

"I'm sick."

"Is it cancer? There's chemotherapy." Her voice broke.

• • •

The magazine slapped the floor. Adam and Marigold turned. Saige could see by the change in their faces they'd been momentarily distracted. She grabbed the napkin under her drink and pushed it against her nose. The soaked paper tore apart in tiny, disintegrating pieces. She couldn't put her head under a pillow and hide. This couldn't be undone. They were staring at her. She squeezed her thumb across her nose, but it didn't stop the tears from rolling down her cheeks. There was no safety here, and she had never felt more alone. She whispered. "I'm sorry. I wasn't trying to listen."

"You could have fooled me," Marigold said. Her hands were shaking.

A lanky young man approached, unfolded a tissue from his shirt pocket, and offered it. "I promise, it's clean, and more useful than yours. I'm Finn. I'm sorry you're having a bad day."

Saige took the tissue and wished she could will herself invisible.

CHAPTER 13

"You're going to be fine," Finn said. "Isn't she?" he said to the couple staring.

"What is wrong with you?" Marigold wagged her finger. "This is a private conversation."

"Sorry," Finn said. "This young lady is obviously upset." He tipped his head toward Saige.

"*She's* upset?" Marigold's ponytail whipped her cheek.

"Just trying to help."

"Thank you for the tissue," Saige said. "But could you excuse us?"

"Sure," Finn said and stepped away with a quick glance behind.

Saige turned to Marigold and Adam. She wished she could explain how her mother's illness had changed her life. How close they had been, how she had become the caregiver. How the loneliness now was so overwhelming with no one to talk to.

"I'm really sorry about how I reacted. I heard your brother," Saige said to Marigold. "My mom died from lung cancer. I know how you feel. I was so confused the day I found out."

Marigold glared at her. "I don't even know how I feel. And he's *not* going to die." She cupped her mouth, turned, and ran. Her elbow hit a display table stacked with plastic cups. The cups crashed to the floor and scattered.

Adam and Saige placed them back on the table. He faced Saige. "Look, I don't know you or what happened," he said.

"Don't take her anger personally. She doesn't understand any of this."

Saige's expression saddened. "She won't, not for a while." And neither will you, she thought.

CHAPTER 14

Marigold turned on the faucet in the Jive's restroom. Water splashed her cheeks and trickled down her neck into her blouse. The metal dispenser's paper stuck together in a tight clump, and she could only manage to tear away small pieces from the center. Marigold wiped her nose on her sleeve. Her back pressed against the wall, her legs buckled, and she slid to the floor. Adam dying? Marigold tucked her head between her knees.

The bathroom door swung open, and Hanna stepped inside. "What's going on?"

"Nothing." Marigold tried to keep her voice level.

"You went all kung fu on my display shelf. Come here." Hanna reached for Marigold and helped her stand. "Finn, the guy in the blue shirt, he comes here a lot. The shy one, I haven't seen her before. They upset you. Is there anything I can do to help?"

"No, I can't talk about it right now."

Hanna took a comb from her back pocket and raked her hair. "I wrote *Today is your lucky day* on Finn's cup. I had the same feeling about the girl. But it doesn't seem to be her lucky day."

"Yeah, their lucky day." Marigold stared at the tiled floor littered with paper and motioned to the door. "I need to find my brother. Thanks for checking on me." She gripped the handle, glanced behind her, and saw Hanna's image in the mirror, watching.

CHAPTER 15

Saige jumped to her feet when Marigold came back to the table. "If I could explain—"

"I'd rather you didn't." Marigold gestured to her brother. "Let's go." She whisked her sweater off the chair and hurried out of the building. Adam nodded good-bye and caught up with his sister.

Saige leaned back in her seat and watched them drive away, holding her crushed cup like a security blanket. A hand on her shoulder caused her to jerk.

"Easy there," a low voice said. "Mind if I sit down?" Finn didn't wait for an answer. He settled into the seat next to her. "I brought some water. You okay?"

"I don't know. I heard him tell his sister he was dying, and it brought back some sad memories. I lost my mother a year ago today." Saige twisted her ankle in little circles. "My mom had complained of back pain, but by the time I persuaded her to see a doctor, the diagnosis was stage IV lung cancer." The words tumbled out. "Six months after the diagnosis, she was gone. It's our first year without her. We didn't even put up a tree at Christmas. My dad won't talk about her. He's angry the doctors couldn't save her. I miss her so much."

"It's a difficult time," Finn said. "I lost my dad years back. We were really close. It hurt like hell. Still bothers me, but the pain, it changes."

He leaned in. "That kid doesn't know what hit her. All this information is a big ol' runaway train in her brain. Some folks lash out. Don't blame yourself. When the facts are overwhelming, it's natural to react in anger or denial. I thought I should try to help when the girl behind the counter went to look for a mop." He gave her a sheepish grin after his attempted joke. "Your lucky day. I happened to have a tissue with me."

His words stirred in the pit of her stomach. She wasn't sure who was smiling at whom, but the draw was undeniable. He was interested in what she had to say, his face lit with kindness, and he didn't break eye contact. Some mysterious pull lured her. *Lucky day* was her cup's message. Finn's long legs extended from under the table, relaxed, as if he had known her for years. He wore jeans and a navy button-down shirt. Its rolled-up sleeves accented his arms. Not too muscular; perfect, really. "I don't think I introduced myself. I'm Saige Santoro."

"It's a pleasure," Finn said.

"Do you live around here?" she asked.

"About ten minutes."

"Me, too, if I hit all the green lights."

Finn's cell alerted him. "Sorry, it's a text from my brother. Excuse me a second." He typed and put his phone back in his pocket.

"Sorry, am I keeping you?" Saige asked.

"Not at all. He'll wait. Are you here by yourself?" Finn asked.

"Yeah, it's my first time to the café. I don't get out much. I'm a bit of a loner."

"I'm glad you came in today. Can I get you another cup of coffee?" Finn said.

"No, I've had my limit. Go ahead if you'd like some."

"I'm all right. I'd rather hear more about you."

"Not much to tell. When I was eleven, my father decided I should be homeschooled. My folks relocated to an older community. There weren't any young children around."

"Sounds lonely."

"It was. My mom was my best friend."

"I admire how hard she must have worked. How does a parent handle all the effort involved to homeschool their kid?"

"A lot of parents work together, but you don't have to. My mom ordered DVDs and workbooks."

"Did you get out of algebra and physics?"

"No way. Or calculus. But I didn't go to college. Not yet. How about you?"

"I'm a computer programmer," he said. "Where do you work?"

Saige told him about the bank, winning the iPod, and the little ceremony.

"Congratulations. I've never won anything. Oh, I did win a spelling bee in third grade. Got two gold stars."

Saige laughed. She was glad she had won the contest. It gave her something to talk about.

"You have a little black flake right there." Finn brushed her cheek.

The unexpected gesture surprised Saige, and his tender expression charmed her.

"Would you excuse me for a few minutes?" she asked.

"I'll be right here."

In the restroom, she stopped in front of the mirror. Saige often received compliments about her green eyes. She'd been blessed with her mother's long, dark lashes and had been told more than once that her mouth formed a perfect Cupid's bow.

But now her eyes were red-rimmed, and bits of mascara stuck to her cheeks, dried in tiny dark ribbons. A small bottle of lotion in her purse and wadded toilet paper rubbed away the streaked mascara. Finn's attention had aroused new feelings Saige wasn't sure how to deal with. Maybe it *is* my lucky day, she thought. She took a deep breath and a last look in the mirror.

In the main room, she stopped abruptly, almost tripping two small children running past her. Saige scanned the café, but Finn was gone. The table, now empty, had been wiped clean. Her coat remained draped over the chair back. She retrieved her wrap, clutched it to her chest, and ran outside. The air stung her face. The sky was gray and tarnished. Saige started the ignition and chided herself for believing the chance encounter had meant something.

CHAPTER 16

Finn stood in the Jive's doorway and watched the red taillights of Saige's car disappear. His phone zinged in his pocket. A text popped up from his brother, Noah: *Waiting. Where are you?*

Finn responded: *Coming!*

Finn went to the room in the back and flopped in the chair. His brother, Noah, put down his phone.

"I was about to call Chelsea for a ride home," Noah said. "Where's the girl you want me to meet?"

"She's gone. I didn't tell her I was here with you. I'm sure she didn't know about this room. It was her first time here. She probably thought I cut out on her." The corners of his mouth turned down. "Great. I didn't have a chance to ask for her phone number."

Noah arched his back and stretched. "Don't you think she should have poked around for you?"

"She was distressed—personal issues."

"Let me guess. You played the white knight. You're always picking up lost kittens."

"Her name is Saige, and she was different," Finn said.

"Okay, so what's up with this one?" Noah squeezed a napkin into a tight ball, tossing it back and forth until it fell on the floor.

"I noticed her the minute she came through the door. Something about her . . ." Finn knew he sounded ridiculous, and he would rather pull off a fingernail than tell Noah his thoughts.

"Where's my brother, and what have you done with him?" Noah said. "You don't even know this girl." His tennis shoe kicked Finn's ankle. "Come on. We've been here long enough. Let's get out of here."

Finn nodded. No sense in hanging around now. Saige wouldn't be back today.

CHAPTER 17

Adam didn't know why he'd chosen a public place to tell his sister the news. Maybe the Jive held a sense of anonymity, the privacy of being lost in a crowd. A place where voices were loud and no one would strain to hear. But his plan had backfired.

"We need to finish this conversation," Adam said.

"Where?" asked Marigold

"Follow me to Queeny Park. We'll talk in my car," Adam said.

• • •

The ride to Queeny was only a few minutes away. The park was vacant. Adam maneuvered against the curb, and Marigold edged behind him and cut the ignition. She slid into the passenger's seat. Neither spoke. Once truth had sliced through the silence, there was no going back.

Adam let the engine idle. "This is hard to talk about. I've tried to think how—"

"Just tell me," Marigold said.

"It's Huntington's disease."

"Not cancer?"

"No, Juvenile Huntington's."

"I've never heard of it."

"This disease affects the central nervous system. Cells in the brain break down, leaving you unable to care for yourself. You eventually lose all motor control, and then . . . you die." He paused. "No treatment. No cure."

"What?"

"The disease is more accelerated in young people. I wish it were cancer. There's no way to fight Huntington's."

Marigold gripped her stomach. "Did you get a second opinion?"

"I've done everything. My internist sent me to a neurologist. He did an MRI, a CT scan, and a blood test."

There was fear in his voice.

"No," she shook her head. "Impossible. You're healthy. There must be a mistake. It can't be true."

"It is. I have symptoms—coordination problems, memory loss, anxiety."

"You must have been scared." She grabbed his arm. "Why didn't you call me? I would have gone with you when you had the tests."

"At first, I assumed it was stress related, a virus or something. I thought I'd wait until I knew something solid. It blows your mind the second they're checking for something serious. The doctor said a lot people with this diagnosis opt not to have the final tests, because they don't want to know for sure. They give up hope after they're told they have an incurable disease. I had to know."

Adam pressed the window's toggle switch back and forth. "I decided to stop going to my classes."

"You're quitting school?"

"What's the point?"

Marigold pressed her palm against her forehead. "What happens now?"

"I have to tell Mom and Dad. The disease is progressive. The research says eventually you can't control your muscles. You get hostile and confused." Sweat beaded on his forehead. "At some point, I'll have to move home. Eventually it'll be too hard for Mom and Dad to care for me. I'll probably need long-term care, like a nursing home. It's different for everybody, but the end is inevitable."

Marigold sank further into the seat.

"The disease is genetic," Adam continued. "For me to have it, wouldn't Mom or Dad have to be a carrier?"

"Or maybe they just haven't developed it yet."

He flicked the car keys dangling from the ignition, not looking at her.

"Nobody in our family has had Huntington's, right?" Marigold said. "I don't understand. Tell me everything again."

He started at the beginning and told her the whole story. "Getting the news was a bomb. I'm kind of numb."

"Are there drugs to help?"

"They all have side effects. The doctor encouraged drugs for depression. You know how I feel about taking drugs."

"But if they help you . . ."

"That's another conversation."

"What happens once you lose motor control?

"Worst case, I won't be able to walk, speak, or feed myself. There will be dementia. I'll lose control of toilet functions and won't be able to swallow." He had a fierce look. "I don't want to die, not like that. I *won't* die like that."

Wet droplets sat on Marigold's lashes and then tumbled down her cheeks. She reached over and squeezed his hand.

Adam wiped his eyes. "How do I tell Mom and Dad?"

CHAPTER 18

Saige's thoughts drifted to Finn, and she was ashamed. What kind of loser falls for a guy because he gives her a Kleenex? Why had he pretended to like her? It had been a rough morning. She'd left the house unhappy, a complete stranger had yelled at her for crying, and then she had been dumped. I'm pathetic, she thought.

Saige stopped at a gas station, fished a crumpled pamphlet from her coat pocket, and spread the paper across the steering wheel. *Join us for a free class. Microsoft Word II. 2 p.m. to 4 p.m.*

Saige sped through the streets, and with five minutes to spare, she questioned the librarian. "Is this class still open?" Saige pointed at the brochure.

"We have quite a few seats left."

"I don't know anything about computers. I've never used one."

"It's an advanced class. It may be a little over your head. But it's just through those doors."

Saige found Meeting Room No. 3, signed the roster, and took a seat. Everyone in the class was as old as her father. The instructor introduced himself to the class. "I'm Sam," he said. "Any questions, raise your hand, and I'll be happy to help."

Minutes later, Saige regretted her decision to join the class. She had trouble with the mouse, the cursor wouldn't move to the right place, and the scroll wheel always went the opposite direction. The class was beyond her skill level. She didn't *have* a level. The instructor came to her computer every few minutes to help get her on track with the other students. The elderly in the class were more adept than she. Humiliation of the day—round two. The minute the class was over, she would thank Sam and not come back.

Sam approached Saige after the others left. "I hope you weren't too frustrated."

"I was. I don't think I'll be back. You don't have a Mouse 101 class, do you?"

"Try the class for beginners. It's pretty basic. Don't give up. This was a level-two class. Perhaps a computer book might also be helpful. Check with the staff."

"Well, thanks for your help."

The class had taken her mind off Finn, how he'd disappeared without a good-bye. Saige strolled to the counter to investigate the schedule. She hovered next to the sign-up sheet, picked up the pen, but couldn't do it. It would be easier to flip through colorful pictures in *Homes & Gardens* and not think about files and edits.

Across the room, the librarian was shelving books.

"Excuse me," Saige said.

"Yes. How was your class? Isn't Sam a wonderful teacher?"

"He was very nice. He suggested I pick up a beginner's computer book."

"Sure, over this way. Anything specific?"

"Yeah, one for dummies would be good," Saige said, her tone sarcastic.

"The computer books start on this shelf and go on to the other side." The librarian plucked a book from the shelf and offered her *Computers for Dummies*.

"Thanks," Saige said, flipping through the book. She headed toward the checkout and did a double take. Third in line at the checkout was Finn. Saige edged toward the wall by the biographies, but it was too late.

"Wait." Finn sprinted toward her. "I wanted to talk about what happened at the Jive."

"Forget it. No explanation necessary. Just leave me alone." Saige tossed the book back on the shelf and rushed toward the exit. She drove away from him for the second time that day. She parked her car on a side street until she saw his car pass. Saige steered her Toyota back to the library and wrote her name on the line under Computers 101.

CHAPTER 19

"You haven't changed your mind about the movie, have you?" Noah asked Chelsea. Chelsea tossed the clothing catalogues into the recycle bin and kissed her husband's stubbly cheek. "No, I'm going to change now. Come on, Chloe, keep me company." Their white Lab followed, her tail swinging like a metronome.

Chelsea changed her blouse, sat down on the bench, and began her ritual. Chloe gave a low woof and put her head down on Chelsea's feet.

"Are you ready yet?" Noah sounded impatient. "You could have clothed half the people in China."

"One minute." The magnifying mirror accentuated tiny lines as small as thread on the sides of her eyes. Chelsea leaned forward, glued on the false eyelashes, and gave them an extra pat.

"Why do you wear all that goop? You don't need it." He kissed the crown of her head.

She bit her lip to refrain from telling him she'd consulted a plastic surgeon for those infant crow's-feet. She'd be thirty in a few years. Didn't want to end up like her mom.

"You never used to wear false lashes," Noah said. "I don't like them. They remind me of a 1960s Barbie in my aunt's doll collection. They're so heavy, so artificial." He batted his lashes.

"You're not funny." She poked his stomach. "They're fashionable."

"We'll be in a dark theater, for God's sake."

"It's a matinee show. And we're going out afterwards, right?

I'm ready. Let's go." She rubbed Chloe's soft belly. "Did Finn decide to go?"

"He called from the library. He'll meet us there."

"I love going to the theater." Chelsea squeezed Noah's arm. "It's more fun since they renovated. The leather recliners are so cozy."

"And we can order food without leaving our seats," Noah added.

"You owe me two chick flicks for this one," Chelsea said. "The review said the whole movie is car chases and bridges blowing up."

They parked and met Finn at the ticket window.

"Good timing." Finn gave Chelsea a hug and leaned toward Noah. "I ran into Saige at the library." The girl behind the glass window swiped his credit card. "Thanks."

"How'd it go?" Noah asked.

"It didn't," Finn said.

"Who's Saige?" Chelsea asked.

CHAPTER 20

After Alana hung up her coat, she checked her phone and counted three missed messages from Michelle. Michelle was her assistant, layout designer, and more than anything, a trusted friend. Alana's staff was dependable and could juggle a multitude of tasks, but Michelle was responsible for the magazine running smoothly. Alana hit redial.

"What's going on?"

"Borg wants a meeting in Los Angeles. Tomorrow," Michelle said.

"We spoke this morning. Why the sudden rush?"

"He didn't say. He sounded anxious to meet."

"Does Jeffrey Browne Jewelers still want a one-third-page ad?" Alana asked.

"He signed a four-month contract," Michelle said.

"Good." Alana flipped open her planner. "Tell E.B. to contact the art museum and start the shoot. The curator gave me the green light. And Murphy's articles look good. My schedule is clear. Go ahead; get me on a flight to L.A. I need to put these questions about *New Heights* to bed. I should have done this sooner. Leave the return flight open. I could use a vacation."

"I'm on it." Michelle's keyboard clicked in the background. "Even if I can find a flight, you know the ticket prices on short notice will be ridiculous."

"No worries. Larson said *New Heights* will pick up the tab for first class at their expense. I can pack and be at the airport in an hour; check standby. If you can't get me on today, try tomorrow. And I'll need a rental car."

"I'm on it," Michelle said.

"Call me back with the flight info if you find anything."

An hour later, Alana was almost at the airport. Michelle had found an evening flight in first class. Alana would get into L.A. before midnight. She boarded the plane with time to spare. The engines roared, and the plane tilted upward into the violet sky. Alana reached for her book, *Medieval History of Europe.*

It all had happened so fast. Had she remembered everything? She had forgotten to call Daniel Stern, her lawyer. Alana yawned, reminding herself to call him later. He would have tried to come along.

She had scheduled this trip to L.A. to get a gut feeling about the deal. Even with her best interests at heart, Daniel could be, well, Daniel. He was smart as a whip but bossy as hell. This was her vision. Not Daniel's. She'd meet with Larson. No deals, just evaluate the situation.

CHAPTER 21

A warm California breeze flowed down Windsor Avenue. It carried a mix of smog and salty air, along with the peppery smell of geraniums in clay pots, accenting the storefronts. Palm trees towered on both sides of the street, and Alana found the colorful splashes of flowers a remarkable contrast to the drab, grayish landscape she'd left in St. Louis. The temperature in Los Angeles was a delightful seventy-three degrees.

The massive building's brass plate announced 280 Windsor. The sleek high-rise dominated the street, contrasting with adjacent squat buildings, especially the old mission at the bottom of the hill. Ten-foot glass doors stood in front of Alana like sentinels, and the Swarovski crystal handles tattooed floating prisms across her fingers.

Inside, the grand ceiling soared to an overwhelming height. At the top, an immense dome with an oculus flooded the lobby with light. The sophisticated black and white decor epitomized elegance. Alana sucked in her lips, mesmerized by its glamour. Her heels flicked against the marble floor and reverberated across the reception area. Behind a wooden desk, the security guard's muscular arms squeezed against his jacket's sleeves, a white shirt was tightly buttoned at his throat. Across his jacket pocket, Alana could clearly see *NH ENTERPRISE* embroidered in gold thread.

"Hello. Alana Hudson to see Borg Larson."

The guard checked his clipboard. "Yes. Mr. Larson's expecting you. Take the elevator around the corner. Place this card under the red light. It'll take you right up." A pistol flashed through his jacket's opening. Alana couldn't imagine Michelle, her assistant, packing heat.

The elevator ascended and opened. Borg Larson was probably six feet tall and powerfully built. He wore a navy crepe Armani suit and a silk tie in bold plum.

"At last we meet," Borg said. His voice was deep and self-assured. His smile could have melted ice cream. "Thank you for flying out on such short notice. My office is this way."

Down the hall, his office door was open. Two men seated at a glass table stood when Alana entered, and they exchanged introductions—Andrew Stinson, the general manager, and Borg's attorney, Stanley Hoffman.

"Ms. Hudson," Andrew said, "we'd like you to review our offer. If we can come to an agreement, we have a contract ready."

"I believe a contract may be a little premature, but I'm interested in your proposal."

Borg shuffled through a stack of papers. "As we mentioned, we're an exclusive supplier of capacitors and specialized electronics to several cities in Asia, and about to open a new factory."

"Articles about capacitors will not work in my magazine," Alana said. "My understanding was we'd sprinkle in a few articles about cutting-edge technology."

"I assure you, there will be no articles about capacitors. We run stories of interest to all readers and advertise products in the back of the magazine."

Borg handed Alana the latest copy of his magazine. She skimmed the pages: "Drones for Beginners," "Best Drone for the Money," and "Best Camera for Drones."

"I like staying current with technology, but I was under the impression I'd retain content control and decide which articles to run," Alana said. "I believe we discussed you would take a percentage from any ad revenue you brought in and would retain a percentage from magazine sales, and I would approve all of your article submissions."

"Both our companies started small and grew." Borg clicked the end of his pen against the desk. "Now we're both major respective players but must rethink our strategy. I'm very interested in an haute couture house in Paris. I believe you received some of the design illustrations?"

"Yes, and I found them appealing," Alana said.

"We would give a great deal to you by offering our European house," Borg said. "Let's say it's my special contribution to the magazine—pages of affordable yet elegant fashion choices. La Chic Boutique has agreed to pay premium ad prices to get their name on the street. Of course, they want to see how they're received in America, so the choices must be carefully selected. They will choose one magazine, and they're ready and willing to commit."

"It's hard to predict what will sell," Alana said.

"I foresee no regrets. The boutique invests in quality materials: tailored, fashionable, and customized," Borg said. "If you agree to promote their collection, they'll sign immediately."

Alana glanced at the other men scribbling notes. "Mr. Larson, why not start up your own magazine?"

"A new magazine requires a lot of time and money. You have the distribution, and we like your layout. It's a win-win. I need a way to showcase the boutique's work, and that's where *Slick* comes in. Do you have any concerns or questions?"

"I should have included my lawyer in this conversation," Alana said. "Would you excuse me a moment? I'd like to try to reach him."

Alana stepped out the door and hit Daniel's cell number. At the voice mail prompt, she said, "Hi, it's me. I had to fly to California for an impromptu meeting with Larson. Call me as soon as you can."

• • •

Stanley told Borg, "Don't you realize you're holding the golden key? Ms. Hudson stands to gain everything in this deal. You're shortchanging yourself. Think about a separate magazine exclusive to La Chic Boutique's work. Martine is offering to customize: color, length, and specific sizing for her pieces. Women will love it. The work is unique. If demand goes skyward, we're talking enormous sums of money."

"Well, it won't sell in *New Heights*," Borg said, his voice firm. "My current readership isn't interested in fashion.

"So start a new magazine. "Be *Slick*'s competition."

"Do you remember the time and work needed to launch *New Heights*?" Borg said. "I have to be in the Philippines. The factory's about to open, and we need to finish the formalities. I don't have the time, and Ms. Hudson's magazine is solid."

"Then let's discuss a merger," Stanley said. "You keep all your articles and advertisements. Make it a blended family. Maybe you take 60 percent. You're providing the candy."

Borg frowned. "Let me think about it. The day isn't over. Nothing's been decided."

Stanley wiped his glasses with a handkerchief. "If the contract is worded carefully, perhaps it could be set up for a future takeover."

Borg focused on the papers in front of him. "Umm . . . uh-huh."

"I'll look into it," Stanley said.

• • •

Alana returned to find Borg, Andrew, and Stanley huddled in conversation. Borg brushed a piece of lint from his lapel and looked at Alana. "Did you speak to your attorney?"

"He's unavailable at the moment."

"Well, why don't we break for lunch? I've reserved a table at an outside café on the Boardwalk."

Alana hadn't eaten since breakfast. "Sounds like a good idea."

Borg shook her hand. Electricity all but crackled. His blue eyes flashed. Alana held his gaze and gave herself a mental kick. You can't think straight if you're attracted to him, she thought.

CHAPTER 22

Rosie settled into the wingback chair with her copy of *Time* magazine. She had just read a couple of paragraphs when a movement outside the window startled her. A five-foot-nine-inch yeti was trudging toward the mailbox. No, it was only Carlos in his thick parka and fur-lined hood.

On the other side of the driveway, a snow-covered puppy disappeared in the drifts, bounded out, and dashed back, pouncing and nose diving into the snow. Rosie was amused by her antics until Jo-Jo spied Carlos and the pup leaped back on the driveway to greet him.

Rosie vaulted from the chair. By the time she ran out the door, Jo-Jo had her front paws on Carlos's legs.

"What the . . . ?" He drew his leg back and thrust his foot under Jo-Jo's belly.

Rosie screamed, "No!"

Jo-Jo went airborne and landed in a snow pile next to the driveway.

"I told you to keep that dog away from here," he said. Rosie ran past him.

"Are you okay?" Rosie cradled her. They both shivered, the dog from fright and Rosie from cold. She carried Jo-Jo to her neighbor's house and hammered the knocker until Penny opened the door.

"Is everything all right?" Penny took the dog, picked up a towel, and rubbed cakes of snow from her paws and belly.

"There you go." She set Jo-Jo on the floor, tossed a ball, and the pup scampered after it. "I let her out to go potty and . . . where's your coat, dear?"

Rosie opened her mouth and closed it, deciding not to tell her neighbor what had happened. She could see the scene play out: Penny in tears, telling Carlos she'd have him arrested. He would shout back that she'd do no such thing because the dog was on his property, was a menace, and tried to bite him.

"There was no time," Rosie said. "I ran outside when I saw Jo-Jo heading into the street."

Penny was flustered. "I only left her for a minute. Perhaps she was confused because of the snow. It's her first winter. We'll have an electric fence installed in the spring."

"Well, I should be going," Rosie said.

"You take care of yourself, dear." Penny gave Rosie an expression of concern, and Rosie was sure she detected sympathy in her eyes, as if Penny could read her mind.

"I'm trying."

CHAPTER 23

Adam revealed the news to his mom and dad as gently as possible, but there was no good way to soften the information. Samantha covered her face, sobbed, and was inconsolable. Luke sagged into the chair, as if someone had kicked the air out of him.

That night, Samantha didn't touch her dinner. Luke did the opposite. He ate everything, as if he could grind away the news with the force of his teeth.

Later, Marigold passed her parents' bedroom. She paused and listened. They were searching the Internet for an explanation, for hope. "This can't be happening," her mother said. "It's like someone has placed a plastic bag over my head. God, Luke, I can't breathe." She began to cry and said, "Marigold has been pressing me with questions: 'Are you *sure* none of our relatives had HD?' I feel so guilty. We can't keep dodging the truth."

"We have to tell them," her father said, his voice wavering.

Barely audible, her mother said, "I know."

Marigold turned and tiptoed back to her room. Max, their fourteen-year-old dog, followed.

• • •

In the morning, Marigold joined her parents in the kitchen. Samantha was sitting motionless. "Can I fix you something to eat, Mom?"

Samantha shook her head.

Marigold filled a baggie with dried apricots. "I'm going out to the bookstore." The dog came to her side. "No, Max. You can't come." She patted his side, opened the refrigerator, and took a slice of cheese from the stack. "Treat?" Max wagged his tail, sat, and waited, looking as dignified and calm as a forty-eight-pound, full-bodied dog could.

Marigold tore the cheese into pieces. "There you go." Max lapped every bite and plopped under the table.

Samantha pleaded, "Can't you stay? We should be together." She stood up and paced around the dinette table, touching the backs of the four chairs.

"I'm researching Adam's illness."

"And you know what the research says," Luke said, his voice gentle. "I think we all need to find counseling."

"And do what?" Marigold shouted. "*Accept* this?" Max jumped from under the table, his ears pointed backward and then forward like satellite antennas. Marigold frowned. "I'm sorry, Dad. I feel helpless being passive." To her mother, she added, "I know we planned to wait, but could we celebrate our birthdays tonight? Have a German chocolate cake, with lots of coconut? Adam loves coconut."

"But today's Sunday."

"So what if we celebrate a few days early?"

"It's a special time for you both, sharing the same birthday. Shouldn't you ask Adam?"

"I feel like I'm going to explode if something normal doesn't happen. By Wednesday, we may not care."

"Maybe a distraction would be helpful." Samantha sighed. "Confirm it with your brother. I'll wrap presents while you're gone."

"Thanks, Mom. I hope the celebration will cheer him up." She kissed her mother's cheek. "Adam and I went birthday shopping weeks ago. We've already bought gifts for each other. I've wrapped his, and I think he put mine in the coat closet. We'll keep our tradition and blow out the candles together."

Marigold had always thought her mother pretty. She was now in her mid-forties, slender, with shoulder-length blonde hair, and the corners of her eyes crinkled whenever she laughed. Always strong, protective of her family, and filled with a love of life, today her mother appeared to be a different woman. Overnight, she'd lost her sparkle, her skin had paled, and her movements were rigid and lifeless, like a piece of wood.

Her mother squeezed the chair where Adam usually sat. Her father's arms tenderly circled his wife, and she leaned into his chest. His sweater absorbed her tears.

Marigold said, "Lie down and rest for a while, Mom." She stroked her mother's hair. "I won't be gone long. I'll call Adam, and we'll cook dinner. You won't have to do a thing." She opened the freezer, found a package of chicken, and placed it on a plate to thaw.

"You're trying to research, but don't forget about school-work. Your scholarship—"

"I'll take care of it. Promise. I'll take Max outside before I go." Marigold whistled. "Here, Max. Come on, old boy. Walk?"

Walk used to be a magic word, synonymous with excitement. Max lifted his head and then apparently changed his mind. He rested his chin on his front paws. Lately, Max, a mix of Australian shepherd and collie, was slow to move. Marigold called him again. "Let's go." She shoved her keys in her jacket, snapped the worn leather leash on Max's collar, and let him lick her cheek.

· · ·

Marigold had been at the bookstore barely twenty minutes when her cell rang and Adam's picture popped up on her phone.

"Hi. I was going to call you." She kept her voice cheerful. "I thought it would be nice to have our birthday dinner tonight."

"Whatever you want."

"Mom's not eating. Can you come over and we'll cook—"

"Mari, turn around."

"Adam! Did Mom tell you I was here?"

"Yeah. We need to talk. Let's sit over there." Adam pointed to an isolated area with vinyl hardback chairs and a small table. From an overhead speaker, Paul McCartney's song "Yesterday" played in the background.

Adam drummed the table. "You realize one of our parents has to be a carrier. I get the feeling they're not telling us everything."

"I get that feeling too. Something's up." Marigold sighed. "Thank God you stayed in St. Louis to go to college, or you'd be all alone. We're here for you." She pushed back from her chair. "Come on, let's go home. We need to be together. Don't say anything until the celebration is over, okay?"

"I won't ruin it. I promise," he said.

• • •

They returned home and climbed the steps to the front door. Marigold wondered if she'd been wrong to insist on festivities. Inside, the aromas of chocolate cake and chicken simmering in the skillet greeted them. The dog waddled over and waited while they hung their coats.

"Hey, buddy," Adam greeted Max, stroking his side.

Samantha gave them a thin smile. "I was restless and thought I'd get a head start."

"You should have waited. Let us help." Marigold turned on the oven light. "Mmm . . . the chocolate cake smells wonderful. I think it's done."

"Test it," Samantha said.

The toothpick inserted in the cake came out clean. Marigold placed the pans on a cooling rack, set the table, and added more basil to the marinara sauce. Luke drained the pasta and put it in a bowl. Samantha sliced the chicken and iced the cake while Adam tossed the salad.

They worked as a unit but ate in silence. After dinner, Adam paced the floor. He needed answers, but he'd promised Marigold he would wait until after presents and cake. He opened his parents' gift first—a pair of tennis shoes. He would exchange them for a pair without laces. Velcro would be more useful. A square black box from Marigold contained a simple silver wristwatch with blue numerals.

"You said you were tired of using your phone to check the time," she said. "Push the button on the side."

The watch glowed, and a pale green light illuminated the clock face. "It's perfect," he said.

Marigold received a delicate bracelet threaded with amber beads from Adam. Her parents' gift was a silver egg-shaped locket with black filigree. Its top unscrewed, revealing a small open area to tuck tiny paper wishes or mantras.

There was no "Happy Birthday" song as Adam and Marigold blew out the candles. A swirl of smoke lingered. The cake was cut. Forks clinked against the plates.

"There's something I'd like to talk about," Adam said after the dishes were washed. He settled on the couch next to his sister, crossing and uncrossing his legs. "You said you're not familiar with Huntington's, but something doesn't add up. For me to have it, one of you *has* to be a carrier."

Luke spoke. "Your mother and I didn't know anything about Huntington's because . . ." He briefly looked at his wife and took a deep breath. "Because you and Marigold are adopted."

Marigold paled. Adams's jaw dropped. Samantha hurried over and knelt in front them. "We never knew how to tell you. We tried so many times, but it became easier *not* to tell you."

"What the hell do you mean, we're *adopted*?" Adam said, standing and moving away from her.

Marigold recoiled and stood beside Adam. "You're not my mother?"

"Oh, sweetheart, of course I am."

"Obviously, you're not. How could you not tell us? All these years . . ." Marigold pointed to Adam. "Is he my real brother?"

"Yes, Adam is your brother." Samantha's voice was raw with emotion. "Your biological parents were killed in a car crash. The police report said they were coming home from dinner. The rain had turned to ice, and their car skidded down a ravine." Samantha pleaded with her daughter: "Please look at me." Marigold kept her head turned away.

"I was working for Family and Children's Services the day they brought you in. You weren't quite a year old, Mari, and Adam was almost four. The minute I saw you, I knew you were meant to be my family. I would die for either one of you. God, this is wrong. I'd suffer this disease for you if I could. I'm sorry we didn't tell you." Samantha began to cry.

"Mom, I didn't mean what I said. I'm sorry. I'm sorry." Marigold embraced her mother.

Adam was silent.

"I guess this explains why we could never find any baby pictures of us," said Marigold.

"You were so young," Luke said. He rubbed the back of his neck. "The only information we were given was that there was no known health history. This is an awful time to tell you, but you needed to know. We don't carry the gene, son. This is horrible, but we *are* family, and we'll always be here for you."

Adam returned to the couch. Marigold sat next to her brother. Samantha blew her nose. Luke grabbed a fistful of M&Ms.

CHAPTER 24

Alana worried that her dark business attire for the meeting wasn't appropriate for lunch on the beach. "I'm staying at a boutique hotel about ten minutes from here. Would you mind stopping so I can change? I'm afraid I'm too warm in this suit."

"Not at all," Borg said. "The news mentioned we'd be in the eighties this afternoon."

Alana thought of the howling winds and snow she'd left in St. Louis.

Borg waved his key card in front of the elevator light. In seconds, they were in the lobby.

The guard presented Borg with a fob. "Your car's out front, Mr. Larson."

A red sports car glimmered in the brilliant sunshine, an automobile cooler than anything Alana had seen in any James Bond movie. She blinked back the desire to drive around the Amalfi Coast and drink limoncello.

Borg pushed a button, and the doors floated up like wings—a mechanical bird about to take flight.

"What is *this*?" Alana stared wide-eyed at the car.

"It's Ferrari's first hybrid. This engine can hit 190 in under fifteen seconds."

Alana was a sucker for sports cars, and this was *the* ultimate. The front of the car was designed with curvaceous lines: an Italian super car.

Two years ago, a convertible had caught Alana's attention.

She'd stopped at the dealership and had taken a test drive. After the wind had tousled her hair and she'd tasted freedom, every dollar she had went toward buying a Lexus SC.

Alana glided across the Ferrari's smooth leather interior, and a moan escaped her. Borg entered the driver's side, clicked a button, and the doors floated down.

They stopped at Alana's hotel. She'd packed a few dressy outfits appropriate for upscale dining and warmer weather. She quickly changed, hurried through the lobby, and joined Borg. The car roared toward the coast.

At the restaurant, heads turned, and Alana experienced what it was like to be a celebrity, even though she was pretty sure they were looking at the Ferrari. They waited briefly for Borg's favorite valet. Borg handed him the fob and his jacket.

Alana was happy she'd traded her business suit for a pale mint ankle-length skirt and sleeveless crop top. Her open-toed shoes shimmered silver, with a thin strap crossing her ankle. Her hair was tied back in her signature French braid.

Borg guided her through the restaurant and outside to the boardwalk. A man in a crisp white jacket ushered them to an ocean side table, and a wide umbrella shielded them from the bright sun. The maître d' adjusted the chair and waited while Alana paused to watch a pod of dolphins diving in the distant water.

Waves rolled against the sand, and shrill seagulls hovered, hoping for a leftover morsel. Tables covered with white cloths were crowned with crystal vases brimming with bright yellow roses. Black napkins, folded like accordions, fanned out of etched water glasses.

"Allow me." A waiter snapped the napkin and dropped it lightly across Alana's lap. They decided on the special, and Borg ordered for two: champagne, crab cake appetizers, fresh grilled sea bass, and asparagus in a light lemon sauce. After the champagne was poured, they sipped from the flutes, and appetizers arrived. Alana took a bite of the delicate crab meat and forced herself not to re-create the famous Meg Ryan scene, "I'll have what she's having."

The entrées followed and did not disappoint. "Perfect," Borg said, wholeheartedly enjoying the sea bass. He dabbed the corner of his mouth. "I find it interesting that people won't take risks and consider owning a business. There's greater opportunity than working for someone else."

"It *is* risky," Alana said, "but I'm working for something I love."

"I'd have it no other way," Borg said. "I'm master of my own destiny."

"I only regret I don't have more free time," Alana said.

"What would you do if you found yourself with more free time?" Borg asked.

"I'm an amateur oil painter. I'd probably spend more time at the easel. Definitely would spend more time with my family. I hardly have time for a social life. I love yoga. If I can't get to a class, I work out at home." Alana pushed her plate back. She hadn't left a crumb. "The meal was delicious. Thank you." She watched the waves lap the shoreline. "I can't believe this weather. I could get used to this."

"It's pretty much the same every day," Borg said.

"Lucky you," Alana said. "What do you do with your spare time?"

"I read. Mostly about business. I used to ski, but it's a long time since I've been on the slopes. I've spent the last few years working on this deal. Retail has turned around, and the time is right. I believe what I have in Paris will be lucrative, Alana. My lawyer believes it would behoove *New Heights* to merge with *Slick* and create a fifty-fifty partnership."

Alana kept her composure and sipped her water. "You didn't say anything about a partnership. It was my impression this was a percentage deal. I control the magazine articles and promote events and fundraisers." She paused, "And your tech articles—"

"Who doesn't love state-of-the-art technology?" Borg said. "Google Glass, Apple watches, 3D printers . . . We'll have space for your content as well as mine."

Alana heard only her heartbeat racing in her ears. She held up her hand. "This is a complete surprise, considering our earlier discussion," she said.

Borg flashed a thousand-watt smile. "Your magazine will be the perfect venue for our tech articles. Everybody wins." He buttered the last piece of bread and took a bite. "We'll combine our magazines and give them a new cover. Add some articles on technology and related advertising, and push La Chic Boutique. A fresh magazine uniting *Slick* and *New Heights* would require a makeover and time to tie loose ends. We can easily implement those changes, but there is some urgency. "We could rename the magazine . . . maybe . . . *Slick New Heights*?"

Slick was her child. Alana's instinct was to protect, to pull in the reins. She stalled but wondered if she was preventing her company from reaching its full potential. "I have a low appetite for risk. Combine the magazines? Why didn't you suggest this earlier? I would need to see a written proposal."

"If I may be blunt, you have less than ideal marketing strategies. We can help. Live large, dream big," Borg said, and refilled her glass.

Daniel's ringtone sounded in her bag. Alana excused herself

from the table and took the call. The hoarse voice didn't sound like her attorney.

"Who is this?" Alana asked.

"It's Daniel. I caught some flu bug, and it went into pneumonia."

"You sound terrible," Alana said.

"I'll be all right. Your message said you're in California."

"Borg said it was urgent. Can I fill you in? This is huge. Are you up to it?"

"I can take notes." Daniel's wet cough went on for too long.

"No, let's wait."

Daniel blew his nose. "Good idea."

"I'll call you in a few days, okay? Take care of yourself."

Alana returned to the table. "Sorry, but my lawyer's sick. I won't sign anything until he reviews the proposal."

"Let me think." Borg tapped the table, his eyebrows raised and knitted together. "Good fortune is about hard work and timing. I have an idea."

"I'm listening,"

"What if you went to Paris? You could visit the couture house, meet the owner, and look at the merchandise. Have you been to Paris?

"I've never been to Europe."

"Would you be interested?"

There was only one answer. "I believe I would," she said. She was glad she always traveled with her passport.

Borg signaled the waiter. "My assistant can schedule all arrangements. Stay a few extra days. Get familiar with the city. If the merger goes through, I'd like someone to check in seasonally and meet with Martine." Borg reached in his wallet, left a stack of folded bills on the table, and checked his phone. "Shall we go?"

Paris. Alana paused as she pieced the parts together. Michelle could contact her if something unexpected came up. Basic layouts were organized and months ahead of schedule. She'd left her return ticket open-ended so she could have a little vacation in California. She could easily change her plans to a working vacation in Paris. How spontaneous. How unlike her.

CHAPTER 25

Rosie swirled on burgundy lipstick and hummed Gloria Gaynor's disco hit, "I Will Survive." She picked up her purse, stuck her head out the bedroom door, and listened for Carlos. If she hurried, maybe she could slip through the kitchen and get away without a confrontation. The back door squeaked across the metal threshold, and heavy footsteps thudded down the hall. Carlos rounded the corner, his eyes narrowed and angry. "Where you think you're going?" His fingers snapped in repetition, signaling his agitation. He'd put on thirty pounds since their wedding, probably from all the beer. She wouldn't have minded the extra weight, to have a teddy bear kind of guy, like Jack Black. But Carlos was no cuddle toy. He grabbed her arm, and Rosie flinched.

"Carlos, please."

"I *said*, where you going?"

"You're hurting me. I have to go to the store. And the car is low on gas."

He released his grip. "What about my lunch?"

"Jeez, Carlos, you can't throw together a sandwich?"

"You're gonna fix it, and watch your mouth. What about lasagna? Tony's wife cooks him pasta for lunch."

"It takes a long time to prepare lasagna."

For the last six months, he'd started telling her where and what time she could go out. "How about I fix you a bologna sandwich and put it on a plate with those potato chips you like?" she said, hoping to pacify him.

Carlos frowned. "Grab me a beer, too. And pick up some black electrical tape while you're out. There's bare wire on the space heater downstairs. And then come home. I don't want you gone all afternoon."

Rosie's shoulders knotted together. She made his sandwich, gave him a beer, and hurried out the door.

She'd pay for her mistake in marrying Carlos. Forever. Catholics might be more lenient these days, but not her family. They were old-school, and Rosie wasn't prepared to fight tradition. I can't do this anymore, she thought. But she knew she would.

Months after they'd wed, Carlos had informed her he didn't like her girlfriends. Said they were a bad influence on her, and it was their fault for making him feel old. Maybe, she conceded, it was their youth. And hers. She was twenty then. He was thirty-three.

He'd hang up on friends who called their landline. He used to apologize and tell her he did it because he needed her with him. Rosie had bought a cell phone, saying it was required for work, but nobody called anymore.

She'd never met Carlos's family. His father had died years before they met. Rosie blamed his parents for not teaching him how to treat a woman with respect. Or how to make a sandwich.

• • •

Carlos watched from the window as Rosie drove away. She could work harder to make him happy. His job was harder than hers. She sat on her butt at a home computer answering calls for a leasing company, while he unloaded trucks in a warehouse.

She left him on the weekends, and he didn't like it. He tipped back his bottle of beer. They'd had a big fight on his recent thirty-fifth birthday. Rosie had wanted to go out with another couple to celebrate. He'd hung up the phone on whatever her name was—the one with the smart mouth who called him "old man." She'd thought she was real funny. He'd shown her who was in charge.

Marrying a woman thirteen years younger guaranteed her friends would be a problem. He didn't want to go to their houses on weekends and play stupid board games. Rosie didn't like his friends, either. She had gotten mad the night his friends came by to play poker, got drunk, and broke a lamp. Big deal, he thought. Carlos preferred hanging at Ray's house anyway. He didn't have a wife complaining about booze spilled on the rug.

Rosie hadn't done anything for his birthday. He'd turned thirty-five, for God's sake. A milestone birthday, and what did he get? Nothing. She hadn't even baked him a damn cake. She had cooked dinner and afterward stuck a candle in a Ho Ho. Rosie had baked desserts for him while they were dating—good cakes, too, with lots of thick icing.

It was Rosie's mother who had suggested he ask for her hand. "Rosie needs a husband. You should propose." Carlos had been surprised when Rosie had said yes.

Acid burned his stomach. He snapped his fingers in agitation and wished he could break something or just hit her once to curb her tongue. He'd been fighting that urge lately. If she did as he told her, he wouldn't feel this way. It was her fault. It always was.

CHAPTER 26

Saige checked out the book *For Dummies* and took Sam's classes, sometimes twice. She set goals in the classes and caught on
quickly. Sam always stayed after class, answered her questions,
and even showed her how to set up an e-mail account she could
access using the library's free computers. Saige spent her spare
time at the library studying.

One evening, Saige stopped Sam in the corridor. "I wanted to
thank you for all you've done for me."

"Happy to help. I'm aware you don't own any devices for
reading e-books, but I'm teaching a class on Saturday on how to
download books from the library. You might find it interesting."

Saige was at her usual seat on Saturday. The door opened. It
wasn't Sam who appeared.

"Finn." She shifted in her seat.

"Saige, what are you doing here?" He sat next to her. "I've
been back to the Jive hoping I'd see you."

"Funny," she said, her voice crisp. "I stayed away, hoping I
wouldn't see you."

Sam entered. "Hello, everyone," he said. "Thank you all for
coming."

"Let me talk to you," Finn said, his voice low.

"No. I learned my lesson. I don't trust you." Saige tucked
her papers in the folder and left. Fool me twice, shame on me,
she thought. He didn't care about her. Guys like him probably
watched for girls like her. Girls with unmet needs. Lonesome and

friendless. She guessed Finn had had plenty of girls. Better to cut things off and not get hurt.

• • •

Saige tried to not think about Finn. If she stayed busy, she could push him out of her mind. She pried the lid from the tomato soup can and flipped the grilled cheese sandwiches. "Dad, lunch is ready. Come on."

Saige's father sat down and trimmed the crust from his sandwich while Saige ladled out the soup. "Mmm. You know how to brown the bread on the outside and melt the cheese perfectly on the inside," he said. "Where did you go this morning?"

"I've been taking computer classes."

"What's the point?" He dipped the corner of his sandwich in his soup.

"The point," she said, "is to stay up to date with the world. Mom did a great job, but you never allowed technology in the house. She couldn't show me what she didn't know, and now I'm struggling to catch up."

Saige pushed her plate away. She wasn't hungry anymore. "You know, our lives are bits and pieces of experiences. Those stories are our struggles, our victories, the wisdom we've gained through life. You've kept me so sheltered, I don't have any stories."

"Saige, you're wasting your time. There's nothing wrong with the old ways. It keeps life simpler. How much do these classes cost? You should be saving. Don't throw away money on computer classes."

"The library classes are *free*. I've been thinking about college. Or maybe," she said, slowly, "if I could get the loan from you, I could quit my job, go to school full time, and wouldn't have to pay interest on the loan. I could pay you back after I graduate."

He shook his head. "I don't think you should quit your job."

"Mom would have wanted me to go to college," Saige argued. "You know I could take out a student loan anyway and—"

"I don't want to talk about this," he said. He threw his crust in the garbage disposal and left the kitchen.

Saige knew the conversation would end. Case closed whenever there was discussion involving her mother.

Saige opened the newspaper and searched the want ads, but there was nothing she was qualified to do. She smashed the paper into the recycle bag.

CHAPTER 27

Saturday evening, Brad called Adam and asked if he wanted to join him on Sunday for a church service.

"I'm not religious," Adam said. "I believe in a higher power but not in the dogma of established faiths. There's too much superstition. I call it the Santa Syndrome."

"What do you mean?" Brad asked.

"You know, be good, follow the rules, or you won't get the goodies. I'm still trying to figure it out," Adam said.

"You won't find this place conventional. It's not like any church I've ever visited. It's mostly music and a twenty-minute inspirational talk. Call it a philosophical message to think about during the week. You don't have to confess anything."

"What do you do?"

"Listen, let go of the noise in your head, and try to find peace. Reverend Barnes quotes the great teachers without imposing religious doctrine. We believe we are our thoughts. Change a negative thought, and the old belief won't weigh you down."

"Sounds logical, but I'm sure it's easier said than put into practice."

"True, but if we fall, the center offers us guidance to help pull ourselves up," Brad said. "All are welcome. Look, I know there's nothing I can do to help, but I wanted to share my community with you. Life's so chaotic; this place has been good for me. I asked because I'm leaving for Truman on Monday to check out apartments."

Adam knew he was going to miss Brad. He was easy to talk to.

"If you're not interested in the service, I understand. It's not for everyone. I just thought maybe . . ."

"Thanks for thinking of me," Adam said. "I'll go with you."

• • •

They stopped in front of a building in an industrial park. No crosses, no statues, no ornamentation, only a small metal sign on a post read Spiritual Well Being Center.

Inside, they drank coffee, and Brad introduced Adam to numerous people. Members of the congregation greeted him. Adam wasn't sure what type of people he expected to see at an unconventional place of worship, but they were just regular folks. The lights flickered, and Adam followed Brad. There was an altar with a podium to the left, but instead of a crucifix or a cross, a screen covered the wall.

Everyone sat in traditional pews. A stylishly dressed woman in a long skirt and russet jacket stood up from a front pew and strode to the podium. Everyone quieted, waiting for her to begin. She adjusted the microphone.

"Hello and welcome. I'm Reverend Cecelia Barnes."

Adam guessed she was about fifty. Her voice was tranquil. She spoke about how to bring harmony into one's daily life, and how human it was to forget to be thankful.

She leaned into the podium. "Gratitude will set you free." She posed questions. "Today, did you appreciate water flowing out of the tap because you turned the handle? Who saw the sun glowing on the snow this morning? Or did you see only the dirty snow piled on the side of the road? What did you *choose* to see? It is about choice, my friends. Change the negative thoughts to positive, and you'll change your life."

Adam realized he hadn't noticed anything at all lately. He was too busy thinking about dying.

"This week, slow down and be mindful. I'll leave you with a quote from Henry Ward Beecher: 'We do not see things as they are. We see things as we are.'" She asked everyone to be still for one minute and reflect on something for which they were grateful.

Adam's eyes closed, and he began to sweat. And pray. And bargain. What did I do wrong, God? I'm a good person. Can you give me more time? If scientists could find a cure, I swear, I'll use my degree to help others.

The minute was up. Four teenagers stood at the altar, strummed guitars, and harmonized to the Beatles songs "In My Life" and "Nowhere Man." As the music floated around the room, some sang along, and others just listened. Another feeling overwhelmed Adam. Profound sadness for all he would miss. Too bad he hadn't paid more attention.

After the service, Adam picked up several pamphlets advertising classes at the center. One class met on Wednesday evenings and offered meditation. The description explained how a deep peace can occur when the mind is calm and quiet. Adam examined the picture of the instructor. He recognized her from the Jive. The woman teaching the course was Hanna.

CHAPTER 28

Rosie moved in and out of the aisles, breathing in perfume from the cosmetics section, enjoying the scent of leather from shelves of purses, and checking clothing fitted to perfect-sized manne-quins. She hoped to bury the intimidation of her husband's vola-tile outbursts by distracting herself with visual stimulation and throngs of people. Rosie combed the racks of clothes at Macy's and reached for a dress with short sleeves and a cheerful green and yellow pattern.

A young woman with long bangs and short black hair reached for the same dress in a smaller size. Her eyes were shockingly black—Cleopatra eyes, worn like body armor—and her creamy red lipstick appeared more appropriate for a night out dancing and drinking. Her gray pearl necklace looked drab when she held the dress against her shoulders. "Don't you love this?" she asked.

Rosie agreed. "I do. Now if only winter were over. The weather's ridiculous. It's the end of March. We're supposed to be enjoying daffodils and flying kites, right?"

"It's the worst winter I remember," gray pearls said. "The whole Midwest got socked. They say the snow isn't letting up. There may be more next week."

Rosie pointed at another stand of dresses and wrinkled her nose. "Nothing on that rack. The patterns remind me of the old Waverly wallpaper I have in my bedroom."

The woman laughed. Rosie sensed she'd be fun to know. It would be nice to have a new friend, because all her girlfriends were married, had babies, and didn't bother to call. She missed her girlfriends. After she and Carlos were first married, the couples had met at each other's homes to socialize. Carlos had always sat alone and sulked. No wonder they were now excluded.

"You have kids?" Rosie asked.

"Nope." She checked the price tag. "Not ready yet."

"Neither am I." Rosie chose a thin, yellow belt, and the two women went together to the dressing rooms. Rosie undressed and scrutinized herself in the mirror. Her fingers, like calipers, grasped the two-inch band of flesh around her belly. A part of her wondered if maybe Carlos would stop the name-calling if she lost a few pounds, but she doubted it. Rosie's mother had always told her she was lucky to be Latina, and to be proud of her full lips, tan skin, and natural breast size. Rosie thought she could do with a little less booty. She zipped up the dress and went to the hallway's three-way mirror. The woman with the pearls was checking the back of her dress.

Rosie offered her the belt. "Try this. It didn't work for me, but you're thinner."

The woman buckled it and admired herself in the mirror. "I like it, thanks. You have great taste." Minutes later, they both ended up together at the cash register.

"Well, good luck," the woman said, taking her bag. "We have the same dress, so we can't go to the same party."

Rosie tried to smile. She could have assured her it wouldn't happen. She never got invited to parties anymore.

Rosie's stomach rumbled, and she took the escalator to the food court for a pretzel. A high school boy removed a tray from the oven. Rosie paid and found a table. She chewed the soft bread, tore the rest into little pieces, and daydreamed about a new life.

Seeing two teenagers holding hands reminded Rosie of her

high school boyfriend. They used to eat at the food court on weekends. Today the food stalls buzzed with activity. Parents at the Chinese buffet struggled to read the menu board, hold on to a wandering toddler, and quiet a crying baby. The father lifted the baby girl out of the stroller. Neither parent noticed the leather wallet the mother had left on the counter.

"Hey." Rosie's voice was lost in the noise. A man in line picked up the wallet and hurried after the family. The woman appeared relieved, and her husband shook the Samaritan's hand.

Rosie admired honesty. Carlos would have pocketed the wallet. She popped the last bite of pretzel in her mouth and made her way out of the mall toward the parking lot.

Traffic was heavier, but gridlock was more fun than being home with Carlos. Rosie stopped at the drugstore and headed for the makeup aisle. A little laugh escaped, and she cleared her throat.

The woman from Macy's did a double-take. "Hi again. Isn't this strange?"

"Yes, and you're holding the same nail polish I'm going to buy."

"What are the odds?" The woman chuckled.

Rosie introduced herself and took a bottle of Tango Tease from the shelf.

"I'm Chelsea. I love the new Blast line." She added two bottles to her basket.

"Did you find bargains?" Rosie gestured at all of Chelsea's lotions and creams.

"No. I'm low on supplies." Chelsea checked her watch. "Would you like to get a coffee or something? There's this great place not too far from here. The Jumpin' Jive Café."

"Sure. I know where it is. I'll pay and meet you there."

Rosie Perón had found a new friend—*if* she could keep the relationship hidden from Carlos.

CHAPTER 29

Saige went to the library every evening after work to use the free computer. A couple of women at work exchanged e-mails with her and sent her links to YouTube videos. With a click, Saige discovered she could watch a symphony in Russia or take a guided tour of the Taj Mahal.

"Dad, it's amazing," she said one night at dinner. "You wouldn't believe it. You can find *anything* on the Internet. Would you like to go to the library with me tonight?"

"No. It's a waste of time to be on a computer," he said.

"I wish you would come along once. What are you interested in? You like to fish. You can find out about lures and rods and—"

"I can go to the Bass Pro Shop and touch real equipment," he said.

"You like Paganini and Debussy. There's this website called YouTube. You can listen to all kinds of music."

"I have a record player," he said. "Or maybe someday you'll play the piano again."

She ignored his comment about the piano. "If you'd have an open mind toward new ideas, you might find you enjoy it." She cupped the back of her neck. They still couldn't talk to each other.

"I have an open mind. I'm just not interested. Don't need it; don't want it."

"Fine," she said.

Her father's stubbornness created more determination in

Saige to learn. One evening at the library, she found Sam in the photocopy room.

"Hi, Saige," he said. "I'm getting ready to teach PowerPoint. Care to join us?"

"No, it's above my skill level."

"I promise it's painless. I know the class isn't full. Why don't you think about it?"

She hesitated.

"If I might offer a quote from Tolstoy: 'Everyone thinks of changing the world, but no one thinks of changing himself.' You're changing, Saige. Don't give up."

"I'm not giving up. But sometimes I'm afraid I'm not smart enough. Afraid I'll fail."

"Then we need to work on your confidence."

"Have a class for self-assurance?" she asked. Saige helped Sam staple papers together. "Okay." She passed him the stack of handouts. "I'll try it."

In the class, Saige powered on her computer. A chair bumped her, as the one remaining seat was taken.

Saige looked over and groaned. "What are you doing here?"

Finn took off his jacket. "Same thing you are. Working on PowerPoint."

Saige shifted her chair to block Finn from her view. Distracted, she forgot where Sam said to find the Font button.

An hour later, Sam said, "Our time's up today. Please look at our list of additional classes."

Saige waited until Finn had left the room. He bent down for a sip at the drinking fountain, and she hurried past him to find her car.

Finn called out in the parking lot. "I didn't leave, Saige. I was still there at the coffee shop. Around the corner. But you ran, and I wasn't fast enough to catch you."

Saige faced him. Finn jostled the keys in his pocket and stepped toward her. "You wouldn't let me explain."

"You disappeared. I was sure you were playing me," she said.

"The Jive has another room. My brother was waiting for me. We talked while you were in the washroom. When I came back, you were gone." He moved closer.

"I didn't know about the other room."

"Do you think we could start over?" Finn asked.

Saige wanted to believe him. He shifted closer. She tried to think.

"I'm sorry. Would you give me another chance? Can I take you out?"

Okay. This was going to be a challenge. She believed him. "Yes. I'd like that."

CHAPTER 30

The plane landed in Paris at Charles de Gaulle Airport at 10:00 a.m. She'd slept the last hour and a half until the pilot had announced their final descent. Although more comfortable in first class, Alana had struggled to sleep in the oversized seat.

The stuffed-to-the-max carry-on she'd brought along instead of a suitcase allowed her to skip the wait at the carousel and plunge ahead to customs. She carried her passport in the zipped side pocket, a habit she developed from her many trips to Mexico. After her passport was stamped, Alana fought her way through the crowd. Outside, at the taxi stand, a man from ground transportation greeted her. "*Bonjour, mademoiselle. Ça va?*"

"*Ça va bien*," she said, trying to be polite.

She realized her mistake too late. He spoke rapidly. "*Voulez-vous votre petit sac pour allez dans le coffre du taxi?*"

"*Je regrette, je parle un peu.* I speak only a little—"

"Where would you like to go?" he asked.

"The Paris Hilton on the *Avenue de Suffren*, near the Eiffel Tower."

"*Bien.*" He gave directions to the driver and raised his arm for the next taxi.

Alana climbed into the cab, collapsed against the backseat, and watched the scenery through heavy lids. The Eiffel Tower appeared in the distance, and Alana perked up and pressed her nose against the glass. "It's so close. I can't believe it." The driver ignored her.

He braked in front of the hotel. A porter opened her door and gestured to the front desk. The hotel bustled with casually dressed tourists, women in crisp Dior suits, and small dogs peeking from women's purses.

"Alana Hudson," she said to the clerk.

"Ah, *oui*." He printed her reservation and asked for a signature. "Rooms are not guaranteed ready until 3:00 p.m., but we will do our best. You have arrived early. You may wait or take a walk outside, perhaps, and see our beautiful city."

Right then, all she craved was a comfy bed and a few hours' sleep to get through the rest of the day. She planned to turn in after dinner, hoping she'd be refreshed and ready for the early meeting tomorrow with Martine at La Chic Boutique.

"It looks like we have a room almost ready. Possibly forty minutes to an hour more. Perhaps you would be more comfortable in the Executive Lounge on your floor. Snacks and drinks are available, and I believe they're still serving breakfast. This key will allow you access." He gave her a plastic card. "We'll send someone for you as soon as the room is ready. Oh, and *mademoiselle*, you have a message from a *Monsieur* Borg Larson: Transportation is arranged for your meeting tomorrow with *Monsieur* Victor Dumont. *Monsieur* Dumont will meet you in the lobby at 8:00 a.m." The clerk put the note in an envelope.

"*Merci*." She tucked the paper in her purse. "You'll find me right there." She flipped her finger in the direction of an empty couch.

Alana sank into the sofa, limp and exhausted. She was dreaming when someone called her name.

"Ahem. Everything is ready, *mademoiselle*. This way, please," the bellman said, and he assisted her to her room.

The room was large by European standards. A miniature

bonsai tree sat on a circular table. The wallpaper's colors were so muted that it was barely noticeable. The lavish king-sized bed had three large pillows stuffed against the headboard. Alana immediately closed the curtains to shut out the bright morning light and set the alarm to wake her in two hours. Just a couple of hours, she thought, to help get on Paris time. She undressed, and the soft sheets settled against her body.

CHAPTER 31

The radio clicked on. Alana sat on the edge of the mattress, her thoughts clouded from jet lag. She opened her carry-on and retrieved a pair of shorts and a blouse. She had planned to walk down the *Champs-Élysées* in style. She felt tired, and her mouth was dry. Style would have to wait. It was almost 1:00 p.m., and the Executive Lounge offered lunch until 2:00. Alana entered, and the concierge behind the desk gave her a hearty *bonjour* and asked for her name.

"Sit anywhere you wish," she said. "Let me know if I can assist you in any way."

The room was quiet. Only one other couple sat at a table in the corner. A muted television played at the far end. There were couches next to coffee tables, and several glass tables were scattered throughout the room. A pleasant woman immediately came to the table. "May I bring you water? *Café*?" she asked.

"Both, please."

"Help yourself. There are hot and cold dishes," the woman said.

Alana was surprised and delighted by the plentiful assortment of food. Counters were laid with trays of sandwiches, breads, fruit, an assortment of cheeses, and hot prepared foods. Eager to see Paris, she was grateful she could self-serve.

The elevator took her down to the Art Deco–style lobby. Alana had been exhausted on her arrival and hadn't noticed the gleaming marble floors, the oil paintings adorning the walls, or the four-foot spray of fresh flowers on the foyer table. The lobby boasted intimate waiting areas decorated with oriental rugs, antique armoires, and impressive balustrades. But Alana knew the most beautiful spot was ten steps away, straight through the lobby doors. Outside was Paris—and it was hers for nineteen hours.

She stopped at the front desk. What was the French word for *map*? *Carte*?

"May I help you?"

"Thank goodness, you speak English."

"We are a very international staff," the man behind the counter said. "How may I assist you?"

"I need a map, *s'il vous plait*."

"Of course." He opened a pamphlet. "The city is easy to navigate. We are here." He circled the street with a red pen. "You are in walking distance of many sites. You saw our Eiffel Tower on your arrival. She is hard to miss. The *Arc de Triomphe* is a few minutes away, and the cathedral is here." He drew red circles all over the map.

"*Merci, monsieur*."

•   •   •

Alana set out on foot, which allowed her to explore the streets and shops of Paris. The Eiffel Tower would be her first stop. It loomed larger and larger as she followed the map, cutting through the quiet neighborhood to the *Champ de Mars*. She approached the iron lattice tower and stopped, and a great joy filled her. She had dreamed of going to France since she was a young girl, and now the dream was real!

Minutes later, she waited in line to buy a ticket. There was one working elevator, and the line was long. Alana decided to walk the stairs to the second floor. Breathless, she leaned against the rail and viewed the skyline. All the roads led to the *Arc de*

Triomphe, and she marveled at the geometric layout of the city and the River Seine winding through the heart of Paris. She would have lingered, but the tower was crowded with tourists.

Back on the street, Alana stretched out the map but was interrupted by an elderly dark-skinned woman in a wrinkled skirt and a wide-brimmed hat. "Something to remember Paris?" she asked and held out a basket of assorted jewelry. Alana picked through the trinkets and paid for a pair of silver-colored Eiffel Tower earrings. She wore her souvenir and continued to the Notre Dame Cathedral. It would take an hour on foot, but the sun was warm and the temperatures were hovering in the sixties, a perfect day to amble along the Seine. The cathedral was located on one of the two islands in the river.

Alana sat on a bench to rest. A young girl, maybe a high school student on break, sat next to her and took off her backpack.

"Are you American?" the girl asked.

"I am."

"Me, too. I'm Audrey from Ohio." The girl shaded her eyes and pointed down the sidewalk to the church in the distance. "Isn't it magnificent? I think Notre Dame is my favorite place in the city. They started construction back in 1163, and it took, like, two hundred years to build." She unzipped her canvas bag, removed two brochures, and offered one to Alana.

"Would you like this? It has great history about the place."

"Thanks," Alana said.

"Ever watch the Disney movie *The Hunchback of Notre Dame*?"

"I have. There's also an old black and white movie from 1939," Alana said.

"I'll check it out. I love old black and white films. I have to go. Enjoy Paris!" She adjusted her backpack.

"Thanks for the brochure," Alana said.

Approaching the cathedral, Alana paused to examine the buttresses holding the walls like slender fingers. Along the sidewalk, couples pressed together, whispering in each other's ears and kissing, confirming this *was* the City of Love.

Alana stopped. The hair on her neck prickled. She turned around. Behind her, a man stood in the middle of the sidewalk. He wore black jeans, a white crew-neck sweater, a black leather jacket, and a scarf wrapped around his neck. His short hair was combed straight up on top. Dark shadows marked where he hadn't shaved. He stepped closer, his boots clanking on the sidewalk.

"You are Alana?"

Her mouth dropped.

"I am Victor Dumont. *Monsieur* Larson asked me to keep you safe while you are in the city today. I've been following to catch you since you left the Tower. I am your ride to the designer house."

"*You're* Victor?" Alana set her jaw. "Do you have identification?"

He took out his wallet and gave her his license. She studied his information and returned it. Alana didn't know whether to be angry or pleased. She didn't know Borg was looking out for her.

Victor said, "I did not mean to frighten you. You are going to tour *Notre Dame*? I would be happy to lead you."

The tour lines were long, and tourists were everywhere. It might be good to have a private guide, although something about him put her off. "All right," she said.

Once inside, Victor began to tell her about the famous cathedral.

"See the soaring spaces? The church became so big, it developed stress fractures. Architects needed to find a way to prop up the outside walls, so they used the buttresses to add support."

"It feels very spiritual," Alana said. The walls carried the faint scent of incense.

After Victor showed her the Rose stained glass windows, they decided to climb the stairs to the Gothic towers and see what Victor called the most special view in all of Paris.

"I don't know how many steps we've climbed, but my legs are on fire," said Alana as she tried to catch her breath.

"There are four hundred steps," Victor said. "We are halfway there. Can you climb the rest?"

They trudged up the spiral staircase. Alana was grateful when at last Victor said, "We are here."

The ledge was open, unprotected without the glass, and the perspective took her off guard. Alana felt lightheaded. Out the window sat a grotesque gargoyle perched on the edge, a monkey-devil, half man, half beast with wings.

"Pretty scary," she said.

"No, they are to scare evil *away*. A secret for you: They are actually lovable monsters designed to divide the flow of rainwater off the roof."

Alana wasn't convinced that the gargoyle was lovable, but she agreed that the view was spectacular. The entire city lay in front of her.

"Thank you for the tour," she said. "I didn't know that almost all the bells were melted and turned into cannons."

"New bells were made for the 850th anniversary in 2013."

Alana chuckled. "Quasimodo would have been impressed."

Victor said, "I love my city. It is the most beautiful in the world, and I have a passion for historic details."

"Yes, it shows." She tried to stifle a yawn, but her lips parted and her nostrils flared.

"Sorry, Victor. It isn't you. I'm jet-lagged and terribly tired."

"Come. I know a little place where we can have a bite to eat."

Alana touched her earring. "Good, I'm starving." She followed Victor to a patisserie on a back street away from the main boulevard. She stopped and examined the samples in the window: mini-croissants topped with chocolate roses, bite-sized caramel tarts, and tiny cakes covered with glazed berries arranged like jewels.

"Those pastries are almost too pretty to eat," Alana said. "They're works of art."

The sun was low in the sky, and Alana was eager for a meal. They sat outside at a table for two on a quiet street lined with trees. She ordered a cold Orangina—a carbonated citrus drink; a *croque monsieur*, thick melted cheese and ham on toast; and one of those flaky dough rectangles with jeweled fruit on top for dessert.

Alana took the chair overlooking the sunset. She watched the sky tint pink where it touched the horizon and fade to yellow where the clouds streaked across the blue. An apricot glow settled on all the distant buildings and trees, silhouetting the Eiffel Tower in the distance. She tried to memorize every detail.

"Are you all right?" Victor asked.

"It's so beautiful," Alana said. "I never want to forget."

For the first time since she met him, he smiled.

CHAPTER 32

Carlos worked several Saturdays a month. When he got off work, he liked to spend the evening playing cards with his buddies if he didn't have to work a late shift at the plant. Those were the times Rosie was free to hang with Chelsea. They talked about fashion, politics, and parents—everything but Carlos.

One Saturday morning, Rosie had planned to meet Chelsea for lunch. Chelsea announced she was bringing her husband, Noah, and his brother, Finn, to the Jive. Lunching on burgers and fries, they all laughed and shared stories. Rosie had forgotten how much fun it was to be with another couple.

"I have an idea," Chelsea said. "Let's go bowling tonight. I haven't bowled in years. Call your husband, Rosie, and ask him to join us. We'll have a blast."

"He can't," Rosie said. "He's playing cards with his friend tonight. Let's make it another time."

"We could still have a foursome if you can come," Chelsea said to Finn. "The battle of the girls against the guys?"

"I'm seeing someone," Finn said. "If she can come, let's do a group bowl. Saturday nights they have laser bowling with black lights, music, and pumped-in fog."

"Great," Chelsea said. "Sounds like fun."

They all agreed to meet at seven-thirty.

• • •

Carlos was in the kitchen. He should have left by now. Rosie had set her phone on vibrate, and there was a soft buzzing coming from her jacket pocket. She stepped into the bathroom, closed the door, and lowered her voice.

"Hi, Chelsea. No, you don't have to pick me up. I'll be there in twenty minutes."

She walked down the hall and Carlos approached her. "Where you think you're going?"

"I'm meeting some friends at the Three Strikes bowling alley. Aren't you playing cards with Ray?"

"He had to help his brother move." Carlos belched. "What friends? Forget it. You're staying home."

"You have no right to tell me I can't leave," Rosie said. "You spend weekends with your friends."

Carlos positioned himself between her and the door and snapped his fingers. "I said you're not going out."

"That's what you think," she said.

Carlos's palms slammed her chest. Rosie's elbow clipped the coffee table as she went down.

"That's what I know." Carlos picked up her purse, removed her keys, and shoved them in the front pocket of his jeans. "I think we've settled this."

Rosie moved into the kitchen and dialed her friend. She cupped the mouthpiece. "Chelsea, I can't meet you. I'm sorry. Something came up. I'll talk to you later."

Carlos had *never* been physically abusive. Rosie massaged her arm and searched the freezer for an ice pack. Surrounded by empty beer cans, the CRT monitor sat on a nearby card table, its tangled cords draped across the floor. Unopened mail lay scattered across the table, and Carlos's unwashed dishes were stacked on the counter. This was her life—dirty, dismal, and now dangerous. She waited for anger to give way to acceptance.

CHAPTER 33

Rosie stayed home the rest of the weekend until Carlos left for work on Monday. At lunchtime, she stood in line at the Jive. "I'll have a chai tea, please." Rosie took a wadded five-dollar bill from her purse.

"Your name?"

"Rosie."

The barista studied her and scribbled on the cup.

Rosie stepped back. "Oh—sorry about your foot," she told the guy behind her. She moved to an adjacent counter and waited for her drink.

"Next. Can I help you?"

"I'll have black coffee. Name's Adam."

The barista swiped his credit card, and Adam dropped some change in the tip jar.

A skinny kid behind the counter called, "One chai tea for Rosie. Coffee, black, Adam."

Rosie stirred sugar in her tea and said to Adam, "It's always packed in here."

"Over there. The mom and two kids are leaving," Adam said.

"Share a table?" Rosie asked.

"Sure."

Rosie slung her purse on the chair. Adam bumped his cup, and coffee spilled across the table. "Sorry," he said.

"I have extra napkins." Rosie dabbed the mess, catching the liquid at the table's edge before it dripped on the floor.

"Thanks."

"You're welcome."

She read the cup's inscription to Adam: "*Sharing can comfort.* Hanna, the barista, is pretty weird. She thinks she's a fortune-teller or something. Sometimes I'm not in her line, and she still writes on my cup."

"I think they help each other filling orders, but her messages are usually on target. Mine says, *Listen and you'll find the right path.*" Adam motioned to Rosie's cup. "So, you have something you need to share? I'm a good listener."

Rosie twisted her wedding band. She whirled it over her knuckle. Vacillating, she pushed it back.

"I know you're married. I was asking because of the comment on your cup." Adam fidgeted in his seat.

The gold band weighed on her hand like an anchor. Rosie hesitated for a moment before saying more. "Isn't a circle the symbol of unending love? This ring is a pretense. My marriage is a sham. How can you hurt someone you said you loved? I know there's no excuse for violent behavior, but how do you stop it?" There. She'd said it out loud.

"I don't know," he said quietly. "Are you all right? You're kind of pale."

"I've never admitted this to anyone. Not even to my family."

Adam was silent for a moment. "Yeah. Saying the words gives it a new reality, doesn't it?"

"Too real. I don't see my situation changing. I'm afraid to leave, and I'm afraid to stay." Rosie inhaled sharply.

"Sometimes it's easier to hide from the truth than to face facts. Abuse is not something to take lightly," Adam said.

"It only happened once." Rosie wondered if he was judging her. "I'm pretty good at hiding things. I don't have anybody to talk to. My husband, Carlos, scared off all my old friends. I have a new friend, Chelsea, but I haven't told her about this."

"Your secret's safe with me. But maybe you need to trust that your friend can handle it. Not everybody will abandon you. Have you thought about leaving?"

"I can't. I took a vow to marry for life. I've tried to live up to my word. My family's old-school and very Catholic. They've attended St. Joseph's Church since they've been in this country. I've thought about divorce, but my parents would be so ashamed." She lowered her voice. "This is embarrassing. I don't even know you."

"Well, then, I think it's time for introductions. My name's Adam."

"I'm Rosie."

"Okay, Rosie, I'll share something private with you. My buddies go to school out of state, so I can't talk to anybody but my family." He let out a nervous breath. "I found out recently I'm going to die in the not-too-distant future. I've been diagnosed with a disease. I'm angry and scared, and I pretty much feel hopeless all the time. It's been hard to accept."

"I'm so sorry." Rosie leaned back in her chair.

"I'm not contagious. It's an autoimmune disorder." Adam swallowed the last drop of his coffee. "It's called Juvenile Huntington's." He put down his cup. "Man, it seems like every time I come in here, I hit a new low."

"I can't imagine," Rosie said. "What scares you the most?"

"Everything," he said. "For now, I have periodic tremors. Eventually they'll affect my ability to drive. Take away the car, and you take my freedom. Or, it could be the thought of wearing diapers someday. A close second. Oops, TMI?"

"No, you're fine."

For a few minutes, they were both quiet. "Are you in any danger?" Adam asked. "I think you are."

She rubbed her elbow. "This has been a bad week."

"Do you have family to help you?"

Rosie stiffened. "I can't ask them for help."

"Sounds like you need to get away from this guy."

Her phone rang, and she signaled him, raising a finger to her lips.

"Hello?"

"Where the hell are you?"

"I have to stop at the post office—unless you want to," Rosie said.

"I'm not going out again. I just got home."

"I'll be there as soon as I can."

Rosie ended the call and dropped the phone in her bag. "God, he doesn't want me out of his sight. Things have been changing. Maybe I'm doing something wrong."

"Believe me, you're not the problem. Listen," Adam said, "if you're in trouble, call me." He wrote his number on his coffee receipt.

"Thanks. If you'd like to hang out sometime, you know, and talk, my work schedule is flexible. I work from home." Rosie gave Adam her cell number. She shrugged. "I don't live far from here."

"I don't want to get you in trouble."

"Carlos tries to monitor what I do, but we have different schedules, so I have free time. You can text me. I'll be okay."

Adam was frowning. "Don't hesitate to call me. And be careful."

"I will. I could use another friend," Rosie said.

"Me, too. I'd like the companionship," he said. "My family is great, but it's comforting to—" He tapped her cup. "To share."

CHAPTER 34

Saige unlocked the front door after work, and the soothing aroma of pot roast greeted her—as did the woman standing in her father's kitchen.

The stranger wore a flowing cotton skirt, a low-cut, scoop-neck blouse, and sandals with turquoise straps. The color matched her painted toenails. Her auburn hair was tucked in a loose bun, and she was simmering stew in Saige's mother's wrought iron skillet.

"Oh!" The woman laughed. "You startled me. You must be Saige. How do you do? I'm Cornelia." She pumped Saige's hand. "I hope you're hungry. I cooked enough food for a week."

Raphael Santoro entered the kitchen carrying a bottle of Shiraz and peeled back the foil from the cork. "Now, where's the wine opener?" he said. "Saige, I didn't hear you come in." He kissed her cheek. "I guess you met Cornelia."

"Yep, we met."

Cornelia was opening and closing drawers. "Hah! Here we go." She waved the corkscrew like a flag. "Pass me the bottle and round up three glasses."

"I'm fine with water," Saige said.

"Nonsense. We're celebrating."

"Celebrating what?"

"I finally get to meet Raphael's daughter." The cork popped out with a thump, and Cornelia poured three good-sized drinks. "Sit and relax, both of you. Let me slice the bread. Dinner's ready in two minutes."

The home-cooked meal she didn't have to prepare tasted pretty good, Saige had to admit. "I didn't know you were dating, Dad."

Raphael winked at Cornelia. "Well, yes," was all he said.

"I guess this explains why he was whistling while shaving last week." Saige wrinkled her nose after sipping the dry wine.

"Now take a bite of beef," Cornelia said. "The wine complements the meat."

It wasn't too bad.

"More bread?" Cornelia asked.

"Sure," her father said. He was grinning like a Cheshire cat—or a man high on endorphins and testosterone. Saige sipped her Shiraz.

She didn't know what to make of her father dating someone. He'd been so lost after her mother died, first angry, then distant. Saige didn't want her father to be alone the rest of his life. She should have noticed the recent changes. He had been gone many nights when she'd come home from the library, had engaged more in conversations with her during meals, and had privately monopolized the phone, now that she thought about it.

Saige hadn't pried, and he hadn't offered an explanation for his new behavior.

"So," Saige asked, "where did you two meet?"

"We met at David's Bar and Grill," Cornelia said gaily.

"Really?" She'd never known her father to go to a *bar*. He was a Denny's kind of guy.

"I got off early one night and stopped in with a couple of guys from work," her father said.

Cornelia passed the mashed potatoes. "They had live music. The band played a lot of Dean Martin songs, very romantic. The little dance floor—"

"You two *danced*?" Saige asked, incredulous.

"We did. Your father is a great dancer."

Saige poured herself another glass of wine. Cornelia opened another bottle.

• • •

Saige dragged herself out of bed and searched for the bottle of Advil. She swallowed three tablets, praying her head wouldn't explode. It was her first hangover. She vowed never to drink so much again.

The three of them had talked and laughed at Cornelia's jokes until after one in the morning. Saige had finally left the table, had somehow managed to get undressed, and had collapsed into bed without brushing her teeth.

Saige called her boss. "Mr. Seers? I'm afraid I can't come to work today. I'm nauseated and have a terrible headache. I'm sorry. I wouldn't want anyone else to catch it. . . . Yes, maybe it's a twenty-four-hour bug going around. I'll probably be fine tomorrow."

Saige crawled back into bed and waited for her head to stop pounding. Two hours later, she wiggled her feet into a pair of thick socks and ambled to the kitchen. She set two empty coffee cups, one stained with red lipstick, in the sink. After eating something, she felt like her usual self and wondered if she should call Mr. Seers and go in to work.

Instead, she decided to play hooky. For the next hour, she read until she was bored hanging around the house. Close to lunchtime, she decided to go to the Jive. On the drive over, she began to worry. What if she saw someone she knew, or worse, a coworker? Maybe she could say she went to a clinic and they told her she wasn't contagious after all. What was wrong with her? Lying to Mr. Seers, ditching work, and plotting excuses. Her father wasn't the only one acting unusual.

At the Jive, the lunch crowd waited to place orders. Hanna's line was the longest. Saige moved to the shorter line, as did the woman behind her. Saige turned to look around the room, and the woman behind took off her jacket. Saige tried not to stare at the purple bruises on the woman's arm.

"This is taking forever," the woman said.

"Are you on a lunch break?" Saige asked. "You can go in front of me."

"It's okay. I work for a rental car agency. I take reservations from home."

"I didn't know companies did that," Saige said.

"Yeah, they install software on your computer. It saves a lot on gas."

"I work at a bank, but I took a sick day. I wish I could think of something different to do—something fun."

"Have a manicure. I always feel good afterward."

"I've never had one," Saige said.

"Seriously?" The woman rummaged through her purse and gave Saige a card. "Here. This gal is great. Tell her Rosie sent you."

Saige hesitated. "I'd have to go home and call. I don't own a cell phone."

"How do you live without a phone? Oh, sorry, not my business."

"Next!" a voice yelled out.

"Black tea, large, and one of those cookies, please."

"Your name?"

"Saige." She counted out exact change.

"They'll have it ready for you over there." He pointed to the next counter, and Saige moved aside.

The woman said, "One small chai tea. The name's Rosie, and I'll take a cookie, too." She tapped on the glass. "The one in the front of the case, please. It has more chocolate chips." She smiled at Saige. "Sometimes it's about the chocolate."

Saige laughed. "You know, a manicure does sound like fun. I'd like to call the gal you recommended."

Rosie handed Saige her phone. "Here, use mine."

"I don't know how to turn it on," Saige said.

Rosie picked up her tea and wrapped a napkin around the cookie. "Let's sit down, and I'll show you how it works. Then we'll see if we can get you an appointment. By the way, my name's Rosie."

Saige introduced herself, and after they sat down, Rosie gave Saige her first lesson on a smartphone.

"If you don't mind my being nosy, how is it you don't have a cell phone?" Rosie asked.

"I've heard they're expensive. I live with my father, who believes technology is ruining our society, so we've never had one."

"Your dad, he sounds kind of . . . Amish or something. Sorry, no offense, but you can't change the way the world works, and we're all about technology. What does your mom say?"

"She died last year."

"Oh, I'm sorry. Your dad's overprotective, huh?"

Saige scoffed. "Try controlling. He resists any change I want to make."

"I understand."

"I was in third grade, and my school had a special performance of "The Yellow Boat," a play about HIV in kid-friendly terms." Saige turned away. All these years later she was still embarrassed. "My father called the school, furious, claiming they had no right to tell me about AIDS."

"I'm not familiar with the play." Rosie brushed crumbs off her shirt.

"Other parents were upset too; it wasn't like Dad was the only one. The principal suggested that parents who objected should keep their child at home. Yep. My last day in public school. From then on, I was homeschooled."

"What a drastic decision," Rosie said. "Your poor mom—I can't imagine the work it takes to homeschool a child."

"She devoted her life to me. We weren't connected to a lot of homeschooled families, so I didn't have a lot of kids to hang out with."

Rosie patted Saige's hand. "So you had a lonely childhood, with a quiet, empty house. I had the opposite—a mother who was so busy with so many little ones, she didn't have time for any of us. Had I known you then, I would have generously offered you some of my siblings."

"How kind of you," Saige laughed. "You know what I missed out on the most? Classmates and friends. I loved my mom. She did the best she could, but—"

"I know what you mean," Rosie said. "Hey, I was thinking, a basic flip phone is maybe twenty bucks, and you could get a plan where you pay for limited minutes. I have some free time until I start my shift, and I need a car charger for my phone. Maybe instead of a manicure, we could take a look at some phones."

"Sounds great! I'd appreciate it," Saige said.

They drove to a Verizon store, and an hour later, Saige was the proud owner of her first cell phone.

"Congratulations," Rosie said.

"Thank you for helping me."

"No problem." Rosie turned into the Jive's lot. "Remember, I put my number in your contacts. I have to get to work. Don't forget to read the instructions. Have fun."

CHAPTER 35

It was a lazy Friday night. Saige and Finn nestled on the couch, and the soft light from the fireplace flickered on the wall.

"What are you thinking about?" Finn asked.

"How happy I am."

"Are you sure you're the same girl I met at the Jive?" Finn said.

"I don't think so," Saige said. "I feel different now. I still miss my mom, and I realize I don't know my dad very well. He's all I have, you know?"

"You have me." Finn snuggled against her.

"I mean, I wish he and I weren't butting heads all the time. I could talk to my mom about anything, but I'm on guard with my father. Maybe, if he stopped telling me every decision I make is the wrong one, I'd be more open with him. No matter what I do, I'm not good enough. I guess he thinks I'm incompetent."

"Why not tell him to lay off the guilt trips?"

"No, that would hurt his feelings. I can't."

"Can't or won't?"

"Can we drop this?" she asked.

"Sure. I didn't mean to go Freudian on you. Do you like the woman he's seeing? What was her name? Carnally?"

"Cornelia. I think so, although it's kind of weird seeing Dad with another woman." Saige shot him a furtive look.

"Okay, moving on to another topic. How's the new online class?"

She rested her chin on his chest. "Navigating the site was a challenge. It's not college, but the classes are free, and I'm learning a lot. I'm grateful to Sam for telling me they were available. As long as I take the test at the end of the course, I can sign up for more."

Interrupted by the vibration of her cell phone, Finn rolled his eyes and grinned. "I know you get excited to get a call."

"It's Rosie," she said.

"Tell her she created a monster."

"I won't be long."

CHAPTER 36

Rosie turned off her computer and phoned Chelsea. "I have a favor to ask."

"Sure. What's up?"

"I met this guy at the Jive. It's a long story, but he's sick with something called Juvenile Huntington's disease. His condition sounds like a mix of Parkinson's and Alzheimer's. It's called Juvenile because symptoms show at a younger age, and the disease progresses faster in young people."

"How horrible," Chelsea said. "How old is he?"

"Not sure. I'd guess early twenties. His name's Adam."

"I've never heard of Huntington's, but my grandma had Parkinson's. She got the shakes so bad she couldn't walk. Does Adam need help getting around?"

"Not yet. His friends go to school out of state, and I think he's lonely. He said he found it so difficult to manage his classes that he had recently dropped out of college. I'm sure he's depressed. I thought we could all go to dinner sometime."

"Noah and I are checking out a new seafood place tonight, Ocean Breeze, over on Fifth Street. They advertised half-price appetizers during happy hour. Call your husband and Adam. See if they're interested."

"Well, Carlos is working tonight, but if Adam wants to go, I'll pick him up. Should you check with Noah?" asked Rosie.

"Naw, I'm sure he's fine. We can meet at the restaurant, but give me a little time to get presentable."

"You always look beautiful."

"I don't feel beautiful."

"You're joking, right? I'd kill for those perfect little dimples when you smile. Not to mention your gorgeous eyes."

"The trick is the makeup. But it's okay if I'm not perfect, because I have a big heart," Chelsea said, adding a quick laugh.

"Yeah, Carlos tells me I have a big butt. You said happy hour, so we should be there by five thirty or so."

"I'd better get started," Chelsea said.

• • •

By the time Rosie arrived at Adam's complex, he was already waiting on the bottom step.

"So, your friends know about me?" Adam asked, fastening his seat belt.

"About the Huntington's? Yeah, I guess I should've asked your permission first. You seemed down this week."

"No, I'm fine talking about it. You're right; I've been obsessing. Some days I feel such despair. Nights are worse, lying there, imagining scenarios about my future."

Rosie caught Adam's shoulders slump, and she hurried to change the subject. "Getting out might cheer you up. You're going to love Chelsea and Noah."

"Did you tell Chelsea about Carlos?"

"Not yet. Don't say anything."

"Okay." He flipped down the visor and checked himself in the mirror. "Thanks for including me. It's good to think about something else. I talked to a counselor today about returning to audit my courses. My parents suggested that."

"Yes, that's a good idea. You should stay busy. You should put together a list of things you'd like to experience. Do you have a bucket list?"

"A what?"

"Things you always wanted to do but put on hold, because you thought you'd do it later."

"What's the point of that now?"

"I'm sorry. I wasn't trying to be insensitive."

"I admit I always wished I could play an instrument, guitar or maybe piano."

"You could take guitar lessons. Freddy's Frets is about a mile from here," Rosie said. "They teach lessons in everything."

"I don't own any instruments."

"Hmm. . . . I have an old Casio keyboard I haven't played in years. It's two octaves short of a real piano, but it works great and has a lot of features. Push a button, and the notes change to sound like different instruments: flutes, harpsichords, jazz guitar."

"I don't know," Adam said.

"I taught myself to play chords from a book. It was pretty easy. I could drop the keyboard off next week. I still have the book, too. You can bang on the thing and play around."

"Sure, why not? I can't travel to Europe, and it's too cold for skydiving. Thanks."

"Good," she said. "I'll get it to you as soon as I can. You need to find activities to keep your spirits up."

Adam hummed along to a tune on the radio. "This should be fun. I love seafood, if it's cooked and doesn't involve tentacles."

Rosie laughed. "We're here. Come meet my friends."

After Rosie made introductions and the group was seated, five appetizers were ordered to share. Noah and Adam hit it off immediately. Both had been on a track team in high school.

"I always enjoyed running," Adam said. "Cleared my mind."

"Jogging always energized me," Noah said. "I could blow

off steam, and it gave me time to think. I still run, but it isn't the same as the carefree days of high school."

"Maybe I should try running," Rosie said, and everyone laughed. "All right, I'm not the athletic type. I never played a sport, except for soccer back in grade school."

"I was on the girls' tennis team for a semester," Chelsea said, "but I wasn't very good, so I dropped it. Shopping's my sport. Walk that mall, lift those earrings . . ."

The waiter placed a basket filled with French bread on the table, poured olive oil in trays, and drizzled dark balsamic vinegar on top.

"Your appetizers will be right up," he said.

Rosie tore her bread in pieces, dipped, and soaked up the olive oil. "Did you guys know each other in high school?"

Chelsea shook her head. "Noah and I met in college."

Rosie smiled nervously. "I never finished college."

"I recently dropped out," Adam said. "But I'm still auditing."

"Jeez," Noah said. "I'm really sorry you had to drop out. I can't imagine how tough this is on you."

"Yeah," Chelsea said. "Rosie told us about your illness. It's hard to imagine how life can change in an instant."

"I didn't mean to bring down the party, but I'm glad you know. It's not something I can hide."

Noah said, "We're glad you're here. Maybe we could try out new restaurants—take turns picking."

"Great." Adam raised his glass. "To new friends."

CHAPTER 37

A good night's sleep would ready her for the early meeting with *Madame* Duprey. Alana kicked off her shoes and stumbled into bed. Even the voices in the hall didn't keep her awake. The phone rang, insistent and loud, until Alana groped for the receiver.

"Good morning, *mademoiselle*. You requested a wake-up call?"

"Yes, *merci*," she dropped the handset back in its charger.

She stayed in the shower until the bathroom fogged with thick steam. Reluctantly, she climbed out, fumbling for the hotel robe on the back of the door.

Alana hadn't packed a lot of clothes and couldn't wear the dress she wore on the airplane until the wrinkles relaxed on the hanger. She decided on another: white with small black polka dots and a red flower sewn on the front. Two inches of black tulle whooshed under the hem. Alana gathered her hair in a French braid, tied it back with a ribbon, and hoped her dress didn't flare too wide. She'd noticed that Parisian women tended to wear narrow, tailored skirts.

Michelle had e-mailed that St. Louis was still fighting snowstorms, yet Paris was having an unusual warm spell for early spring. Alana slid into her shoes and found a jacket to counter the chilly morning air. She stuffed a mini-notebook and her iPad into her purse and set off for the Executive Lounge. Alana reviewed her notes and nibbled two chocolate croissants.

She had no trouble locating Victor in the lobby. A leather jacket lay over his arm, and his rumpled white shirt was half-tucked in his jeans. He escorted her outside to a moped and tossed her a helmet.

"What? No, I don't think so. I'm wearing a dress, in case you hadn't noticed."

"One is not late for an appointment with Martine," Victor said.

Alana didn't have the address of the boutique. "Fine," she said. She hiked her leg over the seat and sat behind him. Victor swerved into the traffic, and Alana's arms tightened around his waist as he wove though the narrow streets. Victor's thin tie flapped against his shirt. Alana pressed against his back for warmth; the air chilled her bare legs. A sharp turn landed them onto a street paved with old, worn cobblestones.

Boutique shops were already open for business. The architecture with wrought iron balconies reminded Alana of New Orleans. Red awnings shaded the store windows. Victor veered off the bumpy street to a wide, tree-lined boulevard. Sidewalks stretched for miles. The sun peeked between tree limbs, but Alana still shivered, partly because the idea of meeting Martine left her edgy. Would they expect her to speak French? Victor could help translate, but she would be responsible for deciding if the clothing line would work in her magazine.

"How much farther?" she yelled. He didn't answer. Her back had started to ache. They were rocking along at a fairly high speed. Signs flashed by for petrol, the ads peppered with flawlessly airbrushed young women in seductive poses wearing lacy bras and lingerie. It was more flagrant than in the States, but the message was the same: Sex sells.

Their destination was an unadorned one-story building, and a metal plaque on a post identified La Chic Boutique. Alana climbed off the Vespa, tossed the helmet to Victor, and patted her hair.

Inside, a section of corridor seemed to go on forever with rooms on both sides. Each area teemed with activity. On the right, bolts of fabric of every color and texture ranged from faux fur to lace. On the left, employees in cubicles scribbled furiously with markers and pencils.

"Come, *vite*." Victor knocked.

Behind the door a voice commanded. "*Oui! Entrez.*"

Victor motioned for Alana to follow.

CHAPTER 38

The woman at the desk kept her arms folded against her chest. Her mid-length blonde hair swept back from her forehead and was tucked behind her ears. She reminded Alana of a young Catherine Deneuve, the film star, except for her unsettling stare, the same one Victor used. Maybe it was a French thing. It was a disturbing look because it suggested disapproval. Or was it distain?

"Ah-lah-nah Hudson?"

"Actually, it's pronounced Ah-*lay*-nah." Alana waited for her to stand and finally extended a hand but received only a cold stare. The woman remained seated.

"Yes, then, Alana." The words were slow and deliberate. She emphasized the *lay* sound, and Alana sensed she was mocking her. "I am Lee-own. Leone Davin," she said.

"I was told I was to meet with Martine Duprey."

Victor rested against the wall behind Alana and said nothing.

"She has been called away. You meet with me." Leone picked up a sample from her desk, rolled her fingers across tiny, shimmering beads sewn into the fabric, and leaned back into the leather chair.

Victor spoke to her in French. Alana couldn't guess what he said, but Borg's name was mentioned. Victor sputtered, Leone hissed, and tension crackled. For several seconds, neither Victor nor Leone spoke. Leone shook her head and flipped her fingers as if dismissing him. She crossed her arms again, and her manicured nails pushed against her black pinstriped jacket. A red blouse blazed underneath.

"So, I understand we are to inspect the designs, *oui*?" Leone pressed the intercom on her desk. "Prepare the runway," she said, lushly rolling the r's in the back of her throat. Alana looked around for Victor, but he was gone.

They snaked through the building to a room with a stage. A closed gray curtain flecked with silver threads sparkled under the bright overhead lights. A long runway projecting from the stage was flanked by rows of chairs. Leone sat down and motioned for Alana to sit next to her. Leone spoke into her headset. "We are ready. Begin."

Music piped through the speakers, and the curtain parted. A tall young woman in copper stilettos wore a tangerine-colored dress with long, sheer sleeves. The front was slit to her navel. Each foot was precisely placed in front of the other. At the runway's end, she shifted her weight, turned, and strutted back.

The next girl modeled brown ankle boots and a beige dress, the texture of burlap, with orange koi printed on each shoulder. The third model wore a white accordion-pleated skirt with miniature painted heads from Edvard Munch's *The Scream* placed at precise intervals around the hem.

Another young woman, skin as pale as moonlight, paraded in a neon-yellow dress covered with spikes of . . . tiny fabric bananas? Those on the sleeves were three times larger than on the rest of the dress.

Alana's eyes glazed. She was a publisher, not a fashion critic, but she knew her readers wouldn't wear burlap sacks with koi fish painted on the shoulders, or spiky banana-sleeved dresses.

Leone's nail tapped against the clipboard. The final ensemble was a vivid green floor-length skirt paired with a bright pink

top. Three stiff pieces of green fabric jutted like petals from the
back of the neckline and over the model's head. Alana imagined
a walking tulip.

Leone clapped twice. The music stopped, and the curtain
closed.

"And so, *mademoiselle*, did you not love the show?"

"It was . . . unbelievable."

• • •

Alana passed the models changing; their faces were smiling,
hopeful. She slowed her pace to examine the clothes. The jackets
had center back seams; the seams were straight, well done. The
beige dress with the koi had a shoulder yoke instead of the back
and front sewn together over the top of the shoulder, a shortcut
often done with cheaper clothing. The workmanship was perfect,
but it wouldn't matter if her readers wouldn't buy the clothes.
She'd have to tell Leone her line wouldn't be a good fit for the
magazine.

Back in the office, Leone opened a drawer and removed a
folder. "Cappuccino?"

"No, thank you."

"So, then, let us begin." Leone pushed a portfolio across the
desk to Alana.

Alana slid the folder back. "I'm sorry. Your clothes are very
creative, but I'm afraid they won't sell successfully in our magazine. My readership—"

"Give the designs a chance. Put them in your magazine where
they—"

"I'm afraid your line is specialized, not tailored to everyday
wear." Alana strained to keep her voice pleasant.

"Perhaps your magazine is not progressive enough to showcase my work."

Alana wouldn't sit and be bad-mouthed by this insulting French woman. "I know my readers' taste, and this clothing will not work." Not progressive enough, she thought, fuming.

Leone stood and leaned against the desk. "We show you our new line, and you have the nerve to—You have insulted me. Leave at once."

"This is no way to conduct business. I'm here merely to inspect the designs."

Leone's upper lip raised and her nostrils widened. She slapped a stack of papers. They flew off the desk.

Alana jumped out of her seat. The woman was crazy. Alana backed out the door and into the hall, where Victor was waiting.

"Come on," Alana said. She tugged his sleeve and bolted ahead. They flew down the narrow corridor, retracing their steps until they found the exit.

• • •

Back in her hotel room, Alana pressed a moist washcloth against her face and speed-dialed her assistant.

"How's Paris?" Michelle asked.

"God, it's good to hear your voice. I don't know. Paris is beautiful, but the haute couture idea blew up. What was I thinking?"

"What happened?" Michelle asked.

"I spent what felt like hours with a woman named Leone, who has the warmth and charm of a Gestapo agent. The clothes are completely wrong for us."

Alana fell back onto the bed and tucked a pillow under her neck. "I guess I'll call Borg. How's everything at home?"

Michelle hesitated.

"What's going on?"

"It can wait. You've had a lousy day."

Alana sighed. "What's wrong?"

"I didn't want to tell you on the phone, but I'm so excited. I'm . . . I'm pregnant. You know we've been trying for years."

Alana's mind raced. "I'm thrilled for you and Steve."

"Thanks. We're excited. You know I'll stay until we can get the right person, but I want to be home with the baby."

"That's amazing news. We'll have to celebrate after I'm home. Oh, I almost forgot; would you send the notes from our last staff meeting? I can't find them, and I'm trying to get a little work done while I'm here."

"Will do. Oh, and Taylor's complaining about doing the piece on the human body exhibit. She said it's gross; they're displaying real bodies."

"Assign Murphy to it," Alana said. "And tell Taylor to find the folder on my desk labeled 'Rehab Centers' and to follow through with the occupational therapist. I want an article about computers for seniors as part of their therapy."

"I'm on it," Michelle said. "Enjoy yourself. Today you can officially say you spent some of April in Paris. Has a romantic ring to it, don't you think?"

"The trip isn't romantic."

"Don't burn your bra yet," Michelle said.

"If you subtract Leone from the picture, I'd say I'm having a great holiday. Los Angeles was perfect. But remember, my work is my vacation."

"Defiant words from my independent boss."

"I don't know when I'll be back. Call me if anything comes up," Alana said. "And congratulations again. I'm happy for you." She hung up and headed to the lounge. How would she find someone as capable and dedicated as Michelle? Forget dinner. She needed a drink.

CHAPTER 39

Finn took Saige to Michelina's, their favorite Italian restaurant, to celebrate her twenty-third birthday.

"I bought you something. You can open it after dinner." Finn set a package wrapped in shiny gold paper topped with a black ruffled bow on the table next to the wall. "Suspense is half the fun."

The waiter brought an iced tea for Saige and a beer for Finn. "I have to wait until we finish the main course?" she asked. After the waiter brought their salads, Saige said, "Please. I can't stand it." She leaned her fork against her plate.

Finn set the present in front of her. "All right." He grinned mischievously. "Happy birthday."

She drew it closer. "It's heavy." Saige tore off the paper and gasped. "Is this for real?"

"It's a mini, but it should take care of all your needs. I loaded it with all the software you might want. Now you don't have to spend all your evenings at the library. You can work on your online classes anywhere you want."

She glided her fingers along the laptop's smooth, cool surface. "I can't believe it. It's the best present I've ever gotten."

• • •

Saige was determined to quit the bank and find new employment. Every day, she searched the ads during her break. One Thursday, a job posting caught her attention: administrative assistant for a graphics company called Two Can Do It. The business was owned by two sisters. In a quick phone call, Saige was able to schedule an interview for the next day during her lunch hour. She felt that the interview went well. The following Monday, they called to ask if she was still interested in the position.

Saige called Finn. "I got the job!"

"Congratulations," he said. "Are you sure you've given it enough thought? You've worked at the bank a long time."

"Kelly and Beth are terrific. We'll work out of Kelly's home. I'm sure it's a great opportunity. It's right. I can feel it."

"What do you think your dad will say?"

She contorted her face. "I don't know, but I guarantee it won't be good."

• • •

After dinner, Saige worked up the nerve to tell her father she'd accepted a new job.

"You want to leave the bank to be a *secretary*? You could be a manager if you stay at the bank. You could work in corporate someday."

"I'm a greeter! Work in corporate? All I do is say hello and direct customers to the right window. I've never even been promoted. There's more to life, Dad."

"They'll take advantage of you, these women. You're working out of somebody's house? Is it a real job?"

Saige flinched. Anything with a paycheck was a real job, wasn't it?

"I'm sick of the bank. I'm taking the job."

• • •

The first day on her new job, Saige arrived twenty minutes early. Kelly and Beth's welcome cured her nervousness. The sisters were in their thirties, maybe a couple of years apart. Beth wore jeans, but Kelly dressed more vibrantly, with a rich, red Chinese silk scarf draped around a white sweater. Several gold bangles clinked on her wrist.

Beth motioned to an office chair. "This is your work space. We need you to take calls and organize our appointments. If you have any questions, ask the client to hold, and press this button to mute the call."

Each desk was equipped with two twenty-four-inch monitors. Bins organized the room. Extra-large dry-erase boards on the wall indicated the day's workload. Oversized calendars flagged work due dates.

For a few days, Saige was like a fish on a bicycle, but the women were patient. Saige answered the phone and set up appointments. Thanks to Sam's classes, she also e-mailed clients, created files and folders, and worked out simple Excel spreadsheets after Beth showed her what was needed. Working at the computer all day increased her typing skills. She remembered the elegant blonde with the French braid her first day at the Jive and how impressed she'd been as she'd watched her ply the keyboard. By the end of the month, Saige was pretty sure she was almost as fast.

CHAPTER 40

Saige's classes were giving her new confidence. Fascinated by the illustrations her bosses designed for their clients, Saige searched through the course brochure for a basic image-editing software class.

After dinner, she told Finn, "I signed up for an online Photoshop class. You loaded Elements on my laptop. I might as well take advantage of it. Maybe after this, I'll sign up for a class on how to set up a blog."

"You don't need a class," Finn said. "There are tons of free blog sites. I can help you."

"That'd be great."

"Come here," he said. "There's something I want to show you." He opened the desk drawer and took out a candle in a glass container covered with a raffia bow.

"Oh, it's lovely, thank you." She pried off the wooden lid and sniffed the soft scent of lavender. There was something else: a silver key lying across the wick.

"The key is to my apartment. I don't want you to go home. Move in with me, Saige."

She focused on the key. "I don't know. My dad—"

"Your dad has Cornelia now. He's spends all his time at *her* place." Finn smiled. "Say you'll live with me."

Saige paused. "It's a big step. I'm not sure. You don't think it's too soon?"

"No. I want to be with you all the time. I'll go with you and talk to your dad if you want."

His handsome face was tender with hope and determination. "You'll move in with me?" he asked again.

"Yes, Finn, I'll move in with you."

Finn whooped and whirled her around in a circle. Saige dropped back her head, laughing, and held on to him.

"Should we get your things tonight?"

"No, I'd rather tell Dad myself first. I'll do it tomorrow." She picked up her keys from the kitchen table and added his key to her ring. Driving back home that night, she worried about how her father would react to the news.

• • •

Saige told her father after breakfast and braced for an argument. He sucked in a gulp of air and puffed out his cheeks. Here we go, she thought.

"You barely know him."

"You think we should be married first?"

"I used to think living together was wrong." Her father frowned. "But the divorce rate is so high, and relationships are so disposable, I'm confused as to what a couple should do. Granted, you don't know someone until you live with them, but I'm sure this is too soon."

"I'm a grown woman. I can do what I want. I'm telling you, not asking you."

"How can you talk to me this way? I didn't raise my daughter to be so disrespectful."

"I don't mean any disrespect, Dad, but I want to think for myself. Let me figure it out."

"I'm trying to protect you."

"Well, don't. Because you're so old-fashioned, I haven't experienced life." She'd never spoken to him this way. Accusing. She didn't want to hurt her father, but he didn't understand. "I have a laptop now, and guess what, Dad, it didn't kill me. I have a new job and a supportive boyfriend who believes in me. He loves me. I'm going to pack and move in with Finn, with or without your approval." She turned and ran up the stairs.

He called after her. "You'll regret this decision. You don't know the boy yet. Love is more than having somebody helping you feel good about yourself. Keep your house key. You'll be back."

CHAPTER 41

Finn noted the time on the microwave's clock and guessed that Saige was telling her father about their plans to live together. He paced around the kitchen and wondered what it would be like to live with Saige; he had never lived with a woman. It was ten o'clock, and he figured Noah was awake by now. Impatient to share his news, he punched his brother's cell number.

"What's up?" Noah answered.

"Hope I didn't wake you," Finn said. "I have some exciting news. I asked Saige to move in with me, and she said yes. Today's the big day. She's getting her things as we speak."

"Wow. I'm happy for you. I really am," Noah said. "I think she's a great girl, but it's a big step. Are you sure about this? You don't have a great track record."

"I've changed," Finn said defensively.

"You said you were taking a break after the Laura fiasco. How long has it been?"

Finn ignored him. "Do you and Chelsea want to go to lunch with us and celebrate?"

"Can't do lunch. Chelsea's out with her friend Rosie. How about dinner?"

"Maybe. Huh—weird. Saige has a friend named Rosie." Finn's call-waiting beeped. "I have to take this. It's Saige."

"I'll ask Chelsea about dinner," Noah said. "Congratulations, bro. Go easy. You don't want to lose *this* one."

CHAPTER 42

Adam hoped he wouldn't be the only guy in the meditation class at the Spiritual Well Being Center. He hadn't been back to the church since the service he'd attended with Brad two weeks before.

He thought meditation was done in a seated position, but the pamphlet said the instructor preferred that everyone lie prone. Adam had bought a yoga mat for comfort's sake. The class was packed, and he felt relieved that it wasn't all women. He found a corner, leaned against the wall, and waited. For Hanna.

She quietly entered and said hello. Her multicolored hair was spiked today, and there was a red gemstone pasted in the center of her forehead. But it wasn't her offbeat hair drawing his attention. It was her eyes. Warm brown with flecks of yellow. They flashed intelligence.

Hanna unrolled her mat. "I hope this session will help you calm your thoughts." Her expression was serene, her brown eyes kind. "Please lie down and get in a comfortable position. Close your eyes." She guided the class through breathing techniques. "Slow. Deep. From your belly. Like babies breathe." Her voice was low and hypnotic.

Adam followed her directions and began to relax. He could hear Hanna as she stirred about the room, her voice moving farther, then closer.

"Put your hand on your chest. Find your heartbeat. Repeat: I am one with my spirit." The class murmured the chant.

"Raise your palm to your crown and slowly work your way downward. Feel your energy radiating from within."

Adam felt heat pulsating.

"Now, brush away any negative energy. Focus on your breath."

Her voice was coming closer. "In, out," she repeated slowly. Adam wanted to peek to see where she was, but he was relaxed and didn't want to break the spell.

A gentle weight rested across his brow; Hanna cupped the back of his head. Adam didn't move. "In, out. Notice the silence. If you have thoughts, let them go." She cradled his head, and he felt himself slip away to a quiet place. He wasn't sure how much time had passed, but the chime of a soft bell roused him. Perhaps he had fallen asleep. There was no anxiety, no tightness in his chest.

After the session, Adam moved toward Hanna, but a crowd had swarmed around her. He took his mat, stepped over a few people whose eyes were still closed, and left.

On the drive home, the worry returned. He wrestled with his negative thoughts and tried to silence them. But by the time he arrived at his apartment, he'd lost the fight.

CHAPTER 43

Tuesday night's traffic was heavy. A woman in a Chevy Tahoe driving in front of Carlos put on her blinker to switch lanes.

Arrogant bitch in her big car, he thought. He tasted envy at the material success the vehicle represented. Success he didn't have. He waved her over. The second she was in front of him, Carlos gunned the engine. He knew she'd panic. She checked her rear-view mirror, tires squealed, and metal crunched. The front of Carlos's car crumpled against her SUV. The car behind him braked, but it was too late. Carlos braced himself.

The three cars edged off the road. The woman climbed out, shaking her finger at Carlos. "Why did you signal me in and then run into me?"

"I didn't do nothin' wrong. This was your fault." Carlos rubbed his neck. "My car. Look what you did to it."

The two other cars had minimal damage, but the twisted metal on Carlos's car was beyond repair. His trunk was almost in the backseat, the hood was mashed, and the front bumper was torn off, hanging like a ripped fingernail.

The man who rear-ended Carlos said, "I'm Jim Simmons. Here's my insurance information, license, and phone number."

Carlos copied it.

The woman said, "I've never been in an accident. What do we do?"

"Get your insurance card," Simmons said. "Nobody's hurt."

He surveyed both cars. "You barely have fender damage," he said to the woman.

"Did you see him wave me in?"

Simmons shook his head. "No, nothing but brake lights. It happened so fast."

She opened her glove compartment and retrieved the paperwork.

Carlos used his phone to take pictures of the damage and of their license plates.

"I'd guess your car's a total loss. What are you going to do?" Simmons asked.

"Call a tow truck," Carlos said, "after she gives me her ID and stuff."

"Okay then."

"We'll be in touch," Carlos said.

The woman shot Carlos a dirty look and got back in her car.

He watched them drive away and turned back to his phone. "Ray, it's Carlos. I have some business for you. Can you tow me to a garage?"

• • •

Carlos hunched over the table and filled out the paperwork for the insurance claim.

"I wonder how much money we'll get."

"I don't like this," Rosie said. "You did this once before. They're going to catch on and put you in jail."

"Shut up. Nobody's gonna know."

Rosie's feet shifted. It wasn't an easy decision. She'd given it considerable thought. Adam's words had haunted her. She knew he was right. Maybe she'd have a chance to start over. She had to try. Stop stalling, she thought. She took a deep breath. "I want to talk to you. I've been thinking a lot lately. About us."

Carlos's eyes narrowed. "Somebody giving you advice? If it's what I think, the answer is no. We're united in the Church forever."

Rosie's chin rose. "You have no right treating me the way you do. Putting me down all the time. I . . . I want out."

He sneered. "You got nowhere to go."

"I'll go back to Mamá's if I have to." Rosie swallowed. She didn't want to go back. All the shouting and whining, her family packed in the two-bedroom house like cattle in a truck. She wasn't free either way. But after her conversation with Adam, Rosie had decided to err on the side of her own safety.

"I've always been fond of your mamá. You might want to reconsider going back home. Wouldn't want anything to happen to her, would we?"

Rosie startled at his statement. "Is that a threat?"

"Consider it a warning. You're staying with me. You don't want to be kicked out of the Church. Never take the Sacrament again." He crossed himself.

She rolled her eyes at his hypocritical gesture.

Carlos pounded across the floor and shoved her against the refrigerator. The glass bottles rattled inside. He grabbed Rosie's shoulders, ripping the side of her blouse, and slapped her. Rosie cupped her cheek and tried to move away. Carlos's hand slid up her throat. She clawed at his wrist, but he was stronger.

"Pay attention. It doesn't matter what you want. I'm warning you, Rosie. Try to leave, and I'll find you." His thumb crushed against her Adam's apple. "You understand what I'm saying?" He released his hold.

The kitchen began to spin. Rosie gripped the counter for support. "I understand," she said.

"Good. I don't want to talk about this no more. I'm hungry. Go do your job." He stormed into the living room.

The thump in her chest was so great she was certain she was having a panic attack. It hurt to swallow. Rosie wrapped her hands around her neck, cradling her throat.

He shouted from the couch. "What are you doing?"

Bastard. Rosie opened the refrigerator and was shaking so hard that she almost dropped the cardboard carton of eggs. She counted out three eggs and cracked them against the mixing bowl. Pieces of shell splintered into the hot oil. She pushed them away with the corner of the wooden spoon. Hot grease snapped and began to burn the white around the edges. Her eyes widened. You'll be sorry, Carlos. So sorry.

CHAPTER 44

Borg hung up the phone with Victor and calculated how to do damage control. He didn't know Alana would be thrown into the lion's den, though *Leone* was pronounced exactly like the French word for *lion*.

Martine had had business in Calais. Instead of representing Martine's personal line, Leone had substituted her own designs, hoping to impress the American. Martine would be furious.

Borg remembered Leone all too well. They'd had dinner the few times he had visited Paris on business. Leone had invited him to her apartment, and they'd slept together, but Borg had told her from the start that he was attracted to her only in a physical sense. Later, he'd informed her he was no longer interested in dating her. There was no heartbreak involved, just disappointment from Leone, who had regarded Borg as a powerful trophy.

She was unlike Alana, whom Borg suspected wasn't capable of an insincere thought. He'd sensed it during their first Skype chat. He had liked her the moment she'd stepped out of the elevator. During lunch at the beach restaurant, her laugh had been contagious. It wasn't only her beauty he was drawn to; he knew roomfuls of gorgeous women. It was the way she met his eyes, firm and unruffled, protective of the magazine she'd created, a determination he understood very well.

The merger with Alana's magazine was crucial. He couldn't let Leone's stunt ruin his plans. Borg called his assistant into his office.

"I need a flight to Paris. Immediately."

. . .

Up at dawn, Alana stayed in her hotel room reviewing possible future articles. After an early lunch, she Skyped Michelle and waited for her image to appear on the screen.

"Alana, hi," Michelle said.

"I forgot about the time difference. I didn't know you were home."

"When has that ever stopped you?" Michelle chuckled, picked up a paring knife, and placed a sweet potato on the cutting board. "How's France?"

"I've been thinking that I'd like to visit a few cities outside of Paris. Maybe take a train somewhere. Since we won't be doing business with La Chic Boutique, I'll have more free time than I'd intended." Alana took a sip of water. "I've been looking at Taylor's notes. I like the article she wrote, but I want to tweak the plan. Have her interview another therapist and then go for media coverage. Maybe we can get some computer donations for the rehab centers."

"I'm on it. What happens now?"

"Well, I hope I never see Leone again." Alana pressed her palm against her forehead. "Such an arrogant woman. The clothes were outrageous, and as soon as I suggested they wouldn't work in our magazine, she snapped. I thought she was going to hit me."

"Were you scared?"

"I was. Victor was waiting in the hallway, and we took off running. I think he was afraid of her, too. I've decided I'm not cut out to decide next year's fashion choices, except for myself. I wish you could have been with me."

Michelle wiped her hands on a towel and leaned toward the screen.

"I'd have given anything to have been there. Actually, it all sounds like quite the adventure. I'm a little envious." Michelle rubbed her belly in a circular motion. "No exciting travel plans for me for a *long* time. We'll have to save for college. See? Travel now while you can."

"Yeah, but you're about to embark on the adventure of a lifetime. How do you feel?"

"I experienced my first morning sickness, but it wasn't too bad. Nothing a few crackers couldn't solve. It came on two days ago, so we'll see."

"Glad it's under control. Let me know how Taylor's interview goes."

"Will do. What are your plans today?"

"I'd like to venture outside the city. There's no way I'll be able to see all the main attractions in Paris. The Louvre was closed yesterday, so I took a Seine River cruise and toured Sainte-Chapelle."

"Don't waste time talking to me," Michelle said. "Experience everything you can. We're organized here. Go," she said and pointed a sweet potato at Alana.

Alana gave her a two-finger salute. "*Au revoir*, Michelle."

"*Au revoir.*"

Alana put on her Nikes, stopped at the concierge desk, and asked if they could arrange for a driver to take her to Rouen and Normandy. After a short wait, she was in the backseat of a mid-sized car. Stephan, her driver, assured her he spoke perfect English and would take care of her for the day.

He pointed out famous landmarks on their way out of the city toward the town of Rouen. Alana knew she couldn't go home without seeing the cathedral Monet had captured on canvas so many times. Rouen was also the city known for honoring Joan of Arc, Alana's childhood hero.

"I'm fascinated with medieval times," she told Stephan. "I've always admired Joan of Arc for her courage. I did a paper on her in college."

"We have great love in our hearts for her," Stephan said.

Alana flipped through her guidebook and stopped on a page with a picture depicting Joan's death. She was tied to a pillar, looking toward the heavens, as she was burned alive.

"It says she was executed at nineteen." Alana couldn't imagine a young girl outlining military strategies and waving a banner instead of a weapon.

"*Oui*, but they had no record of her birth. They could only guess her age. If not for her, we would still be under English rule. The voice of God guided her. Such a miracle."

Alana didn't tell him that doctors and scholars had diagnosed the saint as having schizophrenia, bipolar disorder, and even bovine tuberculosis. What mattered was that the woman believed in her convictions enough to die for them.

"She was very brave, *monsieur*."

Alana recalled the image of herself running down the corridor to escape Leone's wrath. She held the page close to her breast and vowed to be a little more of a fearless warrior, a little more like Joan.

CHAPTER 45

On the way back to the hotel, worlds away from the past, she reflected on the day. Alana decided her favorite part was the beach at Normandy. So haunting and beautiful. She hadn't expected to be so moved at the American Cemetery overlooking Omaha Beach. White crosses had marked the graves of the more than nine thousand U.S. servicemen who died during the D-Day invasion.

"Thank you, Stephan. I had a fantastic afternoon touring the countryside. You were a wonderful guide."

"My pleasure," he said.

The lights in front of the hotel illuminated the water in the fountain. Even in the shadows, she knew who it was. He turned. "Alana."

"Borg . . . what are you doing in Paris?"

He smiled broadly as if to reassure her. "I spoke with Victor yesterday, and he explained everything. He was powerless in this situation. I booked a flight the moment I was informed. I understand there was an unpleasant encounter with Leone."

"An understatement," Alana said, still flushed with surprise.

"I'm very sorry. Allow me to explain. Leone is *not* in charge. She can be very aggressive. She was eager to show her work and used the opportunity to have you view her personal line." His distrust of Leone was clear.

"Oh! So those weren't Martine's designs?" The bellman opened the door, and they moved into the lobby and found seats near the piano bar.

Borg apologized again. "Martine is back, and Leone and her line no longer exist at La Chic Boutique. Martine is at her office and wondered if you would give her another chance, this evening . . . now, actually."

Alana's eyebrows rose. "It's late, and I've been out sightseeing all day."

"She said she would wait if you would come back."

Clearly, Borg was upset that she had been duped by Leone. He *did* fly all the way to Paris hoping she would give Martine a chance. The poor man probably had jet lag. Alana yawned. "Okay. I'll go with you. Give me a minute to change. I don't want to meet Martine dressed so unprofessionally." She pointed at her tennis shoes. Alana crossed toward the elevators.

"*Mademoiselle Hudson, s'il vous plait.*" The concierge approached and extended a note. "This arrived for you a short time ago."

Alana opened the memo and read, "You will need to pay." She flipped the paper over. It was blank, and there was no signature. "I don't understand. Where did this come from?"

"A woman stopped by the desk less than an hour ago and asked if this could be delivered to Alana Hudson. This is all I know."

"Odd. I haven't purchased anything. I'm sure it must be a mistake. Could you throw this away for me?" She gave it back to him.

Alana went to her room and changed. She returned to find Borg conversing with an attendant. "Everything is arranged," Borg said. A bellman motioned, and a limousine edged to the curb.

Alana greeted the driver, followed Borg toward the back, and sprawled across one of the spacious seats. They left for La Chic Boutique.

Exhausted from the day tour, Alana collapsed against the leather cushion and breathed the faint scent of Borg's cologne.

From heavy lids, she saw the refrigerator door open. Borg removed a tray lined with biscotti, cookies, and fat strawberries dipped in chocolate.

"I arranged for some snacks. Are you hungry?" he asked, and offered her the tray.

She shifted in the seat. "Very. Tired *and* famished." Alana plucked a fat strawberry from the tray and popped it in her mouth. The chocolate dissolved on her tongue. She reached for a cookie. "Aren't you exhausted?"

"I slept a bit on the plane and caught another couple of hours at the hotel. Tea?"

"Please."

Borg poured them each a cup, took a piece of biscotti, and softened it in his drink. "After Victor told me what happened with Leone, I knew you'd want to end all association with the boutique."

"So you flew all the way to Paris to convince me?"

"I did, because I'm certain you'll like Martine's line. Leone poisoned your view, which was unfair to Martine. She's a good person."

The ride was smoother than the motorbike. The driver turned into the lot and parked.

Alana and Borg traversed the hall farther than she'd done on her previous visit. A door's nameplate read M. Duprey. Borg rapped twice.

"*Oui, entrez,*" a melodic voice called out.

Seated on a bold black and white striped couch, a trim woman in her early sixties rose to greet them. "*Bonjour, mon ami,*" she said and kissed Borg on each cheek. "You must be Alana. I am Martine Duprey. Lovely to meet you." Tiny charms on her bracelet jingled.

The office was small but intimate. Two chairs covered in luxurious fabric rested on either side of the settee. Fashion books were stacked neatly atop the coffee table. *Madame* Duprey smoothed her skirt against the back of her legs, sat on the couch, and invited them to join her.

"Please forgive us for the terrible treatment you received from Leone. You are under no obligation to like our clothing line. Leone's work has always been quite different. We encourage individuality, but she was deceptive. It is not tolerated."

"Thank you, *Madame* Duprey—"

"No, I insist, call me Martine. Is this your first time to Paris?" she asked.

"Yes, it has always been a dream of mine to visit France."

"Welcome. May I offer you a drink? Perhaps you would like some champagne or wine?"

"Champagne would be superb," Alana said.

"*Deux*," Borg said.

A delicate laugh escaped Martine's lips. "*Trois, c'est ça.*" She called her assistant, and in moments the bottle arrived, uncorked, with three glasses. Martine poured the champagne and raised her glass. "Let us now examine the line you were *supposed* to see."

On the way to the showroom, Martine talked about her company. As soon as they were seated, the lights dimmed, and the show began.

The clothes Martine presented were a mix of solid, bold colors and unique prints—designs much more acceptable to *Slick* readers. Alana was particularly impressed by several outfits printed with French Impressionists' and Cubists' paintings on the fabrics. The show concluded, the models bowed, and the curtain closed.

"What did you think?" Martine asked. "Our desire was to keep it simple, yet stylish."

"I loved the way you paired the jackets with the dresses. The jacket with Picasso's *Three Dancers* was my favorite."

Martine's smile indicated she was pleased. "I look forward to your comments. We want our choices to be appropriate for your magazine."

"They were all wonderful. Choosing what *not* to include will be difficult."

"If we go forward with negotiations, I would like the first run to start with eight outfits," Martine said. "If your schedule allows, perhaps tomorrow we might oversee the final selections."

"All right."

"Is ten o'clock agreeable?"

"I'll be here in the morning, and we'll conclude our meeting," Alana said.

They said their good-byes, and Alana and Borg crossed the parking lot to the waiting limo.

CHAPTER 46

"Are you glad you gave the boutique a second chance?" Borg asked on the ride back to the hotel.

"Ask me tomorrow."

"If the line is successful, the number of ads can be raised—meaning increased revenue for the magazine," Borg said.

"I think we're getting ahead of ourselves. I've only seen a sample of their work. We need to consider consistency in demand and analyze consumer buying patterns. I have many concerns."

"We'd be lucky to get an exclusive with her," Borg said.

The limo halted under the Hilton's canopy, and Borg spoke with the chauffeur a moment.

The bellman opened the door for them. "I've hired a car to provide transportation for tomorrow. Unless you'd rather ride with Victor." Alana could see Borg was trying not to smile.

"Oh, trust me, that wasn't funny."

"Victor told me he would provide transportation. I didn't know he drove a motorbike." Borg handed Alana two business cards. "Here is Martine's information. I've arranged for a different driver; the other card is his number."

"You won't be there?"

"No, I have a conference call, but I'll meet you here afterward, and we'll fly back together. I'm used to quick business trips. Would you like to have dinner tonight?"

"I'm tired. I think I'll order room service." She could have sworn she saw disappointment in his face.

"Probably a wise plan."

In the elevator, Alana pressed the button for the fourth floor, her finger still poised. "Your floor?"

"Same. I'm in room 422."

"Oh, I'm in 428."

The elevator door opened. They started down the hall and paused at his door.

"I guess I'll see you tomorrow," she said. "Good night."

"Good night, Alana."

She walked down the hall and slid her card in the slot. Borg waited by his door. Maybe she should have accepted his dinner invitation, but she feared it would have been perceived as a date. Everything was business. Why should she expect anything else?

• • •

Borg wiped his face with a hot washcloth and went to the lounge for appetizers and a glass of wine. Back in his room, his thoughts turned to Alana. She seemed to like Martine, which was important. Martine was a trusted friend he had known for years. They were close to making the deal, and now he could relax, comfortable the two could work well together. But he needed to persuade Alana to take the final step: agree to sign him on as a partner. It was mandatory. Borg had plans for the new magazine. Who knew where the venture could lead?

He thought of Alana, down the hall, only three rooms away. Suddenly, the room seemed warm, stifling. He turned up the air-conditioning, hung up his clothes, and put on his robe. He had learned not to let personal feelings get in the way during a transaction. This is a business deal, he reminded himself.

CHAPTER 47

The room was stuffy. Alana raised the window and propped herself against the sill. The cool night air brushed her face, and the curtains fluttered in the gentle breeze. The French, like most Europeans, preferred windows without screens. The Eiffel Tower glimmered in the distance, and Alana lingered at the window, taking in the panorama.

She hadn't eaten since lunch, with the exception of the few snacks she and Borg had shared in the limo. Too tired to go to the lounge, Alana reviewed the room service menu and called in an order for soup and salad. The woman on the phone told her it would be at least half an hour. Alana snacked on a bag of chips before she cleaned up.

This had to be the longest day of her life. Alana turned her back and let the hot shower rinse the shampoo from her hair, sending her fatigue down the drain with the suds. She dried off and found a comfy T-shirt, sweatpants, and supple ballet flats.

Borg seemed certain she was up to the task of selecting retail. It was she who carried the doubts about being right for the job, especially now, a world away from home. Maybe, with Martine's help, they could come up with a strategy to analyze trends. Borg desperately wanted to carry Martine's line. Alana was confident the ads would be successful, but she remained unconvinced that Borg should get a share in *Slick*.

The quiet was broken by a soft, insistent tapping. "Coming," she said.

It wasn't room service. Alana hardly recognized her. Leone's face was contorted with fury. She held a pistol in her right hand, unhidden. Alana shoved the door, but Leone's foot wedged in the opening. She forced her way in, and the door clicked behind her.

"You've made a terrible mistake." The gun was low, aimed at Alana's stomach. "You have ruined me. I lost my job and have no references. Martine will destroy my reputation. I've been disgraced, and you're responsible."

"No, this was your fault. You tricked me," Alana said. She scanned the room. There was nowhere to run. Nothing to protect her. "Think of the consequences if you shoot me. You'll go to jail, prison."

"My pistol is equipped with a suppressor. I will be gone, and there will be no trail."

Alana took a step back. "What if I told Martine I changed my mind? Said I loved your clothes?"

Leone shook her head. "It is too late."

A sharp rap on the door startled them. "Who are you expecting?" The gun waved back and forth.

"Room service. I ordered dinner."

Leone crept into the bathroom, raised the revolver, and squinted down the rear sight. "Get rid of him. I came for you, but I have many bullets." She left the opening cracked wide enough to accommodate the gun barrel.

Alana opened the door.

"*Bonjour, bonjour,*" the young man said. He placed a plastic stopper at the door's base to hold it open and pushed a cart covered with a white tablecloth into the middle of the room. A single rose in a thin vase was flanked by a bowl and plate, topped with silver covers.

"You have ordered some dinner, *oui?*"

He was thin, gangly, and boyish. Too young to die.

"Thank you. I'm sure I'll enjoy it. Just leave it there, please."

"Oh, *mais non*. My papa, he is chef. He has prepared pumpkin soup and *Salade Nicoise*. *C'est très bon!* A meal is a celebration to be enjoyed, *n'est pas?* Allow me to move the chair for you. Do you wish to order some wine?"

She took euros from her purse to tip him. "No, nothing more. Thank your father for me, uh . . ."

"*Je suis Eric.*"

"That will be all. *Merci, Eric.*" Her heart raced. He seemed disappointed. She guessed he was new and enthusiastic, and aspired to please the American—and his papa. The bathroom was dark, but Alana saw the crack had widened, and the hall light illuminated the glint of metal and Leone's faint reflection in the mirror. Leone's shoulders were raised, her arms straight, the gun poised and ready.

"Your meal has been beautifully prepared. Allow me." Eric gripped the metal covers and removed them with dramatic flair. "*Voila!*"

A faint click was barely perceptible. Maybe Leone had taken off the safety. Eric followed Alana's gaze. The gun was now visible through the crack of the door.

Eric froze. "*Mon Dieu!*"

Leone slinked from the shadow, shifting the gun between them. She paused an imperceptible beat. In that split-second, Eric loosened his grip on the tray covers and hurled them at her. He shoved the cart into her legs. The vase toppled onto the plate, and the soup splashed the tablecloth. Leone fired and missed. Eric bolted out the door, feet stomping toward the stairs. Leone stumbled into the hallway, cursing.

An inner voice urged Alana: Run! But her feet were implanted like tree roots. Heavy. Cemented to the floor with fear. The stairway exit was to the right, two rooms past hers. Leone wouldn't follow Eric down the steps. Leone had come for her.

Alana bolted to the window, tore back the curtain, and hoisted herself onto the sill. She climbed out onto the thin perch and screamed, a primal reaction, alerting danger. Below her, the ground rose and fell. There was a heaving sensation in her stomach. Alana felt lightheaded, and some unknown force nudged her, trying to pull her over the edge. A chill ran down her arms. She closed her eyes, hoping to regain her equilibrium. She rose on the balls of her feet, arms stretched wide, searching for a fingerhold, and she prayed to not slip. The only light was from the slice of moon tattooed in the sky and the two lampposts in the deserted courtyard below.

Where was Leone? Alana pressed her stomach against the wall, inching along the ledge. The next window was dark. The last room, the one by the stairs, cast a dim light. The faint glow beckoned. Surely the guests would help her—if they didn't think a woman standing on a ledge outside their room was crazy.

Four floors up had never seemed high, but she had never been trapped on a five-inch-wide ledge with nothing to protect her. Like walking a tightrope. Damp hair stuck to her forehead. Her breathing came fast and shallow, making her dizzy.

Alana stopped and clung to the wall, paralyzed. A strong image of Joan of Arc flashed in her mind, Joan on horseback leading men into battle. Alana slowed her breath and prayed. Help me, Joan. Somewhere in the distance, sirens sounded, but she could barely hear them. The pounding of her heartbeat was too loud.

Breathe slowly, she thought. What was it her teacher had said? *Deep. From your belly. The way babies breathe.* Alana focused on her breath and willed her legs to move. The narrow ledge demanded she walk on tiptoes. She shuffled along, counting steps in her head. Palms to the wall, her cheek scraped against the stone.

Her calves cramped, sustaining the awkward position, and she desperately wanted to knead the spasm to stop the pain. Panic interfered with her perception. She miscalculated the next step and swayed backward. Alana thrust her weight back toward the wall and regained her balance.

She turned, expecting to see Leone and her pistol taking aim. She was alone except for a pigeon roosting on the gutter. The bird cooed and fluttered away. Garbled noise drifted from her window. Definitely voices, but the wind and the distance broke the words, leaving only muffled tones. Maybe the boy had sent help. Were the police in her room? She couldn't risk calling for help until she knew Leone was gone. Surely Eric had reported what had happened.

Two more steps. Thank God. Alana hammered the glass with the side of her fist. No one came. She peered inside. The room, illuminated by a desk lamp, appeared empty. At the bottom of the window was a slight gap. Alana pried underneath the sash and lifted until she could crawl through the opening.

"Hello," she called out and stepped into the room. Two suitcases were open on the floor, the bedspread was rumpled, and a pair of men's slacks were draped across a chair. Alana collapsed on the edge of the bed. Who was in *her* room? She rose, yanked a towel from the bathroom shelf, and propped the door to keep it from locking behind her. The elevator dinged. A chambermaid clutching bottles of shampoo rounded the corner and knocked on a guest's door. Alana waved her arms to get her attention, but the woman disappeared into the room for a few only seconds, emerged, and stepped back into the elevator without looking up.

Alana stole down the corridor. The plastic wedge still propped her door. She heard Borg's voice. "It's over. Give me the gun and walk away. You haven't done anything we can't forget."

Alana raced back to the empty room and dialed the operator. "I need help. No, *not Madame* Allard, I'm Alana Hudson, and I need you to connect me with security. No, se-cur-i-ty. Do you speak English?"

A shriek echoed in the corridor. "Let go *maintenant!*" Alana dropped the phone, darted to the door, and pulled it opened a few inches. The hall was quiet. A snap broke the silence, and Leone bolted from the room, the pistol still locked in her grip. Alana kicked the towel out of the way. The door closed, barely touching the frame. Alana watched through the crevice. Leone ran toward the exit. Her tread echoed only seconds on the stairway and then disappeared.

Alana raced to her room and found Borg leaning against the nightstand, the color drained from his face. The receiver had dropped to the floor. His white robe was darkening with red. Blood. There was so much blood. Alana lunged for the phone. "Hello! Is anyone there? A man's been shot. We're in room 428. You understand? Send help. Hurry!"

Borg's legs folded. Alana tucked a pillow under his head. She sprinted for a towel, crouched over him, and held pressure against his shoulder.

"Am I hurting you? We need to control the bleeding." His skin was gray, and his mouth had gone pale.

"Hold on. It shouldn't be long. They've called for an ambulance. Borg? Borg?" The robe was soaked red. It smelled metallic, strong, and the sight of it sickened her. He had come to protect her from Leone. Now she wished to protect him. Alana put her head against Borg's chest and listened for a heartbeat. He touched her arm. "I'm so weak."

She whispered in his ear. "Please. Don't die."

• • •

Footsteps thundered down the hall, the heavy stride of an army. Voices grew closer. An entourage of men barged into the room: two paramedics rolling a gurney and two police officers. The hotel's night manager trailed behind them. The taller officer began to shout at Alana. *"Qu'est-il arrivé?"* but she shook her head. One of the medics brushed her aside to attend to Borg.

"Elle ne comprend pas. She doesn't understand," Borg said, his voice barely audible.

The other officer tugged his mustache. His English was understandable, but his accent thick. "You were spotted on the ledge outside the building, *mademoiselle.* That was most dangerous."

"At the time, it seemed more *dangerous* to stay in the room and let a mad woman shoot me." She read his badge. "Officer Barreau."

Officer Barreau's thick eyebrows furrowed together like a long caterpillar. He scribbled notes on a pad. "This was done by a woman?" he asked.

"Yes, her name is Leone Davin," Alana said. "What took so long to get here? She attacked the boy from room service. Was this not reported?"

"Pardon, mademoiselle, the boy was found hiding in one of the storage rooms. He was most frightened," the night manager said.

"Enough. We have questions about the shooting," Barreau said.

Alana tried to answer but was distracted. She tried not to look at the robe. The medics moved Borg, exposing the hole in his shoulder. He moaned, and Alana fought the nausea rising to her throat.

"I am going to give you morphine for pains, *monsieur*. Are you allergic?" the medic asked.

"No."

The medic injected the drug into a vein, took a roll of gauze from his bag, and wrapped the wound. The men hoisted Borg onto the gurney.

"*Attendez*," the manager said, "for his privacy." He quickly covered Borg's shoulder with a bath towel.

"I have to go with them," Alana said to the officers. She picked up her purse and followed them to the elevator.

The wheeled stretcher took most of the space. "It is too crowded for any more persons in the lift," the officer said. "We will wait for the next one."

"No, they can't leave without me." Alana ran down the hall to the stairwell.

"*Mademoiselle,* you must wait . . ."

But Alana was already racing down the steps.

CHAPTER 48

"I think your phone's ringing," Rosie said.

Chelsea handed the necklace back to the salesclerk and dug inside her purse. "Hey, babe. . . . Really? . . . Okay, talk to you soon."

"What's up?" Rosie asked.

"Noah's brother asked his girlfriend, Saige, to live with him—"

"Saige?" Rosie interrupted. "What's Saige's last name?"

"Santoro."

"God—small world. Is this the girl Finn mentioned might meet us at the bowling alley?"

"You know her?"

"Yeah, she's a new friend."

"You never mentioned her," Chelsea said.

"We met at the Jive. Saige talked about him. I didn't know he was Noah's brother. She always called him 'my boyfriend.' Did she give him an answer?"

"She said yes! Finn's practically doing somersaults. We're having dinner to celebrate," Chelsea said. "Want to come with us?"

Rosie wondered if now would be the right time to tell Chelsea her secrets. She wanted to talk about last night. Carlos had left the house with Ray, and Rosie had packed her Casio keyboard to take to Adam. On the way home, she'd stopped for a few items at the grocery store.

Back in the kitchen last night, she'd set the bread on the counter and passed the dark living room. Her heart had jumped at Carlos's shadowy outline, barely visible in the dark room. She hadn't known he'd be home.

A gruff snort followed by a whistle had broken the silence. Rosie had hurried to the bedroom, undressed, and climbed under the covers.

The thud of Carlos's shoes hitting the floor had jolter her, but she'd pretended to be asleep. The mattress had sunk under his weight, and stale beer breath had signaled that he was hovering above her. Without warning, he'd coiled a fistful of her hair, jerking her neck back.

"Don't!"

"Shut up. I don't want to have to be wonderin' where my wife is. You got to understand the rules." Rosie had tried to reach over her shoulder to stop him, but Carlos had driven his knee into her back.

"Don't be fightin' me. Where'd you go so late?"

"Bread. . . . I went out for bread."

"You be home from now on. You hear?"

"I hear you."

"Good, because it seems to me you keep forgetting." He'd unthreaded a few strands of her hair from his thumb and flicked them onto the floor. He'd rolled on his side, and minutes later, loud snores had vibrated in the back of his throat. Rosie had moved to the edge of the bed, afraid to sleep.

Chelsea touched Rosie's arm. "Rosie? I asked if you could come celebrate with us."

"Not tonight, Chelsea. I'll pass." She smoothed the back her hair. "Maybe you and Saige could come over to my place this weekend. I need to talk about something."

CHAPTER 49

On Saturday, Ray picked up Carlos to go downtown to a baseball game. Rosie straightened the house and watched out the window. By the time Chelsea and Saige parked in the driveway, Rosie had unlocked the door.

"Come in." She guided them toward the kitchen.

"I think this is great," Saige said. "Finn and I are a little cramped in his apartment. Can I ask you about how much your house payments are?"

"I don't really know. Carlos controls the money."

In the kitchen, Rosie filled glasses with ice and poured tea.

"I wondered if you'd ever invite me over," Chelsea said.

"I couldn't."

"What do you mean?" Saige asked.

"My husband doesn't like me having friends. Carlos's been like that since we were married, and it's gotten worse. Lately, he doesn't even want me to go out."

"But we go out." Chelsea looked confused.

"He doesn't balk if I do errands, my usual excuse. I work a lot of 3:00 until 11:00 p.m. shifts, and he has to work at least two Saturdays a month, so that gives me some freedom." She scratched her cuticles. "Usually I have to hide my activities from him. But it's gotten worse. He's more aggressive."

"What happened?" Chelsea asked.

"Do you remember the night we were supposed to meet at the bowling alley? He knocked me down and took away my keys."

Saige gasped.

"Last week, I told him I wanted out of the marriage, and he hit me." Rosie ducked her head, embarrassed to share the story. She untied the silk scarf she wore, exposing blue thumbprints on her neck.

"Rosie, oh my God! You have to *leave*," Chelsea said. "Tell your parents, call the police . . . do something. Why are you still here? Go home. You have family."

"I can't. He threatened to hurt my mother if I leave him."

"He's a jerk!" Chelsea said. "You shouldn't stay another minute. Did you warn your mom?"

Rosie shook her head. "No. I didn't. I don't know if she'd believe me. Her ways are different. She believes women should be subservient to men. She told me God doesn't believe in divorce. I wondered if I showed her my bruises . . ." Rosie trailed off. "I was going to ask if I could come home, but I'm scared."

"Can you afford to make it on your own?" Saige asked.

"I don't think so," Rosie said.

"There are places that help women—safe houses. Or you can stay with us. Rosie, the police would help you," Chelsea said.

"I don't want to live in a shelter. If I stayed with you and Carlos found out where you live, I don't know what he'd do. To either of us. Haven't you heard the stories about the men who find a way to come after their wives? I'll take care of the situation. My way."

"I'm not afraid of your bully husband," Chelsea said. "Do you hear yourself? If he's hurting you, you have to get out. You deserve happiness—a man who will treat you right. Let us help you."

Rosie scoffed. "Another man, right." Rosie's expression changed. "I really just wanted you to know about my situation.

I don't want you to try to fix it, okay? I'm going to lay low for now. And I don't want either of you to tell the guys. This is private. If you tell, it could end badly for me. I just needed to talk."

Rosie saw Chelsea exchange a look with Saige and hoped she'd been right to confide in them. And she *was* going to take care of things.

CHAPTER 50

Alana and the officers caught up with the crew in front of the hotel. She caught a glimpse of Borg's ashen face as the medics hoisted him into the ambulance.

Alana pleaded with the officer. "Please tell them I want to be with him. I don't speak French. I don't know where the hospital is . . ."

One of the medics motioned for her to enter the ambulance. She climbed in and sat beside Borg. She drew a deep breath to calm the fear gnawing inside her. The ambulance raced through the streets of Paris. Buildings blurred into hazy shapes and streaks of light until the vehicle stopped at the hospital emergency entrance. A set of double doors swung open and automatically closed behind the medics. A receptionist wagged her finger at Alana and shook her head. She pointed to chairs in a small waiting area and gave Alana a clipboard with papers to fill out.

The police, moments behind, ushered her into a separate room for further questioning. "We received this picture. Is this the woman in question?"

"Yes."

"Can you explain a possible motive for this behavior?"

"I don't know, greedy, delusional . . . psychotic?" Alana told them why she was in France, and what had happened. She retrieved Martine's card from her wallet and gave them her information.

After they took her statement, *Monsieur* Charette, the taller officer, thanked her, and the men left. Alana completed the paper-work as best she could, leaving much of it blank, and returned it to the receptionist, who told her in broken English that the bill would need to be paid in full prior to the patient leaving the hospital. So much for universal health care. Alana was glad she had brought her purse.

· · ·

An hour later, the police returned and asked Alana to come with them. She followed them into a small, windowless room and sat at an empty table with four chairs. A small metal crucifix hung on the wall. Barreau removed a document from a folder tucked under his arm and skimmed the page. "We obtained evidence that *Mademoiselle* Davin purchased the suppressor only yesterday. We believe this violence was premeditated. Leone Davin has a previous record of assault." His smile indicated he was satisfied. "We have traced her address. We *will* find her."

Alana wasn't so sure. She feared she might encounter Leone anywhere—on the street, back at the hotel, or in an elevator. Borg had taken the bullet intended for her. "If you have no further questions, I'd like to go back to the waiting room."

"Of course," Barreau said with a small bow. "Please do not leave the hospital, *mademoiselle*."

The minutes ticked by. Alana approached the reception desk. The woman shook her head. Alana paced the floor. She was alone in Paris.

An older gentleman who had been seated across from her left and returned with a cup of coffee. "Café au lait?" he asked, and offered the cup.

"*Merci, monsieur.*" She gulped the coffee. Another hour passed. Alana waited until Borg emerged in a wheelchair pushed by a woman with curly red hair. A balding man wearing a lab coat trailed behind. Alana assumed he was the doctor and hurried toward them.

Dark circles hung under Borg's eyes. "I told them I could walk."

"No." The nurse sniffed. "It is policy."

They stopped at the door marked Sortie. The doctor gave Borg two bottles of pills. "The white ones are for pain, and the blue one is an antibiotic." The doctor addressed Alana. "The bullet has been removed. It entered the arm near his shoulder and was lodged in the muscle bundle."

"How many stitches?" Alana asked.

"None. To suture could cause infection."

"Are you sure he's ready to leave?" She couldn't believe he didn't need to stay overnight.

"The bullet was embedded in the soft tissue and removed. There were no internal injuries. He does not need to stay. He has pain, but he will be fine."

"*Monsieur*," he turned to Borg, "you must take *all* the antibiotics, *vous comprenez*?" he asked.

"Yes, I understand. Thank you for everything."

"Do not hesitate to call if you have questions."

The police returned, took the bullet from the orderly, and placed it in a bag. They showed Borg the copy of Leone's picture. Borg confirmed, "Yes, she's the woman who shot me."

"You have no more to worry," Barreau said. "She was packing a suitcase when we arrived at her apartment. *Mademoiselle* Davin was restrained and is now behind bars. We have the gun, which will no doubt match this." He held up the bag with a single bullet smeared with dried blood.

Alana's stomached tightened at the small pellet intended to end her life. "Thank God," she said, exhaling a sigh of relief. The

French police had moved so quickly, she no longer had to fear Leone stalking her.

"Her jacket has provided additional evidence." The officer ran a finger around his upper lip. "The soup on the tablecloth matched the stains on her sleeve. The server, Eric, and several others in the hotel also identified *Mademoiselle* Davin. This case is, as you say, 'ironclad.' You are free to go, of course. *Bonne nuit.*"

"Right," Alana said, not caring if her tone was sarcastic. "*Bonne nuit.*" Tonight had been anything but good.

The receptionist accepted Alana's credit card, discharged Borg, and called for a taxi. An aide helped Borg into the backseat. "You are weak, *monsieur*. Be careful," he said, and shut the door. The taxi sped toward the Hilton.

"You okay?" Alana tugged at Borg's seat belt and adjusted it off his shoulder.

"Yes. And you?"

Alana nodded, collapsing against the seat.

"Good pair of lungs you have, *Mademoiselle* Hudson. The commotion in the hall, along with your scream, alerted me. Let's say Leone was very surprised to see me." His amused expression changed. He squinted and breathed in through his teeth.

"Does it hurt very much?"

"It does. I'm right-handed, so I'm lucky the bullet hit my left shoulder. You must have been petrified out there on the ledge. I'm sure it took a lot of courage."

Alana smiled at his word choice. "Yes, courage. I was praying for it."

"It's over now, and you're . . . we're safe. I do feel a bit ridiculous riding in a taxi wearing this vile robe."

At the hotel, a doorman rushed to the taxi. "We will compensate the driver," he said.

The hotel was quiet and the lobby empty. The night manager hurried over to them. "*Ah, monsieur, ça va?*"

"I'm fine, Robert."

"We are so glad you are fine." He cleared his throat. "A shooting in our hotel . . ." He tsked. "*C'est terrible.* No one knows exactly what happened—"

"We will keep this discreet."

"*Merci, Monsieur* Larson. *Mademoiselle,* we have cleaned your room, and everything is spotless. Perhaps you would like to move? May we assist you in any way?"

"I'm tired. I don't wish to change rooms," Alana said. "I didn't have a chance to eat. Are you hungry?" she asked Borg.

"A little, but I'm mostly exhausted," Borg said. "Would you come to my room for a while?"

"Yes, I'll help get you settled."

"We will have food brought to your room immediately, complimentary, of course," the manager said. "Chef prepared a chicken vegetable stew earlier."

Alana nodded her thanks. "Could you send an extra key to his room? I may need to check on him. And another robe, quickly, please."

The bellman assisted Borg to his room, and housekeeping arrived with the new robe within minutes. Alana held up a finger to the woman. "One moment."

Borg winced and strode to the lavatory to change. Alana followed him. "Let me help." She untied the bloody robe and carefully eased it off his shoulders. She then guided his arms into the sleeves of the new robe and tightened the belt around his waist. She passed the soiled robe to the housekeeper. The woman wrinkled her nose, held the garment at arm's distance, gave Alana the extra key, and left.

"I appreciate your coming to the hospital," Borg said.

Alana's mood darkened. "You saved my life."

A quiet knock signaled that their food had arrived. Borg eased into a chair, and they sat to eat. "Smells delicious," Alana said. The soup was filled with vegetables, hearty and soothing, but after a few bites, Borg put down his spoon.

"What's wrong?" Alana asked.

"I . . . I don't know." His eyes glazed. "It's probably the pain medicine. I'm woozy."

Alana helped him to his feet. They were steps away from the bed. "Easy does it. Lean on me." Borg was heavy, and Alana struggled under his weight as he sagged against her. She feared they would both fall. He slumped forward, his arm dangling loosely around her neck.

He crumpled onto the bed. Alana removed his shoes and drew the coverlet across his chest. She placed a glass of water next to the bottle and jotted a note. *You'll probably sleep through the night. Your medicine is on the nightstand. Call if you need me.*

In her room, she hung the Do Not Disturb sign and climbed into bed, where most of the night, hazy nightmares interrupted her sleep.

CHAPTER 51

Adam lay on his back and waited for morning. Since the diagnosis, he didn't sleep much. His parents informed him they planned to pay the rent on his apartment. They were pleased that he had changed his status at the university and was auditing his classes instead of taking them for a grade. Adam knew his parents were trying to give him a purpose, a *raison d'être.*

He finished breakfast, waited until after seven, and telephoned the Jive. "This is Adam McGuire. Is Hanna working today?"

A pleasant voice answered, "Another fan. Everybody wants coffee from Hanna. Let me check the schedule. I think she works this morning. Hold on." After a minute: "She comes in at nine."

Adam drove to the Jive and waited in his car until he caught sight of Hanna near the side entrance.

"Hanna!" Adam hurried from the car.

She waited at the door.

"I don't know if you recognize me."

"Adam, of course. Coffee, black." She smiled. "You want to talk. You think I have answers."

"Yes."

"I start work in twenty minutes." She led him to a table in the back where they were alone.

"I went to your meditation class." Did she remember him? There were so many in the class.

"You haven't been back in a couple of weeks. You shouldn't wait," Hanna said. "It's good to know how to quiet the mind.

You're not sleeping well, are you?"

He shook his head. "You know I'm sick?"

"You have shadows under your eyes, you've lost weight, and I overheard you talking to Rosie."

"I've lost control over my life."

"You have control."

"I don't see how."

"Your mind was born for logic. You'll know what to do."

"You can't tell me?"

She shook her head. "It's up to you to find the answers. Remember, you *can't* force your body to heal. You have to find peace and accept what is happening to you. Practice meditation to lessen your anxiety. Come back to the center. I'll help you."

CHAPTER 52

Saige kissed Finn good-bye.

"How about I pick up Chinese on my way home? General Tsao's chicken and rice?"

"Yum. And egg rolls?" Saige asked.

"And egg rolls."

"Sounds perfect." She checked the time. "I have to leave. I don't want to be late."

"Don't worry. You're always early." His arm slipped around her waist. "Did you talk to your father?"

"Not since the argument about us living together. I'm more annoyed about all the flack he gave me regarding my decision to leave the bank. I think he should call me."

"Somebody has to yield. Call him. Make it right."

"I didn't do anything wrong. It's my life, my choice. But maybe I'll stop by Saturday and talk to him."

The entry area was crammed with smashed cereal boxes, discarded mail, and empty tin cans in paper bags. Finn had a habit of letting the recycling pile up. It was invisible to him. To Saige, it was an unsightly, annoying mess. "Will you take out the recycle stuff, please? It's so sloppy stacked by the door."

"I'll try to remember."

"Try hard, okay?"

"Oh, getting a little bossy?"

His word choice irked her. She wasn't asking for much. "It

doesn't take but a *minute* to run it out. The dumpster's a little tall for me."

"I *said* I'd try to remember. It's the way I've always done things. I hate lots of little trips."

"Well, I hate the mess. See you tonight."

Her parents had taught her not to stir up conflict. Had Finn detected the anger in her tone? Didn't he know how difficult it was for her to speak up and ask him?

Saige's mood lightened when she spotted a deer grazing by a stand of trees in the field below the bluffs. Kelly, one of her bosses, lived in Glen Brook, an undeveloped section on the west side of town. Her Cape Cod home served as their office.

Saige's first two months on the job had passed quickly. She always arrived early, and some mornings, Beth gave her a basic software lesson using Photoshop. At lunchtime, they congregated in Kelly's kitchen, discussing new projects and current events. Saige was always sorry to see the day end. Every night on her way home, she told herself she had found the perfect job.

This morning, as usual, the door was unlocked. Saige let herself in. The sun's rays sparkled on Kelly's collection of blue glass.

The women were at their computers in the makeshift office set up in Kelly's former dining room. "Good morning," Saige said, her voice cheery. She reached in the wire basket next to her station and retrieved the folder with the day's work.

Kelly pushed back her chair. "I have some bad news. We didn't get the Meyer account."

"Oh, no," Saige said.

"It gets worse. I got an e-mail from Koehler yesterday. He cut out 50 percent of the work he originally indicated he needed.

Beth shook her head. "The loss will significantly affect our budget."

"I spent last night crunching numbers." Kelly rubbed her temples "Beth and I can't afford to pay for extra help."

Saige's stomach twisted. "You're firing me?"

"We love having you on our team. But losing these accounts, we can't afford to employ you. We'll give you some time to work this out. I am so sorry."

Tears welled in Saige's eyes. Finding this job had been a fluke—blind luck. Here she was again, stuck behind a door without a knob. "Would you like me to leave now?"

"No, of course not," Beth said.

Saige snatched her purse. "You'll never know what this job has meant to me. But I think I should go."

"I wish you'd stay," Beth said.

"No, really, I think I should leave."

"Well, please call us if you need references," Kelly said.

Saige was bewildered on the ride home. Back in the apartment, she tripped over a cereal box. Emotions swirled like water down a drain. How to tell Finn she'd lost her job, and worse, how to keep the news hidden from her father and avoid a litany of "I told you so."

• • •

Finn put the bags of Chinese food on the table. "Hey, you're home early tonight. What's wrong? Have you been crying?"

"I was let go. I lost my job."

"What happened?"

"My bosses lost two important accounts. They can't afford to keep me on."

"Oh, babe, what a shame. I'm sure you're sick about this," Finn said. "But you were let go because of circumstances, not because you were a bad employee. It'll be all right."

Saige wasn't so sure.

• • •

The first week, Saige scoured the employment ads and moped around the house. Her chances for a new job appeared bleak.

On Friday night, Finn came home asking the same question he did every night. "Any luck today?"

"No."

"Something will turn up." He tucked his arm around her waist, and she leaned against him.

"I thought about advertising piano lessons for children."

"You mentioned you played the piano. Are you good?" Finn asked.

"I guess I am. My mother started teaching me at age five. She taught other kids until she began homeschooling me."

"Did you enjoy it? Or were you one of those kids dragged to the bench, kicking and screaming?"

"No, I really loved it. Mom and I played duets. I had a knack for memorizing pieces."

Finn said, "Well, if you can teach . . ."

"No. It was a crazy idea. I don't know why I brought it up. I'd have to use the family piano."

"Call your father. This has been eating at you."

"He'd tell me how wrong I was to quit the bank. I don't want to hear it. *Especially* now."

Saige was glad Finn didn't pressure her about the piano lessons. She wasn't sure why she'd even entertained the idea. The thought of touching the keys left her sad. She recalled evenings at the piano, her mother patiently guiding her fingers, making up games so learning would be fun. Later, when her mother was sick and too weak to get out of bed, Saige would play for her. It had been over a year since she'd touched the keys that used to bring her joy.

The second jobless week, Saige searched Craigslist. Finn said the site had become a haven for people looking for occasional part-time work, and many found full-time jobs. Two advertisements sounded promising, but when she phoned, Saige was turned down due to her lack of experience. By the third week, she drove back and forth past the bank, but the nerve to ask Mr. Seers to rehire her didn't materialize.

•   •   •

Saige sat in her pajamas and leafed through the classifieds section. A tiny ad at the bottom of the page caught her attention. Surely, this is a joke, she thought. Finn had warned her about scammers.

The notice sounded innocent enough, but Saige wasn't sure. It required her to go to a house in Webster Groves for an interview. Webster was a nice suburb of St. Louis, but Saige hesitated. She inspected the rest of the paper, flipped back to the little ad, and read the paragraph again. She dialed the number and cleared her throat. "Hi, I'm calling about your ad. . . . Yes, I'm free now." She grabbed a tablet. "Take a left on Langley, then two rights. I've got it. My name is Saige Santoro. All right, I can be there in about twenty minutes. Thanks, Ms. Warwick. Okay . . . Katie."

She penned a note for Finn, decided on a dress, and slipped the address in her pocket.

CHAPTER 53

If there ever was a time she needed confidence, it was now. Saige surveyed the grand house in front of her. The impressive manor lazily sprawled across the lawn. The rustic wooden siding, cedar-shake roof, and walls of windows reminded Saige of a mountain lodge.

The wide wraparound porch was decorated with hanging flowerpots and white wicker furniture. Oak trees probably centuries old towered, shading the yard, their massive limbs protecting, holding back the sky.

Saige pressed the bell. A woman about Saige's age answered the door. Her dark hair wound around Velcro rollers, and a royal blue kimono hid her figure.

"I'm here about the job as a stand-in bridesmaid," Saige said. "We spoke on the phone."

"You might do," the woman said and stepped aside. "I'm Katie Warwick. Pardon my appearance, but I have to leave in a couple of hours, and I'm trying to get ready. Come in."

Saige followed her to the living room. Katie sat on the couch and patted the cushion, motioning Saige to sit beside her. Katie's speech was rapid, with hardly a breath to separate her sentences. "You must think this sounds a little crazy, but I'm desperate. The wedding is *this* weekend, and my best friend, Suzanne, came down with mono. I'm now one bridesmaid short, and my fiancé wouldn't dream of dropping one of his groomsmen. I can't believe the bad timing. I'm heartbroken about my friend, but it's absolutely impossible to change the date." Katie kneaded her sleeves. "Well, let's get started. Would you mind standing and walking to the door and back?"

"Sure," Saige said. She shot Katie a confident smile and sashayed across the room.

"Okay, good. Come back and sit down. You're the right height, and you're cute. I need someone attractive for the pictures but not too gorgeous. You know, it's my day."

Saige tried to think of something witty, but nothing came to mind, so she nodded in agreement.

Katie unwound a few curlers from her hair. "Tell me about yourself."

Saige took a deep breath and remembered Sam telling her she could do anything she wanted. Saige gathered every ounce of confidence. "Well, I've currently been working for a graphic design firm. Prior to that, I was employed at a bank."

"Great," Katie said. Saige sensed that Katie was restless, eager to move on with a decision. Saige smiled while Katie scrutinized her like a bug in a glass jar. Katie bobbed her head in approval. "I think you'll fit in just fine. You're smart. You'll look good in the photos. I have a good feeling about you. Okay, if you want it, the position is yours. The job has a few conditions. Sorry I didn't mention them, but I had to see if you qualified. I guess you were a little uneasy too."

"Yeah, I wasn't sure if this was legit."

"Oh, it's legit. Everything is standard wedding etiquette. You'll have to have a fitting for the dress tomorrow, and attending the rehearsal dinner is a must. Do you have a husband or boyfriend?"

"A boyfriend."

"Will he mind you pairing up with a groomsman for the weekend?"

"He'll be fine with it. Would I have to give a toast?"

"Nah, just mingle with the guests, be in the pictures, and walk down the aisle with Michael. Dance if you want." Katie studied her. "You're about Suzanne's size. The bridal shop will adjust the dress. Do you own a nice pair of black shoes with a little heel?"

"I do," Saige said with enthusiasm.

"That's my line." Both women laughed.

Saige was uncomfortable talking about money, but that's why she was here. "What will the job pay?"

"My father said if I found someone I was happy with, he would pay a flat rate of three hundred seventy-five dollars."

Saige struggled to remain composed.

"But you have to sign a contract. It's a legal document," Katie said.

"All right, but I'd like to read over the terms."

"Let's go to the table, and you can have a look. One more question. Is your employer flexible?"

"Oh, yes, *very* flexible." Saige hoped her face wasn't betraying her fib; she didn't want Katie to know she'd lost her job.

"Good. We need tomorrow for the fitting. Suzanne's mother will bring the dress over tonight. Jeez, I'm getting the jitters with all these changes. Have you ever been a bridesmaid, Saige?"

"No."

"You'll have a good time. The dress is burgundy, by the way. I think it'll be a good color on you. The rehearsal dinner is Friday night, down on the river. Daddy rented a steamboat. It's coming all the way from New Orleans. The wedding is at one o'clock

Saturday afternoon at the Missouri Botanical Garden. Do you know where the garden is located?"

"I know it well. I adore the garden," Saige said. One of her favorite activities was to hike to the Japanese section by the lake, put a coin in the machine that dispensed dried pellets, and feed the koi. Their giant gaping mouths vying for food as they surfaced always amused her. She used to tell her mother the garden was food for the soul.

"You're not holding the rehearsal at the ceremony site?" Saige asked.

Katie frowned. "If I hear one more person say—"

"Oh, sorry. Sounds like the subject is a sore spot."

"Everyone's set on tradition. I want the rehearsal dinner on the boat. We'll do a practice run. We walk down the aisle the same way, explain where the parents will be seated, etc. It's *not* complicated.

"It's a great idea," Saige said.

"Thanks. Don't bring it up in front of my mother. We've gone around and around on this. Dinner will be served *before* we rehearse." Katie's eyes glimmered with defiance. "It's my wedding."

"Sounds like fun."

"The day of the wedding, we meet here," Katie said. "Dad hired a chef to make omelets. We'll have breakfast and take photos, and a limo will drive the wedding party to the Rose Garden. The reception's at the Top of the Riverfront after the ceremony. You know, the revolving restaurant downtown? My wedding party consists of twelve people, counting my fiancé and me. You're signing on for two *very* busy days."

"I understand. Am I a secret? That you're renting me?"

Katie laughed. "No, we're up front about this. My father was uncomfortable about a stranger as a stand-in, but my best friends are in the wedding. I have no cousins or sisters, so this was an easy solution. I didn't know what kind of person would answer the ad, but I lucked out. You're perfect."

"Thanks. I'm honored to be chosen for this."

"My father's old-school and wants to be sure the person I hire will be accountable, so he had his lawyer prepare a contract. You're over twenty-one?"

"I am."

Katie led her into the dining room. "Read the terms and be certain you're comfortable signing the document." She left Saige to review the paperwork.

The contract seemed straightforward, no legal mumbo jumbo. "Katie? I'm done."

Katie came back into the room. She'd changed into a short black dress, the curlers gone. "Do we have a deal?"

"We do."

"Fine. You sign by the X, and I'll sign underneath."

Katie gave Saige the bridal shop's business card. "Can you be at this address by ten o'clock tomorrow morning?"

"I'll be there."

The glamour of being in a wedding was new and exciting. Saige couldn't believe the Warwicks were paying her almost four hundred dollars to party all weekend.

· · ·

Saige came home, and Finn was pacing the floor. A scowl settled around his mouth. "I was worried."

"I left a note so you would know where I went."

"Yeah, I found it *and* the ad on the table. What were you thinking, Saige? This doesn't even sound like a real job. You shouldn't have gone to a stranger's home."

"Well, it *is* a real job, and I've accepted. I have to be in the pictures, go to the ceremony, walk down the aisle with a guy named Michael—"

"No. I don't think this is a good idea."

"Listen for a minute." Saige told Finn about Katie, the contract she had signed, and the money she would earn.

"I don't care. I don't think you should do it."

This lecture sounded familiar. Straight from her father's mouth.

"Didn't you hear what I said? Almost four hundred dollars *and* I get to keep the dress *and* have dinner downtown. I'm not worried. This is legit. What's wrong?"

"Rent-a-bridesmaid? I've never heard of such a thing. And I'll tell you, I'm not wild about you linking arms with some guy."

Saige was disappointed in his reaction. He'd always been so supportive. "Finn Hamilton, I believe you're jealous. You know you're my one and only. Come on. I got a job."

"It's not a real job. It's a gig."

"Okay, so it's a gig. It's this weekend, and then it's over. It will put money in my bank account. It's going to be amazing." She smiled. "Want to go out tonight? See a movie? My treat."

"I already have plans to take Sam's PowerPoint 3 class. Excuse me." Finn huffed out of the room.

Saige questioned why Finn was making her feel like she'd done something wrong. She needed the cash and trusted Katie. She was going to take the job.

CHAPTER 54

Saige waited at the entrance outside the bridal shop. Katie and her mother, Helen Warwick, arrived promptly at ten o'clock.

Katie introduced Saige to her mother. "We have the dress," Katie said. "Did you bring your shoes?"

"Right here." Saige patted a bag resting on her shoulder.

Inside the shop, a middle-aged woman wearing oversized red-rimmed glasses approached. Strands of thread stuck to her blouse and skirt, a pincushion was strapped across her wrist, and a pair of antique sterling scissors with ornate scrolling hung from a chain on her chest.

"Hello, Evelyn," Mrs. Warwick said. "Saige, this is Evelyn Donald, the owner of the shop. She could turn a potato sack into a gown Cinderella could wear to a ball. Thanks for working us in, Evelyn. This is Katie's new bridesmaid, Saige." Saige said hello, and Katie escorted her to the changing room.

Saige returned, and Evelyn motioned her onto a platform. Saige admired herself in the three-way mirror and felt glamorous. Evelyn shortened the hem three or four inches to keep it from dragging across the floor and took a tuck at the waist. The strapless gown was elegant against Saige's bare neck and shoulders.

"Don't hold in your stomach, dear," Helen Warwick said. "You don't want the dress to be too tight." She turned to her daughter. "Everything is going to be simply wonderful."

"If the weather cooperates," Katie said, playing with the tiaras in a glass case. "What if we have another freak snowstorm?"

"We'll adjust the plans if there's a problem."

"Don't even say that," Katie said. "It's my wedding day, Mother. You know I've always *dreamed* of an outdoor ceremony."

"Be a realist, but don't fret. If the weather turns bad, we've arranged to hold the service in the pavilion."

"All right, then," Evelyn said. "These are easy adjustments. The dress will be ready in a few hours."

Saige changed into her clothes and waited for Katie and her mom. Outside, they stopped at the Warwicks' car, and Katie retrieved an envelope from the backseat. "I printed a copy of the schedule of events. We'll meet at Union Station at five tomorrow night. Allow extra time for traffic. Daddy's arranged for a limo to take us to the boat. We'll have drinks, hors d'oeuvres, dinner, and then the rehearsal."

"Did you tell her the rehearsal isn't at the wedding site?" Mrs. Warwick asked.

"I told her, Mother." Katie sighed and passed the envelope to Saige. "Wear a dress or nice pants and a blouse."

Katie's mother said, "Don't forget. Everyone must be at our house by ten thirty Saturday morning. There will be a photo shoot of Katie getting ready and whatever else the photographer, Chris, has in mind."

Katie checked the time. "Have to scoot. You have my number."

"Thank you," Saige said. "See you tomorrow night." On the way home, Saige bought a simple black dress and a new pair of shoes. She had no qualms about her decision to fill in as a bridesmaid but was puzzled by the shift it had caused in her relationship with Finn. He'd been acting odd since she told him about the job, and she was growing weary of trying to pacify him.

CHAPTER 55

Rosie knelt in the damp mulch, scooped up another load of dead oak leaves, and crushed them into the yard-waste bag. It would take hours to clear the leaves around the shrubs and ready the yard. Spring cleanup was always a necessary but disagreeable task. Usually she loved tinkering in the earth, planting and nurturing, but today the soil was cold to touch. The lifeless leaves brought no pleasure.

She tented her hand to block the late morning sun and surveyed the street lined with oaks the builder had planted some forty years ago. The trees provided shade in the summer, a beautiful canopy, but Rosie wished they were maple trees. Their warm-colored foliage would crumble and disintegrate, unlike these tough, broad oak leaves trapped against her house.

Even though the air had been chilly two hours earlier, the sun and the physical work had dampened the back of her shirt with perspiration. Tomorrow was Saturday. If she got the beds cleaned, she'd pick out a flat of annuals—red geraniums, golden-yellow marigolds, and salvia to attract hummingbirds.

This had been an unusual winter, and the weather was still unreliable. The gardening rule of thumb in St. Louis was to wait until after Mother's Day to plant, to be on the safe side. Rosie hated to wait. Flowers brought her immeasurable joy. Many a year she'd planted in early spring and had been tricked by a hard freeze that killed. As much as she wanted new life, maybe she should practice playing it safe. Rosie carried the rake into the garage. Timing was everything. She considered the need to plan early to avoid risk. Rosie changed clothes and reflected on what was safe, what was hazardous. And she wished she knew the answer.

•   •   •

Rosie met Chelsea and Saige for a quick lunch at the Jive. They ordered soup, sandwiches, and fizzy soft drinks. Rosie poked a straw through the top of her plastic cup. "I almost changed my order to a latte because Hanna doesn't write on soda cups."

"A missed opportunity," Chelsea said. She sipped her root beer.

"I could have used her wisdom today," Saige said, nibbling bites of her turkey sandwich.

"Why?" Chelsea asked.

"It's difficult discussing this, because you're married to my boyfriend's brother."

"If you guys get married, you'll be my sister-in-law. Don't worry. Girl code always trumps." Chelsea gestured as if locking her lips and tossing a key. "Now spill."

Saige let out a sigh. "I guess Rosie told you I was laid off?"

"Yeah, too bad," Chelsea said.

"I answered an ad to fill in as a stand-in-bridesmaid and got the job. I had the fitting this morning."

Rosie slapped the top of her leg. "Really? Somebody's paying you to be a stand-in at their wedding? Excellent." She tore off a piece of her sandwich, and a slice of crispy bacon fell on the plate. She popped it in her mouth. "What's the dress look like?"

"Gorgeous—burgundy, strapless. And I get to keep it!" Saige wiggled her shoulders for effect and filled her friends in on the details. "There will be dinner, dancing, and, to top it off, they're giving me a nice, fat check. The celebration starts tomorrow tonight with the rehearsal dinner." Her smile faded. "But Finn's spoiling the excitement. He follows me around the apartment and tells me he doesn't like my decision. I tried to reason with him, but he told me I shouldn't take the job. He shuts down and won't talk. Just like my dad. I told him it was my decision, and we had a fight." She jabbed the straw in and out of her plastic lid. "We argue a lot lately. This relationship's taking a downward spiral. I don't understand *why* he's so negative."

"Uh-oh," Chelsea said.

"What?" Saige asked.

"Nope. I can't get in the middle of this." Chelsea swirled her spoon in her minestrone soup.

"What happened to girl code? What do you know? Did he mention it?"

"No," Chelsea said, quickly. "It's just that . . ." Her voice trailed off.

"What?" Rosie asked.

"I don't want to portray Finn in a bad light, but he can be a little, uh, possessive. His relationship was solid with his last girlfriend . . ."

The image of a red flag waved in Saige's mind. "And?"

"We thought they were going to marry, but she broke up with him. Her name was Laura. Finn was devastated." Chelsea leaned closer. "It was his jealously that destroyed them. Please don't tell him I mentioned this."

"I won't," Saige said. "Trust me. Finn's actions are speaking louder than your words." Saige's statement hung in the air until she changed the subject. She turned to Rosie. "How have you been? I've been worried about you."

"Life is peaceful at the moment. Carlos is working overtime, and my boss has me on later shifts. If I'm home and have dinner on the table, everything is all right."

"*If* you're home and have dinner ready? What is this, freakin' nineteen fifty-five?" Chelsea said. "I'm concerned about what will happen when your late shifts end and you're back on his schedule."

"Yeah, I don't know what I'll do then."

"Maybe it's time to run."

Chelsea's words startled her.

"I don't trust him, Rosie." Chelsea finished her last bite.

"Somebody please explain this dysfunctional machismo attitude with the guys in our lives," Rosie said. "Finn's not supporting your decisions. He's bossy, and my husband feels he has the right to bully and intimidate. I don't get it. Why do they act this way?"

"A genetic defect?" Chelsea suggested.

They all laughed, but Rosie recognized the expression Saige hid behind her pasted smile. It was one Rosie had memorized. Fear. Different reasons. Same emotion.

CHAPTER 56

"Hello?" Adam stepped inside. "Mom?" The house was quiet. Adam opened the refrigerator and poured a glass of orange juice. "Hey, Max, you didn't come to the door. What's going on, buddy?" Max was lying on the kitchen floor curled on top of the braided rug. His golden eyes followed Adam's every movement.

Adam lifted the leather leash from the counter. "You want to go for a walk?"

Max's tail thumped once against the floor. His paws twitched. Adam knelt and supported the dog's body to pull him to his feet. Max yelped. His head hung low, his legs unwilling to walk. He sank back onto the floor.

Adam phoned his mom's cell. "Something's wrong with Max. I don't think he can walk."

"Call the vet. I'll meet you there," Samantha said.

Next, Adam dialed his father. He snatched Max's favorite blanket, carried the dog to the car, and gently set Max on the seat next to him. Adam gripped the wheel hard driving to the veterinarian's office and accelerated through a stoplight as it switched yellow to red.

He hurried into the office and kept Max tucked across his lap. Samantha and Marigold arrived soon afterward.

"What happened?" Samantha asked.

"I don't know, but he can't walk. I had to carry him in. Look at him."

Max looked up but didn't wag his tail. Marigold and Samantha knelt down next to him. "What's wrong, baby?" Samantha said.

"I called Dad," Adam said. They all waited in silence. An assistant finally appeared and offered to take Max. "No, I've got him." Adam carried Max into the exam room. Minutes later, Luke joined them.

The vet, Dr. Gardner, a stocky woman in her forties, about five foot seven, tapped on the door and entered the room. She greeted the family and asked about Max. "Has he seemed fatigued lately?"

"I walk him most of the time," Marigold said. "I thought he was limping a little."

Luke thought for a minute. "You know, I don't think he ate much yesterday. His bowl was hardly touched."

Dr. Gardner gently petted Max. "Hey, boy, how are you doing? Okay," she said, to the family in a calm voice. "I'm going to examine him for puncture wounds or bruising." With light strokes, she brushed over his body. She touched his shoulder, and Max growled. Marigold took a step back. "He never does that."

"It means he's in severe pain. I'd like to get some X-rays."

"Anything you need to do," said Samantha.

Marigold teared up. "Max has to be okay." Adam exchanged a look with his father.

The family waited for the radiographs to be processed. Dr. Gardner returned, her hands tightly tucked in the pockets of her lab coat. Her expression was grim.

"Max has osteosarcoma," the vet said. "It's a common form of bone cancer in dogs. It has spread from his upper limb and metastasized in his lungs."

"Max has cancer?" Adam said incredulously.

"I've never found an easy way to say this to families, but Max is suffering. I know this must come as a shock, but I think the kindest act would be to consider euthanasia. I'm sorry."

"This is so sudden. He was fine." Marigold leaned her head against Max and kissed his snout. "You don't understand." Her face had gone pale. "He's not a pet. He's family."

"I know he is." Dr. Gardner's tone was gentle. "But he's been sick for a while. Dogs often suffer in silence. When they vocalize, it's generally because they're in intense pain."

"Doctor, could we talk about this?" Samantha said.

"Of course. Take your time. I know this isn't easy."

The family stroked and hugged Max and talked about the right thing to do. What they didn't want to do. Max lay on his blanket, not moving. They agreed. Luke stepped into the hall to tell the vet they'd arrived at a decision.

The family took turns saying good-bye. There were tears when the assistant put the catheter in Max's vein. Luke spoke to Max in a soothing tone. Samantha cuddled Max, and each said, "I love you." Max watched them. Trusting.

The doctor came in the room, took a large syringe filled with a lavender liquid, and slowly injected it into the catheter.

Marigold took off Max's collar and stroked under his chin. "I love you, love you so much. Such a good boy." Tears streamed down her face.

Adam was sure his heart was tearing into a hundred pieces, but he kept his voice composed so Max wouldn't be afraid. He leaned forward and whispered, "I'm not going anywhere, okay? I'm right here, buddy. Jeez, I'm going to miss you."

Adam rubbed Max's soft underbelly and struggled to stay strong. "Don't worry. It won't hurt. I promise."

Max twitched and took a final breath. Dr. Gardner confirmed with her stethoscope that his heart had stopped. And the family cried.

• • •

Adam didn't go to his apartment. Instead, he drove home to be with his family. Everywhere he went, he imagined the dog following him, room to room. Samantha washed and dried the doggie bowls and put them in a bag. Luke picked up the scattered chew toys, including Max's favorite, an old plastic squeaker mouse. The noisemaker was long gone, and in its place was a hole where Max had carried the thing. The toy had been reduced to a flattened remnant with a cartoon smile, but Max would find it, drop it on the floor, and nudge Adam with his wet nose, hoping for a game of tug.

"What should I do with Mouser?"

"Put it in the trash," Samantha said, sniffling.

Marigold wandered into the kitchen holding the leather leash, looking lost. "Mom . . ."

Samantha took the worn strap and put it in the bag.

"It hurts so much," Marigold said. "Maybe we should've brought him home."

"No, sweetie, it was the right decision. Like the doctor said, Max was suffering."

"His death was painless," Adam said. "He knew we were with him, loving him."

"Remember how he would put his paw on our lap to tell us he wanted to go outside?" Samantha said. "Later he just stood by the door and stared at us. Waiting."

Luke swallowed hard and cleared his throat. "When you kids were little, he'd wait under the table for you to drop any bite of food. Mari, do you remember the time you were standing in the kitchen, talking to your mom, holding your cheese sandwich? Max thought you were offering it to him."

"Gone—in one gulp," Marigold recalled. "He loved cheese, didn't he, Adam?"

Adam nodded. He had so many memories. It was hard to remember a time without Max.

In the doctor's office, Adam had felt the thumping in Max's chest beating against his fingertips. Adam hadn't needed a stethoscope. He'd known the exact minute his dog's heart had stopped, the very second his spirit was gone. Adam thought about how effortless the shift had been for Max to go from life to death, and he was grateful for the easy transition. No more pain. In his intense grief over the loss of his beloved pet, Adam wondered why it couldn't be the same for humans.

CHAPTER 57

Alana called the service Borg had hired to shuttle her to La Chic Boutique. Martine was waiting at the entrance and took her hand. "*Cherie, je regrette.* I've been troubled since the police contacted me last night. I had no idea Leone's mind was so unsettled. I'm so glad you and Borg are all right." Martine shuddered. "People come to Paris and discover romance. It has been known as the City of Love, *n'est-ce pas*? You have quite a different story to tell. Come. Let's not disappoint him after all of this."

They sorted through the outfits on the rack. An hour later, they narrowed the choices to twelve. Martine asked Alana if the skirt lengths were appropriate for her readers, showed her different belts they could substitute, and asked if she was comfortable with the shoe choices paired with the outfits.

"Martine, you're the expert. I'll voice concerns if the style appears inappropriate."

"We are confident America will be a good market for us. Look at this." Martine held up a sketch pad.

Alana studied the designs, the paper colored with markers, precise strokes evoking texture and mood. "They're fantastic."

"We will not only customize color but tailor for body types for a more appropriate fit," Martine said. She lifted two dresses from the rack. "A woman can choose: sleeveless, V-neck, scoop, empire, or drop waist. But . . ." She hung the dresses back. "Sales are final unless we caused the error."

"*C'est ça*, it is so," said Alana, and Martine laughed.

By late afternoon, they finished. "I think your readers will be happy with the selections if you and Borg accept the boutique as a client. I don't know if we will see each other again, but I wish you success. It was my pleasure to meet you."

"And you," Alana said warmly. "I have a lot to consider. Good-bye, and thank you."

"*Adieu.*" Martine kissed her on each cheek. "Tell Borg we will speak later after he has recovered."

Alana returned to the hotel, eager to check on Borg and tell him about the meeting.

In the lobby, the hotel manager motioned to her. "*Bonjour, Mademoiselle. Monsieur* Larson asked you receive this note."

Alana,

By the time you read this, I will be on a flight to New York. Everything is arranged for you. Your flight to the States leaves at 8:15 tonight. I assumed you would need extra time with Martine. I hope today was productive. If you need a different flight, call my office and have my assistant arrange a more convenient one.

Borg

• • •

Alana tore open the envelope and removed a boarding pass. Borg had taken care of every detail, yet she regretted that he'd left without a word, not even a good-bye. His note sounded cold and unfeeling. "*Monsieur,* do you know what time he checked out?"

"About one hour ago."

"May I check the room?"

"*Oui.*" He handed her a key. "Do not be long."

"*Merci.*"

She needed to see for herself. Alana placed the key card in the slot, and the light blinked green. Inside, the room was spotless. No hint that Borg had slept in the bed, no indication that it hadn't all been a dream. A flash of white caught her attention, a crumpled piece of paper partially hidden by the fold of the drapery. Alana smoothed out the creases and read:

Thank you, dear Alana, for your tender care last night. I'm sure the pain will affect my traveling, but I must attend a meeting in New York. I've arranged for your return flight. Hopefully, the time will work for you. Please call the office if this doesn't meet your satisfaction. I'm sorry we couldn't fly back together. I'll call you as soon as I return.

Borg

CHAPTER 58

"I don't understand why you're against this." Saige refreshed her lipstick. "You act like you're angry with me."

"I'm not mad, but I think it's weird. You shouldn't be involved with these people," Finn replied.

"You don't get it. I *want* to do this. And don't refer to them as *these people*." Saige picked up her purse. "I'll be home . . . later."

Rush hour traffic inched along, giving Saige time to consider Finn's behavior. Again, she was certain his attitude was no different than her father's controlling way of dealing with her. She tried to distract herself, but the thought kept pricking her consciousness like a sharp pin.

Saige arrived at Union Station and passed the imposing stone structure with its red roof, clock tower, and turrets. She marveled at the design of the elongated fountain in front. Fourteen bronze figures spraying arcs of water depicted the meeting of the Missouri and the Mississippi.

The famous St. Louis landmark was once the busiest train station in the country, before flying became the preferred mode of travel. After the station was renovated into a hotel with a shopping mall and restaurants, Saige's father had taken the family downtown to see what he claimed was a treasure reborn. Her father might remember the architecture and the statues, but Saige's memories were of the men at The Fudgery, singing in harmony, stirring the creamy mixture on long white slabs, and cutting samples of the sweet confection. It had been almost ten years since her last visit, and now the mall parking lot was vacant.

She caught sight of Katie surrounded by three other young women in short dresses and high heels, and she hurried to join them. They were talking at the same time, a buzz of disturbed hornets.

Katie was pointing at a stretch limo parked by the lake. She quickly introduced Saige to the other women and yelled at the driver, "What are you going to do?"

A young woman with high cheekbones took a step back. "I'm *not* getting in the limo."

"Just wait, Marie."

A man in a blue jacket opened the hood. "It's somewhere in the engine."

Marie paled. "Gross."

"Did the limo break down?" Saige asked Angie, a young woman with short blonde hair.

"No, we have a different problem," said Angie. "So, you're the stand-in for Suzanne?"

"Yes, I'm Saige." She squinted at the limo.

"Marie spotted a black water snake right as it crawled underneath the front of the limo."

"It was huge," Marie said. "I can't stand snakes. Their eyes scare me, and their weird, forked tongues. They have no legs, for cripes' sake."

"If they're not poisonous, what's the big deal?" Tessa asked.

Marie made a face. "You don't understand. I *hate* snakes."

Katie dialed her cell. "Daddy, please, can't you get another limo? . . . You don't *know* it's gone. . . . Hold on, I'll get him." She motioned to the driver. "Thomas, could you come here?"

He took the phone and listened a moment. "No, sir. We've searched all over. ... Yes, sir. We'll be there in twenty minutes." He returned Katie's cell phone.

"Sorry, miss, we have to leave. It's probably gone by now." Thomas opened the passenger door. None of the women moved.

"My father won't pay for another limo," Katie said. "We need to get to the boat."

Marie wasn't convinced. "What if it attacks us?"

"Black snakes are actually harmless," Saige said.

"Oh, God," Marie said. "I can't. Please . . ." Her voice trembled. "I'll take a taxi and meet you there."

Katie scowled. "We should stay together. Come on, it's gone." Louder, she said, "Let's go, everybody." Katie ushered the women into the limo, gave Marie a push, and scrambled in behind her. Saige climbed in last and closed the door.

"Can it slide in through the air vent?" Angie asked.

Marie lunged for the door.

Katie shoved away her arm.

"It can't. A filter blocks the entry," the driver said. "You all sit back and have fun. There's wine in the refrigerator."

None one stirred. Thomas removed his cap. Keys jingled.

A security guard from the hotel ran toward them, waving his arms. Thomas rolled down the window.

"Sir, don't start the engine! If a snake's next to the fan, it will be killed, and you don't want that to happen. Nasty business. My supervisor had a suggestion. He thinks a cold spray of water might drive the snake out, if it's still there."

The guard took off his gloves and unrolled a hose from the side of the building. Thomas popped the hood. Water splashed the windshield like heavy rain, blurring the view. Saige reached around Katie and patted Marie's back to calm her.

Then she glimpsed the creature. The snake slithered from under the limo—very long, very black. Before it could crawl back into the warmth of the engine, Saige yanked open the door and jumped out of the limo.

Katie leaned over and yelled, "Get back inside. You can't leave!" The girls pushed toward the window, generating a chain reaction of hysteria.

Saige kicked off her heels and seized the security guard's gloves, jamming her fingers inside. The yellow vinyl, too large, nearly reached her elbow. Saige grabbed the snake by the tail and held the reptile at arm's length. The snake thrashed. Its head writhed toward her face.

The driver's jaw had gone slack, and the guard dropped his hose. Saige grasped the snake beneath its skull. She had a good hold, but the serpent was strong. It whipped and contracted to get free. Saige ran toward the bushes, pointed the thing toward the undergrowth, let go, and stepped away. The snake disappeared.

Saige marched back to the limo, water from the hose swishing under her feet. She tossed the gloves to the guard and climbed in the back. Everyone gawked.

"What happened?" Angie said. "Jeez, weren't you scared?"

"Our first house was surrounded by woods. Snakes would get caught in the garden fence. We had one in the house once. I've watched my dad handle them. They're just as afraid of us." Saige shrugged.

Saige perceived the awe on their faces. She wiped her feet and slid on her new high heels. Everyone in the car clapped, including the driver.

CHAPTER 59

"We're here," Katie announced. The entourage of young women made their way across the uneven cobblestones toward the steamboat docked in the river. The *Dalliance* was three decks high with white gingerbread trim, and a paddle wheel at the back end was flanked by four American flags. A whistle pierced the air; a jet of steam shot into the sky.

"Drinks and dinner will be served prior to the rehearsal," Katie reminded everyone. They trekked up the ramp and hurried to the cabin lounge. The room hummed with activity. Servers in dark pants and crisp button-down shirts hurried to take drink orders and offered guests plump shrimp artfully arranged on silver platters.

Saige scrutinized the other women's chic cocktail dresses and sparkling jewelry and was thankful she'd purchased a new dress and a pair of vermillion-red heels.

Windows wrapped around the sides and front of the prow, ensuring an expansive view for the passengers. The tables and posts gleamed in the early evening light, boasting a fresh coat of varnish. The ceiling was thick with white beams. The carpet, dark blue and gold, was barely worn. In the center of the room was a glass case with a miniature replica of the ship.

A man in a tuxedo hammered jazzy, toe-tapping tunes on a piano. Saige remembered the hours her mother had spent teaching her to play, a time Saige always had her father's approval. "You give life to the notes on the paper," he had often said.

Her thoughts drifted to the last time she had touched the keys, playing "Ave Maria" at her mother's funeral.

Katie poked her. "Come with me. I want you to meet my father." A trim man in his mid-fifties approached, dressed in a charcoal suit and yellow tie. Saige thought he was attractive for an older man. His tanned face suggested he spent time outdoors. "There's my girl." He greeted Katie with a kiss on the cheek.

Katie turned to Saige. "This is my father, James Warwick. Daddy, this is Saige."

"Ah, our stand-in bridesmaid. A pleasure to meet you," he said.

"We would have been absolute basket cases if it weren't for Saige." Katie relayed the earlier events with the snake.

"Well played." He beckoned to a young man wearing a navy sport coat. His shoulders were broad, and he wore an easy smile. "Saige, this is Michael Anderson. He'll be your escort this weekend."

"Hello," Saige said. Michael was about six feet tall with sandy-brown hair and a dimple in the center of his chin. Saige thought he resembled a professor with his wide, black-rimmed glasses. His hair was short. Michael's laid-back demeanor put Saige at ease.

"I'd like to say hello to Nick's parents," said Katie's father.

"I'll come with you," Katie said. They excused themselves and greeted the couple.

"Are you an old friend?" Michael pushed his glasses back a little, Saige thought more from habit than necessity.

"Actually, I answered an ad. I'm what you might call a rented bridesmaid."

The corners of his mouth curved and Michael laughed. "I didn't know. Leave it to Katie to be so resourceful."

A young woman came to take their drink order. "A White Russian," Michael said.

"For you, miss?"

Saige paused. "I'll have the same."

Saige and Michael chatted until their drinks arrived. Saige took a sip. "It's kind of sweet—very good. What's in it?"

"Kahlua and vodka mostly," Michael said. "Careful, the alcohol can sneak up on you. Hey, there's Nick, Katie's fiancé. Have you met?'

"Not yet."

"Come on, I'll introduce you."

The steamboat whistle blew once more, and the boat slowly drifted down the river, carried by the Mississippi's current. A calliope began to play "Hello, Dolly."

The drink relaxed Saige, and she mingled with the guests. "I know traditionally the rehearsal takes place where the wedding is held, but this is great," she said to Michael.

"Katie isn't conventional."

"One of the qualities I like about her." Saige finished her drink.

Michael sat next to her at dinner, and they chatted about music while dining on roast beef and soggy vegetables. Afterward, the wedding party went to the lower deck to practice the ceremony. Michael linked his arm in Saige's. Pachelbel's "Canon in D" played while the setting sun cast a fiery red-orange on the normally muddy Mississippi River. The music reached a crescendo, softened, and faded as they approached the minister. Michael squeezed Saige's hand.

Katie said she had never cared for the time-honored "Wedding March" song. She and her father started down the aisle, and a CD played "Somewhere Over the Rainbow," sung by the Hawaiian artist known as Iz. Saige could hardly believe they were paying her to be there. She'd have done it for free.

After the rehearsal, the bridesmaids told stories about the couple and how they came to know them. It was her turn. Saige felt her cheeks flush, but she got a nod from Katie, who had her arm securely linked around Nick's. Saige told about answering Katie's ad in the paper, and they all laughed.

"Gotta say, you're one gutsy gal," Angie said. Saige beamed a wide smile.

Sometime after midnight, Mr. Warwick announced, "The limo's here and will take you back to your cars. You girls be careful on your drive home."

The night was dark and moonless. Saige rolled down the window, cranked up the radio, and sang along to old Motown music.

• • •

Finn was alert on the couch with a bowl of chips. Saige jumped on the sofa next to him, knees digging into the cushion. "I wish you could have been there. I had a wonderful time." She stopped. "What's the matter?"

Finn put the bowl on the table. "I'm supposed to be happy you stayed out with a bunch of strangers and came home at one in the morning? The guy you were paired with? Did he put the moves on you?"

"What? No, of course not. Why would you ask that question?"

"I think we should talk in the morning." He folded his arms—an iron gate she couldn't unlock.

"Tomorrow will be hectic. I have to leave early for the wedding pictures at Katie's house."

"Of course you do," he said, his tone scornful.

"You're accusing me of something. Why?" Her voice was high-pitched, like she'd sucked on a helium balloon.

"It seems like you're enjoying this event a little too much."

She followed him into the bedroom. "I enjoyed it a *lot*."

"More than being with me?"

"Completely different situations." Her lips pressed together. "I had a fantastic time." She unzipped her dress and kicked off her shoes. "I thought you'd be happy for me. Why are you acting this way?"

"You know you didn't like this whole bridesmaid idea, and you did it anyway."

"I have bills, you know."

"I'm more than willing to help you."

"Well, I wanted the job, the money, *and* the experience of being part of a wedding. We'll do activities without each other sometimes."

"We just started this relationship, and you want to be apart from me."

Saige hung her dress on a hanger and brushed her teeth. Finn gestured for the toothpaste. She slapped it in his hand and marched out.

He climbed in bed and reached for her. "I'm sorry. I get a little possessive. I missed you tonight. You were gone a long time. Then I imagined the guy—what's his name?"

"Michael."

"Yeah, *Michael*." He said it like he'd bitten into a bad persimmon.

Finn turned over and clicked off the light. For the first time, there was no good night kiss.

CHAPTER 60

It was good to be home, in her own bed, the soft covers tucked under her chin. It was four in the morning, but Alana felt wide awake and refreshed. Last night, she had fallen asleep by eight thirty. Her days and nights were still mixed up from all the time zone changes.

She lay in the darkness, and Paris now seemed like a dream: Victor, Martine, Borg, and Leone. Except Leone was a nightmare. Alana hugged the blanket. Borg would survive, but would *Slick* if the merger didn't go through? She needed to examine the pros and cons.

An hour later, the office's familiarity embraced her. She rummaged through papers stacked on her desk and reflected on the clothing line and how easy it had been to work with Martine. Yet she was still uncomfortable for some reason. Maybe the problem was about Borg. It was difficult to feign indifference around him.

Muffled noises drifted from the reception area and then the conference room. "Hello?" It was most likely Sean. He liked to start early on special projects.

Alana flipped through the stack of mail Michelle had organized in a container and then turned on her computer. An e-mail from Martine said she hoped Alana had arrived home safely. Alana's thoughts strayed to Borg, breaking her concentration.

Scuffling filtered through the door. "Sean?" She retreated into the main office. A choir of voices bellowed in unison, "Surprise!"

A "Welcome Home" banner was taped to the wall. Purple and white balloons floated about. Trays of mini-quiches and a basket of fruit sat on the conference table. Her staff cheered and clapped.

"You guys, what are you doing?" Alana smiled at them. "Jeez, I wasn't gone that long."

"We missed you," E.B. said.

"Yeah. And you're not supposed to be here this early," Murphy said. "You should be sleeping."

"Who knew balloons were noisy? They thump together." Taylor laughed. "Did you hear us?"

"I did, but I had no idea what you were doing. Thank you for the party."

Michelle gave her a big hug. "Welcome back, Alana. The office wasn't the same without you, and we wanted to show you we appreciate your leadership."

"I appreciate you, too." Alana patted Michelle's stomach. "Congratulations, Mom." Alana knew it would be only a matter of time before Michelle turned in her resignation.

E.B. reached for a quiche. "Tell us about France. I'll bet it was the best trip of your life."

Alana laughed. She hadn't even told Michelle about her ordeal in Paris. She started at the beginning. After her tale, they all gaped at her.

"It was the trip of a lifetime. But not quite the one I'd always dreamed about."

Taylor said, "It sounds awful. Thank God you're home."

"No, Paris wasn't awful, but Leone was. The police arrested her the same night."

"The woman was nuts," said Sean. "Let's hope they keep her locked up."

The phone rang, and Michelle answered, "*Slick Magazine.* How may I help you? One moment please." The caller was put on hold. "Alana, Borg's on line one."

"I need to talk with you," Sean said.

"Give me five minutes. Thanks again for the party, you guys. It's great to be back."

At her desk, she took a quick breath. "Borg, hello. How are you?"

"Good morning. I'm rested, thanks to pain medication. I'm so sorry I had to leave you in Paris. Are you over the jet lag?"

"Almost, if waking at four is normal." She laughed.

He paused. "Any decision yet?"

"I'm meeting with my lawyer this morning."

"I spoke with Martine," he said. "She has had other offers. I was afraid of this. I want an exclusive."

Alana was silent.

"This experience with Leone has no doubt clouded the situation for you."

"No," Alana said. "It's not only—"

"I have to be in Atlanta tomorrow. I could plan a layover in St. Louis and meet with you as early as this afternoon."

Papers rustled in the background.

"Let me check my schedule." Alana flipped open her planner. She had a meeting with Sean in five minutes, and Daniel would be at her office in two hours.

"My calendar is clear." Her pulse quickened. "If you don't have to be in Atlanta until tomorrow, maybe you should consider staying overnight in case we still have details to negotiate. You know how these discussions run." She hoped her voice didn't betray her nervousness.

"Can you recommend a hotel near you?"

"The Ritz-Carlton is close."

"My assistant will make the arrangements."

Alana gave him her work address. "Call me when you land."

"I'll see you very soon."

As soon as she hung up, Sean came in, a pencil behind his ear, his arms full of manila folders. "What happened? Did we get the contract?" he asked.

"No, but Borg's coming into town this afternoon, and I hope we can iron out some decisions." Alana caught the worry in Sean's eyes but couldn't offer him any certainty regarding the future.

She was lucky to have Sean on her team. They'd met in college. He'd been with her since the magazine's conception. He was conscientious and dependable. Sean had been concerned when Alana had mentioned her apprehension about the magazine and the possibility of Borg bailing them out.

"Be careful, Alana. You know the saying about sleeping with the enemy," Sean said.

Alana bristled. "I'm not sleeping with him, and he's not the enemy."

"He is if you take on his staff and *we* get the boot."

Alana gasped. "How could you think such a thing?"

"I know you confided to Michelle and me about Borg's offer. We didn't mention it, I swear. Maybe Taylor or one of the others overheard, but the buzz about it is all over the office. E.B. asked me if she should start looking for another job. Got all emotional and said this was her home."

Alana swallowed the lump in her throat and tried to reassure him. "Sean, there are so many variables in the mix, but I'll take care of the business. Leak the word there's nothing to worry about."

Alana glanced at the clock on her desk. "I'm sorry, Sean. What were you saying?"

Sean said, "I said, what are your plans? *Are* we joining forces with the other magazine?"

"He lives in California—" She let out a puff of air. "I'm beginning to think it's not realistic."

"Are you sure we're talking about the magazine merger?"

Unable to decide, she shrugged off the answer.

"Would you move the business to California? I can't afford to live there."

"Don't worry, okay? Let's dig in, finish the issue, and put together a winner."

They worked on new topics for the magazine, articles to assign, and potential interviews. An hour later, they wrapped up. "I feel good about this," Alana said. "Tell E.B. I want three photos for each article. Call Simon at the art museum for a heads-up on which paintings they want covered in the shoot. He wants a full-page ad to promote the new exhibit. I'll need a mock layout as soon as possible."

"This should be a great show." Sean gathered his notes. "Too bad you didn't have time to visit the Louvre."

"Maybe next time."

Michelle stuck her head in the door. "Your sister's on line three. Can you take it?"

"Put her through." She waved good-bye to Sean and picked up her phone.

"Hi, Natalie. Thanks again for picking me up at the airport."

"I wondered if you could meet tonight for dinner."

"Can't. Borg's on a flight to St. Louis with a possible layover. It's conceivable we'll have dinner."

"You like him."

"We have business to discuss."

"I'll bet he likes you, too. Sometimes you have to take a chance. Have some fun."

"Why? He must live two thousand miles away. What would that get me?"

"Kisses, maybe." Natalie giggled.

"You've got it figured out, huh? I have to go. Daniel should be here soon."

"Tell him I said hi," Natalie said. "I was worried about him. He was in the hospital."

Daniel was not only her lawyer but a longtime friend of the family. Natalie considered him a big brother.

"He's okay now, so don't worry. And leave Borg to me. Maybe we can have dinner next weekend."

"Okay, have fun."

Daniel arrived, punctual as usual.

Alana smiled. "You look well. Natalie's been worried."

"I'm improving, but a week away from my clients means I'm behind schedule."

"I hate to be sick," she said. "It's unproductive and a pain to catch up on work. I go out of town and come back to this." She gestured to the many papers on her desk.

"It seemed you were gone a long time," Daniel said. You had your trip to California, then Europe."

"I'm sorry I didn't let you know about California. Trust me. I regretted not keeping you in the loop. I'm worried." Alana indicated the room. "I've worked hard for this. Do I want to share my magazine?"

"The plus side," Daniel said, "is there could be considerable growth if you merge. Do you stay in your little pond or move into uncharted waters? Borg will want to run his own articles, so the magazine size will be larger. You'll have increased production costs, but those expenses would be shared."

Daniel removed a paper from his briefcase. "I've gone over the boutique's information. The company is solid. Bringing them on board with a contract could be a good investment. Regarding the merger, the negatives might be negotiating which articles you run and commuting to Paris, if you decide to take on the extra responsibility. Traveling could be a strain after the excitement wears off."

"How do our subscriber numbers compare to Borg's?"

"Pretty comparable," Daniel said.

"I think Martine is reliable. Her work is high-quality, and revenue from the boutique's ads would offer *Slick* more security," Alana said, thinking out loud. "Borg said Martine is hungry for exposure and would consider signing a long-term contract. Expanding the magazine could be positive, but I like my company's size, and that would change. How would Borg and I combine the staffing? I haven't asked how many employees he has."

"I think Borg will do what it takes to get this fashion section operating," Daniel said. "He can't put the fashion ads in *New Heights*. You can't take a tech magazine and turn it into *Elle*."

"He wants a fifty-fifty split." Alana squeezed the bridge of her nose. "He said he'd keep his products' advertisements in the back of the publication. No full-page glossies in the middle. I've always hated magazines choking you with so many ads you can't find the articles."

"You're going to have to bring your website up to date to increase online sales. It's not user-friendly, Alana."

"I know."

"I researched the few past issues of *New Heights*," Daniel said. "The articles in his magazine are high-tech, more for the computer-savvy. But everybody's interested in gadgets and technology, so he could be an asset. Are you afraid this type of content could turn readers off?"

"I am, although my readers might enjoy his articles if they aren't *too* technical." She rapped her pencil on her desk. "Something is nagging at me."

"Details," Daniel said.

"All right. I have a problem that could monkey-wrench the whole deal." She hesitated. "I find Borg . . . attractive."

Daniel's eyebrows shot up. "A key fact. You didn't mention you withheld information."

"Easy, counselor."

"You shouldn't mix business and personal feelings," he said. "It's a dangerous combo, bound to backfire."

"I know." She sighed. "He's scheduled a stop in St. Louis this afternoon."

"Do you want a meeting with the three of us?"

"Not yet. I want to spend more time getting to know the man who would be co-owner of my magazine. What's your take on this? Can a long-distance business survive?"

"Of course. It happens all the time. But I don't know if you're posing the right question. Maybe you should ask yourself if you can run a business with a man for whom you have feelings. Answer that, and let me worry about the contract."

Michelle tapped on the door. "Natalie stopped by and left this. She was running late. Said to give you both a hug."

Alana took the paper from Michelle and read to herself. A small smile tugged the corner of her mouth. It was hard to be annoyed with Natalie. Her heart was in the right place.

Alana,

I have the perfect solution for you. Don't go out to dinner.

Invite Borg to your house. It's about time you used your kitchen! Explore the other side or you will always wonder.

Love,
Natalie

• • •

Alana folded the message and tossed it on her desk. Everybody has advice for me, she thought.

"Tell you what, Daniel. I'll meet with Borg today and call you when I have something definite to report. He needs an answer, and I need to move on. If I go through with this, you figure out a contract giving me complete control over the articles we run. I don't want to compromise my integrity and lose the essence of the magazine. The work has to feel like *Slick,* not *New Heights.* Excuse me one second." She stepped out to speak with Michelle.

Alana returned, positive the note from Natalie was in a different spot. She suspected Daniel had read it. He always watched out for her. Although his snooping irked her, she didn't call him on it. He scrolled through the messages on his phone.

"Everything all right?" she asked.

"I was wondering if we can trust this guy," Daniel said. "Keep me informed, and don't sign any paperwork until I review it."

CHAPTER 61

Adam gripped his mat and squeezed between two young women in the meditation room. A woman with long blonde hair in a French braid was positioned in a downward dog stretch pose, and the petite brunette on his right lay on the floor next to him, her eyes closed.

The floor was crowded. Throngs of bodies were packed in neat rows like sardines in a tin. Since Max's death, constant obsessive thoughts had swarmed inside Adam's head like little bees stinging—sharp, sudden, alarming.

Without warning, his worry turned to agitation, dread, and despair. It would be easy to blame his edgy mood on Max's passing. Adam assumed that the loss of his pet wasn't the reason for his anxiety but probably the catalyst. Fear of days to come began to consume him. He needed this class. He needed Hanna.

She entered and rolled out her mat. Hanna scanned the room, met his eyes, tipped her head a brief second, and then greeted the class.

The gentle cadence of her tone immediately soothed him. She guided the group through a series of exercises, again with the focus on breathing. "Don't try to stop your thoughts," Hanna said. "Let them pass. Be the observer. They can't hurt you. The tension associated with the thoughts will. What you resist persists."

The breathing in the room took on a life of its own, and Adam stopped to listen. A rustle, maybe the fabric of her blouse, signaled that Hanna was next to him. "Let go of the worry," she whispered, her lips near his ear.

He whispered back, "I tried. I can't."

"You have to." She took a finger and gently tapped the center of his forehead, repeating the motion until he sighed and his jaw relaxed. Periods of silence and Hanna's words alternated as her voice drifted farther away and became an indistinguishable sound in the corner of his mind. He was sleepy. Floating.

Adam twitched, breaking the trance. His arm went rigid and jerked from his side. He hit the blonde lying next to him. Hard. She startled and let out a cry.

"Oh, God. Sorry." The class stirred from their reverie. Some sat upright to see what had happened; others held their position on the floor, watching him. Adam stood, but the rigidity in his legs caused him to stumble as he fled the room.

He hoped no one would follow him, but a patter of footsteps trailed behind. Soft but relentless. Adam clutched his abdomen and wondered if he was going to be physically ill, which only exacerbated his embarrassment. Outside, at the bottom of the concrete steps, he supported his weight against the metal rail and faced the grass in case he retched. A tiny squeak from the door told him she was there.

"Come back to the class," Hanna said.

Adam took a breath, commanded his stomach to be quiet, and faced her. "I just whacked the woman next to me. Am I supposed to explain to the class? Tell them about my disease?"

"You could. Everyone will understand. You won't be judged."

"I'm not able to do that."

"Don't try to bury what's happening to you. Feelings never stay locked away. They claw their way out and find you. You can't stop living because you lost control and you're embarrassed," she said, her voice gentle. "There is no crystal ball with answers."

"Twenty-one years of a life lived in vain," Adam said. "I haven't had time to do anything meaningful."

"Much of humanity lives without reflecting or contemplating."

"I wanted more," he said.

"What's troubling you the most?"

"There's no one thing. It's everything. I may not see my sister finish growing up. I'll never have children, travel the world— snorkel in Tahiti. Win a case. An important case." He gripped the railing. "Or go to Boston. I had applied to law school, you know?" He watched her. "I think I just figured out the worst thing. After a while, the memory of *me* will fade. Time and life will go on as if I never existed. I expected to leave a footprint. Those dreams are gone."

"I'm sure you've effected change. We all do. Every day. Actions have a ripple effect, not photographable but there all the same."

"It doesn't seem enough," he said.

"If you leave, you'll go home and brood. Ruminating will only intensify your anxiety. Come back. It's too soon to hide. The day will come, but not now."

Adam searched her face and saw kindness and love. Simple, unforced. Inherently Hanna. The sour feeling in his gut was easing. She reached for him. He accepted the lifeline.

CHAPTER 62

Rosie's car idled in her parents' driveway. This way would be so much easier. No risk. No guilt.

The house in front of her, its blue paint curling away from the warped clapboard and exposing the wood beneath, was her childhood home. The yard was covered with bare dirt patches, and untrimmed bushes blocked the windows.

She stayed another minute and rehearsed her speech to ask her parents if she could come home. They would disapprove of her decision to leave her husband. The last time they had spoken, her mother had told her she should stay with Carlos. And try harder. That was before the physical violence. What would Mamá say now?

Rosie stepped over the fractured concrete on the drive. She pressed the buzzer, waited a full minute, and twisted the knob. The door was locked.

Rosie retrieved a key from under the front doormat, a scrap of tattered fabric on which the black *L* and *C* had worn away long ago, leaving *WE OME*.

Inside the house, the silence unnerved her. Her five siblings, ranging from six to twenty years old, all lived at home. She was the only one who had left.

Rosie walked down the hallway to the cramped kitchen, tossed her purse on the wooden picnic table, and repositioned the bench. She could see her younger self sandwiched at the back end of the table like a book wedged too tightly on a shelf.

During holiday dinners, a card table was set up to accommodate extra family. Rosie always claimed the table for herself and Carlos in order to separate them from her wrangling siblings—the name calling, spit-the-watermelon-seeds games, and all the kicking legs. Rosie wondered if her mother ever wished for a different life.

Mamá's words echoed in her head. "Good Catholics aren't supposed to use contraception. A big family is a good family." Papá drove a bread truck across the state and was gone more nights than he was home. Rosie doubted her mother's wisdom. Maybe Mamá had been too busy to hug. Too tired to teach manners, consideration, and respect. One thing Rosie knew for certain: No way would *she* be saddled with a six-pack of kids.

Rosie examined the family portrait on the wall just beyond the kitchen, and her shoulders drooped. She could never look at the photo without thinking how she'd been forced into the role of motherhood—the unpaid nanny, an arrangement she hadn't asked for. The responsibility had stolen her childhood because she was the firstborn. Rosie turned away. *That* girl thought she'd found a way out with Carlos.

But there was no escape hatch. Like Alice, she'd fallen into a rabbit hole and didn't know how to get out. She'd been warned. What had Carlos said? *"I've always been fond of your mamá. You might want to reconsider going back home. Wouldn't want anything to happen to her, would we?"*

Rosie glanced at the family photo and reconsidered confiding her problems to her mother. She loved her family, and though she had to get away from Carlos, she could never come home. Rosie locked the door behind her and hid the key under the *OME*.

CHAPTER 63

Alana struck her pencil against the notepad. Tap-tap. Tap-tap. Borg—a potential business partner. Michelle—leaving. Tap-tap. New staff needed. A heavy knock interrupted her thoughts. "Come in."

Borg opened the door. "Don't blame Michelle," he said. "I hoped to surprise you."

She knew she was staring. "Mission accomplished."

Michelle stood behind him and mouthed the words, "Oh, my God, he's gorgeous."

Alana wanted to make a face but asked Michelle to shut the door. How long had it been since Paris? Alana had missed him. She searched his face for any indication he had missed her as well. She debated whether to give him a hug. Instead she cleared her throat.

"You were going to call me from the airport. I wasn't expecting you for a while."

"I didn't fly commercial today. I own a private plane," he said. "All I needed was to line up a pilot. We flew into your smaller airport, the Spirit of St. Louis, instead of Lambert International."

"You *own* a plane?"

"It's a BizJet, nothing fancy, but it gets me where I need to go. I do a lot of commuting, and the convenience it provides is enormous." He took off his jacket. "It's good to see you, Alana." Borg scanned the shelves mounted on the wall behind her desk. "Your office is captivating. Are these carved chess pieces?"

"Yes, I collect them."

"My God, they're incredible: Civil War pieces, Viking ships, nutcrackers, ancient Egyptian . . ." He moved closer and picked up a grinning Cheshire cat. "Alice in Wonderland?" He chuckled. "Fantastic." He pointed to the shelf below. "Are those African masks?"

"Yes. They're quite special. Did you know the masks have a spiritual and religious meaning?"

"No, I didn't." Borg examined the details with apparent fascination.

"I've been collecting sets for years," Alana said. "The boards are packed away. Since I can't put all thirty-two pieces on each shelf, I put out so many and then rotate the sets every few months. My friend Jim sculpted many of these. He's quite an artist, don't you think?"

"He is indeed. They're all stunning. Mmm. . . . This metal set's intriguing. The pieces are abstract, like tiny sculptures. Do you play chess?"

"A little, but mostly I display them as artwork. I promised myself no more purchases, but there is one more I want to add, then I'll stop."

"Which one interests you?"

"It's a King Arthur set. I have a passion for medieval history."

He appeared curious. "Mention the medieval period, and most people associate it with famine, the Black Plague, and public executions. What attracts you to that era? It's usually not first on the popularity list."

Oh, he should not have asked that question, Alana thought. "People think our technology is so advanced today, but think about it. They discovered printing using movable type. Examine Gothic architecture and try to compare *that* to a skyscraper." She tempered her enthusiasm. "Not everybody shares my passion. The chess pieces remind me life's a game. Don't forget to have fun playing it."

"Ah, a perfect segue for my question. What are you thinking with regard to the merger? Are we going to play the game?"

"I don't have an answer yet. I thought we could use today to get to know each other. We'll need to compromise, I suspect. How do I know we can work together?"

"You're right. We should use this time to get to know each other. Your lawyer, Mr. Stern, will he join us?"

"Not this time."

"Well, what would you like to do?"

"The Medieval Festival's in town."

Borg opened his phone and typed in the information. "We could attend the three thirty show. I see it includes a meal. Have you eaten?"

Alana shook her head. "No, I haven't. It's a wonderful idea. My car's parked out front."

"Good, because I took a taxi from the airport."

"Okay, it's settled." She opened the door and stopped at Michelle's desk. "Text me if you need me. Otherwise, see you on Monday."

CHAPTER 64

Saige woke up early, too excited to sleep. Finn lay next to her, snoring, his arm draped over her waist. She raised his arm gently, trying not to awaken him, and slipped out of bed. She wouldn't return home until late and wanted to finish the new piece for her blog.

It had taken awhile to get the hang of blogging. After hours of watching YouTube tutorials and researching, she submitted her first post. The topic was cancer, a tribute to her mother. She used the site as a personal journal. Saige found writing to be cathartic. She didn't expect anyone to read what she had written, but the stat counter recorded the number of visitors reading her posts. Her website averaged thirty hits on a good day. It comforted her to express her thoughts and read the comments others left.

Saige started up her laptop. Today she wanted to write about domestic violence. Ever since she and Chelsea had visited Rosie, Saige had been thinking how frightening it must be for Rosie, wondering if at any minute her husband would berate or strike her. Saige couldn't understand why Rosie would stay with Carlos. Why would any woman stay with an abuser? Was it worth the cost?

She researched and learned that the subject was complicated. Saige discovered the media center for the World Health Organization online and contacted the Center on Violence Against Women. She discovered that many factors kept a woman locked in an abusive relationship: fear, lack of money, low self-esteem, even love.

The previous week, she had driven to a shelter for battered women and found three women willing to talk to her. Each feared her husband, and Saige came to understand the reason her friend hadn't left. Rosie's words to Chelsea echoed back to her. *"I don't know what he'd do. To either of us."*

Rosie's bruises had appalled Saige. Maybe another woman in a similar situation would stumble across her blog, read her story, and find courage from her words. Saige examined the rough draft one final time and created a new blog entry.

Dear Reader,

This post is dedicated to women suffering from spousal abuse. I recently discovered a friend of mine is in an abusive relationship. Let me preface this article by saying I am not an expert. Let me also say that no man—or woman—has the right to control their significant other, physically or mentally. If you are a victim of physical injury, ask yourself why you are tolerating violence.

To anyone suffering abuse, it may seem impossible to have the courage to leave, but you must find shelter elsewhere and remove yourself and your children from potential harm. It's hard to take this step, not knowing where you might end up. Fear of the unknown is scary, but the unknown is preferable to a black eye, or worse, serious injury or even death. It might be the most difficult decision you ever make, but with only one life to live, why let precious minutes drag into years because of fear? I encourage you to call a hotline and talk to a trained advocate, and to check your area for free legal advice.

Words can wound as badly as a knife or a fist. The difference is words will leave scars on your heart—invisible to others, but every bit as harmful. Don't tolerate verbal abuse. If you have an abuser in your life, seek protection immediately. Talk to a friend, a member of your family, or your church. Don't wait. Again, I am in no way an expert on this matter, just someone who cares.

Saige added links to helpful resources and included a number for pro bono counseling she'd found on a St. Louis law site. She clicked send.

Saige closed her laptop and headed back to the bedroom. Finn passed her and said, "Good morning" on his way to the kitchen. Saige carefully unpacked her bridesmaid dress and wondered if Katie was nervous. Finn banged pots and pans in the kitchen while she was getting ready. She joined him as he was setting the table.

"You look spectacular," Finn said. He had made a full breakfast: scrambled eggs, pancakes, bacon, and a pitcher of fresh orange juice.

His attitude had changed drastically from last night, when he'd distanced himself from her. Saige said nothing.

Finn moved the chair for her. "Breakfast, it's the most important meal of the day." He forked three pancakes and passed the platter to Saige.

The tension from last night troubled Saige, but she didn't want to start an argument. She'd let it go. For now.

Saige scooped out a few tablespoons of eggs and picked the smallest pancake. "Katie's parents hired a chef. I don't want to eat too much. I'll burst out of the dress."

Finn was silent.

Saige poured a half-glass of orange juice. "What are your plans today?"

He pushed back his plate. "Guess I'll wait for you to come home. What time is the wedding over?"

"Katie said to plan on all day." She chewed her food.

"The Botanical Garden, huh? Then out to dinner?"

"That's right." Saige took her empty plate to the sink. "I should leave. Can't be late."

"No, don't want to be late," he said.

She checked herself in the mirror and gathered her purse and keys.

"Call me," he said.

"If I can."

He mumbled, "We'll see about that."

She didn't ask him what he'd said. She'd heard him.

CHAPTER 65

Marigold hadn't seen Adam since the family put Max down. She closed her book and called her brother.

"Hey. I've been studying for hours and could use a break. How about I pack lunches and we go to the park? Pick you up in an hour?"

"I don't feel like it."

"Come on, the fresh air will be good for us both."

"I'll pass."

"Please? I miss you."

Adam gave in. An hour later, they parked near their favorite trail at Queeny Park and ambled down the concrete path. Wild honeysuckle, impatient and ready, was fuzzy with green buds. Spears of tulip leaves poked through the mulch. "Crazy spring, huh? Thank God the snowstorm didn't kill the flowers." Marigold stepped into the soggy grass and tugged a few needles from a pine branch. She crushed them and inhaled the woodsy scent. The two of them paused on the wooden bridge spanning the creek.

"Do you wonder about our biological parents?"

"Sure," Adam said. "From my perspective, I wonder why the hell they had kids if one of them was a carrier of Huntington's. Were they selfish? Or stupid?" He snorted. "Irrelevant now, isn't it?"

"God, it's like my life's an incomplete jigsaw puzzle," Marigold said. "I want the missing pieces of my heritage." She stooped to retrieve an acorn and tossed it in the creek. Tiny waves undulated in the stream. "Mom and Dad should have told us we were adopted. The person I believed I was is not who I am." The water went still. "The bottom keeps dropping out of my life. First your diagnosis . . ."

Marigold was instantly contrite. "God, here I am complaining. Your situation trumps everything."

"Forget it. You're entitled to your feelings. Let's stop." Adam found a seat by the sidewalk. "Why didn't they place the bench over there?" He pointed to the pond thirty feet ahead. "I love the water. It's so peaceful."

Marigold reached into the paper bag and retrieved two peanut butter and honey sandwiches. A gust of wind rushed a cluster of shriveled leaves. Adam and Marigold sat at the bottom of the slope, and Marigold silently questioned how many more spring seasons she would share with her brother.

Adam admitted, "I think of our biological parents as ghosts who fluttered into our lives one evening, and now they've drifted away." He tipped his head toward the sky. "Like wisps of clouds."

"I keep replaying the moment their car crashed over the ravine," Marigold said.

"Stop torturing yourself. Let it go."

"I'm a McGuire," she said. "Mom and Dad are my parents—my only parents. I love them. So why can't I shake these feelings?"

"The information's a shock."

"I can't begin to guess how difficult it is to deal with your diagnosis. Are you all right by yourself in the apartment?"

He didn't answer.

"Adam?"

"I'm okay," he said.

"Come home," she said, softly. "Don't stay by yourself. You belong with your family."

"I'll have plenty of time for that." Adam turned back the foil cover and bit into the bread. He stiffened, and the sandwich dropped to the ground.

"It's clean. It landed on the foil." Marigold brushed away pieces of dirt from the wrapper and offered it to him.

"I'm not hungry," he said.

"It's fine."

He shouted at her. "I said I'm not hungry!" Marigold's eyes brimmed with tears. "I'm sorry, okay?" he said. "It's not you. Let's go. I'm tired."

They were quiet on the ride to his apartment. "I'll walk with you," Marigold said. He didn't argue. On the top landing, he took the key.

"Don't forget who I *was*." He crossed the threshold and closed the door.

• • •

Adam leaned against the wall. Poor Marigold, he thought. She was trying to help, and he had sulked and been in a funk the whole outing. He'd managed to ruin everything. Once his depression came up to feast, it ravaged him *and* the people he loved.

He called his sister.

"I wanted to apologize," Adam said. "I didn't mean to be harsh. I get frustrated. I'm feeling down again. I don't want your memories to be of that pitiful guy, okay? That's what I meant when I said, 'Don't forget who I *was*.'"

"I could never stay mad at you."

"Good, because I have a favor to ask you."

"What's up?"

"Rosie asked me if there was anything I'd regret not doing with my life, and I thought of something."

"Are you going to tell me?"

"I want to go to Boston. See Harvard. Eat clam chowder. And I want to go with you."

"Oh, wow," she said. "I did *not* see that coming."

"I found some good deals on airfares. If you can skip class Friday, we could go this weekend."

"Like *this* Friday? I don't know. I should clear it with my teachers tomorrow. I guess I could study on the airplane."

"I don't want this trip to just be about me. Why don't you write down places of interest to you?"

"No, this is your time. Are you sure it's safe for you to travel?"

"I can do this."

"It would be special to have the time together," she said.

"Great. Check with Mom and Dad. Don't worry about any expenses. I'll book the flights and figure out the details. The airline will hold the reservations for twenty-four hours. I'll wait to pay until I hear from you tomorrow. I caught a break on the hotel rates, too."

"Adam?"

"Yeah?"

"You know there will be a lot of walking."

"I know. I didn't say it would be easy," he said. "We won't need a car. I read Boston has a great subway system, the MBTA; they call it the 'T.' I probably could go by myself, but I never know . . ."

"No, you shouldn't risk going alone. I want to be there with you," she said.

"Thanks. I've had some lessons dealing with humility. Not feeling ashamed of this disease is liberating, but I backslide. I'm not proud of my actions."

"I'll always forgive you, whatever you do."

"Remember, I'm holding you to your promise," he said.

• • •

Adam put on a Maroon 5 CD, lip-synched to "Moves Like Jagger," and booked the flights. He cranked the music louder and stacked three sweaters, two shirts, a pair of dress slacks, sweatpants, socks, and boxers on top his dresser. He retrieved a book he had purchased last summer, *A Guide to New England*, and lay down on his futon and began to read. A note slipped from between the pages and fluttered to his chest. Adam read *Places to Visit in Boston*, a list he'd prepared last year. He folded the paper and tucked it inside his wallet.

Within the hour, his phone zinged a text.

Mom and Dad said yes.

Ha! I'm so excited! I'm almost packed.

I'll go in early to confirm with my teachers.

Adam texted back, *Good. Let me know ASAP.*

He plugged his phone in the wall, fell into bed, and watched an old rerun of "Cheers." He slept soundly. In the morning, he detached the phone from the cord and powered on. There was one unread message. *Got the okay from my teachers. We're going to Boston!*

Adam punched his fist into his palm. Take *that*, Huntington's, he thought. Life blazed inside him. He couldn't restrain the smile stretching across his face. He wrote a note and placed it on the counter: *Pay for tickets. Deadline 7 p.m.*

Adam composed an e-mail to share the news with Brad:

How's it going? Getting excited about Truman? I'm auditing my classes but don't attend much. I miss basketball and hanging out with you guys. I guess you're busy preparing for finals.

FYI—I took a couple of meditation classes at the center. Oh, big news! My sister and I are going to Boston for the weekend. Two nights from now, I'll be looking at the Charles River. The anticipation is stimulating. Good luck at Truman.

He typed Marigold a text: *I can pick you up today after school and we can talk about what we're going to do on the trip.*

She replied: *Meet you in the front.*

He set the phone on the counter. *Bah-stin.*

CHAPTER 66

Alana and Borg cruised down the highway, and along the way, Alana pointed out Forest Park, its treasure of attractions, and various neighborhoods like The Hill, a community known for its Italian heritage and great food.

"Oops, here's our exit." Alana maneuvered the car onto the ramp. "This is an amazing city. There's so much to do, such diversity. I want to swing by the courthouse and show you the Arch."

"That's impressive," Borg said. Alana slowed the car so he could snap a picture with his phone.

Alana wasn't comfortable driving the streets downtown. One wrong turn, and she'd end up on a one-way street sending her in an unintended direction. Thank God for GPS. She swerved to avoid a pothole but caught the edge. The car jolted, and Borg winced.

"Does your shoulder still hurt?" Alana asked.

"I'm pretty sore," Borg said, "and I have one heck of a bruise."

"What did it feel like to be shot?" Alana asked.

"Like a searing hot piece of metal was driven through my flesh."

"You lost a lot of blood."

"I've spent a lot of time thinking about how fragile life is. What's meaningful in the big scheme?" he asked.

Alana wasn't sure why her heart was beating faster. Was it Borg opening up to her, or was it that she had been asking herself that same question?"

"You're completely powerless against a bullet," he said. "I underestimated Leone. I never imagined she was capable of murder."

Alana focused on the cars speeding past her. "The moment I met her, she struck me as cunning and calculating. The night she forced her way into my room, I was sure I was a dead woman. I still have nightmares." Alana's grip tightened on the steering wheel. "I worried what would happen to my staff if I died. I asked myself, what would Joan do?"

"Who's Joan?"

"Joan of Arc." Alana paused. "I pictured that young girl in battle, and a strange calm quieted my panic. I can't let *my* troops down. They're my team, and I can't screw up this decision. That's why I must choose wisely." Alana blinked and thought back to the day at the Jive. What was that message Hanna had written? Hadn't it been *Choose wisely*?

The space between Alana and Borg was twelve inches at most. Borg laid his palm against her arm, strong and gentle at the same time. "Quite a powerful analogy," he said. "In my business, I care for the people working for me, but they're my employees, not my friends."

"We run our businesses differently," she said. After a few minutes, their speed was reduced to a crawl. "Oh, great." She gestured to the line of red taillights. "The cars are lined up for blocks."

"There's a parking garage ahead," Borg said.

"Good," Alana said.

Their tickets were waiting at the box office. Alana and Borg perused a kiosk before the show. Alana inspected a Renaissance hairpiece, a delicate wreath wrapped in satin. Pink silk roses covered the headband, and a thin diaphanous piece of veil was attached to the back.

"Something for my lady?" Borg asked.

Alana took the circlet from the hook and adjusted the garland on top of her hair.

"You are most beautiful, fair Alana," Borg said.

"Why, thank you, kind sir." She included a regal mock curtsy.

Borg picked up a faux gold metal crown and tried it on, tipping it slightly off to the side.

"What do you think?" he asked.

Alana laughed. "Very nice. As long as you don't get any ideas about being king."

He didn't miss a beat. "No promises."

Borg paid for their headpieces, and they strolled toward section C to find their seats.

A photographer stopped them. "Souvenir?"

"What do you think?" Borg asked.

"Let's do it," Alana said. The photographer gestured, guiding them closer until their shoulders touched. Borg leaned his head next to Alana's, and the flash fired.

"Two copies of the picture will be in an envelope at booth number six," the photographer said. "You can pay now or later. Sign here."

Borg signed the invoice, wrote their seat numbers, and removed three twenty dollar bills. "Could you deliver them during the show? And keep the change."

"Yes, sir. You got it."

The arena was a circle divided into four sections. Alana tallied the number of people in costumes. "There must be seventy-five actors and twenty horses. Watch the stallion over there."

A white horse decorated with purple and yellow cloth draped across its flank leapt into the air.

"I believe the horse is an Andalusian," he said. "My father owned one. The most beautiful breed in the world, in my opinion."

"I don't know anything about horses, but I'd agree with you."

Four men lifted their trumpets and signaled the games to begin. In each section, there was jousting and sword-fighting on horseback. Live falcons soared overhead. Men in costumes waved colored flags and marched along the sand floor. The audience roared as the horses galloped across the arena. Knights touting weapons dismounted for combat.

A woman served them soup, oven-roasted chicken, and herbed potatoes after the show began. During the meal, the photographer slipped into the aisle, passed Borg two envelopes, and disappeared. Alana didn't take her eyes off the two men battling steel.

· · ·

The sun set below the horizon as they returned to the parking garage. "I had a great time," Borg said.

"Me, too. The show was so authentic. Like stepping into a time machine and being whisked back to the 1400s." Alana touched the veil on her wreath. "We're still wearing our headpieces."

Borg stopped under a streetlight. He drew her close and brushed his lips softly across hers, lingering, barely touching, as if asking permission. Her head tilted upward, desiring more. His kiss was gentle, revealing, like coming home. Her skin warmed under Borg's touch, and her heart raced. She kissed him back, oblivious to anyone around them. Her tongue flicked, seductive, wanting. A quiet moan escaped her.

He whispered, "I've been wanting to do that."

"Let's go to my house," she said.

For a brief moment, Borg tensed.

"What is it?" she asked.

"Maybe I overstepped. We know this could complicate things."

"Right. The proverbial 'Don't mix business with pleasure.'" Alana thought they were like children caught with their hands in the cookie jar. She had no doubts. She wanted the cookie.

• • •

They approached Alana's front door. "Do you mind taking off your shoes? I don't wear them in the house." She flipped on the foyer light and questioned her impulse now that passion wasn't overriding reason. Her smile wavered in the awkward silence, but as they walked through the great room, she began to relax.

"Your house is beautiful," he said.

"I purchased a furnished display home. My offer included the furniture and accessories. I don't have time to decorate."

"Country French," Borg said. "Charming." He sat down on a barstool at the kitchen's long granite counter.

"Would you like a drink? Tea, wine, or a new martini I've been dying to try, called April in Paris?"

"I'll go with the martini. Do you need some help?"

"Just keep me company." Alana shook the ingredients, filled two martini glasses, and sat on the barstool next to Borg's.

Borg sipped his drink. "I like it." They moved closer and clicked their drinks. Neither drew away.

"Tell me about you," Alana said. "Do you have family?"

"My parents and my older sister live about two hours north of San Diego."

"I have a sister, Natalie, a few years younger than I am," Alana said.

"And your parents, do they live in town?" Borg asked.

"About twenty minutes from here. Of course, in St. Louis, everybody says they're about twenty minutes from everywhere." Her skin flushed. Was it the alcohol or sitting so close to him? Focus, she thought. "I also have two aunts and two grandmothers here. We're a close family."

"So would it be difficult to leave permanently?" Borg asked.

"Pretty much impossible," Alana said. "What about you? Could you ever move?"

"I've never considered leaving the West Coast." He moved his drink to the side and lightly touched her shoulder.

Alana's stomach gurgled. "Well, that's embarrassing. I know we ate a few hours ago, but I'm hungry."

"Let me take you to dinner."

"I have an idea. How are you with a grill?"

"Pretty handy. What did you have in mind?"

"A light meal. If you can grill chicken, I'll chop up a salad."

"Consider it done."

After preparing the food, they carried plates, flatware, and a bottle of wine outside, sat on the patio, and ate under the stars, listening to the distant mating calls of deep-throated frogs.

A gentle breeze cooled the night air, and they talked about college, their dreams, and their magazines. "You remember my assistant, Michelle?" Alana asked. "She's pregnant. She recently announced she'll leave the firm to stay home with her baby. I'm really going to miss her."

"It sounds like she's a good friend." He rubbed his chin. "Babies can change relationships. I lost touch with some special friends after they had a child. All they could talk about was their Sarah. Can't say I blame them. She was a cute kid."

"I'm sure I won't lose my friendship with Michelle," Alana said. Her napkin lifted in the breeze, and she grasped it. "Maybe we should go in."

They cleared the table. Inside, Alana opened a bag of mini Dove chocolate bars and scattered them in a bowl. "I'm afraid this is dessert."

He removed the wrapping and took a bite. "That's all I need," he said. Before she could reply, Borg moved around the table and stood next to her. Alana's breath was unsteady when Borg moved her hair off her shoulder, and she felt his warm lips slowly move down her neck, and then back to her mouth. His kiss tasted of chocolate.

Alana shivered with pleasure. It had been such a long time. She knew exactly what she wanted. She led him to her bedroom.

He unbuttoned her blouse. It fell away, revealing a satin camisole.

Borg's shoulder was still bandaged. Her cheek grazed his smooth flesh, and her lips softly pressed against his chest. Alana lifted her head and gave his lip a gentle nip. He stroked the back of her neck and followed the curve of her body. She pressed against him. He reached under her camisole and moved gently over her breast, and she felt her entire body responding.

Alana whispered, "Do you have protection?"

Borg fumbled for his wallet, peeling apart the fold where cash was kept. His expression answered her.

He thumbed the wallet again. "Do you?"

"No." She sighed. "It's been a really long time." Her need

was palpable, but she managed to take a step away. Borg drew her back, close enough she could feel his ache. She traced the ripple of his abdomen and fought a deep yearning for something lost. She gently pushed him away. "I think we should stop."

He moved behind her, caressed her. She wanted to beg him not to stop. Instead, she said, "I have only so much willpower." She handed him his shirt. "Besides, this may not be the best road to go down if we end up working together."

• • •

Back in the kitchen, Alana leaned against the counter and played with Borg's empty candy wrapper. The kitchen was quiet except for the ticking of the clock on the counter.

"I think I should go," Borg said.

Alana wrapped her hand around her cup, wondering what sex with him would have been like, and her nipples hardened under her blouse. She inhaled a sharp breath, brought her arms in front of her, and took a long drink of water. "Yes, it's after midnight."

Borg put the cork in the empty wine bottle and called for a taxi. "Someone will be here in about ten minutes. Let me help you clean up some of the mess. It's late. You don't want to wake up to this tomorrow morning."

"Thanks," she said, surprised by his offer. Borg scraped the dishes and put them in the dishwasher. By the time Alana finished wrapping the leftovers, the taxi's headlights in the driveway splashed the kitchen window.

"Well, then, I guess I'll say good night." Borg slid his feet into his leather loafers.

A breeze rustled through the treetops, and the moon slid in and out from behind the clouds. They said their good-byes, and Borg reached for her and grazed her neck with a soft kiss. She shivered. The electricity between them wasn't going away.

CHAPTER 67

Adam backed into a space in the visitor parking lot. He spied his sister in the crowd and flashed his lights. Marigold waved in acknowledgment. She cut across the grass toward the car. She was almost to the walkway, and Adam watched her right foot twist in the grass. Books flew in the air. The scene played like a slow-motion video. There was nothing he could do.

Seconds later, Adam knelt beside his sister. Marigold lay crumpled on the lawn, her eyes filled with tears.

"I heard it pop. God, it hurts."

"Can you stand?"

"I don't know." Marigold rolled up the cuff of her pants. Her ankle had already started to swell and bruise. She gripped Adam's arm, struggled to her feet, winced, and fell back.

"Lean on me," he said. "There's an urgent care down the street." Adam picked up her books and steadied her as she hobbled to his car.

• • •

"The good news is that the doctor said you don't need surgery, since your ankle isn't broken," Adam said, assisting Marigold to the couch. He couldn't stand the regret on his sister's face, and he tried to mask his own disappointment, knowing the trip was off.

"Whatever," she said. "Everything's ruined. The doctor said not to travel and to keep my leg elevated. It hurts so much. Don't ever let anyone tell you a sprain hurts less than a break. And those stupid crutches rub under my arms."

"I'm sorry, Marigold. At least, with the weekend coming, you can rest."

"Can you reschedule the trip?" she asked.

"I don't think so," Adam said. "You'll have to study for finals, and the airfare goes up after school lets out. This was the best weekend."

"Are you going to cancel the tickets?"

"No, they'll expire if I don't pay."

"I'm sorry, Adam."

"It's fine."

"No, it's not," Marigold said.

She was right, Adam thought. "I'm going to the Jive to get some coffee," he said. "Would you like anything?"

"No, just hand me my book. And the ice pack."

• • •

Adam ordered a coffee and stepped aside. Hanna poured his drink and called his name.

"No words on my cup?" he asked.

"You're pale. What's happened?"

"It doesn't matter."

"Find a seat," Hanna said. "I'm taking my break."

She joined him at a high-top table, and Adam confided the events of the past day. His words carried more than a hint of melancholy. "I'd go by myself, but I'm afraid to be alone so far from home."

Hanna's soft brown eyes never left his. "I know what this journey means to you. It would have been extraordinary for your sister to have these memories. I'm not Marigold, but I'd be glad to accompany you to Boston."

Adam blinked. "We hardly know each other. Why would you offer to come with me?"

"Because," she said, "you'd volunteer to help if someone were in need. The idea you can't go has destroyed your spirit."

She was right. He hadn't anticipated the desperation. "I hate for you to think of me as weak."

"You're vulnerable."

"You'd really come with me?"

"I'd just have to cancel a class."

"And pack," he said.

Her laugh was delicate. "And pack."

"I'll cover all expenses," Adam said, "everything."

"You said the tickets will expire this evening?"

"Oh, jeez. Almost forgot. I'll take care of that right now." Adam picked up his phone and deleted his sister's name from the reservation. "Hanna, I don't know your last name."

"It's Tallaway."

"You're sure about this?" he asked, his finger poised on the keypad.

"Yes, I'm sure it's Tallaway."

"No." He smiled. "I meant about taking the trip with me."

"Just adding a little levity. And the answer is still yes. I wouldn't have offered if I thought otherwise. My break is over. Let's meet here Friday."

They agreed on a time. "I don't know how to thank you," Adam said.

"Don't thank me yet." Hanna uncapped her marker and scribbled on Adam's cup.

"I have to get back to work," she said.

He rotated the cup. *The best-laid plans~*

CHAPTER 68

The sky was white and lilac, laced with wispy clouds, and the forecast predicted a strong chance of storms. Saige hoped this was wrong for Katie's sake, so her day would be perfect. At the Warwicks', cars already lined the street. Saige rang the doorbell, and someone yelled, "Come in."

The party congregated in the great room, all dressed for the ceremony. Almost everyone. Katie waved from across the room. Relaxed, wearing slacks and a T-shirt, she sipped her drink. The groomsmen wore white jackets and black bow ties. Nick had spiced up his tux with a burgundy tie, the color of the brides-maids' dresses, and Saige was pretty sure he was wearing Star Wars cuff links.

Katie's father came forward, tugging at his collar. "Hello, Saige," he said. "Oh my, all you girls look lovely. Down the hall is the kitchen—enjoy the food and drinks."

Across the room, Tessa, one of the bridesmaids, raised her mimosa and mouthed the words, "Want one?"

"I'm fine," Saige mouthed back.

Katie approached Saige. "Good, everybody's here. Grab some food. In twenty minutes, Chris will start the photo shoot. He brought props. It'll be a blast," she said and disappeared into the crowd.

At the pass-through bar, a man in a white fluted hat intro-duced himself as Chef Mark. "What can I get you?" Saige ordered an omelet.

Michael crossed the room, flashed a smile, and tossed an empty paper cup in the trash. "You ready for the big day?"

"Sure." She took the plate from the counter. "Everybody's so happy and friendly."

"We're a tight-knit bunch," Michael said. "We've known each other since grade school. It's too bad about Suzanne, but maybe it was fate. I'm glad I had a chance to meet you."

"Thanks. It's great to be here. Have you ever seen two people more in love than Nick and Katie?" Saige watched the couple separate, talk with their friends, find each other, touch, turn back to their friends, and then reach for each other. Their private dance. "They look so right together," Saige said.

"They are. Like two halves of a whole." Michael adjusted his glasses. "There's Chris, our friend and photographer extraordinaire. Chris, come here a second."

The young man strode toward them, cameras dangling from his neck, with another one across his shoulder. "Michael. Looking good. Hi," he said to Saige. "I'm Chris."

"Saige is the girl from Katie's ad."

"Nick told me."

"Why do you have all those cameras?" Saige asked.

"This is my primary camera," he patted one near his hip. "This other one is a backup. The third is my new toy. It's a 3-D camera. The pictures are a surprise. Don't tell."

"I won't." Saige was pleased to think she was in on the secret.

The bridesmaids went to Katie's room and helped her change into her gown.

Saige stood back, privileged to be there, yet an outsider. Mrs. Warwick clasped a pearl necklace around her daughter's neck. "Something borrowed." She opened a jeweler's box, took out a sapphire ring, and slid it onto Katie's finger. "Something blue—a gift from your father and me."

"It's beautiful, Mom. Thank you." Katie hugged her mother.

Saige's heart wrenched, knowing her own mother would never help her get ready for her wedding. She hoped Katie knew how lucky she was.

• • •

The photographer asked the girls to take off their shoes, pair with Katie, and jump on the bed. They obliged, leaping mid-air, giggling. Click.

Saige was last. She stood on the bed, face flushed. Katie clasped her wrists. "It's okay. You're part of this. On three," she said and counted. Click.

It was Mr. Warwick's turn to be photographed with his daughter. Saige knew Chris captured a special moment between father and daughter: the tender expression, the way the corner of his eyes crinkled with happiness and sadness at the same time. His cheek pressed against his daughter's. Click.

"Nick and Katie, I need you outside." The wedding party followed, curious. Everyone was stunned to see an inflatable white heart the size of a double bed sprinkled with red rose petals. "Katie, lie down. Nick, you on the other side. Now reach for each other." Chris stood on a stepladder and took "aerial" shots of the couple lying on the giant white heart. Click.

"What a creative guy," Saige said to Michael.

"He loves his work. Are you having fun, Saige?"

"I've never been a part of anything like this. My life's dull."

"Well, it's not today. This day is about joyfulness."

"I know. I'm happy to be here and to have met all of you."

"It's mutual," Michael said, his eyes fixed on hers.

"Let's go to the garden and have us a wedding," Mr. Warwick said.

"Yee-hah," Nick said and laughed.

"Yee-hah," said Michael.

They all shouted yee-hah, and the wedding party stepped into a shiny limousine.

Saige sat quietly, remembering how much she had loved working for Kelly and Beth. Most people weren't lucky enough to be as passionate about their jobs as Chris was. After the wedding, she'd be back where she started, jobless and without people she could count on, except for Finn. And the way he was acting, even that was up for debate. With this group, it was hard to draw the line between family and friends. They were all so close.

More than anything, Saige wished to belong somewhere and have friends she could count on. She wasn't even sure she could count on herself. That might be a place to start.

CHAPTER 69

"Welcome to Boston's Copley Back Bay," the woman behind the hotel counter said. "We have you down for one queen room, staying two nights, checking out on Sunday."

Adam removed his credit card. "Wait. There's been a mistake. We need *two* rooms."

The woman frowned and clicked the keyboard. "I'm sorry, sir. We're fully booked. We're a small hotel. We only have forty rooms. If you like, we can provide a rollaway bed."

Adam tugged his collar. "I'm sorry, Hanna. I didn't . . ." He turned back to the clerk. "Would you mind checking again?"

The woman sighed. "The hotel is booked through the entire weekend."

"Just one second, please," he said. The line behind them grew longer. Adam whispered to Hanna. "What about another hotel?"

"We'll be fine," Hanna said.

• • •

They settled in their room, and housekeeping set up a rollaway bed.

"Do you mind if I rest?" Adam asked Hanna.

"No worries. I'll scout a café for dinner."

"Do you like sushi?" Adam asked.

"Sorry, but I don't eat anything with eyes. No problem. Most restaurants offer plenty of choices."

"Would you mind if we eat soon? I'd love to get an early start tomorrow."

"Of course," she said.

Adam sat on the bed. "I hope this isn't weird for you, sleeping in the same room and all."

"Worry is a thief. It steals time and never gets you anywhere. I'll see you in an hour."

• • •

Hanna was breathless. "We're in trouble."

"Are you all right?" Adam sat on the edge of the bed. "Tell me what happened."

She laughed, and her face radiated pleasure. "Down the street—there's a chocolate bar."

Adam tsked. "I'd never have guessed you're a closet chocoholic."

"Everybody has secrets. Hungry?"

"Starving."

The sun set behind the city's skyscrapers, and long shadows painted the street in darkness. Dessert First was two blocks away. They waited at the bar, and Hanna ordered hot chocolate with chili pepper and fresh whipped cream. Adam selected thick hot chocolate topped with coconut.

"Delicious," he said. "Think we could talk the Jive into serving this?"

"I'll speak with management right away." Hanna took a sip. "Why are you grinning?"

"You have a chocolate mustache."

Hanna ran her tongue around her lip.

"Nope. You missed." He wiped a spot under her nose. "Got it." Half a cup later, they were seated at a table with vinyl placemats. Adam talked about the city and tried to teach Hanna how to drop her *r*'s and imitate a Boston accent.

"I want a veggie *bur-gur*," she said.

"Try again. You *almost* nailed it. *Buh-guh*."

The waitress came to the table, and Hanna ordered with her best Bostonian accent. The woman took their orders and scurried away.

Adam frowned. "I'm disappointed. How can they not offer clam chowder?"

"We'll find a place tomorrow."

"Sounds good. What'd you find out while you were exploring?" Adam asked.

"Boston is a fascinating city, a treasure trove of history."

"*This* city is where it all started—great thinkers rebelling against tyranny. Can you imagine? The Freedom Trail leads to sixteen important historical sites."

"Hmm. It's over a two-mile walk if you want to see it all."

His smile vanished. "What about the trolley?"

Hanna shook her head. "We're too early. Opens in May. The good news is we're close to one of the subway stations. The system has five lines to get travelers around the city, and they're color-coded. I don't think we'll have any trouble. Did you bring your list?"

Adam took a paper from his wallet. "Right here."

"What are the three most important 'must do's'?"

"If I have to pick, I'd say the Paul Revere House, the Boston Latin School, Granary Burying Ground, and . . ."

"Keep it simple."

"Okay. Harvard. First is Harvard. That's why I'm here."

The waitress served their food and hurried to another table.

"We can take the Red Line to Harvard, have lunch, and see how you feel," Hanna said.

"Good plan." Adam tasted his sandwich. "Can you eat waffles?"

Hanna smiled. "Yes. And dairy."

He passed her a forkful. "So I assumed, watching you polish off your drink."

"Tell me why you want to see the Boston Latin School," she said.

"Four signers of the Declaration of Independence went to school there, but only three graduated. One of the greatest minds, Ben Franklin, dropped out. Now there's a statue erected of *him* in front of the school. I'd say he had the last laugh," Adam said.

"He persevered. Tell Rosie he was one of seventeen children."

"Are you serious? How'd they get anything done back then?" he asked.

"Hard work, I guess. And drive. A driven man can achieve impossible results—especially with a woman at home taking care of the kids," Hanna said.

After dinner, they strolled to the arts district on Newbury Street and peered through the glass of one of the galleries. Adam pointed to a portrait of Mickey Mouse in a storefront window. "Now there's an icon. Probably valuable; it looks old. Do you have a favorite artist?"

"It's impossible to pick just one," Hanna said. "Today, I'd say Odilon Redon and Élisabeth Vigée-Lebrun.

"I'm not familiar with either of them. Are you into art?"

"Didn't I tell you I have a master's degree in art history? I have favorites in every period."

"I had no idea," Adam said.

"Don't look so surprised. We're constantly changing paths."

"Wouldn't you rather teach than—"

"Serve coffee? I do teach."

Adam didn't press. Hanna the mysterious barista was now Hanna the woman who took on many roles. He liked knowing another side of her. That she liked chocolate. And had secrets.

They circled back to the hotel. The boulevard was busier. Heat lamps stood near tables along the sidewalks, and the night was dynamic and full of life. A street musician at the corner played "Amazing Grace" on his guitar, and Hanna threw some coins in his velvet-lined case. Laughter drifted through the open doors of pubs and fine restaurants. Crowds of tourists and locals wandered the streets as Adam and Hanna trekked back to their hotel.

"I feel like a dud. Maybe you'd rather stay out and enjoy the evening."

Hanna opened the door to their hotel. "I'd rather be here with you."

CHAPTER 70

Alana didn't sleep well, her thoughts confused, a tumble of dark ruminations. She lay in bed imagining Borg's arms around her and what might have been. The tug of disappointment persisted. She'd never fall back asleep now. Alana secured her robe and crossed barefoot over the cool wooden plank floor.

She debated making coffee or going to the Jive, and opted for coffee at home. On her way to the kitchen, a manila envelope tucked among some photos on her desk, like a half-hidden Easter egg, caught her eye. Borg must have placed it on the table last night. She tore open the packet. Inside, she found a picture of the two of them, cheek to cheek, at the Medieval Festival. The happy couple. Alana propped the picture against a frame. Too late to wish one of them had prepared for last night. She'd forgotten how good it felt to have a man's company. To be kissed.

Alana ground the beans and questioned how this man could throw her life off balance. She was attracted to his self-confidence and how he lit with excitement when talking about a new project. Alana had always been drawn to intelligence. Add warm lips, consideration, and a great body to the list. Another tingle went through her. Her mind wandered to the kiss they had shared under the streetlight, the image of him wearing the gold crown, cocked on his head sideways like a halo dropped from a fallen angel.

If they had slept together, how would it have affected the business venture? A basic rule in any industry: Never have a relationship with someone in your office. Blah-blah-blah. How many times would the recording play in her head? Of course, their professional relationship hadn't been determined yet. Alana drained the cup and thought about her staff. The magazine was everything to her. Too important to give up. Emotions had blurred her analysis. And suddenly, she had her answer. Alana poured another cup, strode to the hall desk, and placed the photo inside a drawer.

•   •   •

Borg answered his phone. "Good morning. I'm about to board the plane."

"I had to call. I have my answer, and I'm ready to counter."

He waited.

"I know you're trying to avoid another start-up, but my instincts tell me all your articles don't belong in my magazine. What if you kept your articles in *New Heights* and we ran the clothing line in *Slick?*" No turning back now, she thought. "I was thinking we could do a media blitz to promote the boutique's clothes."

"You're telling me there will be no magazine merger?"

"No merger," she said. "This has been an incredibly difficult decision. I have struggled with it every day. You have so many business ventures, but this is *all* I have. I want full say on everything."

She took a deep breath and continued. "Since the boutique was your idea, if we use my magazine to showcase the line, we could split all profits from Martine's ads fifty-fifty. I know *Slick* would lend itself to Martine's style. If you want to run Martine's ads in *New Heights,* I'll step away. But no merging the magazines. I can't do it any other way."

"You need the control."

"I can never tell with you if it's a question or a statement," she said. "It doesn't feel right to merge and have to vie with each other for article space. This decision keeps the arrangement simpler."

"So you'll cut me a check each month?" he asked.

"All paperwork relating to the fashion house and sales can be duplicated and sent to both of us. Am I picking up some hostility? Or is it sarcasm?"

"Sarcasm. I'm adjusting to your proposal. Martine and I discussed using my name at the top of the ad, *A Borg Larson Line*, with her company name sewn inside the back of the collar."

"No problem."

"Let me talk to Stanley, and you discuss the proposal with Daniel."

"About our, uh, situation." Alana reached for nerve, not wanting to cut the tie. "Maybe we should keep our relationship strictly about business."

Borg was silent, the moment awkward. He answered, "Business it is. I'll call you or have Andrew send a written plan to your office after Stanley reviews it."

After she hung up, Alana faced the fact that she was lonely and her life was missing something—something very important. But she knew Borg wasn't interested in a relationship. He'd made no attempt to argue when she suggested they keep things professional, not personal. For him, it was all about the magazine—*her* magazine.

CHAPTER 71

Adam called his family while Hanna showered. After he hung up, he expected to hear the buzzing of the hair dryer, but Hanna slid under the covers, freshly scrubbed, her hair damp.

Adam took his time cleaning up to give her space. He dressed in sweatpants and a T-shirt, climbed into the rollaway at the foot of the bed, and tried not to watch as she read her book. "This is definitely weird," he said. "I'm in Boston in a hotel room with Hanna." She laughed at him as though it were the most natural thing in the world that their beds were ten feet apart.

"Are you ready to turn in?" she asked.

"If it's okay with you. I'm tired."

Hanna clicked off the light on the nightstand. "Good night, Adam," she said in the darkness.

"Good night." It was difficult to sleep. He was warm and tossed the blanket away, replaying the day. He thought of Hanna's laugh and how she tried to lick the chocolate foam from her lip. Adam felt little butterflies in his stomach. But he wasn't thinking about butterflies. Was she awake? He waited for the pattern of her breathing. The familiar guide relaxed him, and he finally dozed.

When Adam awoke the next morning, Hanna was gone. A note on the hotel stationery left next to her pillow told him she would wait in the café. It took him all of fifteen minutes to shave, dress, and find Hanna in the lobby bistro. She was sipping tea and chatting with the waitress. Her fair complexion glowed baby-soft, and her eyes sparkled when he approached the table.

"Hey, sleepyhead," she teased.

He shot back, "Hey there, wide-awake-at-dawn girl."

Hanna smiled. "You did say you wanted to get an early start."

Adam protested. "It's only eight fifteen. I doubt anything's open."

"Harvard never closes."

Adam waved the waitress over. "Coffee, black, and two eggs with toast. And for you?" he asked Hanna.

"Your girlfriend already gave me her order. She asked me to wait for you before I turned in the ticket. I'll have coffee right out, sir," she said.

"She's my *friend*," Adam called after her, uncomfortable with the comment.

After breakfast, they easily found the station to board the T to Harvard Square. It was an easy fifteen-minute commute, and the campus was open for tourists to roam the grounds. Adam and Hanna stepped through the black iron gates, and he allowed himself a moment to daydream about a life he would never know—finding new friends whose interests matched his, cheering on the football team, and receiving the coveted Harvard law degree.

Later, they waited behind a procession of tourists for their turn to rub the toe of the left shoe on the bronze statue of John Harvard, supposedly for good luck. Hanna snapped Adam's picture with his smartphone, along with a selfie of the two of them with the university in the background. He found a smile, but the magic was ebbing. There was something surreal about the hub of students and tourists mingling. Adam suspected it was because he was a visitor, not a student.

They lingered in the Harvard Yard. A tour guide pointed out the red dorm buildings for freshman students. "I wonder which one would have been mine," Adam said to Hanna.

"Maybe over there," she said, "by the elm that looks like a wineglass."

"Would've been perfect," he said.

They hiked the Quad, climbed the grassy slopes, and rested on the library steps. The day was clear and sunny, but the cement was cold and hard. After five minutes, Adam stood. "Would you mind if we browse the Harvard bookstore? I want to buy a souvenir for Marigold."

"Let's go," Hanna said.

After rifling through merchandise, Adam decided on a crimson sweatshirt. Emblazoned in white across the front was the word *Harvard*. "I think your sister will love that," Hanna said as they left the store.

Adam glanced back at the old campus with the ivy-covered brick. He'd never be back. There'd be no statues of him—nothing to leave behind. No last laugh. The horns honking at the street corner caused his head to pound. He had experienced a piece of Harvard, and he silently crossed it off his list.

• • •

"You're quiet," Hanna said.

"I thought this trip would make me happy."

"You're not?"

"I'm disappointed and angry that I won't get my chance. The best-laid plans, right?" Vibrations from the ground increased as the train approached.

"You knew you couldn't have Harvard," Hanna said. "But you got a glimpse of what would have been. You can stop wondering."

"I'm chasing a future that can never be. It's a wasted journey."

"Adjust your expectations. Accept that nothing will be normal. A question has been answered. You'd have more regret if you hadn't seized the opportunity. This trip was your fantasy, and it's not over."

They filed onto the T and watched the city blur through the subway windows. "You're right," Adam said. He addressed a man checking his phone. "Excuse me. Where's the best place around here to get clam chowder?"

"We all have our favorites, but mine isn't far." He gave them directions to Fresh Catch.

"Okay," Adam said to Hanna. "Let's get a real taste of Boston."

The restaurant was easy to find. The lunch crowd had thinned, except for a group in the back. Adam and Hanna nestled in a cozy booth, and Hanna ordered an artichoke salad, and Adam, New England chowder. After the sliced loaves of bread, their lunch arrived, enough for each to split four ways. Adam's spoon dove into the dish.

"Can you try this?" he asked. "It's heavenly."

"No, I don't eat seafood, even mollusks. Describe it to me."

"It's creamy, with tender potatoes and onions. I think I taste bacon and, of course, clams. Soft, not chewy. Perfect." He smacked his lips. "The herbs, I'm not sure. Fresh fennel, I think. Maybe bay leaves and pepper. No tomato."

"Sounds like you know your way around a kitchen."

"I do. Well, it's a family thing; we each take turns picking recipes and cooking together. Not so much since I got my own apartment. How's your salad?"

"Wonderful," she said, "but I'll never finish it. I'm stuffed."

"Why don't we get the food wrapped? We have a mini-fridge

and a microwave. I'm not letting this go to waste." Adam flagged their server, and Hanna insisted on picking up the tab.

After the bill was paid, Hanna bent to retrieve the bag and looped the handle in the crook of her arm, exposing the lacy rise of her bra. Adam found it difficult to look away. At the Jive, Hanna always wore an apron over a white button-up shirt.

"Shall we find the Paul Revere House?" she asked.

"After you." He followed, admiring her slender frame maneuvering down the narrow aisle.

"'scuse me!" A busboy zigzagged between the tables and whizzed around the corner, his tray stacked with dishes. Adam grabbed the booth on impact. A circular platter teetered overhead and pitched forward. A crash echoed around the room. Floorboards were covered with olive oil, broken glasses, and shattered plates. People in the restaurant cheered and applauded.

The boy stammered an apology and picked a piece of asparagus out of his hair. Splatters of red wine dotted Adam's khaki pants. A woman rushed from behind the reservation stand and glared at the young man. "I've told you to slow down. Get someone to help clean this up."

"Sir," she said to Adam, "we insist you send us the cleaning bill." The woman huffed to the register, entered a code, and presented Adam with two coupons: *Your next meal is on us.* "I apologize," she said. "Is everyone all right?"

"We're fine." Adam stuffed the coupons in his pocket. "Thank you."

"What happened?" Hanna asked.

"It was the busboy. I'm sorry for him but happy to report that, this time, I was not responsible." Adam grinned. "He plowed into *me.*"

Outside, a homeless man in jeans and a dirty gray sweatshirt sat propped against a storefront. His possessions were in a plastic bag by his side, a tin can with some change by his knee. Adam focused on the man's torn tennis shoes. The holes revealed he wore no socks. They stepped around him.

"Wait," Adam said. He reached inside the sack, removed the cardboard container of soup, and offered it to the man. "Boston's best clam chowder," Adam said.

"God bless you," the man said and smiled a toothless grin.

Adam retrieved the coupons from his pocket, removed a twenty from his billfold, and folded them inside the man's tin container.

Hanna gave him the bag. "Salad and bread will be a nice addition to the chowder. You'll find plastic utensils inside."

Knotted fingers poked through the frayed cloth glove. He picked up the bag. "I thank you kindly."

"Our pleasure," Adam said. After they left, he turned to see the man plunging a spoon into the container of chowder.

They found the subway and exited at Haymarket. Adam and Hanna meandered through the narrow streets to the Paul Revere House. After the self-guided tour, Hanna admitted she was tired, and they backtracked to the hotel.

In their room, Adam packed his carry-on. "I'm enjoying our trip. Thanks for coming with me."

He gave her a hug. Her skin was soft. She lingered before stepping back.

"I'll print our boarding passes for tomorrow," Adam said.

Hanna draped her sweater on the swivel chair next to the desk. The garment fell to the floor. They both reached at the same moment, and Adam brushed against Hanna's back. She circled to face him.

He was dizzy. His pulse raced. Adam couldn't explain his desire to stroke her bare shoulder—his overwhelming desire for all of her. He kissed her forehead, her cheek. Her full lips. His boldness surprised him, as did the accidental passion. But he held her, and she didn't draw away.

"Before we go any further," Hanna said, "we need to be clear so there isn't any confusion. You have enough to deal with. A relationship would be too painful. We only have this moment, because to kindle anything more would be asking for sadness too heavy to carry. Are you *sure?*"

Her question forced him to be brutally honest. His action had been impulsive, and he considered the consequences. Tonight, if he took her, tomorrow he'd have to let her go.

"I know I want you. That's all I know." He had to be honest so he wouldn't disappoint her. "I don't have a lot of experience."

"Nor do I," she said.

His arm wrapped around her waist, and he pulled her onto the bed. A romantic melancholy stirred unexpectedly inside him. He never suspected he would fall for Hanna.

•   •   •

Adam awoke to an empty bed. Another note rested on the pillow beside him. The message read the same as the one yesterday. She would meet him in the restaurant. Tender memories of last night commingled with the dark thought that he would never lie with Hanna again. He was startled, afraid of the emptiness consuming him.

Adam quickly dressed and went to the lobby. He spied Hanna sitting near the window. A shard of sunlight illuminated the side of her cheek and the color of her hair. He paused, savoring last night's intimacy.

Now he'd live forever in Hanna's memory. She'd done that for him. If there was some miracle cure, he'd never forget her, either. And not just because the passion they'd shared had been so intense, but because—as dangerous as it was to admit this one-sided secret he carried—his heart had opened to her in a way he'd never experienced.

CHAPTER 72

Nothing gladdened her spirit like flowers ablaze in color, and Saige wished she could linger at the garden's border, where the perennials and annuals were anything but quiet. She hated to hurry past the serpentine columns of bright daisies and tall lines of pink lupines. This fairy-tale wedding was everything Saige had imagined, except for the sky—clear and light an hour earlier, now a silver-plate gray. A westward breeze rushed in a sea of clouds.

In the rose garden, five-foot-wide white umbrellas on pale bamboo poles surrounded the guests. Blue hydrangea topiaries, carefully placed on each side of the podium, waited for the bride and groom's arrival. White chairs arranged in neat rows faced the wooden gazebo where Katie and Nick would exchange vows. A porcelain vase contained umbrellas for the wedding party in the event of bad weather.

Saige picked up her bouquet, and a strong wind flicked her hair across her face. "Do you think the weather will cooperate?" she asked.

"I don't know," Marie said, "but the caterer told Mrs. Warwick the wedding could be moved inside." She pointed to a pavilion about thirty yards away. "They're getting ready for the champagne toast after the ceremony."

"Katie really wants the service outside," Tessa said. "She told me they'd do their nuptials in the rain if they have to."

An announcement asked the guests to take their seats. Saige

studied the crowd. There were so many people. She swallowed. Her mouth was dry as chalk. "Does anyone have water?" Marie found her a bottle. "Thanks. I feel kind of dizzy," Saige said and leaned against the curved wall wrapping behind the gazebo.

"You're hyperventilating. Take slow, deep breaths," Michael said. "We'll do it like we rehearsed, okay? You'll be fine." He patted her shoulder.

"Get your hands off her, buddy," a voice said. Finn stepped out from around the corner.

Saige gasped. "My God, what are you doing here?"

"I suspected something like this might happen. You have a lot of nerve, dude."

"Who *are* you?" Michael asked.

The girls spoke to each other in hushed voices. Mr. Warwick burst into the group. "What in the world is going on?"

"This guy is trying to put the moves on my girlfriend," Finn said.

"I assure you, son, the only thing happening here is a wedding, and we need to get started. Do I have to call security?"

"One second, sir." Saige grabbed Finn by his sleeve and dragged him to the side. "Are you insane? You have to leave."

"I was looking after you."

"You're embarrassing me, is what you're doing." She pushed his shoulders. "Go home. We'll talk about this later." Saige rushed back to the group.

"What happened?" Tessa asked.

"Tell you later. I'm so sorry, everyone."

Mr. Warwick stepped toward her, frowning. A vein running down his forehead bulged. "I hope you can reassure us nothing will disrupt my daughter's wedding."

"Yes, sir. I took care of it. Again, my apologies."

The music started, and the first bridesmaid and groomsman stepped down the aisle.

"It's okay," Michael reassured her.

"I'm not sure it is." Saige frowned, unable to justify Finn's irrational behavior. She sucked in a big breath because all around her the air was thin and evaporating.

"We're up," Michael said. "Ready?" He offered her his arm.

Saige gave him a weak smile and scanned the grounds. She didn't see Finn. "Yes, ready."

Thunder rumbled in the distance. Saige was certain the sky flicked bits of moisture on her nose. She and Michael took their position behind Angie and Will and waited their turn.

Music from a CD crooned from the speakers, and Michael escorted Saige down the aisle toward the podium. Behind her, guests whispered with excitement. Saige was unable to quiet the small voice inside her, warning. She couldn't imagine making marriage vows to Finn. They had a hole in their relationship, and she wasn't sure they would find a patch strong enough to fix it.

"Canon in D" played on cue. Mr. Warwick wrapped his daughter's arm in his, and they slowly moved toward the minister. Light rain began to fall on the concrete. Saige brushed a drop from her arm. Plunk. Another hit her cheek. The pastor read from the Benediction of the Apaches: "For each of you will be warmth to the other. Now there is no more loneliness for you."

As he pronounced them husband and wife, a huffing wind blew two of the umbrellas and lifted them momentarily airborne before they toppled to the ground. Saige wondered if they should run for cover. "What a Wonderful World" sounded from the speakers. Nick grabbed Katie's hand, raised it in the air, and yelled, "Follow us! Drinks in the pavilion!" They bounded across the white runner, and the guests followed.

The sky released plump drops now, hurling at the guests like missiles, but Saige focused on the quiet messages, the gallant gestures. The groomsmen grabbed umbrellas from the vase and held them over the bridesmaids as they trotted down the concrete walk. Mr. Warwick supported one over his wife, and she leaned close to him. There was something sweet about the whole scene. The rain didn't ruin the wedding; it created a memory.

Michael propped an umbrella above Saige and started to hum "Singin' in the Rain." She laughed at him and pulled a soaked strand of hair from her eyes.

Saige was almost to the pavilion. She glimpsed Finn in the distance, hunched behind a marble statue, his hair plastered against his head, his soaked clothes stuck to his body. He waved, but Saige lowered her eyes to avoid his gaze, and her pace quickened. Michael held the door open, disengaged the umbrella, gave it a few shakes, and followed her inside.

Drinks were served, and everyone toasted the newlyweds. Outside it thundered, and the rain poured in torrents, but no one paid attention except Saige. She sipped her drink and stole glances out the glass panes. In the excitement, no one remembered Finn. If anyone asked, what could she say about his irrational behavior?

Finn was nowhere in sight. Saige sighed, relieved. She saw only soft, wet grass and, down the path, the marble statue of *Juno*, standing silent.

CHAPTER 73

The loud ringtone startled him. Adam used the counter for support and uncurled his stiff fingers to pick up the phone. His body had decided not to cooperate with his mind.

"Hi," Rosie said. "We're going to the movies tonight. Care to join us?"

"I'd love the company."

"Don't you want to know what the movie is?" Rosie laughed.

"Not really. I'm feeling sorry for myself since I quit driving."

"I noticed your symptoms worsened after your trip," Rosie said.

"Yeah, my arms and legs thrash without warning, like a jack-in-the-box." He paused. "Hey, Rosie, I apologize for being so irritable lately."

"No worries," she said. "I'm so glad you managed a vacation. Have you talked to Hanna? I was at the Jive last week, but she wasn't there. They said she was on vacation leave. Funny she took another vacation so soon."

Adam said nothing. He had told family and friends that Hanna had gone with him and they'd had a great time, but he hadn't mentioned that the hotel had screwed up the room reservation. Hanna was a secret only his heart knew. It was his job *not* to miss her. He'd been home from Boston three weeks already. Adam hadn't realized not seeing Hanna would hurt this much. He couldn't tell anyone. Not even her.

"Maybe we could go to the Jive next week," Rosie said.

"Yeah, maybe," he said. Maybe not, he thought. Was Hanna avoiding him?

"I'm happy you had Boston. Now we need a new idea for your bucket list."

"I'm planning something," Adam said. "What time are we going tonight?"

"Depends. Do you want to get something to eat first? Carlos's working until eleven, so I'm free."

"No, thanks. I'll make a sandwich. The movie is enough excitement."

"Chelsea wanted an early evening show. Is around five all right? We'll pick you up."

"I'll watch for you," Adam said.

He tossed the phone on the counter with more force than intended. It slid onto the floor. He bent to pick it up, and his body stiffened. Maybe he should have told Rosie he couldn't go. Avoid the whispers, the insinuations from strangers who didn't know him. Adam scrawled the words *Rosie—movie—5 tonight* on an old envelope. He forgot a lot these days.

Adam laid clean clothes on the bed, stripped, and stepped inside the shower stall. He lifted the bar of soap, and the familiar tightening in his legs warned him he was going down. Adam tried to break his fall but wasn't fast enough. His head struck the tile. The water pooled red and washed down the drain.

• • •

When Adam hadn't answered after Noah knocked several times, everyone was concerned and got out of the car. Adam eventually managed to answer the door.

"Jeez Louise," Noah said. "Are you all right? What happened?"

"My God, there's blood matted in your hair," Rosie said. "And it's trickling down your neck."

Chelsea ran to the kitchen and took a dish towel out of a drawer and ice from the freezer. "Hold this against your head. I think you need stitches."

Rosie called Adam's parents. By the time Adam and his friends reached the hospital, Adam's family was waiting at the entrance.

Luke filled out the paperwork and accompanied Adam to the procedure room. While the doctor sutured Adam's scalp, he questioned him. "How did you fall?"

"It came on suddenly." Adam told him about the Huntington's.

"I see. Is this falling new for you?"

"No, but it's worse now."

"Do you have in-home help?"

"No, I live in an apartment by myself."

"Would you like us to help you find a rehab facility?"

"That's not necessary," Luke said.

Adam was taken aback by the doctor's comment but too tired to argue. It's time, he thought.

As they left the hospital, Samantha examined Adam's wound. "Thank God your friends came by. This could have been worse."

"I'll give up the apartment," Adam said, and the words ricocheted inside him, shattering what dignity he had left. "You free tomorrow, Dad?"

His father didn't hesitate. "Of course."

"I can help," Noah said.

"We'd appreciate it," Luke said. "Say, ten o'clock tomorrow?"

"I'll meet you at the apartment."

• • •

In the morning, Samantha greeted Adam and offered a cup of coffee. "Are you sure you want to go? Dad and Noah can pack your things."

"I need to be there," Adam said. "It's the first place I lived away from home. It'll give me closure."

They arrived at the apartment complex. Noah climbed out of the car, and the three men carried empty boxes inside and packed Adam's belongings. He didn't own much. The usual college student necessities: a couch, coffee table, futon, and computer desk. A few hours later, the place was empty and cleaned.

"Ready to go?" his father asked.

"Actually, there's one drawer left," Adam said. "I'll meet you downstairs."

"I can get it for you," his dad said.

"Just give me a couple of minutes, all right?"

Adam filled the last box with kitchen utensils. He said a final good-bye to the empty room. A life he would never reclaim had come full circle. His first apartment and his last. Adam locked up and left.

Luke slammed the van's rear door. Adam wanted to tell his father he'd slammed the door on his life. A moving van drove past; its motor growled as gears shifted up the hill. A young girl was pointing at one of the apartments and laughing. Her new life was beginning.

Noah clasped Adam's shoulder. "We'll have to rain-check the Nicholas Cage movie."

"Sure. I'll see ya. Thanks for your help."

Noah gave him two thumbs up and got in his car.

"I guess we're done," Luke said.

"Almost." Adam dug in the bottom of his pocket, fished out his key, and squeezed the metal in his palm. This was the turning point he'd dreaded all along.

Luke steered the van toward the leasing office so Adam could sign papers and surrender his key. As they drove away, Adam watched his apartment building disappear from sight. A wave of depression hit him. *Now* it was real.

• • •

"Are you comfortable here in your old bedroom?" Samantha asked.

"Guess so. Glad it's on the first floor and close to the kitchen."

"Lunch will be ready soon, hon." Her efforts to sound cheerful rang hollow.

Luke was at work and Marigold at school. It was the two of them trying to get through another day. By late morning, the breeze had vanished, and heat was casting a haze over the city. Sometime after noon, lightning cracked across the sky, and the trees bent so viciously that Samantha listened for sirens warning of a tornado. But none came. She stirred macaroni and cheese at the stove, and a release of thunder startled her. The rain changed to hail, which banged against the gutters. Out the window, a white grocery bag blew down the street. Adam staggered into the kitchen, confused.

"I forgot what I came in for."

Samantha reminded him. "Lunch."

Some days were easier than others. Today was not a good day. Adam sat down, unsteady, weaving in the chair. He could feed himself, but every morning Luke helped with tasks like shaving.

"I want to talk to you, Mom. You always said I could come to you about anything."

Samantha ladled the pasta into two bowls, set them on the table, and handed Adam a spoon. She knew exactly what he wanted to discuss. He talked about it all the time.

"You used to say Kevorkian was ahead of his time. Don't force me to go through this." The spoon dropped in the bowl and sank to the bottom. He fished it out, orange sauce dripping from his fingers.

"For God's sake, I'm your mother. What do you expect me to say?" She reached in the drawer for another tablespoon and napkins.

His voice was desperate. "I need you to listen."

Samantha set a new spoon on his place mat and sagged in her chair.

"Look at me. The disease is progressing faster than we thought it would. I want a choice. Why can't Missouri be a state with a Death with Dignity law? Too late for me to move to a state that has it."

Samantha said nothing.

"I don't want to lie in bed like a vegetable. I don't want hospice and morphine. I *want* the right to die."

His words stabbed Samantha's heart. "I can't talk to you about this. What if there was a new drug that could save you?"

"That's false hope, Mom, and you know it. Max was sick, and we put him out of his pain. Don't I deserve as much? I found a way—"

"We shouldn't have this conversation." Her voice was so quiet, she wasn't sure if she'd said the words out loud.

Adam's tone was shrill and irate. "If I weren't sick, I'd be out there fighting for this cause. Who the hell has the right to tell me I can't choose for myself? I can still think and speak, and I want the right to die without suffering."

She hoped she wouldn't anger him more. "I know how frightened you must be. You hate the drugs' side effects, but maybe you could try them again." Samantha was at a loss to advise him. Adam's doctor had told them the new drugs could treat some symptoms and at the same time worsen others. Drugs for depression could worsen his tremors. Drugs for tremors could worsen his depression.

Samantha stood up and moved toward Adam. "Take some time and think about this." She cradled her arms, making a frame around him. His body jerked.

Adam wrenched free. "I don't have time. It's running out."

CHAPTER 74

Borg took his seat on the plane, buckled his seat belt, and reached for an envelope in his pocket. He studied the picture, frowned, and tucked it back in his jacket. Normally, he didn't bother to look out the airplane window, but today the sun had burned a hole through the clouds. The jet climbed through the opening into the exposed blue.

Borg removed a stack of papers from his briefcase. The decision hadn't been easy, but he knew what had to be done, and it pained him. Unfortunately, this was the only way. He placed his laptop on the plastic tray and spent the next hour revising notes. His plane landed. Borg rolled his carry-on out of the airport and flagged a taxi to take him to the hotel. Later, he called Stanley from his room.

"Did you get my fax?"

"I got it," Stanley said, "but I don't agree."

"Just do it," Borg said. "I don't pay you to argue."

"It seems wrong," Stanley said.

"Do what I tell you. Send it FedEx and require a signature."

CHAPTER 75

Samantha read the clock: two thirty. She slid off the sheets and eased from the bed, trying not to wake Luke. He hardly slept through the night anymore. Most nights, she'd turn over and his side of the bed would be empty. She'd go downstairs and find him seated at the table, staring into space.

Samantha clicked on the kitchen's dimmer light, barely illuminating the room, and filled a cup with tepid water. How would they get through this?

Adam had become more despondent as the weeks had passed. His doctor had recommended family therapy. Samantha picked up a card left on the table, traced the edges, and ran her finger across the name embossed on the top: Laura Peterson, Marriage and Family Therapist. What help could she offer them? Certainly not hope. Samantha turned the card around, dropped it, and flicked it away. It was up to her to stay strong. She put her head on the table and prayed.

Footsteps padded on the stairs. Luke came around the corner, worn and rumpled. The furrow between his eyebrows had deepened to a dark groove. He gathered up a bowl, spoon, cereal, and milk. Samantha sipped her water, and Luke chewed his cereal. They left the dishes on the table, climbed the stairs, and tumbled back into bed. Luke stared at the ceiling, Samantha at the wall.

"Adam's very depressed. He told me he wants to die," Samantha said.

"Oh, God. Did you talk to him about seeing a therapist?"

"He refused."

"He's desperate. You won't change his mind," Luke said.

"I can try." She turned out the light.

CHAPTER 76

Rosie rang the bell and waited, repositioning one of the red carnations. Within seconds, Samantha opened the door. Rosie presented the bouquet wrapped in cellophane. "I hoped these might brighten your day."

Samantha inhaled the flowers' spicy fragrance. "How pretty, thank you. Come on in. Adam's on the computer. I'm sure he'll appreciate the company."

Rosie rapped on the door and entered. "Adam?"

He sat in front of the computer, completely engrossed. "Whatcha doing?" she asked. Adam struggled to turn off the monitor but failed.

"What's wrong?" She moved closer.

"Don't," he said.

"Assisted Suicide" was bold on the screen. "My God, what is this?"

Our clinic in Switzerland treats anyone suffering from an illness or an unendurable disability that would end in death.

Tears rose in her eyes. "No."

"Go on. Keep reading," he said.

A lethal, fast-acting, painless barbiturate will allow the patient to fall asleep and in minutes pass peacefully into death. Rosie scanned pages of information, the light from the screen reflected on her face. *There must be two people present at an accompanied suicide. The patient must possess mobility sufficient to self-administer the drug.*

Rosie turned Adam's chair so he would face her. "Is this place for real? How horrible. You can't consider this. It is not up to us to take our own life. It's up to God."

"It's my life. I decide what my best interest is. I've asked for their help," Adam said. "I'm seeking aid, the right to die with dignity. I *will* not go into long-term care." He spoke calmly. "They have my application and the medical reports about my diagnosis and prognosis. I meet all the requirements. I've been given the 'green light.'"

Rosie stared at the screen. "Does your family know about this?"

"No, not yet, but they will. I have to have someone with me."

"They'll have to *go with you*? Your family is barely holding together, Adam. Your mother *gave* you your life. You want her to watch you take it away? And Marigold—how do you think she'll handle this? Your choices for her are to wave good-bye as you board a plane or wait by your side while you take poison and die in front of her?"

"And you don't think she'll be *here* doing the same thing? Holding my hand, watching me die?"

"That's different."

"No, it's not. I didn't think you'd understand. It's my life, or what's left of it, and I don't want my family's last memories of me in hospice. I choose my death to be quick and peaceful. Did you know Oregon, Vermont, Washington, and California have passed physician-assisted death laws? New Mexico and Montana have court rulings pending. Unfortunately, I'm not a resident. There are other places in Europe, but this is the only one that doesn't require me to be a citizen."

"I'm begging you not to do this. It's wrong."

"I've heard you mention before that you think suffering is

some kind of 'gift' in your religion. That's *your* opinion. Suffering isn't good or evil, it just *is*. So don't act like I'm a bad person, Rosie, or even bother to present your beliefs. You weren't supposed to see this." Anger swelled in his chest and roared out his mouth. "Who decides these rules mandating that we have to suffer and die a slow and miserable death? Well, screw that, Rosie. I'm the victim in all this. I don't know why you can't understand my feelings."

A shuffling sound distracted him, and Adam saw his family in the doorway.

CHAPTER 77

Alana's cell broke the silence, and Michelle's name lit the display.

"Hey, Michelle."

"You don't have to sound so disappointed."

"Yes, well—"

"He's gone?"

"Left last night."

"Oh. Want to talk? I could meet you," Michelle said.

"I don't feel like going out. Come by for lunch?"

"Sure. Give me an hour."

Michelle was always prompt. Alana invited her inside, and Michelle followed her to the kitchen and sat down at the counter.

"Care for something to drink?" Alana asked. "I have water, tea, lemonade . . ."

"Lemonade would be great."

"Okay," Alana said. "I just made some turkey sandwiches. Let's talk first."

Alana poured two tumblers of lemonade and sat next to Michelle. "I've wondered if the radiant new mother saying was a myth, but you're a walking testimony."

"I think I'm glowing from the megavitamins." Michelle took a sip of her drink. "Alana, we need to have a discussion about finding someone to fill my position."

Alana's smile faded. "Are you sure you have to leave?"

"I'm sure."

"You've been with me since I started the magazine."

"I know, but once Steve became partner, the decision to leave was easier. I thought I'd never give up my job. But I want to stay home with the baby, and now we can afford it."

"You might change your mind down the line," Alana said.

"Maybe, but I think this is the right decision. I won't leave until we get someone, but we need to start the process."

"God, everything's changing. I thought I knew what I wanted. Since Paris, *nothing* is a sure thing anymore," Alana said.

"Okay, we aren't talking about me staying home with the baby. This is about Borg, isn't it? Are you falling in love with him?"

Alana shifted in her seat. "How does anybody really know? I'm not naïve. There's definitely an attraction. We have fun, complementary personalities, want-to-tear-each-other's-clothes-off chemistry . . . but we're working on a business deal. How can I say *love*? We haven't known each other very long."

"That's the surprise in a relationship," Michelle said. "The heart doesn't understand a timeline. It decides on its own. Besides, sometimes . . ."

"What?"

"You just have to take chances."

Alana sighed. "My feelings changed after Borg was shot. There was a different connection. I knew I cared the minute he left Paris without me. I was *so* miserable. Now he's all I can think about."

Michelle nodded. "I knew Steve was 'the one' after our first date. The pursuit was so much fun. Now we're just an old married couple."

"Oh, please." Alana laughed. Michelle and Steve still held hands in public, Michelle loved Steve's corny jokes, and Alana could see Michelle's face light up when Steve called her cell. "I don't know how to feel. I don't know *what* to feel. How can I seriously entertain the idea of a relationship? Borg's so far away."

"True, the two of you don't have a conventional relationship." Michelle laughed and fanned herself with her napkin. "By comparison, I lead an uninteresting life. Dare I ask for details about last night?"

Alana hesitated. "It was a perfect day with a depressing end. He kissed me after the show, right in the middle of the sidewalk."

"You're usually so reserved about public affection."

"It was sweet," Alana said. "And wonderful. We came here after afterward, cooked dinner, and talked until after midnight." She didn't reveal anything about the passion they'd shared. "He helped me do the dishes. He said I probably wouldn't want to get up to the mess in the morning."

"He helped clean up? The man's a keeper."

"Yeah, well, I called this morning and told him I can't share *Slick* and that we should keep our relationship on a professional level. He didn't argue the point."

"Appears you laid down the rules and maybe diminished his masculinity a bit," Michelle said.

"You think? Part of me wanted him to protest, but . . ." Alana shrugged. "He agreed with me."

"How did you expect the guy to react when he heard you didn't want him to touch you again? The day he came into the office to surprise you, I liked him," Michelle said. "We all did. He conversed with the staff and was interested in everyone. The man's a powerhouse, but he struck me as the real deal. Genuine."

Alana gazed out the window. The branches of pine trees swayed ferociously, limbs opening and closing, letting in sun, clouds, darkness, light. Repeating. The same chaos roiled inside her.

"I *was* happy with my life."

"I wish I had a tape recorder." Michelle sighed. "You're missing the bigger picture."

"Before I left for Paris, I had it all," Alana said.

Michelle reached over and patted her arm. "The change is within you. Everything's the same."

"No, it's not. You're leaving me."

"I'm leaving work, not you. Doors close; windows open. It's part of life. I loved working together. If you called on a weekend and decided you needed something done, I was there. Just keep in mind that you might not find someone willing to give up their life for the magazine."

Alana got the sandwiches out of the refrigerator and took off the plastic wrap. "Do I ask too much? Am I such a perfectionist?" She cut the sandwiches in four neat sections and served them.

"You're Alana, and you're driven. For the client, that's good. For a relationship, maybe not so much. Life can get messy. You know the saying—better to bend than to break. I think it goes for your heart, too. Remember what's important."

"Well, I already told him no merger."

"I knew you would." Michelle sipped her lemonade.

"I won't move away from my family, and Borg said he'd never considered living anywhere but the West Coast." Alana breathed a heavy sigh. "I suppose I have my answers. All right, start searching for a replacement."

"I'm on it," Michelle said.

Alana knew she would miss those words.

CHAPTER 78

"Come in." Adam motioned to his family. The lines of worry across his forehead had softened, replaced by relief. Rosie jumped to her feet.

Adam's family sandwiched together on the edge of the double bed. Marigold gripped her mother's knee.

"I've agonized over how to tell you," Adam said. "You know how strongly I feel about the right to die. Well, I've found a way."

Samantha bit her lip. Luke walked across the room and knelt to read Adam's computer screen. "I didn't know there was such a place." His voice choked. "I can imagine it gives you a sense of peace to know you have a way out. But Rosie's right. How could we stand by and . . ."

"I know this shocks you. But now I have options. I'm not so afraid."

Marigold went to the window and opened it. Beyond was the street where they had learned to ride their bikes and played kickball with the neighbors, the backdrop of her childhood. "I tell you everything, Adam," she said. "You're my best friend. When I think of a world without you . . . where I could never talk to you or see you again . . . I don't know how I will bear it." Tears stung her eyes. "But I'll stand by your decision, whatever it is. I'll go with you, if it's what you need. I don't want you to be alone."

Rosie begged Samantha, "Please don't let him do this. He can't go without your help."

"Rosie, please," Samantha said. She steadied herself against the desk and read the page. Her face drained of color. She turned to Adam. "I know how important this is to you, but I can't go. I don't think I could live with myself."

Luke put his arm around Adam's shoulder. "I refuse to spend what time we have together arguing whether this is right or wrong. I'll be there for you."

Adam hugged his father. "This means a lot, Dad. There are other countries that offer physician-assisted suicide, but they require you to be a resident. Even in the States. This is the only place I can turn to for help."

Samantha covered her mouth and turned away.

Rosie said, "No, this is wrong!"

"*Stop* it!" Adam said. "I'm the one living this nightmare."

"My son tells me what a good friend you are, Rosie," Luke said. "I also know you are a person with deep religious beliefs. I respect them, but you're not here every day to see his depression worsen, his fits of anger, his rage from loss of control. Our family needs support, not guilt."

Rosie stood. "I can't condone this. Please think about it."

"I do," Adam said. "Every day."

Rosie ran from the room. The front door slammed behind her like a gunshot.

• • •

Samantha hadn't spoken to Luke since Rosie had stormed off. All evening, Luke had tried to catch her eye, but she'd refused to meet his gaze. At nine o'clock, she'd used a headache as an excuse to escape to their bedroom.

She settled into the soft swivel chair and tried to read but couldn't concentrate. Samantha put down the book, unsure what she would say to Luke. She clicked off the reading lamp.

Her family was like the filament inside the glass bulb beside the nightstand: fragile and easily broken.

Samantha changed into her pajamas. Behind the closed door, Marigold's voice was choppy and distorted, as though she was speaking into the blades of a fan. She'd stayed in Adam's room throughout the evening. It was important they had time alone. Samantha didn't call out good night.

Luke came up the stairs. After he closed the door, she said, "I know you meant to be supportive, but you should have discussed it with me instead of blurting to Adam that you would take him to Switzerland."

Luke hung up his shirt. "We were caught off guard. I didn't want him to think he had to bear the weight of this alone. I figured it might help to let him know I was there for him."

"You and Marigold said you'd get on a plane with him, but I said I couldn't. So now I'm the bad guy." Samantha picked up a brush off the nightstand and ran it through her hair, trying to keep her cool. "I'm not so sure we *should* do this."

"He's scared," Luke said. "Think of all the work necessary to prepare for this. He's thought it through. Our son's a man now, not a child. This must have been a difficult decision for him."

"You sound like you're proud of him for planning this."

"It takes courage to arrange your own death." Luke's chin dropped. "And he *is* going to die, Samantha. Suffer in ways we can't imagine."

"I don't want to help him kill himself, and I don't want you to, either. Can't you understand?"

"I told him I'd take him. I won't go back on my word."

"Maybe you should have waited." Her shoulders tensed.

"Damn it, Sam, what do you want from me?"

"I want you with me on this—to be on my side."

"Keep your voice down. I didn't know there were sides. How about we're on our son's side?"

"I can't believe what you're saying. How can you dispose of his life so easily?"

"Don't put this burden on my shoulders. I'm trying to understand Adam's point of view." Luke rubbed his forehead. "He has a right to his feelings. Maybe you're acting a little selfish."

Without a word, she slid on a pair of jeans.

"What are you doing?"

"I'm not sleeping here tonight."

"What do you mean? Where are you going?"

"To the Marriott."

• • •

Luke checked the clock on the nightstand every half hour. He couldn't remember sleeping without his wife. Now the bed was cold and deserted. How had life unraveled so quickly? He and Samantha often lamented how days seemed long, yet the years raced by. One summer had blurred into the next. A Christmas would pass, and there they were, stringing lights on the tree again. Time had moved swiftly without the advantage of a pause button. All the family vacations, Marigold in her little tutu and tiny pink ballet slippers. Cub Scout camping trips with Adam. Luke realized he had taken it all for granted. Everything. He had always assumed his family would *be there*.

Adam had yearned to get away from Missouri to pursue a degree in law. His son, the lawyer. Another assumption Luke had made. He'd objected to Adam moving out of state, not liking the decision but accepting. Now his son would die far away from home. The cruel reality was unimaginable.

So was surviving Adam's death without his wife. Luke's feet slid into his slippers, and he went to the closet to dress. While he put on his pants and fumbled with his belt, he recalled Samantha's expression. Not anger, but disappointment. He might have coped with her fury more easily. Letting her down crushed him. He'd never hurt her intentionally, but that's what he'd done. Through their years together, Luke could always depend on Samantha, and she on him. Tonight, everything important had crumbled in a few heated exchanges. Adam needed them. Together. Supportive. The family unit.

If Luke were in Adam's place, what would he choose? It would be easier, he thought, to cross from sleep to death. No fighting for a last breath, just peaceful sleep after saying painful last good-byes. He *was* proud of his son for fighting for what he believed in, as difficult as this was for the family. Hadn't they taught him to be an independent thinker?

Luke slid his wallet in his back pocket, trying to remember where the Marriott was. As he descended the stairs, the lock clicked. Samantha rounded the corner of the staircase. She ran up the steps and met him midway, clinging to the rail.

"I checked into the hotel, and I've never felt so alone in my life. I didn't know what to do." She was sobbing. "I *have* to spend every last minute with my son. You said you'd take him, and I wanted to blame you for stealing some of the time we had left. For making it *real*. I don't agree with what you are doing, but I'll go. I refuse to stay here by myself without my family."

"Shhhh . . . it's okay. I've got you." He stroked her back. "I was coming after you. I won't lose you, too. We have to be here for each other. There's no other way we'll get through this."

CHAPTER 79

Rosie opened the trunk and unloaded the groceries. Carefully balancing two plastic handles in the bend of her arm, she reached for the other three bags. Inside the kitchen, she let the sacks fall onto the counter.

Carlos waited next to the computer table. "You left your computer on." Contempt blazed across his face. He clicked the mouse. The headline from Saige's blog, "Don't be a victim of abuse anymore," glared on the screen. Rosie's heart pounded.

He edged next to her. "Spreading rumors about me to your friends?"

Carlos grabbed her and yanked her off balance. "I'll give you something to blab about." He balled his fist and struck a blow to her stomach. A wave of nauseating pain cramped her belly, her breath knocked out of her. A sickening thud crashed against the side of her head. She stumbled and fell to the floor.

Rosie scrambled backward across the floor. Carlos charged and caught the fabric of her pants. Rosie's legs were strong, and she yanked free. Leg cocked, she kicked his kneecap with a boot heel. Carlos yelped and bent over, clutching his leg.

Rosie scrambled to her feet and raced to the counter. She yanked a kitchen drawer open. Over her shoulder, Carlos crossed the linoleum, hobbling closer.

Ladles, spoons, and spatulas clattered. Rosie grabbed a butcher knife and whipped around. She raised the knife over her head. "You son of a bitch! I'm not putting up with this anymore."

Rosie clamped the knife and waited. Carlos lunged. She brought the knife down. The blade tore his sleeve and sliced the flesh beneath. Blood trickled onto his torn shirtsleeve. He clenched her wrist and twisted. The knife skidded across the floor.

Carlos gripped her throat and violently shook her. A heave slammed her into the counter's edge.

"Try that again," he said, "and I'll shove you so hard, I'll break your back."

Rosie doubled over, gasping for air. The knife was in the middle of the floor. Out of reach.

"Bully!" She screamed at him.

He stepped closer. She didn't budge. Her breath came in short, shaky bursts. She braced for another blow.

"Hit me again and, swear to God, you won't be alive in the morning. I'll kill you. I swear." She didn't take her eyes off the knife. One of them was going to die.

Carlos wiped at the red smear on his arm. "You watch yourself." He trudged toward the bathroom.

Rosie vomited in the sink until there was nothing left in her stomach but fear. She seized the knife, ran to the car, and locked the doors. She backed out of the drive, knocking over the mailbox.

It was time.

CHAPTER 80

Alana examined E.B.'s photos to promote the new Impressionist exhibit. They were soft but bright, soothing, dreamy. Perfect. Michelle's nails lightly tapped the office door. "There's a FedEx delivery guy waiting at the front. He won't let me sign for you."

Alana accepted the delivery, noting the return address was *New Heights*. She tore the envelope, and three pages fell across her desk. Alana skimmed the papers and recoiled as if slapped. "Michelle? Get Daniel on the phone. *Hurry.*"

Her attorney strode in thirty minutes later. "Only for you would I cancel an appointment with my golf instructor." He took a visitor's chair. "What's so urgent?"

"Here." She thrust the papers in his face.

Daniel examined the document. "This is ridiculous."

"Borg's rearranging the deal. This is *not* what we talked about. I told him in no uncertain terms I was to keep *Slick*. No merger. He knew my conditions. Now I'm supposed to agree to this contract or we terminate the association?"

"Well, the man's either deaf or ignoring you," Daniel said. "As far as I'm concerned, this is dead."

"Can he seriously believe I'd sign a contract giving him 70 percent of the advertising income *and* 20 percent of my magazine sales? What's he thinking?"

"This is ludicrous and just plain greedy," Daniel said.

Alana exhaled hard. "It's *definitely* dead. Borg always said the boutique was his contribution, so I suppose he believed he was entitled to more." She struggled to keep her composure. "I'd like to send a reply."

"I'll help you construct a draft, but you don't *have* to do anything. You don't have a signed contract."

"No, I want to respond."

"Then let's get started. Would you like to go to lunch afterward? You can vent."

"Sure," Alana said. "Give me a minute to think about what I want to say. Michelle? Hold all my calls."

It didn't take long. Alana wrote the letter, and Daniel changed a few words. She sealed the envelope with a bang of her clenched fist. She'd send it registered mail. The roller coaster ride was over.

CHAPTER 81

Saige stood outside the apartment door. She inserted the key in the lock, desperately trying to shake off the mental image of Finn standing in the rain. Instead of feeling pity, she judged his actions as pathetic. Hurried footsteps sounded behind the door. The key turned, and the door swung open before she could turn the knob.

"Baby, I'm so sorry. Come on, come inside." Finn reached out to put his arms around her.

Saige jerked away and stepped into the foyer.

"Embarrass any other women tonight?" she asked.

"I know. What I did was stupid."

"You stalked me, Finn. You stalked your own girlfriend."

"I'm sorry. I'm kind of a jealous guy. I admit it. Forgive me?"

"*Kind of?* No! I don't forgive you. You scared me. What were you going to do? Punch Michael?"

Finn lowered his eyes. "He put his arm around you, and I went a little insane."

"But you shouldn't have even *been* there. You were spying on me. We're supposed to have a relationship built on trust."

"I'm crazy about you. Don't be mad."

"It was too soon to move in together. We should have dated longer." She raked her hair behind her ear. "Jealousy is a powerful emotion. It was odd the way you kept showing up at the library. You bought me a laptop so I wouldn't have to leave you at night."

"Come on. It wasn't that way at all."

"I think it's best if I go to my dad's. I'll get the rest of my stuff tomorrow." She threw some clothes and her toothbrush into a plastic grocery bag.

"I don't want to lose you. Stay, and let's talk about this."

"Not now." Saige hurried out the door and almost reached her car.

Finn called after her. "Wait—you forgot your laptop. It was a birthday present." He opened the back door and set it on the seat. "Sounds to me like we're breaking up," he said as he stepped back from the car.

"We'll talk tomorrow." Saige turned the key and drove away. The car idled at the stop sign at the bottom of the hill for several moments until she humbled herself and drove home to see her father.

CHAPTER 82

"Please . . . help me get out. I can do the rest." Adam strained to lean over the edge of the bed.

There was no answer.

"I won't change my mind." He extended his arms, ready to break the fall.

"Stop!" Hands reached out, helped him back onto the bed, and wheeled a computer chair within his grasp. "Here, use the chair. It might explain how you got to the garage."

Adam grunted, hoisted himself, and slid into the seat. His baggy shirt hung over his shrunken frame. "Go."

The right wheel squeaked as it moved across the carpet and down the hall.

"The trip overseas would have been even more difficult," Adam said. "But knowing I had options gave me peace."

This way came with its own terrible price. Adam knew who would find him, and he felt like an animal, an evil beast. The thought was hard to bear. But whether his life ended here or in a foreign country, the blow would be devastating. He hoped everyone would forgive him. He'd left notes apologizing, but he knew his explanations would never be enough.

"Wait . . . one minute." The chair stopped. Adam's breathing was labored and heavy. He took a deep breath and spoke louder, not wanting to slur his words, his latest symptom. "Okay, I'm ready. I'm not afraid," Adam said. "Remember, you have to get out quickly. This is a one-man show."

Adam knew he had lied. He *was* afraid. Somewhere he'd read that to do something difficult, you had to want it more than you feared it. He had no doubts. This was what he wanted.

Behind him, there was silence, except for a sniffle suppressing tears.

"You're brave to help me," Adam said. "Thank you. I know it was terrible to ask you to be with me."

"No, you're the brave one. I couldn't . . ."

The chair halted. A door stood in his way.

"Should I help you?"

"No. Just stay with me a little longer," Adam said.

Adam shifted his body, using the doorknob to pull himself upright, but he couldn't support his weight, and he began to drop to the floor. The knob rotated, and the door to the garage opened as he fell.

"One more step to navigate. I'm almost there." Adam slid onto the floor and edged into the garage.

"I'll get the car door."

"No, don't help me." He writhed against the cold concrete and crawled on his belly. His white shirt was grimy with dirt. Dead leaves stuck to his pants.

A lawn chair was propped against a wall. All that was left was to scoot it up to his car, tug himself up, and climb inside. His lips trembled as he tried to suppress his emotions.

The aluminum chair opened, and Adam struggled into the seat. He looked into eyes that mirrored pain and sadness.

"It's time for you to go," he said. "We've said our good-byes. It can never be enough, can it? I'd say give everyone hugs from me, but you can't. You understand, right? There can be no implication you were here. Never speak of this." Adam pleaded. "Swear it!"

"I swear."

Adam opened the door, crawled onto the front seat, and took the keys from the console. "Go out the back. Press the lock."

After a final embrace, the car door closed. The back door shut, and he was alone.

Adam began to question his decision. *Am I really going to do this?* He analyzed painful thoughts and memories. He summed up his life, his milestones, his legacy of accomplishments and truths. What did he have? What was he left with?

Triumph. He'd never stand in a courtroom but would win the most important case he'd ever come up against: Adam versus the anti-right-to-die groups.

Regret. There was so much he'd wanted to do with his life. He had saved no one from injustice. Or perhaps he had. Himself. He couldn't decide.

Guilt. His mother would find him. He was sure she would blame herself for not being home and hold herself responsible for not having stopped him. Adam let go of the key. He could still get out and crawl back to the door. Or wait.

He recalled each morning when he would awaken, unable to shake off the nightmares. Last night, he'd stayed up replaying YouTube videos of people in the final stages of Huntington's and listening to the tributes to loved ones who'd passed on. The posts had sucked him deeper into despair. Adam had hunted for answers, but they didn't exist. His hand reached for the key, and his mouth went dry. *Forgive me, Mom,* he thought.

The engine started. He lowered the windows slightly, knowing it would help the lethal gas to find its way into his lungs.

The long wait was over. Adam began to count the things he was grateful for: family, friends, and love. Invisible carbon monoxide. He was sleepy. He switched on the radio and waited.

Shapes became indistinct. His head began to ache, and he fought the nausea in his stomach. Adam closed his eyes and breathed deep breaths, from his belly, like a baby.

• • •

Samantha examined the fresh produce. She found three plump tomatoes and tested the button mushrooms for firmness. Tonight for dinner she'd make chicken chili, Adam's favorite. She rarely left him for more than an hour, now that he needed assistance to walk, but he had assured her he was tired and would rest while she bought groceries.

Two weeks ago, Adam had announced he would book the tickets and pay for them when the time was right. Lately, he'd been unusually quiet. Samantha worried the decision would happen any day.

She hurried down the aisles, referring to her list. A pound of chicken, and she was done. Samantha checked her watch. She'd been gone almost an hour. The lines were long, and she decided self-checkout would be faster. At the car, Samantha unloaded the cart and set the sacks of food, along with the box of adult diapers, in the backseat.

She quickly drove home. In the driveway, she tapped the garage door opener and waited. The door rose, and the taillights on her son's Subaru glowed. Soft music she could barely hear drifted from the garage. She could see Adam slumped behind the steering wheel. His chin rested on his chest.

Samantha tore into the garage and jerked the handle of the car door. Locked. All four windows were rolled down but not far enough for her to reach inside. She pounded on the glass. "Adam! Adam!" Shaking, Samantha pulled her phone from her pocket and called 911. She screamed into the phone. "I think my son is trying to commit suicide!"

The garage's interior door to the house was locked. Samantha ran back to her car and yanked her keys from the ignition. She stumbled through the front door and raced to the kitchen. She opened the drawer where they kept the spare keys and remotes. Fumbling. She couldn't tell. She scooped up all of them.

In the garage, Samantha held out her hands, frantically clicking the fobs. Finally, the lock released. Adam sagged lifeless, his skin a cherry red. "Oh, baby, no." Her voice broke. "No, no . . ."

She slid in next to him, turned off the car, and pressed his limp body to hers. She gently rocked him. "You're okay now, aren't you? You're okay. I'm sorry I couldn't help you. I wasn't here. I should have been here so you weren't alone." She held him against her breast. "Oh, God. Oh, God . . ."

CHAPTER 83

Rosie waited in the cul-de-sac until Carlos's car passed. His routine was dependable. It was Saturday. He always played poker with Ray. She wondered if he'd tell his friend about her, how she'd fought back, sliced his arm—and was willing to kill him.

But she knew him. He'd keep quiet, fearing emasculation. She'd stood up to him. Rosie drove back home and carried the knife inside. Dried blood stained the blade. She scrubbed it clean, wiped the sharp edge, and placed the knife in the drawer. Her jaw set in rigid determination. Now, she told herself, stick to the plan.

She'd take her most needed possessions, maybe a few sentimental pieces, and hide them in the trunk of her car. All their furniture was old and used. None of it mattered. There was no sadness. No remorse.

She tucked a small box of jewelry and a makeup case in her purse, carefully wrapped the china cups from her grandmother in layers of newspaper, and placed them in a canvas tote bag.

Rosie dug through her closet. Afraid of arousing suspicion, she chose only two skirts and a couple of sweaters and blouses. She stashed the clothes with several pairs of shoes in a plastic bag and moved to the living room. Rosie closed the curtains and quickened her pace. Decisions. No time to get emotional. She chose five favorite books, a few CDs, and two family photo albums. She sneered at the small wedding album and left it on the shelf. *Burn.*

A fireproof box sat on the top shelf. Rosie checked again, confirming that mortgage papers, Social Security cards, and insurance policies were secure. She closed the lid, satisfied it would do the job.

Now it was time to hide her little stash at her parents' home. Every Saturday, St. Joseph's Church held Bingo Smackdown, an event that started mid-afternoon and lasted until eight—a social occasion her family never missed. There was something to be said for routine.

Rosie closed the trunk of the car and drove to her parents' house. She found the key and unlocked the door. The house was silent. Rosie dragged the bags to the basement and hid them behind the Christmas ornaments.

CHAPTER 84

Borg had called her cell phone ten times in three hours. Alana had given Michelle explicit instructions not to transfer his calls or respond to his e-mails. There was nothing more to say, even though she had sympathy for Martine, who would be caught in the middle. Maybe later she would contact her and apologize for the messy way the situation had ended. The phone stopped ringing. Alana ignored Borg's voice mail and hit delete. Again.

The search for Michelle's replacement had begun. The first applicant was a woman whose monotone voice and dull personality drove Alana to the Flavia machine for a cup of espresso. Candidate number two was a competent but bossy young man who suggested rearranging the office space feng shui–style. The third applicant informed Alana that the job was temporary until her fiancé finished grad school. Alana tore the applications in half and tossed them in the trash basket.

Michelle poked her head around the door. "There's a package here. Are you expecting something?"

"I haven't ordered anything," Alana said as she took the carton.

A letter opener split the seam of tape. Inside, a sealed envelope was half-covered with strips of black confetti. Alana lifted the strands, exposing an exquisitely carved box. She removed the lid and was astonished to see an Arthurian chess set.

The pieces were engraved figurines cast from pewter. The finely carved details were astounding—Queen Guinevere's robe,

King Arthur's chain mail cloak, and the metal flames from the dragon-pawn's mouth. The set was definitely a collector's edition.

"Wow," Michelle said. "It's beautiful. The pieces are so intricate. Is it from *him*?"

"Yes. I told Borg it was the last set I coveted to complete my collection."

The story of King Arthur and his knights was special to her. It represented a time of chivalry and good deeds, the very opposite of Borg's trickery.

"Are you going to keep it?" Michelle asked.

Alana shook her head and carefully placed the figures back in the box. She picked up the envelope without opening it, set it in the box, and buried it with the confetti.

CHAPTER 85

The porch light went on. Raphael Santoro's expression mixed bewilderment with surprise. "What are you doing here so late? Why didn't you use your key? This is your home. You don't need to knock."

He stepped aside. Saige's purple toothbrush had poked a hole through the plastic grocery bag hanging from her arm.

Saige waited for some sort of "I told you so," but her father just scooped her up in his arms into a big bear hug. "It's been a while," he said. "I've missed you."

"Me too. Can we talk?"

"Sure, sure. Let's go sit at the table. Are you hungry?"

"I'd take a glass of milk."

Saige tossed her bag onto a chair. Her father took a milk carton from the fridge and poured her a cup.

"Did you and Finn have a fight?"

"Yes, but I think we have a bigger problem than the fight." She told him about losing her position with Kelly, the rent-a-bridesmaid job, and Finn crashing the wedding.

She wasn't prepared for his reaction. Her father's chuckle escalated to a hearty, deep belly laugh. It was contagious. She didn't know why, but she started to laugh with him.

"I know I'm old-fashioned, but that's the funniest story anyone's told me in a long time. Rent-a-bridesmaid . . . crazy world. My, what you've been through. Life's certainly given you some interesting experiences."

He went to the cupboard for bowls and spoons and took a carton of ice cream from the freezer. A nightly childhood ritual the family had shared—ice cream before bed.

"Can I come home until I can sort things out?"

"This is always your home."

"What do I do about Finn?" She sensed he was fighting the urge to counsel her. "This time, I'm asking your opinion, Dad."

"I don't know," he said. "Jealousy can turn into accusations, demands, and punishment."

"I think he feared losing me," Saige said.

"Doesn't matter. I've had time to reflect since you've been away. I've not always done right by you, and I hope you can forgive me. No one owns you, Saige. Including me. Don't forget that."

This advice from her father? "I need time to think," she said. "I haven't asked about your life. How's Cornelia?"

For a second, guilt crossed his face.

"Dad, do you want to tell me something?"

He swirled his ice cream in wide circles with his spoon.

"Now is as good a time as any, I guess. I'm thinking about asking Cornelia to marry me."

Saige inhaled a bite of ice cream and started to cough. She put out her palm, signaling him to wait, and gulped her milk. "What? You're kidding. You've known her less time than I've known Finn."

A kernel of resentment gnawed at her. Dating was one thing. Marriage smacked of betrayal to her mother. "Have you mentioned the subject of marriage to her?"

"No. I wanted to talk to you first. Nobody can take your mom's place. You know that."

"I'm surprised, that's all."

"First you were busy with all those classes. You spent all of your evenings with Finn, and then you moved out. I accepted it. But I wasn't prepared for the loneliness."

Saige silently nodded. Her father had touched a chord she understood.

"Cornelia means a great deal to me. She's a fine woman." He smoothed his still thick, dark hair. "I'm not in pain anymore, and it feels good. Do you know how good it feels to laugh again?"

He hunted for a reaction. "Yes, you know. It's a precious thing, isn't it? The way we laughed just now. Cornelia and I aren't jumping into anything. Her sister's out West, and her son and daughter live in Florida. We've talked about traveling together so I can meet them."

Saige put her bowl in the sink. "I'm not sure what to say. I want you to be happy."

"I am." He returned the milk to the refrigerator. "Would you do something for me?"

"What?"

"Play the piano. It's been such a long time."

His request took her off guard. "I'm not sure—"

"I miss the music."

She hesitated. "All right." They went into the family room together. Saige sat on the bench and attempted to raise the top. "It's stuck," she said, puzzled.

"You never played after the funeral. I locked it the night you left to stay with Finn." He inserted a key in the brass lock. "Your mother was gone, you moved out, and the music disappeared."

Saige was just beginning to know her father. "For you, Mom." Delicately touching the keys, she played Claude Debussy's "Arabesque No. 1."

NANCY DONNELL

"Thank you," he said afterward. His eyes glistened. "Your mother gave you a wonderful gift."

"She gave me so many things." A picture of her mother rested on the piano, and Saige felt a twinge, missing her. "I started a blog, and my first story was about Mom's death. About the cancer and how it changed me. It helped me a lot to write about the experience. Strangers visit the site and leave messages under my stories." She braced and waited for his reaction.

He caressed her cheek. "Do you know how proud I am of you? You're a strong, intelligent, young woman. I was afraid you'd leave me after your mom died. That was the main reason I fought you about college, but the tighter I held on, the more you tried to run. In the end, you left anyway. I lost both women I loved."

Her father began to talk about his own heartbreak in dealing with her mother's death. "She was everything to me. I watched her suffer and couldn't help."

Tonight, they both listened.

"I know how much you want an education," her father said. "I can help you with a loan. I have some money put away."

She put her arms around her dad. "I'll pay you back."

"I'm not sure what a blog is," he said, "but I want to read everything you write. I think you might have to teach me a few things."

"I'll teach you." She grinned. "But you'll have to get a computer first."

CHAPTER 86

A wedge of soft light between the bedroom drapes woke her. Disoriented, Saige reached across the bed for Finn before remembering where she was. She and her father had stayed up late, talking and healing old wounds. She squinted at her digital clock, groaned, and put her pillow over her eyes for a few seconds before climbing out of bed. She dressed, went in the kitchen, and plugged in her laptop. By the time she'd booted up, her dad ambled in, yawning. He squeezed Saige's shoulder, flipped on the coffee maker, and sat down next to her.

"What are you doing?"

"Checking my blog." She turned the laptop toward him. "This is the piece about Mom."

He picked up his reading glasses and studied the page. "How do I see the next part?"

She showed him how to hold the mouse, and together they guided the scroll wheel.

Her dad read a few paragraphs. "Those were hard times. I wish we could have been there for each other."

"Now is what's important," Saige said.

"Finn helped you, didn't he?"

"He was very supportive. I believed I loved him."

"Love is never easy. I don't think this problem will go away without help." Her father turned back to Saige's article.

"I didn't know love was this much work," she said.

• • •

Saige ignored the dull pain in her head and drove through town. No sense delaying the inevitable. She found a parking space, and Finn met her at the door. "Don't move out," he said, his voice husky with emotion.

"I tried to talk to you for days, and you refused to have a rational discussion with me. I believe it's best to have some space and take a little time apart," she said woodenly. Saige moved through the apartment, collecting her belongings. She folded a stack of blouses and set them on the bed.

"How much time?" he asked.

"I don't know."

"I admit I have a problem with jealousy." He took her arm. "But you run at the first sign of anything you perceive as negative."

"I'm not running."

"I don't want to be apart," Finn said.

"You fought me about my bridesmaid job. I swear, you were so controlling, it was like replaying old issues with Dad."

"I'll seek counseling and get it figured out."

Saige didn't believe it would be so easy. "I'm moving in with my dad for now. I'll find another job and sign up for college classes at night."

"It's what you've always wanted."

She could see he was happy for her. "I should finish getting my stuff." She put her clothes in a compact suitcase and removed the apartment key from her key chain.

"No," Finn said. "Keep it. Please."

She scanned his face, looking for the Finn she thought she knew. "It doesn't feel right." Saige held the key out to him. He wouldn't take it. She placed it on the kitchen counter and closed the door behind her.

CHAPTER 87

Chelsea cooked dinner and set the last potato pancake on Noah's plate. "I'm telling you, I have a bad feeling about Rosie. I've been calling, and she doesn't pick up. Her phone jumps straight to voice mail."

"You two talk every day," Noah said. "Is there a problem between you two?"

"No. Something's not right. She'd at least text me." Chelsea frowned. "I'd like to check on her."

"She's probably busy. Maybe her phone's off. I wouldn't worry. It's not like she's alone. She has a husband."

Chelsea stifled a retort and then reconsidered. "I'm breaking a confidence, but I think I should tell you in case Rosie's in trouble."

"What kind of trouble?"

Chelsea told Noah about Carlos, the bruises, and the promise not to tell.

"That's a secret you shouldn't have kept," he said. "Let's go."

CHAPTER 88

Two hours into the card game, Carlos had lost twenty bucks. The side of his arm ached, but he could handle pain. What bothered him most was how Rosie had taken off. He hadn't told her she could leave. She'd cracked the mailbox post, and he'd have to make a trip to Home Depot. Damn her. Carlos couldn't concentrate. He threw his cards on the table. "I'm done, Ray. Got a situation at home I need to deal with."

Carlos considered a detour to the hardware store but decided it could wait. Instead, he made another stop. Varney's Liquor was out of the way, but he was low on beer and needed something to calm his nerves. Carlos pulled into the lot and hurried through the store to the checkout line. The cashier greeted him by name. Carlos rubbed his fingers in anticipation as the clerk rang up his purchase. "What's taking so long?" Carlos asked. He snatched the bags, loaded the booze onto the front passenger seat, and started the motor. He reached for a bottle, twisted the cap, and took a long chug.

A block later, the empty hit the floorboard. He belched and reached for another. At a traffic signal, a police car passed him on his right. Carlos slumped in his seat and lowered the bottle. A few months ago, he'd been stopped for open alcohol in the car. He couldn't afford to have his license suspended. The police car turned at the next light.

Six cars were stopped in front of him. He honked the horn and yelled out the window. "Come on! Come on!" Carlos turned the corner and veered onto a side street, leaving the traffic behind. This route was longer but without all the cars and stoplights. He could relax and drink his beer in peace.

A house with a neatly manicured lawn drew his attention. He scanned the street. This neighborhood was worlds apart from the shack he'd called home outside Guadalajara. I'll never live in a house like this, he thought. The night before he'd left for the United States, his father had said, "You'll be rich. All Americans are. Learn to work their system."

That was three years ago. Carlos wondered if his father would have been impressed with the life he'd created. He'd gone home once since his move to the States, to attend his father's funeral. Afterward, he had settled in St. Louis in a low-rent district bordering Kirkwood, Missouri, a neighborhood of Victorian houses with gingerbread trim and wide lawns. His home was nothing like those fine houses, and it made him aware he hadn't achieved the success his father had wanted for him. A reminder he had failed.

Carlos turned off the ignition, placed another bottle between his legs, and steadied it while he twisted the top. A garage door opened. An old man emerged—aware and suspicious. Carlos started the car. I don't want no trouble, he thought. Tires screeched as he drove away.

Bottles littered the floor and rolled across the rubber mat, clanking into each other. At the next stop sign, Carlos searched the sack for another cold one. The lines on the road began to blur. He dug in his pocket for his driving glasses and squinted down the road. Worthless. He cursed them, yanked the earpiece from his temple, and tossed them on the seat.

His father had worn glasses. He tried to remember his mother, but the details were fuzzy. He could barely remember her long brown hair. Or was it black? One thing he'd never forget—his mother running away in the middle of the night. She had come into his bedroom while he was sleeping. "You are too young to understand. I hope one day you'll forgive me," she had whispered in his ear. He had cried, but she'd hushed him, warning him to be silent. She'd kissed his forehead, murmured her last words, "I'm sorry," and was gone.

Carlos hated her for abandoning them and admired his father, who raised him alone. His father's advice: *Keep tight reins on your wife, or you'll end up like me, and there will be trouble.* He had a vague recollection of his father punching his mother, slapping her. After she'd left, the memory had given him pleasure. It served her right for leaving us, he thought. Carlos ground his teeth. He hadn't done a good job keeping Rosie in line. He was the man of the house. Who was she to threaten him? She needed a lesson she wouldn't forget.

He snapped his fingers together. The habit usually discharged some of his anger. Carlos reached in the bag, but the beer was gone. Only empty slots of cardboard remained. Didn't matter. In the other bag was his liquid gold. Rum. He reached for the bottle, unscrewed the cap, and drank. He bit his lower lip, but it was numb, and the liquor drizzled down the stubble from his chin onto his T-shirt. Feeling sleepy, he adjusted the window so the cool air hit his face.

A few more minutes and he was home. The car idled in the driveway. Carlos waited for the garage door to open. Eyes closed, he tilted the long bottle up into the air, and gravity pulled more rum into his mouth. His eyelids flickered. The door was still closed. Had he pressed the button? Carlos jabbed the opener. It was taking too long. The garage door rose. Carlos eased on the accelerator and edged closer, waiting. He fed the car more gas and surged forward, crushing the front headlight against the drywall inside the garage.

Damn her.

Carlos stumbled out of the car, stabbed the button to shut the door, and staggered through the house. Arms extended, he flopped across the couch face-first, his head turned slightly. The rum bottle rolled across the worn carpet.

The room spun. He couldn't tell if he was thinking or dreaming. His father hit his mother, and her arms rose to block the blows. His father's face morphed into his own, and the woman under the hammering fist was no longer his mother. It was Rosie. A drunken smile crossed his lips.

He needed water. Carlos's tongue stuck to the roof of his mouth like muddy clay. Nausea rolled over his stomach in waves. Acid burned his throat. A puddle of vomit mounded around his face and into his hair. He could neither breathe nor gag. The alcohol had stopped his reflexes. Carlos blinked, and the room dimmed to gray, enveloping him in an ominous fog.

CHAPTER 89

Rosie returned from her parents' house and parked in the driveway. Her bravado wavered. A rush of guilt caused her to shiver. If she followed through with her plan, she feared she was no better than Carlos and his insurance fraud. But this was different. It was her only way out. What if something went wrong? The thought of going to a women's shelter depressed her. Carlos might look for her there. The run-down motel on Watson Road would have to do. Rosie tugged the ends of her hair. She had played this scenario in her imagination so many times, she was losing sight of logic.

She had this week's grocery money, a small withdrawal from their savings account, and her credit card. Did she have enough money? She'd called her boss to cash in on her weeks of vacation days due. How much time and money did it take to get a divorce? Rosie decided it was too risky to seek counsel. Too soon.

She'd stalled long enough. It was now or never. One click released her seat belt. Rosie hurried into the house.

Leave the computer, she thought. No way she could take it and explain if there was an investigation, but she needed it for her job. Checklist: Get a laptop, a divorce lawyer, and a restraining order.

Her palm grazed her neck. The dull pain in her throat, a reminder she'd survived. This time.

Rosie no longer cared if she was outcast from the Church or if she disgraced her family. She hadn't told them of Carlos's violence. How the house had become her prison. She knew Carlos couldn't force her to stay if the house and all their possessions were gone. She'd finally be free. She wanted every part of their marriage destroyed, as if it had never happened. Wipe the slate clean.

A lawyer could speak on her behalf, and Rosie hoped there would be no more contact with Carlos. She'd say they'd had a fight and she'd left to cool off. She would tell the lawyer that there were irreconcilable differences and that the house fire made her realize she didn't want to find a new home to share with him. This was her ticket out.

Rosie opened two windows in the dining room and the windows over the kitchen sink. Fuel. To keep the home fires burning. The soup was in the saucepan. All that was left was to flip on the gas burner. A light breeze, with a little help, would push the roll of paper towels near the stove. The paper would ignite the nearby stacked towels and catch the rows of cookbooks on fire.

The domino effect would escalate. Carefully placed objects would spread flames to the curtains, the chairs, the table, the room. Towels and paper products were placed everywhere to ensure that the fire would stay properly fueled. Like a game of Mouse Trap.

Rosie wanted a quick look in the basement, although she was certain there was nothing there of value. The wooden steps creaked under her weight as she descended. The basement, always cold and damp, produced an immediate chill. Near the bottom step, her grandmother's old heater lay against the wall. Rosie struggled to find an electrical socket. Locating one, she stacked two containers and set the heater on top. It hummed as it came to life, and she waited for it to warm her. Cardboard boxes from Carlos's father banked the length of the wall. Unopened, old, and forgotten. Her nose wrinkled at the damp, musty odor.

Rosie hurried to the laundry area, passing the stained porcelain sink, the washer, and the dryer. A forgotten sweatshirt hung on an old rope clothesline. Rosie unhooked the clothespin and tugged the shirt over her head.

Paperbacks lay across the plastic bins. A flash of shiny metal caught Rosie's attention—an empty picture frame, the glass across the front cracked. She shoved it aside and lifted the bin's lid, exposing forgotten mementos of her childhood: a middle school soccer trophy, a Koosh ball, a rainbow heart bracelet, and a box of sixty-four crayons with a sharpener in the back. At the bottom lay a cloth doll her grandmother had crafted from remnants of old clothes. The doll, with its button eyes and yarn smile—a forgotten friend. Rosie stroked it against her cheek.

A smoky smell had her sniffing. She turned, dropped the doll, and ran toward the stairway. The old space heater's frayed cord and exposed wire crackled like a Fourth of July sparkler, igniting papers strewn across the floor, leaving a pile of thick glowing dust.

The sparks leapt onto the nearby cardboard boxes. Devouring. Growing larger. Flames engulfed the wooden floor joists. The stairs, her only escape, were no longer an option. The roaring spires had consumed them.

In seconds, the fiery *thing* became alive, and Rosie could only watch as the inferno swallowed everything around her. There was a hum and a loud snap, like a branch breaking from a tree.

Rosie cried out, batting an ember searing her cheek. She swatted her singed hair, sniffing the foul smell. A spark flickered onto her blouse, igniting her sleeve. Rosie dropped and rolled, but the fabric stuck to her flesh. She scrambled to the sink. Water poured from the faucet but didn't stop the pain burning her arm and face.

The basement was a furnace of hot air and growing darker. Coughing, Rosie drew the sweatshirt over her nose. The room was gray and hazy, its objects indistinct. There were two windows in the laundry room. One was above a shelf, the other over the washing machine. Rosie groped for the appliance, working her way along the wall until a metal edge gouged her hip.

She jerked her skirt above her knees, hoisted herself up, and balanced on the washer. The window had probably never been opened. It was rusted, blanketed with decades of dirt, and draped with cobwebs.

She wrenched the lever out of the locked position. The window tilted toward her, opened several inches, and stopped. A small screen was easily unlatched and shoved into the grass. She leaned forward and sucked in the cool, fresh air.

Rosie yanked the metal frame back and forth, hoping it would dislodge, but the window didn't budge. She tried again. And again.

The window slowly began to yield. Rosie rocked and strained, lurching back and forth. Then, like a child's loose tooth, the frame popped out. Rosie heaved it behind her. The window shattered, spraying glass across the concrete floor.

On tiptoes, she boosted herself into the gap. Her arms and chest pitched forward through the opening, but she could go no farther. Rosie wriggled and twisted, but her hips were wedged in the cavity.

Rosie screamed for help. The only reply was the sound of crickets chirping in the brush. She prayed: Don't let me die like this. Sweat drenched her blouse. How much longer? Heat scorched her exposed skin, but she couldn't turn. She ducked her head in surrender.

Footsteps rustled on the lawn. Shadowy figures crossed the backyard. Rosie's voice cracked. "Help me, please."

"Rosie. Oh, my God." Noah knelt in front of her. "I'm going

to get you out of there. Don't let go," he said. Noah grabbed her wrists and pulled until her arms strained in their sockets. She pleaded with him to stop. Instead his grip tightened. He braced his foot against the wall and used his weight for leverage.

Rosie moaned. Her belly scraped the sill, and she fell into the grass. Noah helped her stand, his jaw set with purpose. Rosie's legs were unsteady. She stepped on her skirt and stumbled, ripping the fabric, but Noah held firm. Chelsea ran across the lawn and wrapped her arm around her friend's shoulder. Rosie collapsed against them. Black smoke formed thick, noxious clouds above the house, and a pungent, bitter smell choked the air. A fire truck's siren pierced the night.

At the front of the house, a crowd had gathered on the sidewalk. Curiosity seekers in cars streamed down the street like a funeral procession. The fire trucks honked for people to move out of the way.

"Noah, can you get my car out of the driveway?" Rosie's voice was hoarse. "The keys are under the seat."

"I saw another vehicle through the window. Is your husband home?" Chelsea asked.

"A car? In the garage?" Rosie's eyes were wild and bewildered.

Noah sprinted. Chelsea called after him. "Stop! Let the firemen handle it."

"God, Chelsea, Carlos's probably inside," Rosie said.

"Rosie, you can't go back in there," Chelsea said.

"I know the house." Rosie stumbled up the front walk. The handle turned without resistance. She stepped into the foyer, a veil of shadows. The right side of her home was a black skeleton. How many minutes until the floor collapsed beneath her? Black soot rained everywhere. "Carlos, can you hear me? Where are you?" Rosie coughed and choked as she tried to breathe.

The night breeze pushed through the windows, stirring ash and plumes of smoke around the room. A voice called from the direction of the doorway. "Get out! There's no time."

It was impossible to hold her breath; the persistent coughing wouldn't allow it. She covered her face. Maybe he was on the couch, sleeping. Ten steps away. He wasn't supposed to die. Rosie dropped to her knees and crawled.

She could feel the square leg of the coffee table. She brushed against the smooth fabric on the corner of the couch. Rosie patted the sole of Carlos's shoe and the cuff of his pant leg. "Are you asleep? Wake up." She tugged. Her arm ached. He was too heavy. Rosie tried to draw a breath, but the smoke was at ground level. Behind her someone yelled, "Get her out. We've got him." Hazy figures in yellow stripes swarmed through the remains of the house.

A fireman dragged her to the grass. Rosie leaned on her elbows, coughing up black phlegm. Rescuers carried Carlos outside. Two paramedics rushed to check his pulse and ripped his shirt with a pair of scissors. Wires were attached to his chest and fed to a cardiac monitor.

A firefighter asked, "Anyone else in the house? Any pets?" Rosie shook her head. She pointed to Carlos, lying on the ground, limp and lifeless. The men exchanged glances. One shook his head. "He doesn't have a heartbeat, but we're still trying to resuscitate him."

The medic secured an oxygen mask over Rosie's nose and examined her arm.

Firefighters advanced the hose line into the building and ordered the crowd clicking photos with their phones to move away: "Hurry!" The neighbors pressed back to a safe distance. Families grabbed their children and ran down the sidewalk.

Minutes later, the house moaned. The fire swallowed what was left, spewing red embers, pieces of glass, and billows of smoke.

The crowd fell silent and watched the remains crackle like a giant bonfire. The firefighters aimed their hoses, and a sea of water pounded the smoldering hot spots.

A paramedic inserted a needle in Rosie's arm, giving her IV fluids and morphine for the pain. They covered her burns with sterile sheets and cool compresses soaked in icy water. Rosie shivered, and one of the men covered her in warm blankets.

"We're taking you to Mercy Hospital," he said.

Chelsea and Noah stood nearby. Noah's face was grave. The medics were placing a mask over Carlos's nose and mouth, squeezing a bag to force oxygen into his lungs. Rosie's eyes rolled back, and she slid into darkness.

CHAPTER 90

Borg's voice thundered and reverberated against the thick wooden door. "Hoffman, you've pulled some stunts in the past, and I've warned you. This time, you've crossed the line."

"I have your back. I always do." Stanley's eyes narrowed. "I'm the one who found the undisclosed, hidden expenses in the retention agreement with our company in the Philippines."

"You also almost cost us the contract. You compromised the legal bill, overcharging for excessive computer time. You had formal charges filed against you your first year out of law school."

"I made a mistake—"

"I took you on as a fledgling lawyer. I believed in you, gave you another chance. I should have terminated our relationship last year when you were dishonest in the land deal. You've disappointed me."

"We knew the boutique line wouldn't work in *New Heights*," Stanley said. "You pinned its success on *Slick*, but you were giving all the profits away to her. I made the necessary changes to the contract. We could have had it all."

"*We* could have had it all?" Borg viewed him with surprise. "There is no 'we,' Hoffman. This is my company. I decide. You had no right to change the paperwork and send it to Alana without my approval." Stanley took a step back. "Your actions were irresponsible and unethical." Borg pounded his fist on the table. "We're finished!"

Borg yelled into the intercom, "Andrew!"

The door opened. "Yes, sir," Andrew said.

"Let Mr. Hoffman pick up his personal items and escort him out of the building. You're fired, Stanley. And if I can't fix this, I'm suing your ass."

CHAPTER 91

The sun bled through the metal blinds. Rosie forced her eyes open, but the light was a painful explosion. She squinted and focused on a silhouetted couple seated by the window but quickly closed her eyes, searching for the comfort of the darkness.

There was something wicked in her mouth. Gagging her. Get it out, she thought. She couldn't swallow. Rosie strained and clawed to rip the thing from her throat.

A woman's voice shouted. "Somebody come here, please! She's awake!"

"Get ready to extubate."

"I have the syringe."

"Deflate the balloon ... pull the tube out."

She felt pressure on her right shoulder. Someone holding her down. Rosie wanted them to know she could hear them. Her dry lips pursed to form words, but she couldn't speak over the voices and the beeping machines. Rosie craved water, anything to moisten the burning inside her throat. Voices drifted in and out as she fell through a dark tunnel. "Breathing on her own now ... tired ... need to observe her ..."

She opened her eyes again and fought to focus. A doctor in blue scrubs looked at a chart. A nurse replaced a bag of IV fluid. Chelsea and Noah stood by the bed. Rosie's mother sat on a chair in the corner of the room, her hands folded in prayer position; her father's arm rested on his wife's shoulder. Mamá blew her nose into the cotton handkerchief she usually kept tucked inside her sleeve. "Oh, my Rosie, God has spared you."

Chelsea held her hand. "You're going to be okay."

The nurse gave Rosie a kind smile. "Rosie, this is Dr. Warner. He's the plastic surgeon who'll be taking care of your burns."

The doctor sat on a stool next to her. "Hello, Rosie. I'm Dr. John Warner. You've been unconscious a little over forty-eight hours. How are you feeling?"

"Tired, and my throat feels like I swallowed razor blades."

The doctor nodded sympathetically. "It's from the endotracheal tube. Your throat will be uncomfortable for a while. I'd say you're a lucky young lady. It looks like you have second-degree burns. I don't believe you'll need a skin graft."

His words didn't reassure her. "There's so much pain. My face and arm—"

"I know. I'm sorry. Let's keep you on a morphine drip and valium for now. We'll talk again when you're stronger." The doctor scribbled on the chart. "You're running a low-grade fever, so I've prescribed an antibiotic. I want to keep you a couple more days to monitor the infection and see how you respond to treatment. Your mother said you're not allergic to anything, correct?"

"No allergies."

"I'll see you tomorrow."

"I'm very sleepy," Rosie said, her speech slurred.

"Why don't we let her rest now," the nurse suggested.

Rosie nodded. Her eyes closed.

• • •

For the next two days, no amount of morphine helped. The nurses changed her dressing daily; Rosie screamed the second the air hit her burns. She couldn't dress or go to the bathroom without assistance. Rosie thought of Adam and his struggles and need for help with everyday tasks. Sweet Adam, poor Adam. She drifted into an uncomfortable sleep.

• • •

Rosie roused from a drug-induced slumber. Two bouquets sat on the window ledge, yellow tulips and a pot of white trumpet lilies. Dr. Warner tapped on the door and entered with a nurse.

"Good morning, Rosie. Let's see how you're doing today." He examined her wounds. "The swelling is down and your wounds are healing. It looks like you're ready to go home."

"I have no home," Rosie said.

"You'll stay with us," Chelsea said from a corner of the room. "I'll take care of you."

"I want you to take a pain pill thirty minutes prior to changing the dressing. Second-degree burns can also form blisters; those blisters can get big and may break open. But don't worry. That's normal," the doctor said. "The nurse will give you an instruction sheet. Make a follow-up appointment to see me next week. I know it's hard, but try to stay positive." He wrote on the chart and clicked his pen when he finished. "Take good care of my patient," he said to Chelsea.

"I will, doctor," Chelsea said.

"Do you know what happened to Carlos?" Rosie asked after Dr. Warner left.

Chelsea hesitated. "I'm sorry to tell you this, Rosie," she said. "He's gone. They weren't able to resuscitate him."

Rosie blinked. "Carlos is dead?"

"The medical examiner took his body. You'll have to make the decisions for the final arrangements. Do you need to think about this? Do you have any idea what you want to do?" Chelsea asked.

"Cremate him," Rosie said.

CHAPTER 92

Rosie wandered down a smoky hallway. Lost and crying. Carlos stood in front of her, covered in flames. She held a cup under the faucet, but no water came out. Fire filled the cup and she dropped it, burning her hand. Carlos snapped his fingers and shouted, "You did this to me!"

An insistent knock roused her from the nightmare.

"Rosie, wake up."

Rosie stirred. Her mouth was dry, her thoughts fuzzy from the pain pill.

"There's a policeman here. He said he needs to talk to you."

Rosie tried to register what Chelsea was saying. A policeman wanted to talk to her.

She bolted upright. Blood rushed to her head, and the room began to spin. What if they knew? Had her preparations in the kitchen given her away? Would they take her to jail?

"Slow down," Chelsea said as Rosie wobbled into the living room. The officer stood ramrod straight, his wrists crossed rigid in front of his waist. His shirt, covered in badges, spoke authority. So did the gun in his holster. She swallowed. He took off his hat.

"Rosie Perón?"

"Yes." Her voice was weak, and she almost stuck out her arms for him to cuff her. "Ma'am, I'm here to give official notification regarding the death of Carlos Perón. He did not die from smoke inhalation. The autopsy report showed lethal amounts of alcohol in his blood, and large amounts of food debris were found in his respiratory system. The cause of death was acute respiratory failure due to aspiration. I'm sorry, Mrs. Perón."

Rosie started to weep. Tears of relief.

CHAPTER 93

Saige put down her book and answered her phone. "Hello?"

"Hi, Saige. I hope you don't mind me calling. This is Michael."

Saige nodded, too surprised to respond.

"Michael Anderson, from Katie's wedding."

"Of course, Michael. Hi."

He laughed. "I got your number from Katie. I've been meaning to call. See how you're doing."

Saige pressed her cheek closer to the phone. "I'm doing okay. It's good to hear from you."

"Sorry about the short notice, but I wondered if you'd be interested in seeing a play tomorrow night. A friend offered me two tickets to *Cabaret*."

Was Michael asking her on a date? She had talked to Finn about needing more time to think about their relationship, but they hadn't officially broken up. Nor were they spending time together. Saige quickly considered Michael's offer, determined to settle on a decision. She made her choice.

"I'd love to," she said.

"How about I pick you up at six thirty? The play starts at seven thirty."

"Sounds great." She gave him her address. "How are Katie and Nick?"

"The newlyweds got back a couple of days ago. They stayed at an all-inclusive ocean resort in Mexico. Katie said it was fabulous."

"I've always wanted to see the ocean," Saige said.

"You definitely have to. There's nothing in the world like it."

"I will someday. Well, I'm excited about the play. Thanks for thinking of me."

"I'm looking forward to it. The reviews were great. I'll see you tomorrow night."

Saige hung up with Michael. It was time to call Finn and tell him she wanted to be free to date. Saige felt like an elephant about to sit on an egg as she dialed his number.

Rosie chewed her lower lip. She'd pick up the pieces of what was left of her life and go through the motions until they became routine. Someday, she'd sleep through the night again, and maybe she'd even forgive herself. Rosie tightened the drawstring on her sweatpants and went to the kitchen to help Chelsea prepare lunch.

"How is Adam's family holding up?" Rosie asked.

"I took them a casserole . . . you know . . . after. Everything was pretty raw. I'm sure it still is." Chelsea paused. "I'm sorry, Rosie. You've been through a lot, and I'm sure this is hard to talk about, but the family is having a memorial service at Queeny Park this weekend. Adam's wish was to be cremated."

Rosie's eyes misted. "I still want to call him, check on him. Then I remember he's really gone."

"His poor mom, finding her son like that," Chelsea said.

Rosie kept her eyes lowered. "There's been so much suffering. I'm glad they waited to have the service. I wanted to attend. I feel bad Carlos didn't have a memorial. Everybody should have something. Carlos might have a few cousins in Mexico, but I wouldn't know how to contact them. He played cards with a couple of buddies here in town. The funeral home still has his ashes. I'll do something for him. Maybe it will bring a sense of closure."

"You were barely able to cope with your crisis. You did what you could."

"It just doesn't seem real, Chelsea, none of it." Rosie looked down at her sweatpants. "I don't have a thing to wear to the service. I've lost so much weight. Do you think we could go clothes shopping this afternoon?"

"Sure, we can go to Macy's," Chelsea said. "You know, that's where we met."

Rosie squeezed Chelsea's hand. "I remember."

• • •

"Let's change your bandages," Chelsea said after they put away their purchases. Rosie knew Chelsea fought the urge to turn away every time she bandaged Rosie's red, blistered skin. But she never did. For more than two weeks, Chelsea had cared for her, helped with insurance claims, and canceled all of her utility accounts.

Rosie had continued to lose weight even after her appetite started to come back. Her doctor said her body was using a great deal of energy to grow new tissue and maintain its temperature. Chelsea drove almost every day to Dairy Queen for hot fudge sundaes. In spite of the weight loss, Rosie felt stronger and had completely quit her prescription pain medicine. Except for trips to the doctor's office, today had been her first day out of the house.

She sat on a chair near the mirror. "I think I can do it myself." Rosie cut the bandage and applied the ointment. "You've been such a good friend. You and Noah have done so much for me. I don't know how I can ever thank you."

Noah emerged from the hallway, and Chelsea waved him to join them. Rosie cleared her throat. "I have an announcement, but I wanted to tell you and Noah at the same time. I spoke with my boss yesterday, and I'm starting back to work. I'll need to get a computer and check out apartments."

"You know you're welcome to stay with us as long as you need. You are the perfect house guest—you sleep a lot. Kidding," Chelsea said. "Anyway, we have a surprise. After you lost everything in the fire, Noah and I started a website to raise donations for you. There are a lot of generous people out there. I think we raised enough money for you to purchase some furniture."

Rosie's hand flew to her mouth. "I don't know what to say."

"We were happy to do it. That's not all. The fire department called this morning. They determined the cause of the fire was a faulty heater wire, and they retrieved a box with all your important papers."

"Come here." Rosie opened her arms to hug them. "I know I've said it a hundred times, but thank you again. I have nightmares about being stuck in the window frame. What if you hadn't come by?"

"You're welcome, for the hundredth time. But you know, it was Chelsea who insisted we check on you," Noah said.

"I know. I love you both so much."

"We love you, too," Chelsea said.

• • •

Chelsea had been so busy helping Rosie bathe, doling out medication, and making all the necessary phone calls that she hadn't had time to dawdle in front of the mirror. One evening, as she was brushing her teeth, she was shocked by her reflection in the bathroom mirror, seeing herself without eyeliner, false lashes, eye shadow, and hair spray.

"I feel stripped bare," she said to Noah as she climbed into bed. "Almost invisible. I hope you still want to come home to me."

"Come here." Noah held her. "I'm your husband. I'm *not* like your father. I'd never leave you. A man who leaves his wife to chase a younger woman is scum. You look beautiful, baby, I swear." He ran his fingers across her hair. "It's like silk without all the spray."

Chelsea smiled and nestled against him.

CHAPTER 95

It was sunny and warm—the first Saturday in June. Too beautiful for such a sad occasion, Rosie thought, as she, Chelsea, Noah, Finn, and Saige piled out of Noah's car and crossed the old wooden bridge. Saige and Finn had decided to put their differences aside to honor Adam and his family. Rosie rushed ahead to join the crowd assembled by the lake.

Marigold's face was blotchy and swollen. "I'm so glad you're here. I don't understand." Her eyes glistened with fresh tears. "Why didn't he wait?"

Rosie wrapped an arm around Marigold's shoulder. "He was suffering. I guess he wanted it to be over."

"I didn't really get to say good-bye. I wasn't ready."

"I know. We're never ready," Rosie said.

Marigold rubbed a tissue across her nose and embraced a young woman waiting to give her condolences.

Samantha came forward and hugged Rosie, careful not to brush her cheek or touch her arm. "I'm glad you're here. Chelsea told us about your accident. And *your* loss. I know we didn't come to the hospital." Samantha shook her head. "There are some days I can't even get out of bed."

"I understand. What you've had to deal with has been devastating. I'm very, very sorry." Rosie stole a glance at the dark box Marigold was holding.

Samantha sighed and looked into Rosie's eyes. "I know the last time you spoke to Adam was the day we found him researching assisted suicide. He knew it was hard for you to accept, but he loved you, Rosie. You were so good to him." Samantha wiped her eyes. "The guilt hurts the most. If I hadn't left him alone, he'd still be here."

Rosie swallowed the lump in her throat. She knew guilt; they were best friends. She wondered if any words would comfort Samantha. "You can't second-guess your choice. Adam was determined. He would have found a way, wouldn't he? I think he was trying to do what he perceived as easiest on the family. Going to Zurich would have been awful."

"So was finding his body in the car," Samantha snapped.

"I didn't mean . . ."

"Forgive me, Rosie. These days, I find myself unreasonably angry or crushed with sadness." Samantha turned slightly to include others in the conversation. "Friends tell me this ceremony is a step toward healing. Do you believe that?" she asked those standing near.

Saige said, "Nobody can tell you how to feel or how long until you wake up and don't cry. It's raw. I can tell you for certain, grief doesn't come with a rule book."

"I'm so sorry, Mrs. McGuire," Chelsea said. "Adam was a great guy. Today we'll honor him for the good man he was."

"Thank you," Samantha said. "We bought a bench and had Adam's name inscribed on a plaque. Think of all the people who'll stop and rest here." Samantha read the inscription: "*As you think, so it will be—In memory of Adam McGuire.*"

"It's beautiful," Rosie said.

"Hello, Rosie." Luke embraced her. His forehead was creased with new lines. Grief had ravaged his face. Luke McGuire appeared to be a broken man.

"I'm very sorry," Rosie said. She wished there were another

word to convey her sympathy. What else could she say? *It's deplorable, tragic, inevitable?*

"Thank you. Did you know Adam's wishes were to have his ashes scattered near water? He loved the lake." Luke was quiet, and it took a moment before he could continue speaking. "I read about the fire in the paper and about your husband. What a terrible experience you've been through. Are you all right?"

"The way to deal with the devil is one day at a time."

Luke nodded. "Yes, or an hour at a time." He excused himself.

Rosie, Saige, and Chelsea approached Marigold. She quietly stood near her mother. Tears filled her eyes and threatened to spill down her face. "Saige—how kind of you to come. I haven't seen you since the day at the coffee shop. I was so rude. I hope you can forgive me," Marigold said.

"Nothing to forgive." Saige held a bouquet of white calla lilies. "These are for your family. And Adam."

"They're beautiful."

"I'll put them on the bench," Saige said.

Finn and Noah paid their respects. Others approached the family and offered condolences.

Rosie whispered to Chelsea, "Look by the sidewalk. I think it's Hanna."

"What's she doing?" Chelsea said.

"I'm not sure, but she knew Adam. I think they were friends." Rosie shaded her eyes. In the distance, Hanna knelt beside a maple tree, holding a stick of burning incense.

After a while, the minister asked the family if they would like to start the service. Samantha, Luke, and Marigold sat on the bench. Samantha held the calla lilies, and Marigold held the wooden box on her lap.

The minister spoke. "We come together to remember Adam

McGuire—son, brother, and friend—who spent the last months of his life struggling with an incurable disease. Adam's request was to be cremated." He paused. "The family will leave this beautiful bench, inscribed with Adam's name. He left letters for family and friends, and he asked that they be passed out at his service but read privately. I would like to present them now."

He called names and delivered the envelopes. "I'd like to invite anyone who has any stories about Adam to share them."

A classmate explained how Adam had stayed up all night helping him study for a math test. Another revealed Adam had gone to pick up a prescription when she was ill with fever. A tall young man with sandy hair spoke about Adam, their easy friend-ship, and Adam's love of sports, especially basketball.

Several of Adam's teachers were in attendance. One woman with curly hair stepped forward and announced she had been Adam's logic teacher. "He came to me when he decided to drop out of school," she said. "Adam's diagnosis stunned all the staff at St. Louis University who knew him. We've all struggled to make sense of this tragedy that logic can never explain."

All had gone quiet by the lake. Even the birds fell silent.

Marigold spoke next. "I want to tell a story." She took a breath. "Those of you who knew Adam from high school will remember how he used to love running track. He said it was simple, like breathing. Adam always told me it was mentally recharging, a time when he could reflect. After school, I'd often wait around and watch him run. He'd grin and wave each time he passed me." Marigold looked at the box in her hands.

"One day, after I had sat down to watch him from the bleach-ers, I heard a voice say, 'Come on, geek freak. Show us what you got.' I looked through an opening in the stands and saw Eli, a new kid at our school. His face was all red, and I thought he was going to cry. There were three guys huddled around him. They knocked him down and started kicking him." Marigold's voice wavered as though the memory was as fresh as yesterday. "I was yelling at them to stop. I guess Adam heard and raced over to help. He elbowed one of the bullies in the stomach and shoved the other off Eli. The third guy took off running. It was three against one, but Adam didn't care. *That's* the kind of guy my brother was."

Marigold reached in her pocket and retrieved a silver spoon. She lifted the lid of the mahogany box. Inside, a plastic bag was filled with sandlike ashes and sharp bone fragments. Marigold dipped the spoon. "I wish I could have said a proper good-bye. I'll never, ever, stop missing you." She sprinkled ashes onto the grass in a heart shape, placed a tea candle in the center, and struck a match to the wick.

Luke took the spoon from Marigold, dipped into the gray, coarse material and flicked his wrist. Ashes fluttered to the earth. "He had big dreams," Luke said. "I believe Adam would have done something special with his life, given the chance. He was a kind man, and I'm proud . . . so proud of him. Good-bye, son. I love you."

Samantha steadied herself on Luke's arm. "I couldn't have asked for a finer son. He was truly selfless. I wish . . . I wish I would have been home . . . more supportive. . . . I regret he had to die alone." Her voice cracked. The spoon spiraled into the grass. Samantha wrenched the box from Marigold's grip and scooped her hand into the ashes. "*This* is my boy? It's wrong. A child's not supposed to die before his mother." She crushed her fist against her lips. Powder smudged her wet cheek and sifted through her shaking fingers. Samantha shielded the box against her breast. And wept.

CHAPTER 96

Waiting for Finn at the Jive, Saige knew the relationship was about to change.

"Thanks for meeting me," she said as he slid into the seat beside her.

Finn circled his coffee with the wooden stirrer. "Yeah, we need to talk. You know I hate it that you're seeing Michael. The last two weeks, I've gone crazy every time I think about you telling me you had decided to go out with him. I remember you said I was your one and only. Or did you conveniently forget?"

He *had* been her one and only. Her first love. She still loved Finn, but she had feelings for Michael. It wasn't like she'd planned for this to happen.

Saige hadn't anticipated Michael's kiss. Or the warmth that had flooded her body. Michael's kiss was different from Finn's. His lips were fuller, softer. She liked the way he rolled little circles on the back of her neck when he held her, how he softly massaged her ear lobes, creating a craving deep inside that had thrilled her. She'd closed her eyes, and he'd kissed her again. She hadn't stopped him, but the guilt weighed on her. Dating two men was so *complicated*.

"Saige?" Finn banged his cup on the table.

"I'm sorry you think I betrayed you," she said.

"Haven't you?"

"I told you we shouldn't be exclusive. I'm trying to be honest. If someone asks me out, I don't want to lie to you."

Finn's palms bobbed up and down, a set of scales weighing the injustice of the situation. "This is impossible. I don't want to date anyone else."

"I do. How can I know for sure? I mean, about us? Except for you, I've never had a boyfriend. You've been with other women. I've only been out with one other guy."

"Who was he?"

"Doesn't matter. He was a friend of my mom's . . . her son. If you have to know, we went to a movie. He was the first boy to kiss me, and it was horrible. Like he was chewing corn on the cob." She winced at the memory.

"Stop! I can't do this anymore," Finn said. "You don't understand. I can't be with you and not kiss you, and I can't kiss you, knowing you're letting someone else touch you. No, we can't date until you can commit solely to me."

A part of her was offended that he could cast her aside so easily. Saige's first instinct was to protest, but she had no right. Wasn't she rejecting him to be with Michael?

Finn continued. "I'm seeing a therapist twice a week to work on the jealousy issue. How's that for being committed to the relationship?"

This must be awful for him, Saige thought. Wasn't this what she had wanted—for the jealousy to end? Saige hadn't expected Finn to say he couldn't be with her. She assumed they would continue to date. Michael hadn't liked the idea that Finn was still in her life. He told her so. But Michael had said he would wait.

Saige blinked back a wave of grief. "I can't commit to an exclusive relationship," she said.

"I guess we have to be careful what we wish for," Finn said. "You were so unsure of yourself once. Afraid of choices. Look at you now." He lightly brushed her cheek. "Do what you have to," he said, his voice sad. "Call me if you're ready to come back." He kissed her good-bye. "So you don't forget me," he said.

Saige had imagined that this decision would bring her some sort of relief. Instead, all she had was a big stone of sadness crushing her chest. Forget him? She stared silently at the ceiling. She wouldn't.

CHAPTER 97

Alana answered the door. "What are you doing here?"

"I've called numerous times, and you haven't picked up. I had to see you," Borg said, "so please, give me five minutes." Alana looked at her watch.

"Did you really think I'd try to screw you with a bad business deal? The contract you received was Stanley's idea. I never endorsed it. He believed we were giving you a financial advantage and made changes without telling me. I didn't know about any of this until I received your letter."

Alana crossed her arms, every muscle tight.

"You don't believe me?" Borg took a thick bundle of folded papers from his jacket. "I'm officially out of the deal. Here. It's yours. I paid Martine to wait for your decision."

Alana unfolded the contract and examined the papers.

"Why would you do this?"

"I want you to be successful, and I believe you need La Chic Boutique. It's security for your company. La Chic Boutique could be the next Ralph Lauren. This is a no-strings-attached deal. If you don't want it, you can release Martine from any obligation."

"It's maddening when I don't know what you want from me or understand what you're doing," Alana said. "When I received the contract, I was sure you didn't care about my needs, my work, or my life. I stopped trusting you. You're handing me this now, but how do I know it's not a trick to take advantage of me?"

"I know you think I deceived you, but I'd never do that. The contract I approved agreed with the terms we had discussed. By the way, I fired Stanley for this." After an awkward silence, Borg looked at his watch. "I see my five minutes are up. Good-bye, Alana." Borg turned, climbed in his rental car, and backed out of the driveway.

• • •

Borg stopped at an Italian restaurant in a strip mall down the road. A glass of wine would ease the sting. Inside, the bar was dimly lit, and the shades had been pulled down to block the glare of the setting sun. Borg dropped onto a barstool at the counter. The place was empty except for the bartender polishing a wineglass.

"Can I get you something?"

"A glass of merlot, thanks."

"You got it."

Borg sipped his wine. Martine's work would do well in Alana's magazine. If only Alana could see what a boon this was for her company—a guaranteed source of revenue. Her magazine would be financially secure. He'd envisioned Alana being shocked by his honest revelation about Stanley's boneheaded stunt. He had expected her forgiveness, maybe coupled with an apology. He'd even remembered to bring protection, just in case. Instead, it was clear to him now that the relationship was over.

He was usually good at reading women. Borg was certain her eyes had lit up the day he appeared at the hotel in Paris, unexpected. The same way she had been happy the day he'd showed up early at her office. Even the day they'd *met*. She'd been so caring at the hospital. At the medieval festival, he'd felt drawn to her. During dinner at her house, he'd planned to tell her of his affection. Somehow, it all fell apart.

He had agreed to keep the relationship all business, as Alana had requested, even though that wasn't what he wanted. His blood pressure had spiked when he'd returned to California and found out Hoffman had the sent an unapproved contract. Alana probably hated him, but he knew he had to explain, to try to correct the damage, and gain her trust. Apparently, it was too late.

Borg phoned Spirit airport and arranged an earlier time slot for departure. He clicked off and put a ten and a five on the table. Borg called to the bartender. "Will this cover it?"

"I'll get your change."

"No, it's fine."

"Thanks. It's almost happy hour. Would you like to see what's on the bar menu? Our house specialty is toasted ravioli—voted the best in *St. Louis Dining* magazine."

"No, thank you."

"Maybe next time?"

"No, I don't think so," Borg said. "I was here on business, and now I'm done."

• • •

Alana spread the papers across the table. Michelle's words came back to her. *Remember what's important.* And then Natalie's advice, *Explore the other side or you will always wonder.*

Alana shook her head. She needed balance and organization, tangibles she could count on. She poured herself a glass of white wine and wrapped a throw around her shoulders. Alana looked at the clock and hesitated before dialing the number. "Hi. I'm sorry to call so late."

"*Cherie*, it is good to hear from you, but you sound troubled. What is wrong?" Martine said.

Alana told her about the unauthorized document Stanley had created and how she'd closed herself off to Borg, believing he

TURN LEFT AT THE CORNER

had betrayed her. Alana poured out the story and another glass of wine.

"All is not hopeless," Martine said. "You have lost nothing. Look what this man has done." She paused. "He gave you the thing he wanted most in the world. We have been working on this idea for years. Borg's passion is starting a fashion house, and now he has handed his dream to you. Do you know why?"

"To say he was sorry?"

"No. To say he loves you."

Alana took a breath. She'd closed the door on relationships in the past, fearful of letting anyone too close, of losing control. "He's gone, Martine."

"It's not over, but if you don't express your feelings, you both will lose. That would be a foolish mistake. Borg is a special man. His will is strong, and he has yielded."

"I'm not sure what to do."

"Look deep, *cherie*. I think you know."

"I suppose I do. Thank you for your advice. We'll speak soon."

"Bonne chance."

Alana sat on the couch and closed her eyes, confused. Life had been unpredictable since that day in Los Angeles when the elevator doors had parted and she'd first seen Borg. Alana remembered shaking his hand and the chemistry between them. His easy smile and self-assured demeanor had attracted her to him. She quickly dialed Borg's cell. "Could you come back? We need to talk."

• • •

It was easy, Alana thought, to fall in love. The hard part was finding someone to love you in return. Alana combed through her closet. She had unfinished business. She picked up her favorite off-the-shoulder dress and then put it back on the hanger. She stroked her satin and lace low-back slip and shook her head. After additional consideration, she chose a long, white nightshirt and carefully unbuttoned the top four buttons.

She stood near the window, waiting, her silhouette reflected in the pane. Don't blow this, she thought. Twilight slipped away, and Borg pulled into Alana's driveway. She ducked back and waited until he hammered the door with his palm. Alana slowly opened the door and stepped aside, smiling at the drop of his jaw, the sharp breath he took, and his raised eyebrows.

"I'm glad you came back. I called Martine after you left. She said I was a fool if I let you go."

"What else did she tell you?"

"If we weren't honest about our feelings, we'd never have a chance together."

He followed her to the couch. "There are more important things than the clothing line," Alana said.

All uncertainty slipped away. She pressed her lips softly against his and moved his smooth hand inside her nightshirt. His palm brushed across her breasts, softly at first, as though they were delicate, ripe peaches he was afraid to bruise. She pressed into his hand and shivered as he explored and caressed her. She needed his lips, his hands, all of him. Borg brushed her hair off her shoulders and held her.

Alana took his hand and led him to her bedroom. She slipped off her clothes, lifted the sheet, and waited for him. Borg undressed and slid next to her. His touch was slow and tender. He kissed the corners of her mouth, traveling down to the hollow of her neck. His fingers teased her until she cried out. Just as the longing became unbearable, she rolled on top of him and lowered herself. Borg wrapped his arms around her and pulled her shoulders forward, as if he were afraid she might leave. She felt an ache so profound that it scared her.

They moved together in a slow, rhythmic dance. Quivering, she raised her hips, and their bodies played in tune, releasing at the same moment. A thousand sunsets flashed inside her, deeper and more brilliant than she'd ever imagined.

Afterward, Borg whispered her name in a way that gave her too many reasons to stay in his arms. They held each other until their breath slowed. Borg rose on his elbows.

He stroked her cheek. "I don't know how to tell you that a day away from you is too long."

"You just did," she said.

"Am I supposed to kiss you good-bye? Fly back to California? Can we talk about . . . us?"

"There's an us?"

He kissed her. "Don't ever doubt it. A lot of couples have long-distance relationships. I have a surprise." He reached into his pants pocket for his wallet and handed her a laminated card.

"You got your pilot's license?"

"Now I won't have to line up a pilot when I travel." He lay back on the pillow. "And there's something we need to discuss. It's a logical step."

"What?"

"I'm talking about a monogamous commitment. And we give it a one hundred percent effort. I imagine a future with you, not a short-term fling. I can't quit thinking about you, Alana. You're smart, you don't quit, and you're the sexiest woman I've ever met. We're alike. So much so that we almost ruined something wonderful." His long fingers tangled in her hair.

"How would we manage?" she said.

"I could fly here on Fridays, leave on Mondays, and miss

you each day we're apart," he said. "If that's not enough, share my home. Come to California and stay with me. This wasn't just about sex, you know."

Alana sat up and drew the sheet around her. "I have to be here to run my business."

"We can figure this out."

"The distance complicates the relationship."

"You know, I can run my company anywhere. I'll open an office in St. Louis. I don't want to lose you again."

"I know." She entwined her fingers in his. "When you're gone, I lose a piece of myself. Does that sound crazy?"

"No. But maybe this does. I have this insatiable longing to be your hero. We probably haven't been together long enough for me to have the right to say these words, but—I'm in love with you. Would you believe I've never said that to a woman?"

"I love you, too," she said.

"I'm sorry." He eased her hair behind her ear. "Did you say something? I couldn't quite hear you."

"I said, I love you, too."

"Don't forget to remind me every day. I quite like the sound of it."

"There's so much we don't know about each other," Alana said.

"What do you want to know?"

"I don't know." She propped a pillow and leaned against the headboard. "I want you to know I'm not looking for a ring. I'd settle for a relationship with someone I can count on."

"I won't let you down. This can work. I know it," Borg said.

Alana smiled. "I think I remember you telling me you'd never considered living anywhere but the West Coast."

"Change is good for a man. Keeps him on his toes. I'll commute to L.A."

"I've considered expanding my magazine," Alana said. Her eyes twinkled. "I'd probably need to take on a chief financial officer. Can you think of anyone who might be interested? There are great perks."

"That might be something we could work out." He slid the sheet down and kissed her.

CHAPTER 98

Michelle handed the clipboard to Alana. "Your next candidate is here."

"Here we go again." The wastebasket was filled with discarded applications. Alana quickly reviewed the paperwork. "Send her in."

Her two o'clock appointment appeared vaguely familiar. Alana studied the woman with the green eyes and shook her hand. "Have a seat and tell me about yourself."

The woman sat up straight. "I'm single and currently attending college at night. I give a hundred percent of myself to every project I work on," she said, without taking a breath. "I love a challenge, and I don't mind working after hours."

Alana examined Saige's letters of recommendation. Her eyes snapped open in excitement. "You have *excellent* references. Your past employers gave you very favorable comments."

Alana chewed on the end of her pencil and glanced at the remaining résumés on her desk. "Night classes, hmm? Good for you." This woman was confident, determined, and seemed ambitious.

Twenty minutes later, Alana asked, "When would you be able to start?"

"In two weeks. I promised myself a vacation. I have a school break coming up, so I booked a trip. I'm about eight years overdue."

Alana laughed. She relied on her gut. Skills could be acquired, but personalities could not. She liked this woman. "I understand. It keeps the juices flowing." Alana stuck out her hand. "This offer is dependent on my calling your references, but I see no point in wasting any more time and energy. I'd like to say welcome aboard, Ms. Santoro."

"It's Saige, and thank you for the opportunity, Ms. Hudson."

"Call me Alana. We're pretty informal around here. Come with me, and I'll introduce you to everyone."

CHAPTER 99

Rosie and Chelsea left Dr. Warner's office and drove to the Jumpin' Jive Café. Chelsea turned left at the corner, and as soon as they reached the parking lot, they spied Noah waiting by the door.

"What did the doctor say?" he asked Rosie when they caught up.

"Everything looks good. This was my last visit."

"That's great," Noah said.

Saige entered, and Chelsea waved her over to join them.

"Hi, guys. This is my treat," Saige said. "I'll explain in a second. What's everyone having?"

Saige took their orders, and Rosie offered to help her carry the drinks. The two women went to the counter and placed the orders.

"I have so much to do before I leave town," said Saige.

Rosie said, "Yeah, like getting packed for your trip."

Saige smiled. "Yes, I'm finally taking the vacation I promised myself."

"You said you have a new swimsuit?" Rosie said.

"I bought it three years ago, but the tags are still attached. Good thing it still fits. I told you this is an all-inclusive resort, right? Listen to what this place has. There's music, a magician, karaoke . . . a giant bubble machine on the beach after sunset."

Rosie laughed. "If you sing karaoke, take a video and send it to me."

"Look what came in the mail." Saige dug into her purse.

"A passport! Let me see. Nice picture." Rosie handed it back.

"I'm a little nervous."

"You'll be fine." Rosie winked at Saige. "There's one strong woman in there."

Saige reached for napkins. "Back at you, my friend."

"Remember," Rosie said, "if you decide you don't want to live with your dad, I have lots of space. I'd love to have you for a roommate."

"Thanks. I'll keep it in mind. Are you managing the bills by yourself?"

"Yeah, my boss bumped me up to supervisor, and the position came with a nice raise. I'll actually have an office. I was able to afford a two-bedroom condo. I love it. The association maintains the outside. I didn't have to buy a lawnmower."

"You can't beat a deal like that," Saige said. "I'll come by after I get back."

"Yeah, show off your tan."

"I don't think I told you. I actually met my new boss here at the Jive the day I met Finn."

"Did you mention during the interview you had met before?"

"I decided not to. She didn't remember me. It seems like a lifetime ago. That girl doesn't live here anymore."

"Life's funny that way."

"Yeah," Saige said, "it sure is. Who knew time came with a lost and found department?"

"What do you mean?"

"All of us lost hope for different reasons, but we found it, and more—confidence, courage, faith in ourselves. Maybe love."

"What about Adam?" Rosie said. "What did he find?"

"Peace."

Rosie nodded slowly. "I hope you're right. I feel so sorry for his family."

Saige sighed. "Me too."

"Samantha told me they're planning to create a charity in Adam's name to help families affected by Juvenile Huntington's."

Saige raised her eyebrows. "What a great idea—a perfect way to channel their grief into something positive."

"They still need support," Rosie said. "We're going to dinner tomorrow night."

Hanna called out, "Order ready for Saige."

Saige and Rosie picked up the trays, and the espresso machine blasted behind them like a steam locomotive. They returned to the table with the drinks and passed them around. Saige grinned at everyone. "We're celebrating my new job. I'm now the assistant to the publisher of *Slick New Heights*." The group cheered. "I start the job in two weeks."

Chelsea said, "Congratulations! You're going to rock."

"Thanks!" Saige turned to Noah. "How's Finn?"

"He's hurting. He couldn't handle being here today."

"I understand. It's probably better that way."

"What does your cup say?" Noah asked Saige.

Saige read aloud: "*It doesn't matter if you fail, only that you dared to try.*"

All the cups' messages were the same. They raised their drinks in a toast. Hanna smiled, started the next order, and removed the cap from her marker.

CHAPTER 100

The view from her room on the ninth floor was like a flawless painting. Puffy clouds spun together like cotton candy. A boat jetted across the waves, towing a woman harnessed to a bright blue and red parachute, a human kite gliding across the sky.

Saige wished she could stay here forever. The flight had been smooth, and except for the long line at customs, everything had gone effortlessly. Saige texted her father to tell him she'd arrived. She'd taken her dad to the store before she left, and he'd returned with his own smartphone. Now they were on a family plan. She chuckled to herself. It hadn't hurt that she'd had a little help from Cornelia.

This break from school was exactly what she needed. She loved college but was relieved to have time off. She hadn't chosen a major yet but was considering music. Saige opened the glass doors so she could hear the waves while she finished the piece for her weekly blog. She logged in, and the words came easily for this week's blog.

Dear Reader,

I started this blog to give women hope, mostly because it was lacking in my own life. If you look back at my blog entries, you'll see my first piece was about the death of my mother and how I found my way through the darkness of grief. It was not an easy road to travel, and I often was without hope. Whatever trials you are enduring today, remember, every situation in life is temporary.

*My second piece was about a friend in an abusive relation-
ship and how she struggled to get free. Today's article repeats the
theme of getting free. Change is always hard and definitely scary.
We can spend a lifetime stuck because we're afraid.*

*Don't fear your fear. My new boss mentioned that life is a
game, and you only get one chance to go around the board. Play
it, but consider that everything you do has a ripple effect. Your
choices will always touch another life, affecting others in ways
you will never know.*

*Take a chance and write the stories that will be your life.
Everyone has a story to tell. I promise you.*

~Saige

She pressed send and turned off her laptop. Saige stuffed a
book, sunscreen, and bottled water into the oversized tote bag,
a welcome gift from the hotel. She found her cover-up, stepped
into a pair of flip-flops, and took the elevator down.

Saige squinted against the sun's glare, put on her sunglasses,
and approached a man seated at a wooden kiosk. Piles of plush
towels towered behind him. "Hi, I'm Saige Santoro. I've reserved
an ocean-side lounger with an umbrella."

The man's dazzling smile contrasted against his cocoa-col-
ored skin. "Yes, follow me, please." He picked up several towels
and guided her past a swimming pool with a bar in the middle
of the water. Men and women floated on yellow rafts, their
drinks propped in cup holders on the side. The air was warm,
and the breeze carried smells of sweat, sunscreen, and coconut
coladas. The sun played hide-and-seek behind the clouds, and
Saige breathed in the perfume of sweet flowers, perhaps from
the jasmine or maybe the red bougainvillea at the pool's edge. A
curved, concrete pathway led to soft, beige sand.

At the ocean, the smell was different—distinct and complex. Saige guessed the scent came from the seaweed or the creatures swimming in the water.

She followed the man to a row of lounge chairs, reclined flat like beds. He set a thick white cushion on top the wooden supports and spread a towel. "Have you stayed with us before?" The man patted his damp forehead with a bandana.

"No, it's the first time I've traveled anywhere."

"Welcome to the resort and to Cancun. I'm Ramón. Let me know if I can assist you."

Saige pushed off her shoes, dug her feet into the smooth sand, and wiggled her toes. She shaded her eyes and watched a boat bounce across the tip of the waves, towing another parasailer, slowing enough to place the parachute over the tips of the palm trees. "Ramón, wait." Saige pointed. "Is that safe?"

"They take people out all day long and never have had a problem."

The silhouetted figure in the harness waved, and a man on the shore waved back and snapped a picture.

"Parasailing would make a good story to tell, wouldn't it?" Saige smiled. "How would I sign up?"

"Go back toward the towel desk. Turn left at the corner, and you'll find the activities desk. Open until six every day." Ramón flashed his broad, white smile again. "Enjoy your stay."

"Thanks."

Saige strolled to the water's edge and sat in the wet sand, squeezing it between her fingers. The tide was gentle at the shoreline. Water spilled over her legs, and Saige found herself mesmerized by the ocean's color, the changing hues of blues and greens. She stood and approached the water, slowly at first, testing the depth with each step, sinking in spots as the tide moved the sand under her feet. An unexpected wave curled and hit her with a force she didn't expect, knocking her off balance. She splashed into the water, dove to the bottom, and let the force of the current push her to the shoreline.

Saige turned again and swam farther, where the water was deeper, and she figured how to ride the waves as they whirled and towered above her, spinning in from the horizon, heaving her toward the shore. She swam out again and again to experience the thrill of a tiny tsunami knocking her off balance, challenging her to stand against the power of the sea. She eventually began to tire and floated to shore.

Saige crawled out on the sand, her body heavy. She found her cot, toweled the water from her hair, and watched a father and daughter building a castle with buckets of sand. They used pieces of broken shells for decoration and topped one of the turrets with a white gull feather the little girl plucked from the beach.

"Excuse me for disturbing you, *señorita*," Ramón said. He placed a cushion on the lounger next to Saige. "*Hola, señor*. I am nearly ready for you." Ramón waved him over, immediately peeled two towels from the stack, and arranged them. "May I offer you something to drink?"

"A margarita would be great," he said.

"May I bring anything for you, *señorita*?"

"No, I'm good," Saige said.

Ramón nodded and left.

"Hello, there."

"Hello." Saige liked his khaki fedora.

"Not too early for a swim, I take it?" He settled in the lounge chair beside her and adjusted his hat. "Are you having fun?"

"It's everything I dreamed."

"Do you need any help applying sunscreen?"

"I'd appreciate it. I can't reach the middle of my back." She sat up and handed him a bright orange bottle. A swoosh exhaled from the bottle as the lotion filled his palms. His hands were gentle, and he crisscrossed her skin with light strokes.

"There," he said with satisfaction and rubbed the leftover lotion on his abdomen.

"Thank you, Michael." She smiled, lay back, and listened to the waves crashing on the beach. Minutes later, a boat returned to the dock in front of the resort. The sudden sputter of the engine caused Saige to drift from her relaxed, sleepy state and focus on the vessel as it slowed to a stop. She viewed the woman in tow, floating in the air, a butterfly landing on a wooden ramp in the water. Saige closed her eyes and told herself, after lunch, she would know what it was like to fly. Although maybe she already did.